# NOW YOU

"There!" Jerry yelled in Charlie's ear, pointing past his head to an utterly unremarkable spot in the desert. Charlie nodded, kicked the pedals to bring them around and gunned the plane's engine for one last burst of speed. Then he stood on the brakes, chopped the throttles and the Kuznetzov radial died in ear-shattering silence.

"Everyone out, folks," Charlie called back into the cabin. "We're gonna have company in just a couple of minutes."

The dragon, wizard, programmer, pilot and Russians all piled out onto the dusty lakebed. "Is this the place?" Gilligan asked. "If so, do it quick."

Coming over the lakebed were three Blackhawk helicopters. Squinting, Gilligan thought he could make out door gunners. Two more columns of dust marked vehicles speeding toward them across the desert.

"Stay where you are!" the loudspeaker on the first helicopter blared. "Put your hands up and stay where you are."

As the helicopters flared for a landing, Bal-Simba raised his hands and began to chant.

The security forces, mistaking the wizard's gesture for surrender, barreled in. When the air around the group began to twist and shimmer it looked like heat rising from the desert floor. As they landed, the helicopters kicked up clouds of fine, powdery dust. Even before the wheels touched, the combat-equipped Air Police were jumping from the ships to secure their prisoners.

But by the time the dust cleared there was nothing in the desert but a dozen bewildered Air Policemen with M-16s at ready....

**BAEN BOOKS by RICK COOK**

*Wizard's Bane*
*The Wizardry Compiled*
*The Wizardry Cursed*
*The Wizardry Consulted*
*The Wizardry Quested*

*Mall Purchase Night*

# The Wizardry Quested

## RICK COOK

THE WIZARDRY QUESTED

This is a work of fiction. All the characters and events portrayed in this book are fictional, and any resemblance to real people or incidents is purely coincidental.



A Baen Books Original

Baen Publishing Enterprises
P.O. Box 1403
Riverdale, NY 10471

ISBN: 0-671-87708-9

Cover art by Newell Convers & John Pierrard

First printing, March 1996

Distributed by Simon & Schuster
1230 Avenue of the Americas
New York, NY 10020

Typeset by Windhaven Press, Auburn, NH
Printed in the United States of America

# Part I: Queen of the Fair

## ONE
## Winter Fair

It was high winter and beyond the town the world lay under a blanket of white. Wiz and Moira stood outside the outer gate of the castle and looked down the long sloping High Street to the scene beyond.

"Oh Wiz! Look at the fresh snow! Isn't it beautiful?"

"If you say so," Wiz Zumwalt told his wife. "I'm a California boy and this isn't my style."

"Oh you just don't like snow."

"It's not that I don't like snow. But I hate slush."

"Still," Moira said firmly, "it's beautiful."

Wiz reached out and circled her waist with his arm. "You're beautiful."

Even an objective observer—which Wiz most definitely was not—would have agreed. Moira was wearing a heavy cloak of dark green wool lined and trimmed with dark fur. Her red hair, sparkled by diamond drops of melted snowflakes, hung down over the collar. The cold brought roses to her pale cheeks and her green eyes were bright under lashes the color of brushed copper.

He had loved her from the first moment he had seen

her, but that had been a magic spell. What had grown between them since then needed no spells.

She clung to him for an instant and then broke away. "Oh, come on," she said breathlessly, "I want to see my domain."

Wiz sketched a mock bow. "Lead on, Your Majesty."

Moira struck a regal pose. "Not until tomorrow. After Our coronation you may address Us as Your Majesty. Meanwhile you may give Us your arm."

Ever since the fair committee had announced its choice it had been a joke between them. When the fair officially opened tomorrow Moira would be crowned with holly and mistletoe and proclaimed Winter Queen to reign over the fair. Normally the queen was one of the women of the town, but this year the townsfolk had chosen Moira. If the truth be known this was due to a deadlock between the two logical candidates, but Wiz and Moira had chosen to ignore the politics and concentrate on the honor.

"What? You don't want the rest of me?"

Moira opened her green eyes wide and gave him one of her patented 10,000-volt looks. "There are other parts of you that are useful," she said, "but let us leave that for later." Side by side they started down the icy street toward the fair.

The Wizards' Keep stood on a great bluff that jutted up at the joining of two rivers. The town known simply as the Capital trailed down the sloping back of the rock to the flatlands below. From where they stood they could see over the roofs and walls of the Capital down to the fairgrounds.

Two days ago the water meadows beside the rivers had been as plain and white as the fields beyond. Now, as if by magic, a city had sprung up. Brightly colored canopies spilled carelessly against the fields of white. Along the dark river, boats lay ashore. Here and there campfires burned against the midwinter's chill and everywhere people bustled like ants, erecting tents and stalls, unloading and setting up to display their wares.

Merchants had come from all over the human lands to trade at the Winter Fair. Wizards, townsfolk, farmers and villagers for miles around came to buy, barter, gossip and just gawk at the spectacle.

"Have you ever seen the like?" Moira asked excitedly.

"In my world we call them trade shows," Wiz said. "Remind me to tell you about Comdex some time."

Side by side they strolled down the Capital's main street, greeting townsfolk and acknowledging greetings. Thanks to his magic, Wiz was a member of the Council of the North, the wizards who ruled and watched over the human lands. With his combination of magic and computer programming he was perhaps the mightiest of the Mighty who sat upon the Council. But most of the hellos were for Moira. Before they met she had been a hedge witch in a village near the borders of the Wild Wood, sharing the lives of the villagers, healing, advising and helping them in their day-to-day concerns. Her magical ability would never be above moderate, but she had a warmth and genuine liking for people that none of the Mighty could match.

There were few enough folk out as they made their way down the cobbled streets. The cold kept as many who could stay inside and as it was midmorning most of the residents were hard at work. Wiz could hear the ring of a blacksmith's anvil carried from some side street in the frosty air. From another street came the steady rhythmic clanging of a coppersmith beating out a vessel on a stake. The women of the Capital liked to do their marketing early and anyone who had free time and didn't mind the cold would be down at the water meadows watching the fair go up.

Wiz and Moira were perhaps halfway through the

town when Moira slowed and clutched Wiz's arm more tightly. Wiz turned to look at her and saw she had gone white, making her freckles stand out starkly against her skin.

"Darling are you all right?"

"Fine," Moira gasped. "Be fine. Just let me sit for a minute."

Wiz guided his wife to a wooden bench by a nearby doorstep. She sank down on it and leaned forward until her head was nearly between her knees. She gasped for breath a couple of times and then held the air in. Wiz stood with his hand on her shoulder, feeling helpless.

"Can you make it back all right?"

"I do not want to go back," Moira said, staring at her toes. "I will be all right and we can go on."

"Nuts. You're going back to the castle."

Moira breathed deeply again and straightened up. Wiz could see the color coming back to her cheeks.

"I am fine," she said in a stronger voice. "It was just a momentary dizziness."

"You're trying to do too much and you know you haven't been feeling well. You need to slow down, or at least let Bronwyn have a look at you."

She smiled up at him and patted his hand. "I will. After the fair, I promise."

Wiz started to protest, then smiled back. "Why is it I never seem to win these arguments?"

Moira's smile grew even brighter and she squeezed his hand in hers. "Because I am always right."

*Cold. Black, bitter, eternal cold and forever-frozen silence. They lay heaped where they fell, as they would lie until the primal forces of weather and earth moved them. Some had lived once, others had lived never. Immaterial. Now the living were as lifeless as the never-living, all mixed together in the dark and endless, freezing cold.*

*Somewhere in the chill mass a thing stirred.*

✧ ✧ ✧

As they got lower into town more people appeared on the street, all going in the same direction. By the time they reached the main gate at the foot of the bluff they were part of a small crowd.

The fair started just outside the gate. The road was lined with a double row of booths and pavilions in various stages of erection. Behind those rows Wiz could glimpse other tents, all brightly colored, all erected without the least regard for the appearance of their neighbors, yet all of them swirling together into an oddly harmonious whole.

The place was a cheerful babble of excited voices chattering, calling, crying wares, and shouting. Here, there was a cheer as a pavilion was raised to its full height, followed immediately by a groan as the center pole slipped on the frozen earth and the tent billowed to the ground again. There, children chased one another between the tents and through the crowds, shrieking their excitement. Over yonder a horse whinnied and a bull bellowed. Somewhere else musicians played on pipe and drum and tambourine. From the river bank came the chant of boatmen pulling in unison to bring their boat ashore.

The frosty air was rich with the smell of roasting chestnuts and mulled spiced wine. It smelled of horses and people, garlic and new leather. Of faraway places and pine smoke. It was a wonderful odor and Wiz drank it in eagerly as they let the crowd carry them along.

*Ice film strained and cracked from motion where no motion should be. Another jerk, and another and another until the ice flaked away from what had once been a human hand. The skeletal fingers convulsed and tightened to form a parody of a fist.*

"Wiz look out!" Moira's words brought him out of

his reverie as her hand on his bicep guided him away from a large and uninviting mud puddle. Every morning fresh straw and tanbark was spread to keep mud from fairgoers' boots, but in short order it was trampled, crushed and dragged into the slushy dirt.

Moira's eyes were laughing. "I believe the expression is 'wake up and die right.' "

"Sorry," he mumbled. "I got distracted." Moira's smile and resigned sigh told him she was all too familiar with her husband's absent-mindedness. Looking at her like that he was reminded once again of how much he loved her.

"Let's go check out the jeweler's row," he suggested. "Perhaps they will have something fit for a queen."

Moira inclined her head regally. "Very well. You may proceed Us to guard Us from the mud."

*Rocks shifted, clods of frozen earth fell free and the once-living sat erect in his icy grave. The misshapen head turned neither right nor left but the eyelids lifted on still-frozen eyeballs. Moving in uncoordinated jerks and broad swipes it began to clear the rest of the rubble from its form.*

*A massive wound left the brain half exposed to the freezing air, but scraps and shards began to return. Of true consciousness there was none, nor soul nor spirit, nor coherent memories. But there were reflexes, and skills learned long and well at very fundamental levels. For the animating intelligence that was sufficient.*

There was snow drifted against the windows, but the room in the Wizards' Keep was warm and cozy. A wood fire crackled and danced in the stone fireplace, perfuming the air with cedar. With its carved furniture of dark oak, stone walls, and diamond-paned windows, the place looked positively medieval. With its overflowing litter of scrolls, wooden tablets, and a large crystal ball on a stand, it looked like a magician's study. With the letters of glowing fire hanging above the two occupied worktables, the remains of sandwiches beneath the "displays," the pot of industrial-strength tea in a corner and the flowcharts scrawled in charcoal on one whitewashed wall, it looked like a programmer's workroom. In fact it was both, and the effect managed to be oddly harmonious in spite of the contrasts.

Wiz's desk was deserted, but Danny and Jerry were hard at work. Actually Danny was surfing the Internet and Jerry was just doodling, but they were both doing it with the fierce concentration which is the hallmark of a good programmer and the bane of a good programmer's Significant Other.

"Going to the fair tomorrow?" the younger, slighter, man asked over his shoulder when he reached a pausing place.

Jerry Andrews shrugged his massive shoulders. He was a big man and if he was somewhat soft, he was definitely not fat. "I dunno. Hadn't really thought about it."

Danny spun his chair around and grinned. "That's the advantage of having kids. You gotta think about things like the fair."

"I'm not sure I see that as an advantage," Jerry said slowly. "If Malkin were here I'm sure she'd want to go." He paused. "But then that's why Malkin's not here. It's bad enough having to return the stuff she's lifted and make explanations here and in town. At the fair . . . " He shuddered.

"Yeah. At least June keeps Ian out of trouble rather than encouraging him. Just wait until you have kids."

"That may be quite a wait," Jerry said dryly. "Malkin and I have talked about it and we're not sure we will."

Danny just smirked.

"Oh, speaking of kids," Jerry said, "take a look at this, will you?"

Danny got up and crossed over to look at the work

on Jerry's "screen"—actually a glowing rectangle of fiery letters floating in the air above his desk.

"It's something kind of silly, really," Jerry went on, "but I wanted to see what would happen. Anyway, Ian's birthday is coming up and I thought maybe I could adapt it into something for him."

Danny frowned.

"It's a screen saver. Here, let me."

Jerry gestured with the mouse, clicked twice (producing two squeaks from the rodent-like demon) and sat back. After a few seconds a fluffy, pink mechanical rabbit wearing sunglasses and beating a bass drum marched back and forth through the lines of code.

"Pretty neat," Danny agreed, watching the bunny rub out the letters with its passage. Then the rabbit hopped down off the worktable and made for the door, still banging his drum. It was out the door and down the corridor before either programmer could react. It had almost reached the corner when Jerry reached the door and gestured at the runaway bunny. It disappeared with a soft pop.

"I didn't expect that."

"Yeah. It just kept going, and going, and . . ."

Jerry shot his colleague a dirty look. "You and Wiz."

"Sorry, it was too good to pass up. Anyway, you're gonna need a way to keep that rabbit within bounds."

Jerry rubbed his chin thoughtfully. "I've got just the solution."

*The frozen thing tottered erect. Now the half-crushed head swiveled left and right in a ghastly parody of a hunting dog seeking a scent. Finding what it sought, it jerked and stumbled off down an unlit corridor half-choked with rubble.*

The fair would not open officially until tomorrow morning. But many of the booths were set up and operating. It was already possible to buy things from the early-arriving merchants and Moira managed quite a regal progress, except when she forgot herself and gave way to bright-eyed excitement. Wiz wished he was walking beside her to watch. But it was faster pushing through the throng single-file.

They were barely three-quarters of the way along the main way when someone came up behind them. Wiz turned and saw Malus, one of his fellow members of the Council of the North. Besides the staff of a wizard and the blue robe of the Mighty, the pudgy wizard also wore the green sash of a fair warden. He was not young and not light and the combination of age and the effort to catch up with them had him red-faced and puffing.

"How is it going Malus?"

Malus sketched a bow to the pair of them. "Ah, good morrow, My Lord, My Lady. Well enough. Well enough." He paused to wipe a film of sweat from his bald pate. "Someone tried to set up a trained dragon show down by the corrals. Horses cannot stand the smell, you know, and it just would not have been suitable. Not suitable at all. But we have him on the other side of the grounds now. Oh, and when your turn comes, keep a close eye on Mother Charisong's booth—the tawdry orange-and-green one, you know? She swears not, but I think some of her love charms have compulsion spells on them. Not that I could find any, you understand, but I have my suspicions."

"Oh, Mother Charisong's not a bad sort," Moira said. "She used to come through my village every year or two." She frowned slightly. "She's not malicious at all, but I think she is a bit of a romantic and the idea of instant undying love would appeal to her."

"I'll keep an eye on her," Wiz promised. "Anything else?"

It was Malus' turn to frown. "Well, I was not going to mention it just now, but since you ask I am having a little problem with one of the spells in the new magic.

To brighten and dim magical lights, you know. The demon is not doing what it is supposed to. I have been over and over the code and I can't seem to find the problem. Do you suppose you . . . "

"I'd be happy to. I'll be back at the castle in a couple of day-tenths. Could you bring it by then?"

"Thank you, My Lord. Two day-tenths it is. Enjoy the fair. Good day, My Lady." With that he wandered off.

Moira looked after him, eyes sparkling with laughter. "He is a dear, isn't he?"

"Yeah, but I wish he was a little more logical when it comes to programming."

Moira shrugged. It was an old discussion. While anyone could use a spell written with Wiz's magic compiler, creating them required the same knack for logical thinking and organization it takes to be a programmer in any language. Traditional magic did not build up spells a statement at a time and so relied on other qualities, notably memory, intuition and courage. It was hard to be good at both the old and new magics, and as one of the Mighty and a member of the Council of the North, Malus was very good at the traditional magic.

"He has an eye for chicanery though," Moira said. "Perhaps I had better have a word with Mother Charisong before you or one of the other fair wardens has to take official notice."

At least one journeyman wizard was always on duty among those overseeing the fair to guard against magical trickery. It was not required that the Mighty take a turn as fair wardens, still less that the members of the Council do so, but many of them did.

"Want me to come along?"

"It would be best if you escorted me there and then went off on another errand while Mother Charisong and I talked of old times."

"Thus implying a threat without having to make it." Wiz nodded.

Moira's green eyes grew wide and innocent. "Why no, My Lord. How can you think I would threaten a poor old woman? We will merely have a quiet gossip."

Wiz put his arm around his wife's waist. "Which will make the point without having to say a word. Darling, did I ever tell you you are brilliant?"

Moira cocked a burnished copper eyebrow. "Only by comparison."

"Hey, Danny," Jerry called, "watch this."

Two mouse clicks, two mouse squeaks, and the rabbit with the bass drum was back on Jerry's desk. It marched up and down, beating the drum and getting closer to the table's edge with each pass.

As the rabbit reached the edge of the table, a green tentacle curled out of the "screen," wrapped around the rabbit's throat and jerked it back into the system, cutting the rabbit off in mid-beat.

"Crude," Danny said, "but effective."

Deep in the Wild Wood, the sun was also shining. The weak winter rays slanted through the multi-paned windows of the great hall at Heart's Ease, throwing diamond-shaped patterns on the table. Two women stood beside it, studying a curiously carved casket. Both of them were tall and slender, but the younger one with raven-dark hair was slightly taller than the older woman with the prematurely white hair.

"Now watch closely," Shiara the Silver said to her pupil. Working by touch, because she was blind, she selected a lock pick from the assortment that lay on the table. "You must keep the tension on the mechanism," she said as she smoothly manipulated the lock. Two heads, one silver-white and the other black with russet highlights, bent over the chest. "Past the first ward. Then past the second ward."

Malkin, sometime thief on the Dragon Marches and

now lady to Jerry Andrews of the Wizards' Keep, nodded.

"And then the tumbler slips like so," Shiara said. "Now you try it."

Malkin bent to it with a will. In seconds the lock clicked and the dark-haired woman straightened up in triumph. Then her face froze, her eyes widened, her features contorted and she let out a thunderous sneeze.

"Had it been real, the blow tube would have been filled with something more lethal than pepper," Shiara said mildly.

"You didn't say anything about that," Malkin protested, sneezing again.

The silver-haired woman smiled. "The lesson is never to trust a lock—or the person who tells you how to pick it."

Malkin grunted.

"Well, that is enough for now," Shiara told her pupil. "Your fingers are getting stiff from the cold and it is best we rest for a bit."

"I can go on," Malkin said stubbornly.

The older woman put her hand on the younger one's shoulder. "Of course you can. But there is no need and it is best not to force such things without need. Now come and have some hot spiced cider."

"How did you know?" Malkin asked as they settled in to high-backed chairs before the fire in the great fireplace.

"Hmm?" Shiara said into her mug. "About your fingers? Why, I could hear them. You were slowing down on simple operations."

If Shiara was blind she still had her ears, her hands, her brains and her memories. Malkin was in the presence of a master burglar and she knew it.

She used no magic, of course. Although Shiara had been a sorceress of high skill, the accident that had ended her career as the Council's master thief had left her so sensitive to magic that its very presence hurt her. That was why she lived in a magically "dead" zone deep in the Wild Wood, away from other people and their everyday magics. It was why Heart's Ease itself, from stone tower to attached hall to outbuildings to surrounding stockade, had been built completely without resort to magic.

"It is kind of you to teach me, Lady," Malkin said as she warmed her hands on the mug of fragrant cider.

"It is my pleasure. There is not much human company here in the Wild Wood in wintertime."

Although she didn't mention it, Shiara was also doing Wiz a favor. Wiz wanted to get Malkin out of town during the fair. The multitude of booths and merchants was just too tempting for someone of Malkin's proclivities.

Calling Malkin a thief was like saying Don Vito Corleone was a little dishonest, or Dr. Jekyll had his moody days. Malkin was that rare combination of aptitude, dedication and intelligence that marks a true adept at any art. In her case it just happened to be the art of separating people from their property.

For Malkin, stealing wasn't just a job and it was more than an adventure. It was business, pleasure and a way of life all rolled into one. She was as dedicated to it as a medieval monk was to his calling—a comparison which would have surprised Jerry, considering her distinctly un-monk-like proclivities in other areas.

"You have a powerful talent," Shiara went on. "In some ways too much talent."

Malkin made a noncommittal noise and raised the steaming beaker to her lips.

"I doubt you have ever been seriously challenged in your skill. So far you have been able to rely on your natural abilities blindly, without having to learn the other requirements of your calling."

"Such as?"

"Patience. Forethought. Perhaps a little humility."

Malkin smiled. "As you say, I've done well enough."

"But will you do well enough if you face something that really tests you?"

The younger woman sighed and set the beaker of cider on the table. "Like as not I'll never find out. Little enough opportunity I'm like to have for a great test. Things are much changed from your day, Lady."

"Indeed they are," Shiara agreed. "And very much for the better."

Humans had little magic in those not-so-long-gone days when Shiara the Silver and her mate Cormac the Golden had plied their trade. The pair had relied more on stealth and cunning than Cormac's skill with a sword or Shiara's abilities as a wizardess to purloin especially dangerous pieces of magic for the Council of the North. It had been the last of these quests which had cost Cormac his life and left Shiara blind and allergic to magic of any kind.

"Still, you should strive to perfect your art." *And be careful what you wish for,* the blind woman thought, *for you may get it.*

"Hey, Danny, I've got a new wrinkle for the screen saver. Take a look." Two quick mouse clicks and the bunny appeared.

This time the rabbit didn't have its drum. Instead it was wearing crossed bandoleers and carrying what looked like the mother of all assault weapons. Its pink ears poked out of folds in a camouflage scarf tied around its head pirate-fashion.

"Uh-oh," Danny said. "This looks serious."

As the rabbit approached the edge of the desk, the green tentacle reached out to grab it. The rabbit whirled and ripped off a burst with its machine gun/grenade launcher. Chunks of tentacle and ichor flew everywhere and most of the screen disintegrated under the force of the blast.

Danny and Jerry dived under the table and nearly butted heads.

Suddenly it was quiet again. The room reeked of powder smoke and plaster dust but there was no more shooting. Danny sneaked a peek over the edge of the table. There was nothing left of the screen but an occasional letter or two. The pink bunny in the boonie rag blew the smoke from the end of the gun barrel, surveyed the damage, hopped down off the table and disappeared out the door.

Danny crawled the rest of the way out from under the table. "What did you call that thing again?"

Jerry coughed and brushed the dust off his tunic as he stood up. "Uh, a screen saver."

"Well it didn't save it, it blew it all to hell."

"Yeah. I guess it needs a little more work."

Danny could only nod.

# TWO

# Foulness at the Fair

Almost at the end of the fair's main row, as far from the Wizards' Keep as possible, a smoke artist was displaying his illusions.

The open-fronted booth was carefully darkened to show off his creations to best advantage and, Wiz suspected, to hide the mirrors and other apparatus that made them possible. There were five or six people clustered in rapt attention before the booth, oblivious to the fair-goers pushing past them.

The artist was small and slender, dressed in a cowled black robe obviously meant to remind his audience of a wizard. For an instant Wiz wondered if it was a man or a woman, but then the artist withdrew an unmistakably masculine hand from the sleeve of his robe to gesture.

At the hand motion, three gouts of gaily colored smoke blossomed within the booth, billowing toward the cloth ceiling and swirling together in a pattern that seemed to pulsate and dance to an unheard melody. Garnet red and peacock blue smoke combined to form a deep, vibrant purple while tendrils of yellow smoke lanced through the cloud. Then the smokes sorted themselves into layers of pure color and began to interweave monochromatic tendrils in an increasingly complex design. At first it reminded Wiz of a simple geometric shape, then it became an ever-more-elaborate piece of Celtic knotwork. Finally the smokes twisted into a design that seemed completely random, yet hinted at an underlying order. It seemed to Wiz that if he could just study the writhing smokes long enough he could unlock that secret.

Wiz had no real ability to sense magic as this world's wizards could, but he understood the basic laws of physics and this smoke was behaving in a decidedly lawless manner. There was something wrong here and the realization sent a chill through him.

It took the better part of an hour for servants under Danny's direction to get the workroom cleaned up and presentable again. It took about as long for Jerry to track down and de-instantiate his fluffy pink creation. By the time they had settled down to work again Jerry had decided to shelve his screen saver and Danny had gotten a bright idea of his own.

"Somehow," Jerry said, surveying the freshly patched plaster and the dusted and neatened-up piles of manuscripts, "I don't think that was one of my better ideas."

"Oh, I dunno," Danny said. "It gave me an idea for something I've been working on." This time Danny gestured with his mouse and an aquarium sprang into being on his desk. It was almost as big as the desk and full of water and life.

"Like it? It's Ian's birthday present."

Jerry examined his companion's work more closely. Against a backdrop of coral and rocks, brightly colored fish darted or hovered or swam lazily, according to their nature. Equally brightly colored crabs and other things crawled along the white coral sand, and here and there something like a sea anemone waved delicately in the water.

It was beautiful, but there was something about the setup that bothered Jerry. Part of it, he decided, was that he didn't recognize any of the fish. Then a black angelfish with pulsing neon-blue lights along its side swam by and Jerry's suspicions were confirmed.

"Those aren't real fish, are they?"

"No, they're demons created by special little programs." Danny spoke a word and the spell listed itself out in bright letters beside the tank. "Look, here's something else too. The code's self-modifying so the fish change over time."

"They change over time?"

"Yeah. They evolve with each generation."

"Hmmm," Jerry said in a voice that wasn't at all approving.

"What's the matter?"

"I'm not sure," Jerry said. "But there's something about that notion that bothers me."

"You don't like fish?"

"No, I . . . Well, never mind. I'm sure Ian will love it" Jerry turned away from the demon fish tank and back to work.

As the smoke artist took a bow to a pattering of applause, Wiz nudged Moira.

"That stuff's magic," he muttered.

"But isn't it lovely? See how it sparkles."

Wiz looked sideways at his wife. Normally Moira was more wary of strange magic than he was. She had learned about magic at a time when the humans of this world were nearly powerless and magic was usually destructive or hostile. Wiz had changed that with his magic programming, but the old attitudes lingered. This wasn't at all like her.

He looked at the robed and cowled figure again, trying to discern what was beneath the flow of dark cloth. Again the smoke artist's hands darted from his sleeves and he began anew with a delicate curl of blue smoke from his outstretched palm. Although Wiz could not see the artist's head, much less his eyes, he got the strong impression that the performer was concentrating on his audience rather than his illusion. The smoke thickened and deepened until there was a column of sapphire blue before him. The crowd pressed close, eager for the next display.

Again the smoke shifted and formed a pattern, this one like an intricately fretted snowflake. The tendrils of blue smoke twisted and wove among each other into a pattern that implied something without quite showing it. As Wiz watched, the pattern began to spin like a wheel, pulling the eye with it in a way that made Wiz's stomach roil. He stared down at his boots, fighting dizziness.

As he looked away he felt Moira stir beside him, pressing closer to the artist and his creation. Without thinking Wiz put a hand on her shoulder, but she shook it off impatiently.

Wiz looked up and saw his wife slack jawed with her eyes fixed on the smoke. She took a hesitant step toward it and then a stronger one.

"Moira?" There was no response. "Hey!" he shouted at the smoke artist, but neither artist nor audience paid the slightest attention.

Wiz went cold with fear and almost instantly hot with rage. In two strides he crossed the distance to the artist and grabbed him by the hood.

As he jerked him around, the hood fell back and Wiz recoiled at what was beneath it.

The face was normal enough, pale with high cheekbones and a long nose, but the eyes were not. Instead of showing a normal white and pupil they were iridescent, as though there were an opaline mist over the whole eyeball, or like an insect's eye when the light strikes it right.

The illusionist hissed like a frightened snake and wrenched away from Wiz. His hand darted out of his sleeve and instinctively Wiz twisted away so the hand struck his wizard's staff instead of his arm. There was a flash of blue lightning and a report like a rifle shot as magic met magic. That seemed to break his hold on the crowd and suddenly people were running and screaming, stampeding away from the booth.

Wiz stumbled back, his staff held before him. From down the row of booths came a shout and a flash of magic. Out of the corner of his eye Wiz saw Malus raise his staff to launch another attack.

The thing looked at Malus, back at Wiz and over Wiz's shoulder where Moira was standing. Without a word it whirled, gathering up the hem of its robe. Black smoke reeking of brimstone poured from the robe and rose in a whirlwind above Wiz's head. Malus fired another magic bolt at the growing black cloud, but it disappeared into the smoke without a trace.

Tall as a tree the black cloud grew, and the wind of its turning whipped and tore at the booths and the robes of the wizards. Then the cloud separated from the earth and darted into the sky, pursued by magical bolts from Malus and lightning bolts hurled by Wiz.

It climbed faster and faster until it was no larger than a hand, then a finger. Then it moved away to the south.

"What? Who?" Malus came rushing up oblivious to the commotion spreading throughout the fair. Then he seemed to realize he would not get answers to his questions and settled for indignation. "To think that they would try it here! Of all places! Why, why the sheer effrontery of it!" Wiz noticed he didn't specify who "they" were.

"Get help," Moira said tightly. "Quickly." Her words brought Wiz and Malus back to themselves and both fumbled for the communications crystals they wore around their necks.

"Are you all right?" Wiz asked his wife.

"I think so." She clung to him fiercely and let out a deep breath. "It was like being pulled along by a strong current, or sliding down a slope of loose earth. I've . . . "

Before she could continue there was a soft *pop* of displaced air and Arianne, Bal-Simba's assistant, appeared before them. Arianne's eyes were unfocused and her lips moved silently as she spoke to the communications crystal about her neck. Off behind her Wiz could see a flight of three dragons soaring away from their cavern aerie in the cliffs below the Wizards' Keep. The Watchers had launched the ready patrol.

"We sensed a flare of magic even before your call," she told the two wizards. "Now, what was this all about?"

"I don't know," Wiz said, "but I don't like it."

"A magical invasion of the fair," Malus added. "A creature posing as a man."

Moira was pale and shaking. "It was magic indeed. Like no magic I have ever felt before."

"Programmer magic?" Arianne asked.

Moira bit her lip. "Not exactly. Something like it, but different—colder. Does that make any sense?"

Since Wiz lacked the natural talent needed to sense magic of any sort he could only nod. He had heard his kind of magic described as "feeling" like a horde of ants as the tiny spells that made up the words of the magic programming language operated, but he'd never felt it.

Arianne, however, had. "Colder?"

Moira hesitated. "Not cold, exactly. Rather, not-alive."

Wiz had an image of zombie army ants. He didn't like the picture at all.

"... so whatever that thing was it had a special attraction for people who are sensitive to magic," Wiz summed up.

Around the table in the programmers' office Jerry, Danny, Bal-Simba and Arianne all listened intently. After more than an hour's rehashing of events, Moira wasn't paying much attention.

"Which explains why it didn't affect you," Danny put in. "Like the rest of us you haven't got any magical talent to speak of. But Moira probably had more than anyone else in the crowd so it really worked on her."

"All it did was make me dizzy," Wiz added. Moira looked down at her hands and said nothing.

"None of the other Mighty have ever seen or heard of the like," Arianne told them. "This is something completely new. Worse, the magic is so different we did not detect it until the Sparrow confronted the thing."

"Where did it come from?" Jerry asked.

"It arrived at the fairgrounds early this morning and set up its pavilion like any other merchant or entertainer," Arianne said. "None of the other merchants had ever seen the thing before but none took special notice of it until the whirlwind began. It so well concealed its nature that Malus walked by the booth several times without seeing anything amiss." She nodded at Wiz and Moira. "He apologizes most abjectly for not discovering it sooner."

"I cannot blame him," Moira said weakly.

"This thing is also," Wiz added, "immune to lightning bolts, and whatever spell Malus was throwing at it. But we still don't know what it is or what it was after."

"We can hazard a guess on the last, I think," rumbled Bal-Simba from his oversized chair at the head of the table. Although he had been physically present for the whole conference he had spent most of it receiving reports and communing magically with others of the Mighty.

"An attack?" Arianne asked.

"More likely a scout," the great black wizard said slowly. "Something sent ahead to spy us out and discover our defenses."

"So you don't think it was alone?"

"It seems unlikely. What we know now seems to suggest a being controlled or commanded from elsewhere, not an independent entity."

"Any idea who or where?"

Bal-Simba shrugged. "That is as yet unknown. Perhaps we can discover more when the Council of the North meets this evening." He heaved himself erect. "Now if you will excuse me, I must consult directly with the Watchers. My Lords, My Ladies." He sketched a bow and left.

"Are you sure you're all right? Do you want to go lie down?"

"No, I am fine."

"You don't look it," Danny put in. "You're white as a sheet and you look awful."

Moira looked up. "A fine thing to tell a woman, I am sure."

"Well, you do," Danny said defensively.

"Perhaps you had better go lie down, darling. You really don't look well."

Moira reached out and patted Wiz's hand. "Perhaps I will. Dealing with strange magics seems to take a lot out of me."

"Well," came a female voice from the door, "all alive I see."

Wiz looked up and saw a stout woman standing at the door. A boy and girl were peeking around her from either side and a dragon was looking over her shoulder.

"Oh, hello Shauna," Wiz said. "Any reason why we shouldn't be?"

Shauna was nurse to Ian, Danny and June's son, and mother of Ian's playmate Caitlin. In addition to looking after the children and mothering June as needed, she provided a strong dose of common sense for the programming team.

"Fortuna, but you should hear the stories being bandied about in the town!" She looked at Moira. "Do you know you and Wiz both are dead a dozen times over? And each death grislier than the last?"

In spite of himself Wiz grinned. "And there are a dozen eyewitnesses to each death, no doubt." He took a pull on his mug of tea.

"Folk are bolting their doors strong tonight," the stocky woman agreed. "Fact is, I've never seen them so frightened. It will put a damper on this year's fair, I'll tell you."

Moira stood up suddenly. "Then I am going back to the fair."

Wiz spewed tea all over the table. "*What?*"

Moira reached for her cloak. "I said I am going back. The people need reassurance."

"You're sick and you're going to bed."

"People need my help and I am well enough for that."

Wiz started to protest, realized this was another one of those arguments he wasn't going to win and changed course.

"Then I'm going with you," he said grimly.

"How much reassurance is there if I am in the company of the mightiest wizard of the North? No, if this is to be effective you must not come."

"Look, we don't know what that thing was or what it can do. I'm not going to let you go down there alone."

Moira put her cloak down on the table and turned to face him. "That 'thing' is gone."

"And what happens if you nearly pass out like you did this morning? That'll be a lot of reassurance for everyone."

"I will manage."

"You'll manage better with the proper company, My Lady," Shauna said, looking closely at Moira. "No, not you," she added before Wiz could open his mouth. "I'm the one to go with her."

Wiz had the feeling he'd just missed something important and an even stronger feeling that the situation was getting out of control.

"Still, I'm not sure it's safe."

"As safe as anywhere," Moira retorted.

Arianne nodded. "Three of the Mighty have examined the rest of the fair and found nothing more. This thing harmed no one and I have alerted the Watchers in the castle. With them on guard it will not be able to sneak close again. Meanwhile, Bal-Simba has summoned the Council of the North to meet to consider what more is to be done."

"Besides, Fluffy will protect us!" Ian said.

Wiz raised his eyebrows and looked past the boy at the twenty-foot dragon standing behind him. The dragon's tongue was lolling out and he was panting like a particularly dumb dog.

Fluffy was a very young dragon, hardly older than Ian. Like all immature dragons he was not very smart. But unlike most of them he was more or less a house pet—a circumstance that aroused considerable comment in the Wizards' Keep and even more among the townsfolk.

Fluffy had attached himself to the programmers as a housecat-sized hatchling. When Ian was born, the two became inseparable. Originally the programmers had called him Little Red Dragon, or LRD for short. But Ian insisted his name was Fluffy and, wildly inappropriate as the monicker was, it stuck.

If there was trouble the dragon was only likely to make it worse, but separating Ian and Fluffy made them both mope, so if Ian went to the fair it was a foregone conclusion that Fluffy was going too. The prospect did nothing to raise Wiz's enthusiasm for the expedition.

Danny, meanwhile, had grasped the critical point. "*Us?*" he demanded of his son. "Who said anything about you going?"

"Shauna's going," Ian said. "You always said we should stay close to Shauna, especially if there's trouble."

While Danny was at a loss over the eight-year-old's logic, Shauna's daughter saw her opportunity and moved in for the kill. Caitlin was a couple of years older than Ian, with a mop of jet-black hair, apple cheeks and great dark eyes. She had her Ph.D. in cute with advanced graduate work in wheedling.

"We want to go to the fair," Caitlin protested.

Danny tried for a compromise. "You can go to the fair tomorrow when it's open."

"Tomorrow's too late," Ian protested. "Everything will be up by then."

Wiz wasn't sure why it was more interesting to watch the booths go up than to see them once they were up and open, but that was clearly the general opinion. Even Fluffy managed to droop sadly at what he'd be missing.

"All right, then I'm going too," Danny said.

"You would be almost as bad as Wiz," Moira told him. "You had best stay here as well."

June stood close behind her son with a hand on his shoulder. "I go too." Which figured, since June was as protective of Ian as a mother tiger is of her cub.

Danny looked over at June and Ian and scowled, but he nodded.

"Well, all right but you stay close, you hear?" And then, as Caitlin and Ian cheered, Shauna added: "And keep that creature on the leash!"

Ian had obviously been anticipating victory because he had the dragon's collar and braided leather leash tucked in his belt.

Fluffy drooped his head so Ian could attach his collar. In fact the leash was strictly for show. Fluffy wouldn't allow anyone but Ian to lead him and there was no way the boy could have held the dragon against his will. As it was Fluffy had a tendency to jerk Ian off his feet with a casual toss of his head. But the sight of the leash made townsfolk slightly more comfortable around the dragon and Fluffy seemed to understand that the leash meant he was to be on his best behavior. Besides, Ian was inordinately proud of his job "controlling" Fluffy.

"Okay," Wiz said to his wife. "You won't take me and you won't take Danny. What about Jerry?"

Moira raised an eyebrow and looked over at Arianne. The tall woman stroked her chin in thought. "Appropriate enough," she said finally.

"I dunno," the big programmer demurred. "I've got this homicidal screen saver I'm working on."

Caitlin tugged on his arm and looked up at him with enormous dark eyes.

"Please, Unca Jerry. It won't be any fun without you. Please come."

Jerry suddenly found he was not at all immune to the wiles of a little girl. In fact, like most men without children of their own, he could be twisted around a tiny pinky almost without effort.

"Sure," he sighed. "I'll go back with you. That way the kids can see what's going on."

Wiz looked down at the dark stain of spilled tea on his shirt. "Well, darling," he sighed, "at least keep your eyes open and yell at the first sign of trouble. I think that thing was after you."

Arianne looked at him closely. "Can you be sure it is aimed at Moira?"

"I don't like the way it looked at her."

"You said it seemed to be surveying the crowd."

"Yeah, but . . . " Wiz lapsed into an unhappy silence.

"Oh, don't brood love," Moira said. "It is perfectly safe and I will have Jerry with me should need arise."

"Plus two kids," Wiz added. There was an insistent *whuff* over his shoulder. "And a dragon."

"Shauna and June will be along as well," Moira countered.

That carried some weight, Wiz had to admit. Shauna could keep the kids under control and June was likely to be at least some help. Danny's wife was strange and half wild from growing up in an elf hill, but she was no one to trifle with. On one memorable occasion Wiz had seen her take out three fully armed hobgoblins with the knife she always carried.

"Well, I still don't like it."

Moira reached out and put her hand on his arm. "Pooh. You heard Arianne. There is no danger now. But the townsfolk must be reassured, so it needs to be done."

"We've got to do something about this Calvinist sense of duty of yours," Wiz said as Moira picked up her cloak.

"Who is Calvin?"

"He designed genes," Wiz said absently, "and he gave you the heavy-duty kind."

Moira did what she usually did when she didn't understand her husband, which was to change the subject. "You're a fine one to talk about duty. All a dragon has to do is show up and make some threats and you go off with him and we don't hear from you for weeks."

"That was different," Wiz said with some dignity—hoping reverently Moira wouldn't ask him how it was different. She settled for cocking a coppery eyebrow and fastening the cloak at her throat.

Then, seeing his expression, Moira reached out and took his hand. "Please, Wiz."

Wiz hesitated and then relented. "As long as it's safe."

She kissed him on the cheek. "Oh, we'll be fine," she told him. "You worry too much."

Far and far away, in a place below the earth, a thing considered.

*It was enough. It had found what it needed. Now there was only the harvest.*

Danny and Wiz stood at a window and watched the group cross the courtyard and pass out the castle gate.

"I guess they're right," Wiz said, as much for his own reassurance as Danny's. "It's perfectly safe." He sighed. "I wonder if I'm getting paranoid in my old age."

"I know *I'm* paranoid," Danny said grimly. "I just don't know if I'm paranoid enough."

## THREE

# THE FAIR AGAIN

The fair was very different in the afternoon than it had been that morning. Intermittent clouds hid the sun and the air that had been crisp and invigorating in the morning was now chill and damp. Even the mud seemed deeper.

All of which could have been her imagination, Moira admitted, but there were other changes which clearly were not.

The crowds of gawkers were gone, leaving only the fair workers, merchants and here and there a knot of guardsmen, armed and alert. There was less shouting and no laughter as people struggled to get their goods unloaded and their tents up.

None of which mattered to the children. Ian and Caitlin went whooping and shouting among the booths, avoiding most of the uninteresting mud puddles and seeming to be everywhere at once. Fluffy trotted along with them, head high like a show dog in the ring. Shauna puffed along behind, calling out admonishments and generally trying to keep them under control. June floated along near Ian, close and silent as always.

It would have been a perfectly normal scene, Moira thought, if June didn't keep one hand always on her knife.

She dug Jerry in the ribs with her elbow. "Smile," she commanded out of the side of her mouth. Then, putting on her best beauty-pageant smile, she and Jerry began to stroll among the booths.

Moira paused frequently to admire goods on display or to chat with someone she knew. Jerry contented himself with smiling until his jaw ached and responding to any pleasantries directed to him.

Ian and Caitlin were disappointed at the pace, especially since June and Shauna would not let them get too far ahead of the others. Still they managed to find all sorts of interesting things to look at and interesting questions to ask. They even cajoled a chestnut vendor into blowing up his fire to roast some nuts for them.

They had gone perhaps halfway down the main aisle when Shamus, the captain of the castle's guards, separated himself from a knot of his men and came over to greet them.

"A pleasure to see you, My Lady," he said loudly as he smiled and bowed. His eyes never stopped moving.

Moira nodded to the guard captain. "Good afternoon, Shamus," she said equally loudly. "Oh, I would not have missed it."

The guardsman took her hand as if to kiss it and used that as an excuse to move closer.

"Thanks for coming," he muttered. "The whole place is nervous as a bunch of half-wild dragons. Want an escort?"

Moira dimpled as if she had been paid a compliment. "It would ruin the effect," she said without moving her lips.

Shamus bowed as if taking his leave. "Need anything just sing out." With that he turned and strolled away as if he had not a care in the world. Moira noticed his sword was loose in its sheath.

What with one thing and another it took them the better part of two hours to tour the fairgrounds. Moira stopped and chatted with everyone she knew even casually and Jerry thought he'd never get his jaw unclenched. Even when Fluffy knocked over a pile of baskets with a careless twitch of his tail, Moira managed to turn the gaffe into a social triumph, getting down on her knees to help the stall owner gather up her spilled merchandise and talking gaily all the while.

By the time the group turned back toward the castle the mood in the fairgrounds had lightened perceptibly. Ian had fallen asleep on Shauna's shoulder with Fluffy's leash still clutched tight in his fist. Caitlin was chattering away, but she was content to walk alongside her mother instead of scampering everywhere.

The older members of the party were doing no better.

"My feet hurt," Jerry said as they picked their way up the muddy main aisle back toward the town gate.

Moira smiled at him. "It was in a good cause, My Lord. Thank you for coming."

Something in the way she said it made Jerry look at her more closely. "You're really wiped, aren't you?"

A vagrant breeze drew a lock of coppery hair over the hedge witch's cheek, emphasizing the paleness of her skin. "I am rather tired, but very content." She sighed.

"You'd better rest up tonight if you want to be in shape for the ceremony tomorrow."

The breeze turned suddenly chilly and Moira shivered and drew her green wool cloak closer around her. "I will," she promised. "Just now nothing sounds so good as a hot bath and a warm bed."

"Momma, I'm cold." Caitlin pressed herself closer to Shauna.

"That's what you get for not wearing so much as a cloak, like I told you to." Then she hugged her daughter close against the cold wind. "Never you mind. We'll be home soon enough."

Jerry shivered and pulled his cloak tighter. "I wish I'd brought something heavier. This wind's picking up."

Even Fluffy seemed to notice the wind. The dragon lowered his neck and turned his head to shelter from the full force behind Shauna's bulk. Ian stirred and whimpered on Shauna's shoulder.

Moira looked at the tents beginning to flap against

their ropes and squinted her eyes against the sting of wind-borne dirt. "Perhaps we had better rest a few minutes inside the city gate," she said. "I think I need to sit down."

Jerry raised his voice to be heard over the wind. "We're only halfway there. Want to rest in one of the pavilions?"

"Let us go on. It is only a few hundred paces."

They had reached the spot in the center of the fairgrounds where the main ways crossed. Here the aisles widened out into an impromptu square and the wind tore at them as they stepped out of the relative shelter of the narrower ways.

It tore and howled at them, kicking up dirt and debris until they could hardly see the far side of the square. The wind moaned through the tent ropes and made the canvas boom until it sounded like a chorus of lost souls. Jerry put his head down and pushed forward against the wind, clutching Moira's arm to help her along.

He felt Moira stiffen and slow in spite of his efforts to help her along. "Jerry . . . " she began, and he looked up.

There were things in the wind. At first Jerry thought his eyes were playing tricks on him, but they seemed to grow darker and more solid as he watched. Then they were black clouds within a lighter cloud, indistinct forms that grew and writhed as they moved toward him.

They had no arms, but they seemed to reach out to clutch. They had no heads, but they seemed to fasten their attention on Jerry and Moira with the intentness of a hunting eagle. They had no mouths, but their voices seemed to call out for them, eagerly, hungrily. Moira whimpered and shrank back against Jerry's shoulder as the things drew close.

Jerry stepped in front and threw up his hands in a warding spell. A foggy tentacle lashed out to touch him and he collapsed like a sack of meal.

In the excitement Ian dropped Fluffy's leash. With

a *wheep* of dragonish rage the young dragon lumbered into the fray, tail lashing left and right, upsetting tables and knocking down a pavilion. He snapped at the cloud things but his jaws closed on nothing at all with the sound of a rifle shot.

"*Wiz!*" Moira screamed.

And Wiz was there. Cloakless, hatless, bootless, his wizard's staff clutched before him in both hands. He looked around wide-eyed, then leaped over his friend's prostrate body to put himself between the shadows and Moira, but he did not let the things touch him. Instead he raised his staff, shouting a magic word as he did so.

Wiz swung his staff overhead in a mighty bash. There was an eye-searing burst of purple fire as magic met magic and an ear-piercing peal of thunder as the thing disintegrated. Without hesitating he lashed out again and another monster disappeared with the same flash and roar. Again and again Wiz laid about him at the encircling fog things. Behind him Bal-Simba popped into the square.

With an inarticulate roar the big wizard charged into the battle. Behind him wizard after wizard popped into existence as the Mighty of the North rallied to protect their own. The square echoed and flashed with the blasts of magic.

Wiz tried to reach Moira but Fluffy was in his way. So he put his back against the dragon and struck out furiously at the things in the whirlwind.

And then it was over.

As suddenly as they had come the things were gone. The wind dropped to nothing, the air cleared and only wizards and their allies were left in the open space.

Wiz looked around. Two of the wizards rushed to where Jerry lay senseless on the ground. The others stood or milled around, alert for their enemy. Pressed up against the tents, Shauna stood with Ian and Caitlin gathered behind her skirts. June stood next to her, knife drawn, nostrils flared, and showing white all the way around her pupils like a frightened animal. She only relaxed when Danny rushed to her side.

The only person Wiz couldn't see was the person he wanted to see most.

"Moira?" Wiz called, "Moira!"

"Here darling."

Wiz turned to the sound of the voice, but Moira wasn't there. Only Fluffy, leaning drunkenly against a post.

"Moira?" Wiz looked around wildly.

"I feel funny," came Moira's voice again. "So dizzy."

Wiz's jaw dropped. The voice was coming from Fluffy, the little red dragon.

"Oh my God!"

FOUR

# The Lady and the Dragon

Wiz Zumwalt stood at the window staring sightlessly at the snowscape below. The wan sun was painting the tops of the clouds sullen red as it sank toward the horizon. Guardsmen manned the castle walls at close intervals and in the growing gloom he could see blue witchfire flicker about one or two towers as the wizards within them worked protective spells.

Listlessly he wiped his breath fog from the diamond panes with his sleeve. He probably should have been with the other wizards but he couldn't concentrate. Instead Danny was handling things. Nothing had happened for hours.

"Excuse me, My Lord." Bronwyn, the castle's chief healer, was standing behind him. Her square face and brown eyes were grave, but then Bronwyn always looked serious.

"How is she? I mean, how is the dragon?"

"I think 'she' is most appropriate for now," the chief healer said. Then she paused to pick her words. "Lord, such things are not unknown. Wizards have inhabited others' bodies by similar methods before. The adepts of the Dark League more commonly, but even the Mighty of the North have resorted to the tactic on occasion. As a result we know a good deal about the condition and its effects."

Wiz brushed all that aside. "But is she going to be all right?"

"Her spirit and her intelligence, her ka, if you will, are safe for now," Bronwyn said.

"For now?"

The healer fixed him with her steady brown eyes. "A human in a dragon's body is not a natural combination. Still less when the dragon is not yet full-grown and intelligent. Such mixtures are not stable."

"Meaning what?"

"If it is allowed to go on long enough, deterioration sets in. The personalities become mixed, degenerate and the level of intelligence descends to match the body. Once that happens there is no restoring the human personality even if it is returned to its body."

Wiz's breath caught in his throat. "How long have we got?"

Bronwyn shrugged. "Weeks, perhaps a pair of moons. Moira's personality is strong, so that works in our favor. But the dragon is an alien animal and not intelligent in his own right. That works against us."

Wiz turned from her and slammed his fist into the stone wall. He left a dark smear of blood where his knuckles hit but he didn't notice.

"We are doing everything we can, Lord."

"I know you are. Thanks Bronwyn. Uh, how's Jerry?"

"I think he will be well. We think the things attempted to do the same thing to him but you foiled them by your attack. For now he sleeps the enchanted sleep. He will awake in his own time, but we do not know how long it will be. Several days at least"

"Well, thanks." He turned back to the window.

"My Lord, there is something else you should know."

Wiz turned and looked at her.

"Telling you this violates a confidence, but you are party to the situation and I do not think Moira will tell you herself."

The healer hesitated. Clearly violating a confidence did not come easy to her. "She was—is—pregnant."

"What?"

Bronwyn regarded him soberly. "She is with child, perhaps two moons along."

"But I didn't know! I mean, why didn't she tell me?"

"She wanted to be sure. Then she intended to tell you, after the fair. She did not want you to worry during the festivities. Now"—Bronwyn shrugged—"I do not believe she is thinking clearly."

Wiz sank back against the stone wall. "Oh my God. Oh my God."

The healer watched him closely but did not move toward him. "I know it is a shock to find out like this. Still, it is best that you know."

"We'd been trying . . . " was all he could get out.

With a healer's instinct Bronwyn ignored his tears. "As you well know it is uncommon for a witch to become pregnant. The practice of magic drains the vital energies and makes it hard for a magician to either father or conceive a child. Still, with patience, persistence and a little luck . . . " The healer shrugged.

Wiz nodded dumbly. Moira had consulted Bronwyn several times in her efforts to conceive. He remembered the earlier byplay between Shauna and Moira. Now he understood.

"What . . . what should we do?"

Bronwyn shook her head. "Lord, this is beyond my experience. All we can do is to do the best we can to reunite Moira with her body." She paused. "I have no reason to believe that the separation will harm the child."

Wiz sat heavily on a bench beside the window. "Thanks, Bronwyn."

"If there is aught else I can do? Something to help you sleep perhaps?"

"No, I'll be all right. There's things I need to do."

The healer nodded and withdrew, leaving Wiz to his thoughts.

Night and fog closed around the Wizards' Keep, black, damp and almost palpable.

The lamps burned in Bal-Simba's workroom where the leader of the Council of the North sat and thought.

There was a single knock at the door. Bal-Simba gestured and Arianne entered.

"Any sign?" the giant black wizard asked.

"The Watchers can find nothing. Not even sign of anything unusual."

"To be expected, I fear."

"Lord, you know that Moira was pregnant?"

Bal-Simba nodded. "Bronwyn told me." He sank his chin into a meaty palm. "I wonder if that was what attracted this creature to her?"

Arianne's eyes went wide at the thought. Then she bit her lip. "That implies somewhat unpleasant things about our enemy," she said neutrally.

"Very unpleasant indeed." He sighed. "Beyond the fact that it was Moira, this business has aspects I do not like at all."

"Our enemy seems powerful."

"Powerful, strange and malign," Bal-Simba agreed. "Since the Sparrow has been among us we have seen the magic of elves and even things not entirely of this world. But never magic of the sort I saw today."

Arianne, who had stayed at the Wizards' Keep to organize the defenses cocked a questioning eyebrow.

"Have you ever dealt with a viper?" Bal-Simba asked. "Something small and mindless yet full of menace and the single desire to harm? That was what those things were like."

"Yet even a viper has reason," Arianne said. "They act so to defend themselves or because they are frightened."

Bal-Simba gave her a tired smile. "And in understanding the viper we become able to deal with it. We may hope that these things act with reason as well and that by understanding their reason we can learn to deal with them." He didn't say it with a lot of conviction.

Both of them were silent for a moment. "Well," Bal-Simba sighed at last. "If the Watchers cannot find anything, best to resort to other methods. Have my scrying bowl brought to me. If it will not show us Moira—and I doubt very much that it will—we can at least learn where this new magic lairs."

"Oh, and Lady . . . " Arianne turned, hand on the door handle.

"We need not mention our speculations to the Sparrow. Certainly not yet."

"Of course, My Lord."

Someone edged into the room. Looking up, Wiz saw it was Malus.

"Excuse me, My Lord," the pudgy wizard said. "I just heard what happened. I wanted to offer condolences—and whatever aid I might give."

"Thanks, Malus. I appreciate it."

"I was going to ask you about my spell." He drew the roll of parchment from his sleeve and looked at it ruefully. "It seems so trivial now."

Wiz held out his hand. "Give it to me."

"Now, My Lord?"

"I've got to keep busy," Wiz said grimly.

"Oh, of course, My Lord. And if there's anything I can do, anything at all."

Wiz clapped the fat little man on the shoulder. "Thank you, Malus. You're a good friend."

After Malus left, Wiz spread out the parchment strips and arranged them on a bench beside the window. Like all spells it was written on parallel strips so the spell would not be activated by the act of writing it. Wiz stared at them for nearly five minutes before he realized he had the strips out of order. With a sigh he picked them up and stuffed them in his belt pouch. Then he wandered down the hall toward the programmers' workroom.

He found Danny hard at it. There were at least six

listings in different colors above his workbench and two emacs below them giving more magical commands. As Wiz entered, his young colleague whispered something to a third emac seated cross legged on the floor and the demon made a note with a quill pen on a strip of parchment in its lap.

June was in the corner with Ian nestled wide-eyed and clinging in her skirt. Her other hand stayed near her knife. She hadn't let her husband or son out of her sight since the attack.

"Have you been able to get a line on the spell?"

Danny turned toward him and made a face. "This thing is real cute. First, you were right. It was done with something based more or less on our magic compiler."

"Which version?"

"I said more or less. It's been hacked, moby hacked. There's stuff in there I've never seen and I've got no idea what it does. There's other stuff that goes back to your original quick-and-dirty interpreter, in a couple of cases stuff we took out of the later versions because it wasn't stable. Then there's stuff that's just been fine-tuned."

He gestured and another screen opened, showing another listing. Here and there lines of code stood out in brighter fire.

"Those things we met in the square are very loosely based, maybe 'inspired' is closer, on our searcher system. The highlighted parts were probably lifted verbatim. But each of the things in the square is considerably more complex than our searchers—and a lot more lethal."

"How do they work?"

"I'm not quite sure. What they do is to suck the life force out of their victim, like a bunch of magical vampires. But there's more to it than that and I'm not sure what. Like I say, some of this stuff is just real strange. Some of it is beautifully tuned, some of it is damn crude and a lot of it doesn't look like it does anything at all." He paused. "You know, I think I saw something like this once on the net. A guy kept posting stuff to alt.c.sources. He was a really good programmer only he was going psycho and in his last articles before they took him away he had this same kind of mix of off-the-wall brilliant and just plain off the wall."

"This guy's too strong just to be crazy. Where's this stuff coming from?"

Danny shrugged. "Bal-Simba and some of the others are working on that. I've been concentrating on trying to understand what we're up against."

Wiz was still looking at the code when the door banged open and Malkin strode in.

The tall thief looked like grim death. Her lips were pressed into a hard bloodless line and her dark eyes glinted dangerously. Clearly she wanted to kill someone. Wiz could sympathize.

"Word reached me at Heart's Ease," she said by way of greeting.

"Jerry's in your apartment . . . " Wiz began.

"I know. I have already seen him, much good that it did me. Now I want some answers. Then I want someone's head."

"I bet you think those are original ideas," Wiz said bitterly.

Malkin softened. "I know they are not, My Lord. Your loss is much greater than mine and I am truly, deeply sorry." Then her jaw clenched and her eyes flashed again. "And it gives me one more reason to want this one's head on a pike."

Even through his own misery Wiz was impressed, and a little awed. Normally Malkin was almost obsessively cheery, even in the face of utter disaster. He had never seen her this angry before—not, he thought, that she'd ever had this kind of reason before—and the effect was definitely impressive. More accurately, it was downright scary.

Malkin let out a sigh through her teeth and seemed

to relax through a sheer effort of will. "Now then, tell me what happened at the fair this day."

Talking in shifts and interrupting each other, Wiz and Danny filled her in on the attack.

"So," Malkin said as the programmers wound down, "does this thing come to us or do we winkle it out of its hole?"

Danny and Wiz looked at each other. Neither of them had gone that far in their thinking.

"I think we need more information," Wiz said. "We don't know where this thing is from, how many of them there are, how their magic works or even much about how they operate."

"What he means is we're still in the fact-gathering phase on this one," Danny said. "We gotta get our information together and work out a strategy."

Malkin snorted. "And once you have done all that? What then?"

"Then," Wiz said grimly, "we are going to kick some serious magical butt."

All three of them were early for the council meeting but they found Bal-Simba already in the council chamber with an elaborately chased bronze bowl before him.

"My Lords, My Lady," the big wizard greeted them as they entered.

"Have you found them?" Malkin asked, noting the scrying bowl on the table.

"We are not sure, but we have located the place where the effect is most powerful."

"Where?" Wiz, Danny and Malkin demanded as one.

In response Bal-Simba gestured. The water in the bowl darkened and then the image sprang up bright and clear. The image of a ruined black city on the slope of an extinct volcano.

"The City Of Night!" Wiz breathed.

"So it would appear," Bal-Simba said grimly. "The force is strongest in the caverns and tunnels beneath the place."

"We should have wiped it off the face of the earth," Wiz said bitterly. "It's been nothing but trouble since the Dark League built it."

"Do not be so eager to upset the balance of the World," Bal-Simba told him. "Still, we have been remiss in how we watched the place."

Theoretically the City of Night was deserted, save for occasional roaming monsters left over from the Dark League's reign. Part of the city had been destroyed in the climactic magical battle in which Wiz and the Council had broken the League's power and killed many of its members.

In practice the place had needed the attentions of the Council twice since, once when Wiz was kidnapped there by a remnant of the Dark League and once to lay the slaying demon Bale-Zur, who had been the League's most potent weapon. Since then the Council had watched the place by magic and occasional patrols of dragon cavalry but otherwise left it alone.

"What do we do now?" Wiz asked.

"That is for the Council to decide, I think."

"Hmpf!" said Malkin, in a tone that left no doubt about her opinion of the Council's decision-making ability. Wiz tried to ignore her and look on the bright side.

Four hours later it was abundantly clear that Malkin *had* been looking on the bright side.

"So we are at least agreed, are we not, on the need for action?" Bal-Simba rumbled wearily. That produced a general murmur and nodding of heads all the way down the table. Of course, Wiz noted sourly, some of the older heads were nodding because they were having trouble staying awake after going around and around over the same issues.

"Oh, certainly," old Androclus said from his seat halfway down the table, "but," he waggled an admonitory finger, "with caution."

"Caution be fornicated," growled Juvian. "We must act before this thing strikes again." He traded glares with Androclus, they being opponents of long standing.

From his seat next to Bal-Simba, Wiz looked over at Malkin sitting against the wall. They exchanged looks of complete sympathy. If some of the older members were having trouble staying awake at this late-night session, Wiz and Malkin were having trouble keeping from strangling the council members. Danny and June had taken Ian to bed a couple of hours ago when it became abundantly clear where this session wasn't going. Wiz and Malkin had stayed and fretted and fumed.

"My Lords," Bal-Simba said. "I think we need to sleep on this before we decide further. "Let us meet again at mid-day tomorrow. By then perhaps we shall know more." That produced the strongest agreement Wiz had heard all evening and the meeting broke up without having decided anything at all.

"Well," Wiz growled to Bal-Simba as they left the room, "that was a complete and utter waste of time."

"Because we did not set out on crusade this evening?" the big wizard asked. "You judge too quickly, Sparrow."

In reply Wiz drove his fist into the stone wall beside them. The scabs on his knuckles broke and blood marred the smooth white limestone.

"Speaking of wastes of time," Bal-Simba said mildly.

"Yeah, but it's so frustrating! We're spinning our wheels wasting time and Moira doesn't have much time."

"A wizard must be the master of his frustrations. If you let them master you they will lead you to disaster entire. Besides, we learned several things this night."

"Name three," Wiz snapped.

Bal-Simba ticked them off on his fingers. "We learned that none of the Mighty has ever encountered this thing before, nor, as far as we can find, have the hedge witches or any other human magician. That means that it struck first at the heart of the human lands. Which in turn means what happened was not some chance encounter but a planned attack with magic we have never seen. That suggests in turn that this thing has been biding its time while it honed its powers elsewhere. And that . . . but there are your three, Sparrow, and several besides."

"So what are we going to do about it?"

"Scant choice in that, is there? We will fight this thing and I hope we shall defeat it. As to the details—" Bal-Simba shrugged "—those we shall decide in Council."

"I wonder if that bunch will ever decide anything."

"Unjust, Sparrow. True, the Council is a deliberative body but would you rather we dash off heedless and ignorant against an enemy who is clearly prepared for us?"

Wiz looked at him narrowly. "You're not real unhappy about the way things went tonight, are you?"

"There are worse paths to follow than to gain information before acting. As we know more I think the Council's position will become more definite."

*And the worst of it is,* Wiz thought as he turned down the hall to his quarters, *he's right.* In spite of his loss and anger, Wiz understood Bal-Simba's caution. They desperately needed to know more about this strange enemy and there really was no good strategy that could be formulated until they knew more. From his time on the Council Wiz also understood that Bal-Simba had deliberately let the meeting drift so the Council would not commit foolishly to a plan. He knew all that, he understood the need for it and he didn't like any of it.

He opened his door and nearly tripped over his wife's tail.

The dragon jerked its head upright with its neck taut. Then the eyes seemed to soften and the body relaxed as Moira asserted control.

"I'm sorry, love, you startled me."

"Sorry. I was thinking about something else."

The dragon slithered around to face him. "It did not go well?"

Wiz forced himself to look into the reptilian eyes. "Well enough, I guess. The Council didn't decide anything, but at least they're not going charging off on a wild goose chase. Why didn't you tell me you were pregnant?"

Moira started at the change of subject. "I meant to, but first I wasn't sure and then with the Winter Fair coming on, I didn't want you to worry."

"I wish you had told me."

Moira sighed, a great sulfurous sigh. "I wish I had too."

Instinctively Wiz moved to take Moira in his arms, but the only part of her he could get his arms around was her long scaly neck and that put her head well above his. She lowered her head and he adjusted his grip to just behind her ears but found he couldn't look at her that way. He settled for dropping into a chair and Moira resting her head in his lap.

One side of Wiz's mouth twitched up in what might have passed for a smile. "Some technical problems here."

"I know," Moira said sadly. "I'm afraid the bedroom is a mess. When I got back my first thought was to throw myself on the bed and cry. But the bed was not made to support this body's weight and I am afraid we shall both have to sleep on the floor tonight."

"That's all right."

Moira twisted around to look at him. "Do you know dragons cannot cry? No matter how sad they are, or how miserable or how frightened, they cannot cry."

Wiz felt the tears flowing down his own cheeks. "I guess . . . " He took a deep breath. "I guess I'll have to do the crying for both of us."

Then his head came up. "I swear I'll get you back. I don't care who's behind it, I'll get you back and make them pay!"

"I know you will, love," Moira said simply and snuggled her head into his lap.

Wiz wasn't sure how much either of them was lying for the other's benefit.

The late-rising winter sun was just a dull glow through the fog and low-hanging clouds, but already the programmers' workroom was full. Jerry was still in a coma, but Danny was hard at work at his desk. June was sitting in the corner with Ian more or less asleep in her lap. Malkin was in another corner, very ostentatiously touching up the edges of a double-edged dagger with a bit of fine-grained stone. Beside her lay a swordbelt with a cup-hilted rapier. Moira was off attending to what she delicately referred to as "dragon business."

"Anything?" Wiz asked as he strode into the room.

Danny didn't take his eyes off the screens. "Not much. Mostly it just confirms what we knew last night. I've got a little more on how this spell works, but boy is it peculiar. I wish Jerry was here, this is more his kind of thing." He turned to face his friend. "Do you want to take a crack at it?"

"Not right now. I've got some other stuff to do."

Malkin tested the dagger's edge against her thumbnail, paring off a nearly transparent scraping. "Like what?"

"Like a little scouting expedition. The one thing we do know is that the Enemy seems to be headquartered at the City of Night. The other thing we know is we need to know a lot more about him. So I intend to go poking around and see what I find."

"What you are likely to find, Sparrow, is more trouble than you can handle."

Wiz turned and saw Bal-Simba standing in the doorway. "This enemy is dangerous enough on our ground," he continued as he came into the room. "He is likely to be far more dangerous on ground he has made his own."

The big wizard settled into his over-sized chair. "I met Moira in the corridor," he said by way of explanation.

"She said she believed you had formed a plan last night and begged me to discover it."

"It's kinda hard to get any sleep when you're sharing a small bedroom with a dragon," Wiz said.

"And it is not wise to plan great matters when you are fatigued," Bal-Simba responded. "This idea of yours does not seem to have much to recommend it."

"Relax. I'm not going to take this character on alone. All I'm going to do is get the lay of the land so we'll have a better idea what we're dealing with."

Bal-Simba raised an eyebrow and said nothing.

"Look, you said it yourself. The Council won't move until we know more. We're likely to find out more by scouting this guy than sitting around here. I've been in those tunnels more than anyone else. Once when I rescued Moira from the Dark League, then when I was kidnapped back there and then when we went back to lay Bale-Zur."

"We didn't go into the tunnels that time," Danny said. Wiz glared at him.

"Anyway, the point is, I'm the logical one to scout it out because I know that place."

Bal-Simba's skeptical silence reminded Wiz just how untrue the last bit was. Wiz had seen only a tiny fraction of that giant maze and, being the kind who loses his car in a supermarket parking lot, he couldn't remember much of anything about the layout.

"At some point we're going to have to scout, and now's the best time. Besides, we can't just react. We've got to act and information is the only thing that will get the Council off dead center. Besides," he added after a brief pause, "Moira doesn't have time to waste."

For a long while Bal-Simba said nothing. Then he sighed. "If I could forbid you I would. But we both know I cannot and giving commands which you cannot enforce is unbecoming of a leader. So go if you must, and we will contrive without you."

Malkin stood up and jammed her dagger home in its sheath. "You'll have to contrive without me as well."

Wiz shook his head. "Sorry, this is a one-man show."

"I have a stake in this," Malkin said, jerking her head back toward the room where Jerry lay. "Besides I've got a feeling you're going to need the best thief you can get."

"Meaning you?" Danny interjected.

Malkin spread her hands, smiled slightly and shrugged.

"Shiara does say she is as good as she herself was in her prime," Bal-Simba put in.

"Shiara's not giving her enough credit," Wiz said sourly, remembering Malkin's escapades as his "assistant" in the Dragon Marches.

"So you need me. I'm coming." Then her face softened and her eyes sparkled. "Besides, it should be a tremendous adventure."

*And if it's not at first, you'll make sure it is.* His previous experience had left him all too familiar with Malkin's taste for excitement. He looked over at Danny for support but June was beside him, clutching her husband's arm.

"I'm in this too," he said.

June paled and bit her lip. Then she took Danny's arm. "And me," she said simply.

"Why doesn't that surprise me? Why don't we just take every wizard in the North?"

"You cannot do it alone, Sparrow," Bal-Simba said mildly.

"This is supposed to be a surgical operation. The bigger the team the harder to hide."

Malkin and June just looked at him.

"Okay," Wiz sighed. "We're four."

"Five, I think," said Bal-Simba, looking over Wiz's shoulder.

Wiz looked hard at the big wizard. "You too?"

"No," came a voice from behind him, "me."

## FIVE

# A Question of Company

There was a dwarf in the doorway. A rather young dwarf with a large and very gaudy sword slung over his shoulder.

Wiz wasn't good at telling dwarves apart, but in all the World there was only one sword decorated in such hideously bad taste.

"Glandurg?"

"I told you once, Wizard, the day would come when you would need doughty fighters. I promised you then that on that day I would stand with you."

"Uh, thanks," Wiz muttered. He and Glandurg had never been formally introduced. That had something to do with the fact that Glandurg had spent most of their acquaintance trying to kill him. This had been the result of some kind of deal between Glandurg's uncle, a very minor dwarf king, and a gang of trolls. That had been patched over, but to say that Wiz wasn't thrilled to see the dwarf again was to put it mildly.

Glandurg reached over his shoulder and patted the gem-encrusted hilt of his weapon. "The sword Blind Fury has dispatched one of your enemies. Now it shall sing in battle against your new foes."

That was the other thing. Blind Fury was not only decorated in eye-searingly gaudy style, it was enchanted and no one could withstand its blows. But like its present wielder the spell was seriously lacking in ept. The sword had indeed slain an enemy programmer-magician by slicing through a suit of heavy power armor like it was soggy toilet paper. However, the blow had been aimed at Wiz, and Craig, the programmer, had the misfortune to be standing next to him.

Wiz cast a look of mute appeal at Bal-Simba. The big wizard simply spread his hands. "If you will excuse me, Sparrow, I have other matters to attend to." With that he rose and left.

"Now then," Malkin said, striding toward the center of the room, flipping her dagger into the air and catching it by the point, "we need to get this expedition organized."

Wiz sighed. This was going to be a long quest.

Two hours later Wiz met Bal-Simba at the turning of the corridor. The big wizard looked at Wiz as he fell in beside him and raised an eyebrow in unspoken question.

"I think," Wiz said brightly, "that I may scream. In fact I'm on my way up to the battlements to do just that."

"I am not unfamiliar with the feeling."

"Want to join me?"

"I have never found it a particularly productive exercise."

Wiz made a face. "Has it ever occurred to you that trying to exercise leadership around this place is like herding cats?"

"Quite recently," his companion said dryly. "Sparrow, you already know what I think of this enterprise."

"Almost, I'm coming to share your view. Almost."

"Concerned about your companions?"

"Wouldn't you be?" He ticked them off on his fingers. "June's crazy, Malkin's a kleptomaniac adrenaline junkie, Danny's still kind of wild and Glandurg is just plain dangerous."

Bal-Simba didn't argue. "Even so, they will be at your side in this business, and if you are determined to do this thing it were best if you counted their strengths rather than their weaknesses. None of them is without skills which you might need."

Wiz thought about it for a minute and looked up at the big wizard.

"Do you really think they'll help?"

"The point, Sparrow, is that worrying about them will not help either. A positive attitude can give you an advantage and I think you will need every one you can find."

"All I wanted was a simple little scouting expedition, to probe around the edges a little."

"Life does not always give us what we want," Bal-Simba told him. "Very often we must choose to accept what it gives us with the best grace possible."

"Isn't the sun ever going to break through?" Wiz growled as he looked out the window of the castle's great hall toward the west.

"Not today," Bal-Simba said, looking over his friend's shoulder.

It was afternoon, but the low clouds and deepening fog had made the day even dimmer than the dawn. The sullen gloom beyond the window reflected Wiz's mood perfectly and that, he thought, was one thing he didn't need right now.

Most of the rest of the party shared his mood. Not entirely, of course. Malkin was bouncing around like a fox terrier, happy at the prospect of action—not to mention slitting a few throats and perhaps lifting some purses. Glandurg struck a grimly heroic pose. Danny was just grim and June was, well, June.

Wiz kept looking out the window. "A blizzard coming on?"

"Perhaps. But I think something more than that."

"What?"

"I do not know," Bal-Simba said, "but I suspect we shall find out after you are gone."

The way he said it indicated he didn't think they'd like what they found.

Wiz turned away from the window. "Look, I know you don't like this, but I have got to do what I can to save Moira."

Bal-Simba continued to look out the window. "You must act according to your nature, Sparrow. Only consider what a victory it would be for the Enemy if something were to happen to you."

Wiz bit his lip. "I'll be careful. I promise."

As he said it, he rubbed his right ring finger, bare for the first time in months. Like the others he was leaving his Ring of Protection behind. The spell, which froze the wearer into invulnerable immobility when facing a mortal threat, had not protected Moira. What's more, Wiz's experience in the Dragon Marches had proven that the spell could be used against the wearer by freezing that person through the simple expedient of keeping up the threat. Wiz knew the rings wouldn't help on this expedition, but still . . .

Bal-Simba turned from the window. "The time draws near."

The scouting party all wore traveling cloaks and each of them carried a pack. They were armed and armored, each in his or her appropriate fashion. For Wiz and Danny that meant their wizard's staffs, since neither of them was proficient with this world's weapons. Glandurg had a mail byrnie to his knobby knees and Blind Fury slung over his back. Malkin had a shirt of light mail and her rapier and dagger—plus who-knows-what concealed about her person. June had her knife.

Since they would be sending themselves along the Wizard's Way rather than being sent there was no need to start from the great hall. However the cavernous hall had enough room for the people who had come to see them off, plus the dozen or so of the Mighty posted at strategic points around them in case something nasty tried to come in as they went out.

Among the others were Shauna, holding tight to a tearful Ian. And of course the dragon that was now the body of Wiz's wife.

Moira stepped close and pressed her scaly lips to his. "Please be careful."

Wiz manfully ignored the dragon breath and hugged her as best he could. "Hey, we're only going for a look-see, remember?"

He looked around one last time. "Okay, I guess we're ready."

With that they took their places, close within the circle. Wiz raised his staff, gestured and spoke and with five small *pops* of displaced air they disappeared along the Wizard's Way into the stronghold of the Enemy.

SIX

# DUNGEON REDUX

**"backslash light exe."**

The darkness around them was replaced with a cold blue light and Wiz and the others got their first look at the dungeons beneath the City of Night.

For the others it was a first. Wiz had been in the multi-layered labyrinth beneath the city of the Dark League during the great magical battle that broke the League's power forever.

Not that he recognized a thing. His only memories were of endless tunnels of dirt and stone separated by doors of oak and corroded iron, and strange furtive movements in the shadows. He hadn't liked the place when he had been here then, he hadn't liked it when a remnant of the Dark League had kidnapped him back to the now-ruined city a while later and he certainly didn't like it now.

They were bunched together in a wide stone corridor apparently hewn from solid rock. The passage was wider and taller than any he remembered seeing in the dungeons and the walls were worked smooth instead of being left uneven and scarred with the marks of the hewers' tools.

"The place seems different," he said, running his hand along the stone. "As if someone's been working on it."

"Probably," Malkin said as she looked around appraisingly.

Glandurg kept his hand on the hilt of Blind Fury and sniffed the stale air in great wheezing breaths. June stayed close to Danny, her head swiveling this way and that. Clearly she didn't like what she was seeing. That was all right, Wiz didn't like what he saw either.

"Well, which way?" Malkin asked. She seemed as calm as if they were out for a stroll in the castle rose garden, but Wiz noticed her hand stayed near the cup hilt of her rapier.

Wiz consulted the amulet around his neck. The amulet looked like an ordinary lensatic compass. The first time he came here he had used a seeker globe that floated ahead to show him the way to where Moira was held captive. That had proved less than ideal when the globe blithely floated into a guardroom full of goblin warriors with Wiz and his party close behind. If the compass was more prosaic it was also not as likely to get them in trouble.

Danny lifted a similar device hung around his neck and turned this way and that. "No sign of hostile magic," he said.

The one thing they didn't have was a map. The magical forces around this place were too strong for the wizards of the North to get the lay of the land and there were no pre-existing maps of the place. Wiz suspected that even the wizards of the Dark League, who had delved this place, hadn't had a complete map. He suspected even more strongly that the dungeons' new tenant had done some major remodeling.

"Off in this direction."

"Then," said Glandurg, striding to the front, "let us away."

The dwarf took the lead with Malkin following, then Wiz, then June and then Danny. It wasn't an ideal formation but it did mean that if Glandurg started swinging that sword the others would be able to get clear.

The tunnel led slightly off to the right and down. Here and there the old dirt walls or rough stone showed through, as if whatever was working on the dungeons hadn't finished yet. Wiz found the thought comforting and he tried to hold onto it.

Every hundred feet or so the tunnel would branch, sometimes into three or four directions. But the directional amulet kept pointing straight ahead. At last they came to a branching where the amulet told them to go right. Right through a large iron-bound door of age-darkened wood.

Malkin studied the door in the light of the magic globe. "No obvious lock," she said more to herself than the others. She ran her fingers over the rough iron surface, pressing experimentally here and there.

Glandurg reached for his sword.

"With a single blow of Blind Fury I shall cleave it asunder."

Danny and Wiz edged away from the door.

"Uh, we're not to that stage yet," Wiz said a trifle desperately. "Just keep watch, okay?"

Malkin nodded and bent before the door. She ran her hands over the lock plate like a pianist touching her instrument. She tapped on the door frame in two or three places and then turned her attention to the iron plate set in the stone to take the lock's bolt.

"Easiest to take that off," she muttered and produced a set of tools from somewhere about her person. "Bring that light over here will you?"

As Wiz moved to comply she began to work on the plate in the wall. It was held in place with three large and quite rusty nuts, he saw, with the bolt ends peened over them to prevent their removal. For some reason that bothered him, but he couldn't quite understand why.

Malkin produced something that looked like a surgeon's scalpel and applied it to the peened-over part of the bolts. The rusty iron cut like cheese under the pressure of the magical knife. Next she produced a small bottle and put several drops of an oily liquid on each bolt. The liquid seemed to soak into the joint between the nuts and bolts. Then she held up a tuning fork and struck it against the wall. A pure clear tone at the edge of human hearing filled the tunnel and Malkin applied the base of the fork to the first nut. There was a fine shifting of powder from the nut and bolt as the rust fell away under the influence of the vibrations.

She applied the tuning fork to each of the other bolts and then reached into the tool roll for something else. Then she stopped very deliberately, exhaled and stood up.

"Someone told me I shouldn't rush these things," she explained. "The next step is to remove those fasteners."

"Then we take the plate off and open the door," Danny said.

Malkin looked at him. "Then we see. Best not to anticipate what you'll find on a job like this. Too much chance of missing something important."

With that she turned back and knelt again before the iron plate. She took the first nut between her thumb and forefinger and carefully, delicately, turned it. The rusty nut came off as if it was on only finger tight.

While the others watched Malkin moved to the center nut. She grasped it, moved as if to turn it and then stopped dead. Then slowly, ever so slowly, she began to turn the nut the other way.

"That's tightening it," Danny said, but the nut backed off and fell into Malkin's hand. She shot Danny a raised-eyebrow look over her shoulder and went back to the third nut, which came off in the conventional direction.

Wiz picked up the second nut and looked at it. "A dummy thread," he said. "The first few turns are cut right-handed, but the bearing threads are actually left-handed."

By this time Malkin had the plate off and the door open and while Wiz looked at the nut the others started filing through.

"Come here and look at this," Danny said from the other side of the door. Wiz followed him through. There, behind the now-open door was an evil-looking black sphere cradled like a nut in a nutcracker between a lever and the wall. One end of the lever was pivoted in place and the other end was fastened to the bolt with the backwards nut.

"Turn that thing the wrong way and you break the sphere," Danny told him.

Suddenly Wiz felt very cold. "Nasty."

"I wonder what's in that sphere anyway?"

"Danny."

"Yeah, Wiz?"

"Never ask questions you don't want to know the answer to."

"How did you know how to open that door?" Wiz asked as he caught up with Malkin at the head of the party.

"Wizard, your problem is you're too trusting," Malkin told him. "If it looks like it is supposed to open by turning deosil, then obviously it opens by turning widdershins."

"Thanks," Wiz mumbled and dropped back beside Danny, lost in thought.

"What's wrong?" Danny asked.

"Malkin opened the door by turning the bolt clockwise."

"Just the opposite of what you'd expect. It was a trap."

"How many bolts have you seen since you got here with right-hand threads, like the ones in our world?"

The younger programmer stopped and looked at him. "I can't remember seeing any bolts—except for the stuff we've made. Here they use pins or wedges."

"Exactly. They don't use bolts, right-hand or left-hand. But that door was gimmicked to trap someone who expected a right-handed thread. What we'd expect."

"You mean this place is full of traps designed just for us?"

"Either that or the traps were designed by people who think like us. People from our world."

Danny let out a low whistle. "Jeez, I don't know which is worse."

"Let me know when you decide," Wiz told him. "Because chances are whichever one is worse, that's the one it is."

The evening came on dark and full of dirty fog. There was no sunset that day at the Wizards' Keep, only the dank fog and the wind keening about the towers where lamps burned late as wizards labored over their spells. Here and there a guardsman paced the battlements, cloak drawn tight against the growing chill.

"What is the time?" Bal-Simba asked as he stared out the window, straining to make out the castle curtain wall.

Arianne glanced at the magic sundial sitting on her work table. "Barely the seventh day-tenth." She paused. "Dark, is it not?"

"Too dark," Bal-Simba agreed. "Unnaturally so, I think."

Arianne's eyes flicked to the window but saw only Bal-Simba's reflection against the darkness. "Our enemy's work?"

"Perhaps." He turned from the window. "Ask Juvian to examine this fog for signs of magic."

His assistant nodded and spoke into a communications crystal.

*So cold,* Shauna thought, *even for winter.* She picked up the wrought iron poker and stirred up the fire. *Listen to yourself. Like someone's old grandmother.* Still she stirred the fire, seeking comfort from the renewed flames.

Normally the apartment in the guardsmens' quarters was snug enough, with whitewashed walls and comfortable furniture enlivened with polished copper pots and examples of Shauna's needlework. But tonight it seemed chill and dank, oppressed by the air that had settled over the Wizards' Keep.

She returned to the high-backed bench and Ian and Caitlin pressed back against her, seeking their own comfort. This deep in the castle they could not hear the keen of the wind, but they felt it just the same.

As she settled her bulk onto the bench she sighed and the children pressed closer. She put an arm around each and pulled them closer yet.

Shauna was a guardsman's daughter and a guardsman's wife and she had lived through the evil days of the Dark League's ascendancy when human magic was puny and the Council of the North had faced constant ruin at the hands of foes human and non-human. For all that, she could not remember a more bleak evening.

Malcolm, her husband, was eating soldier's stew, taking the common meal in the guard room. Supper was done, the dishes washed and put away. Normally she would be gently hinting about bedtime by now, but no one was sleepy and, truth to tell, Shauna preferred their company.

"I wish daddy was here," Caitlin said without raising her head.

"Your daddy's got duty," Shauna told her daughter, "special duty like half of 'em tonight."

"I want my daddy too," Ian added.

She stroked the boy's ash-blond hair. "Hush. It will be all right. You'll see. The Sparrow and your daddy and mommy have gone off to fix everything."

Neither child said anything, but both seemed to snuggle even closer.

For a bit they watched the flames in silence. "I wish Fluffy was here," Ian said finally.

"You'll see him soon enough," she said. "Moira promised to stop by later."

Ian looked up at her as if he would cry. "We can't see Fluffy."

"He's not Fluffy any more," Caitlin explained sadly into her mother's bosom. "He's Moira."

"You were right, My Lord," the middle-aged man in the crystal sphere said to Bal-Simba. "The fog is not natural and it bears the mark of the Enemy's magic."

"Is it dangerous?" Bal-Simba asked Juvian's image.

The wizard frowned until the lines of his forehead nearly matched the angle of his widow's peak. "Not now. But there are stirrings within. Perhaps it builds toward something. Shall I attempt to disperse it?"

It was Bal-Simba's turn to frown. "I think not yet. Make sure that we are protected against it and continue to watch it carefully. Meanwhile, prepare spells to disperse it if need be. And report any changes to me."

"I shall, My Lord. I am not sure we can disperse it, but we will begin work on spells immediately. Merry part."

"Merry meet again," Bal-Simba replied and the image blinked out.

"On our very doorstep," Arianne said over Bal-Simba's shoulder.

The big wizard turned to face his assistant. "Our enemy grows ever bolder ever more quickly. A bad sign, I think."

"Perhaps he will overreach himself."

Bal-Simba looked over at the dark window. "Perhaps. And if he does we must be ready."

Halfway down this stretch of tunnel there was a branch that ended after barely a dozen paces. Wiz sent the light globe floating in and examined it carefully before he motioned the others forward.

"Okay people, rest period."

Glandurg looked at him as though he was crazy. "We have barely begun."

"True," Malkin said. "I do not think any of us are tired."

"The idea is not to get tired," Wiz told them. "We don't want to be worn out if we run into something nasty. Besides," he added, seeing Malkin's hesitation, "we can cover more ground if we rest regularly."

Malkin grunted and sank down next to the others. Glandurg ostentatiously remained standing, guarding the entrance.

Wiz sighed as the pack's weight came off his shoulders. He wasn't tired, exactly, but he found he was glad for the break. None of them was hungry, but they all took sips of water from their canteens.

"Well," Danny asked after several minutes. "Now what?"

Wiz shifted his pack. "Now we check in."

"Are you sure that's safe?"

"No, but Bal-Simba insisted on regular reports or he'd have a gang of wizards haul us out of here."

"If we are to be scouts we must needs report," Malkin said quietly. Wiz noticed that even when she talked her eyes kept searching up and down the tunnel.

He hefted the special communications crystal. "Besides there's no sign our enemy understands spread demon communications, much less knows how to tap into the signal."

"This guy seems to understand an awful lot we didn't think he does," Danny pointed out.

Wiz ignored him and whispered into the crystal. The crystal glowed more brightly as the spell within it came alive. Suddenly there were twenty small demons floating in the air in two ranks before them. They hung silent and motionless. Wiz paused, cocked his head and whispered into the crystal again. Again the crystal glowed but the demons did nothing. Wiz frowned and tried a third time.

"What's wrong?" Danny asked.

"I'm not getting any response. It's like there's nothing there."

"Jamming?"

"No sign of it." He tried again.

"Maybe the demons got out of sync," Danny suggested.

Wiz considered. Unlike a normal communications crystal, the "spread demon" crystals used many pairs of demons with the message split into tiny parts and switching from demon to demon in an apparently random but carefully calculated pattern. The system depended on having each demon listening at the right time and in the right sequence.

"Have you ever known anything like that to happen?" Wiz asked.

Danny shook his head. "In our stuff? No."

Malkin had been watching them intently. "If it is not working we had best assume that it is the result of malign action."

Wiz nodded. "Probably best." Then he dismissed the demons and motioned his companions close around him.

"Now we've got to make a decision. If we can't communicate, do we poke around some more or head back right away?"

"We have barely arrived," Malkin pointed out. "Nor have we encountered anything dangerous."

"Nor have we seen anything interesting," Glandurg said. The way he pronounced the last word left Wiz in no doubt that "interesting" translated into "liquid assets."

"We haven't learned anything either," Danny added. June just grasped her husband's arm.

Wiz considered and drew a deep breath. "All right then. We're going on." There were smiles all around, but somehow Wiz didn't feel quite that cheerful.

"Ah, Fortuna, it's cold!" Elias the wizard exclaimed.

"I need no magic to tell me that, My Lord," Malcolm said, never taking his eyes from the darkness beyond the castle walls.

Dark as it was and muffled as they were in their cloaks the only obvious difference between them was size. The guardsman was a good half-head taller than the wizard. Their cloaks hid both his chain mail armor and the wizard's robe of office. Malcolm's soldier's reserve hid his opinion of his companion.

Full wizard this Elias might be, but in Malcolm's eyes he was still a youngster, and a bumptious one at that. The guardsman wished for a more experienced magician, one who didn't chatter so. But the Mighty and most of the journeymen were tucked warmly away, preparing spells against this new enemy. For duty on the walls he'd have to take what he could get.

Malcolm, who had tramped these walls for a goodly number of years, had never seen colder weather. However talking about it made it no warmer. Besides, he wasn't going to give this stripling the pleasure of hearing him say that. So he only shrugged and the pair continued on their way.

"Never like this at home," the young wizard added breathlessly as he tried to keep up with Malcolm's measured stride.

The guardsman spared a glance for his companion out of the corner of his eye. Like Bal-Simba, Elias was a wizard and a black man from the hot lands to the north. But there the resemblance ended and as far as Malcolm was concerned it didn't extend near far enough. It was said they bred mighty magicians in those lands, and in truth Bal-Simba was mighty enough. But either the line had run thin since Bal-Simba's day or this was an unusually poor specimen.

In theory the castle was already guarded against enemy magic. Which might be well and good for them as put their trust in it, Malcolm thought. But to his mind a place wasn't properly guarded until the sentries were at their posts and the sentinels patrolled the perimeter. In theory he even approved of adding magicians to the patrols. *Give them something useful to do instead of idling about in their towers,* he thought. *Show them what the world is really made of.* However after a couple of hours in Elias' company Malcolm was beginning to change his mind.

If only this one wouldn't talk so! To his way of thinking, talking distracted guards from their duties and many's the time he had had a junior guardsman marching his post with a pack full of sand for a week for talking one-tenth as much as this wizard.

He peered out into the darkness, trying to pierce the night and roiling fog. The air was close and cold, inserting clammy fingers into clothing and pulling out heat. It was said there was magic in it of no friendly sort and certainly the guardsmen were nervous and uneasy at their posts.

*Not that that's a bad thing,* he thought as he strode along at a measured pace. *Keeps them on the alert.* Still, this fog and cold could get to a man. It was easy to start seeing things in the swirls of darkness out at the edge of the light. It was almost as if . . .

Malcolm stopped dead in his tracks. "What's that?" he barked.

"What, why noth . . . " The words froze in the wizard's throat as he peered out into the blackness. "No wait. Yes there's something there! It's magic."

But Malcolm needed no wizard to tell him that. Things were moving in the mist, dark things. As Elias gabbled into his communications crystal, Malcolm was already blowing the first blast on his whistle.

There was a note like a crystal bell and Juvian's image appeared in the crystal ball on Bal-Simba's work table.

"My Lord, the magic fog! It changes."

"Raise the wards. Quickly," Bal-Simba commanded, "seal the castle against it."

Juvian nodded and even as his image blinked out, he had begun to raise his staff.

Arianne looked at him and raised an eyebrow in question.

"Alert the others. Our enemy begins his move." His assistant nodded and spoke into her own communications crystal.

Dimly through the fog, the walls of the castle began to glow.

Bal-Simba studied other forms in his crystal as the reports began to pour in.

"Recall the guard into the shelter of the towers," he ordered.

"More of the fog things?" Arianne asked, looking up from her communications crystal.

"It appears our enemy begins his attack." Outside the wind began to keen and sing. "I think I know what it wants," he added grimly.

The adventurers slept that night in an empty room with a guard posted at the door. The stone floor was cold and uneven and everyone was so keyed up that in truth they got little enough sleep. But after a decent interval they ate a hurried breakfast, packed up and moved out again, following the magic indicator toward where Moira—or Moira's body—lay.

"This looks like the section of the tunnels I was in before," Wiz said as they moved away from their resting place. "At least it's built the same way."

"Can you say what lies before us?" Malkin asked.

Wiz shook his head. "I can't even be sure it's the same section. It just looks like it."

"Hmmpf," Malkin said in a tone that indicated how much help *that* was. Then she turned again and led off.

The tunnel was much as Wiz remembered it. Same

musty smell, same dirt floor and walls, same occasional wooden beams for bracing and the same twisting, turning meandering that would confuse a homing pigeon. Wiz was a long way from a homing pigeon and he didn't have the faintest idea where they were.

Malkin rounded a corner and stopped short, rapier half out of its scabbard. Glandurg hissed and stepped out beside her, whipping Blind Fury free. Wiz took a firmer grip on his staff and peered around Malkin and over Glandurg.

Nothing moved. It had been a guardroom, Wiz realized. The same big fireplace and benches and tables he had seen when he had stumbled into such a room full of goblin guards on his first trip here. But the fireplace was cold and dead, the tables and benches were smashed and littered across the floor out beyond the range of the glow globe's light, and there were other things mixed into the litter on the stone-flagged floor.

Nearly at his feet was a halberd, its thick oak shaft neatly sheared off a foot behind the head. Beyond that lay a conical metal helmet and further out in the room was a scattering of other pieces of armor and bones.

Halfway out in the room was a set of leg armor, from shinguards to tassets. Because it was all together Wiz thought for an instant there might be a leg still in it. Then he looked more closely and saw it was empty. The armor had been split open, as if someone—no, some*thing* had been at it with a giant can opener.

"What the . . . ?" Danny breathed in Wiz's ear.

Sword and dagger at the ready, Malkin eased catlike into the room. Wiz shifted his grip on his staff to provide covering fire if needed. But there was no movement, no sound but their own breathing.

Malkin knelt beside the leg armor and carefully turned it with the point of her dagger, wincing slightly at the noise. Then she turned and examined an unrecognizable bit of bone nearby.

"This is old," she announced. "Several years I would say."

Wiz turned up the glow globe and flooded the chamber with blue light. Then he and the others eased into the room in a tight knot.

"How many?" he asked the kneeling thief.

Malkin glanced around and shrugged. "More than half a dozen, perhaps as many as twenty. It would be a pretty puzzle to reassemble enough pieces for an accurate count." She looked more carefully. "But I would say they were all killed at the same time."

"It probably goes back to when the Dark League ruled the city, or a little after," Wiz said. "Even then these tunnels were full of nasties."

"Perhaps it departed with its masters," Malkin suggested.

Wiz looked skeptical. "The Dark League didn't exactly have time to clean up after themselves. And I *know* there were some pretty unpleasant things left when I was kidnapped back here. A couple of them almost got me."

"Then best assume our foe lurks here yet," Glandurg said, shifting his grip on Blind Fury.

"Best assume whatever it is is pretty potent," Wiz added. "These guards were not pushovers."

"There is another thing we can assume," Malkin said as she stood up and brushed the dirt from her knees without letting go her grip on either her rapier or her dagger. "These bones show cut marks. After they were killed their flesh was stripped from their bones and probably consumed on the spot."

The group left the guardroom walking softly and peering into the shadows and silence with every sense alert.

"Nice thing to find," Danny muttered to Wiz as they continued down the tunnel.

"In a way it's good we found it. People will take this place more seriously now."

"I already took this place plenty seriously."

"Well, take it even more seriously."

At the Wizards' Keep, the day dawned on a castle under siege. There was no sun, only dark fog full of darker shapes that swirled about the castle and poked and pried at every nook and cranny. Nor were the fog's powers growing any less.

"Three wing beats out and you're lost," Dragon Leader told Bal-Simba in the latter's workroom. Dragon Leader was a compact man with blond hair and ice-gray eyes, still muffled in his flying leathers. His teeth did not chatter but that seemed more from an effort of will than warmth. "The cold sucks the life out of you, heat spell or no."

Bal-Simba looked at his wing commander over the remains of his breakfast. He had worked the night through and eaten at his desk, much good it had done! He stood up and walked to the window, scowling out into the swirling fog with its half-revealed shapes. Arianne, who had been listening from the corner, moved beside him.

"Lord, say the word and we will go again. But I am not sure how many will return."

"No." The wizard shook his head and turned from the window. "You have done well and I thank you, but best that we husband our resources until we know more."

As unobtrusively as possible a castle page slipped into the room and began to collect the breakfast things.

"I'm sorry, My Lord."

"There is nothing to be sorry for. You have done all you could while this magic fog hangs over the whole land."

"But it doesn't," the page piped up.

All of them turned to face him and the boy colored to the roots of his ash-blond hair. "Well, it doesn't," he added half-defiantly. "It starts thinning almost as soon as you get outside the castle walls and by the time you're across the river it's almost gone."

"How do you know?" Bal-Simba asked.

The boy studied his toes. "I've been there," he admitted finally. "I know I wasn't supposed to but Henry bet me and . . . " He ran down, reserves of courage exhausted.

Bal-Simba and the others studied the page. Look at him once and you'd think he was fifteen or sixteen. Look closer and you'd see he was a couple of years younger, just tall for his age.

"Who are you?"

"Brian, My Lord. The cook's son."

"Do those things in the fog hinder you?"

The page shook his head. "They sort of talk to you, but mostly they ignore you. You can walk right through them. It's cold and you can't see anything, but if you stay on the path you can follow it right down to the river and take one of the boats across."

"It appears," Dragon Leader said, "that this cub is a better scout than any of my riders."

"Or the thing is attracted by ridden dragons," Arianne said, "and perhaps the magic you carry." She looked back at the page. "Did you have any magic upon you?" The boy shook his head.

"Brian, do you think you can get back across the river?" asked Dragon Leader.

The boy nodded.

"Your plan?" Bal-Simba asked Dragon Leader.

"The boy can go where my riders cannot. We must know more about this cloud and how far it extends."

"A dangerous mission for a child," Arianne pointed out.

"I'm almost thirteen!" Brian said and then blushed again as the others looked at him.

"Almost old enough for the apprentice squadron," Dragon Leader said.

"If he cannot carry magic, the boy cannot communicate with us once he is out there."

"I know," Bal-Simba said. "It will have to be in and out."

"I can do that, My Lord," Brian said enthusiastically.

"Very well," Bal-Simba said finally to Dragon Leader. "Take the cub, outfit him warmly and tell him what to look for. But no magic, mind!"

Dragon Leader put his hand on the beaming page's arm and guided him from the chamber.

"The shifts we are driven to!" Bal-Simba sighed when they were out the door.

Arianne laid her hand on the wizard's shoulder. "I believe you are the one who said we do what we must."

Bal-Simba reached up and patted her hand. "That does not mean we have to like it."

## SEVEN

# Trouble in the Tunnels

In spite of his concentration Wiz nearly ran into Malkin when the tall thief stopped suddenly. Almost instinctively the others clustered around her.

Malkin peered ahead intently. "I think there is a light at the end of this tunnel."

"Daylight?" Danny whispered.

"More likely a gorilla with a flashlight," Wiz whispered. The others looked at him oddly. "I mean, let's be careful about this."

Malkin in the lead they crept down the tunnel, with the rest of the party following in a tight knot. Before they had gone another twenty paces Wiz was sure there was light ahead. Another hundred and the glimmer had resolved itself into an eerie blue glow.

Malkin looked over her shoulder at Wiz and raised her eyebrows in silent question.

"I don't know," he whispered. "I don't remember anything like this." He turned to the others. "Stay close and stay cool, people. And don't make any noise."

Cautiously the party crept up the tunnel toward the glow, Malkin flitting along without a whisper of sound and the others coming as quietly as their natures permitted. Wiz tried to watch where he put his feet, keep up with Malkin and not make any noise. He winced every time one of his companions made a scrape or dislodged a loose rock with a clatter.

There was no sign of life ahead, just the glow which gradually got stronger as they approached. It filled the tunnel with a soft cool radiance that seemed to radiate evenly from the top third of the tunnel. There was no sound and not so much as a breath of air moving. But there was a smell that reminded Wiz somehow of the basement of an old house, musty without being damp.

At last they stepped out into a section of tunnel with a flat floor and walls that looked as if the rock had been adzed smooth. At this distance they could detect irregularities in the glowing surface as if it had a somewhat lumpy undercoat. There was still no sign of life.

Wiz motioned Danny forward to take a reading with the magic detector.

The younger programmer came up beside him and swept his talisman over the glowing surface. "I'm not getting any magic from it," Danny whispered.

Wiz reached out and touched the glow. It felt like dry wood pulp and some of the glow came off on his hand. "It's fungus," he said quietly. "Nothing but fungus."

"Hmmf!" said Glandurg, striding up and yanking off a large handful of the glowing material. The move filled the air around him with dust and he sneezed thunderously. "All that over a little fox fire."

"Quiet," Malkin hissed.

"Bah!" the dwarf roared. "There's nothing here but some fungus."

"And whatever planted it," Malkin said quietly. "Something has been bringing it wood to feed upon."

"And what," demanded the dwarf, " do you suppose this oh-so-dangerous farmer of fungus might be?"

Wiz saw indistinct shadows moving in the blueness ahead. "I think we're about to find out."

*An ant!* was Wiz's first thought. But it wasn't. It was insectile and proportioned something like an ant, with divided body and long, spindly legs. But ants don't walk erect. Nor are they six feet tall. True, some ants do have oversized heads with enormous pincers that open and close reflexively, but Wiz had never heard of an ant with polished steel blades riveted to its pincers.

The thing came on, stopping every couple of steps to swing its head this way and that as if testing the air. Wiz and Malkin began to creep backwards, one slow step at a time. The ones behind them backed up as well, to the end of the smoothed part of the tunnel and then into the unworked portion.

It was then that Glandurg's undwarf-like clumsiness betrayed him. He put his foot down on a loose rock, which went scooting out from under him, taking his foot and leg with it. Glandurg went down with a crash and a curse and the ant-thing lowered its head, opened its pincers and charged.

"Drop!" Wiz yelled to Malkin and hurled a lightning bolt at the attacker. The bolt struck home and the creature shriveled and blackened under the impact. The fungus-impregnated wood pulp around it began to smolder, releasing clouds of noxious black smoke. Malkin rolled past Wiz and bounced to her feet, rapier and dagger ready. Beyond her the light from the tunnel was blocked off as a mass of ant-things swarmed toward the intruders.

"Let's get out of here," Wiz shouted.

No one needed a second invitation. They turned and ran with Wiz bringing up the rear and throwing lightning bolts to slow down pursuit.

Another ant-thing appeared out of a side tunnel. It barely had time to open its jaws before Danny dropped it with a fireball. Two others poked their armored heads out of side crevices as the party fled past. Wiz struck one with a spell and Malkin cut the forelegs out from under the other with a deft stroke of her rapier. The thing stumbled, rebalanced itself on its remaining legs and came on after them.

Wiz cast his anti-friction spell on the tunnel. The creatures slipped and slid, but they were more nimble than a dragon and they kept coming, skating down the tunnel toward their fleeing prey.

Wiz stopped dead in the middle of the tunnel and took a deep breath.

"Are you mad?" Malkin yelled. "Come on!" But Wiz ignored her, raised his staff and began to chant.

There was a rumble and a shiver and the loose rocks began to move. At first they shook where they were, as if the earth was quaking. Then they began to move. Gradually at first and then faster and faster the rocks flew down the tunnel like a reverse explosion. Two boulders tried to get through a space not quite big enough and caught. Three other smaller pieces piled up against them and then a host of rocks from pebbles to boulders jammed against them blocking the tunnel solid.

"Cute," Malkin said, admiring Wiz's handiwork.

"It's a variation on Jerry's rubble-moving spell, which we used the last time we were in the City of Night," Wiz explained. "Now let's get out of here before they get the tunnel unblocked." He looked around. "There aren't enough loose rocks here to do that trick again."

"Now what?" the thief asked as they hurried along.

"Now we find a place where the roof and walls are solid rock and cave in this whole section of the tunnel. We can't do it here because the ceiling is too unstable. We'd probably get caught in the landslide."

"Hey," Danny yelled from up ahead. "There's a door here."

As Wiz came puffing up he saw that there was indeed another door of iron-bound oak set in the solid rock wall.

"Can you get us through that?" Wiz asked Malkin. "It looks like the rock is solid enough on the other side to let me use my cave-in spell."

Malkin bent and examined the door, running her fingertips over it.

"Hmm," she said. "Ah, yes. Yes indeed."

"Can you open it?"

"Of course."

"How long will it take?"

Malkin looked at him as if he were simple. "As long as it takes, of course."

Behind them they could hear a faint scrabbling and shifting as the bugs worked to clear the tunnel.

"We may not have that long. We're gonna have to cut our way through this one."

"Stand aside, Wizard," Glandurg said. "It is time for Blind Fury to sing."

That wasn't what Wiz had in mind, but Glandurg had already unsheathed the gleaming blade and was waving it above his head. Obviously something—or someone—was about to get cut and on quick reflection Wiz decided it would be better for everyone if it was the door. He motioned the others back and stepped well clear himself.

Malkin indicated a spot on the wall to the right of the door. "Aim here." Then she joined the group well behind the dwarf and out of range.

Glandurg nodded, raised the sword over his head and brought it down with a mighty blow. Naturally he missed completely. Instead of striking the rock wall, he hit the door along the hinge line, shearing wood and hinges from shoulder height to floor. The door, not made to withstand such an attack, simply collapsed into a pile of boards.

"Missed," the dwarf said sheepishly.

"That's all right," Wiz told him as Malkin winked at him over Glandurg's head. Then she stepped through the doorway and into the room beyond. As soon as they were through a couple of quick blasts from Wiz's staff collapsed a hundred yards of tunnel.

Danny was looking down the tunnel after the dwarf. Then he caught Wiz's arm as Wiz came past. "Wiz," he whispered, "you're sure he's on our side, right? I mean you checked out his credentials and everything?"

"He thinks he's on our side," Wiz whispered back. Then he hurried on, leaving Danny puzzled in his wake.

✧ ✧ ✧

Even a small dragon was an uncomfortable fit in the Watchers' chamber. The sunken floor was crammed with stations for those who used their scrying skills to see far beyond the borders of the Capital or to communicate across the length and breadth of the lands of mortals. The tables were wood, the men and women sitting one or two to a table wore the robes of wizards and they stared at crystals or bowls. There was barely space between them for humans to move, much less a dragon. Nor was the raised platform that ran around three sides of the room really large enough for a beast the size of Moira's new body to be comfortable.

Moira grimly ignored that, even when a hurrying Watcher tripped over her tail. She and Bal-Simba had come for a more important purpose.

"And they still have not reported in?" Bal-Simba asked the Chief Watcher.

"As I said, My Lord."

"Have you tried to contact them?"

"I felt it was best to ask your advice before doing so."

"Then do so now. Tell them to return. We can still bring them back along the Wizard's Way, but if this thing continues to grow we will not be able to do so for much longer."

The Chief Watcher spoke a spell and two dozen demons appeared in the air before him. He spoke again and the demons began to speak, each but a fraction of a syllable before the next took up the message.

"There is nothing, Lord."

Bal-Simba frowned mightily.

"Perhaps the new crystals are not working," Moira said.

"Perhaps," the Watcher said neutrally.

"Try to reach them," the wizard commanded. "See if you can get a reply. If you cannot reach them on the special crystal, try other means. If you cannot reach them, convene a coven of wizards and pull them back unawares."

The Watcher nodded and turned back to his work, trying to ignore the scaly nose thrust over his shoulder.

The Watcher was still bent over the crystal when Bronwyn came hurrying into the Watch chamber.

"My Lord, My Lady, you had best come. Jerry is stirring. I think he may be awake."

Jerry Andrews was tossing restlessly on the infirmary pallet when they arrived. Two of Bronwyn's apprentices were beside him, bathing his brow and keeping him from falling out. They looked up and withdrew slightly as Bronwyn led the others in.

"He has become increasingly agitated in the last daytenth," the chief healer explained. "That usually means the subject is returning to his body."

"Will he be all right?" Moira asked.

"Ask me after he awakens." She cast a professional eye at her patient. "I do not think that will be long."

"Jerry," Moira called. Then more loudly. "Jerry, wake up!"

"Wha . . . " It was a mumble rather than a word, but the apprentice healers brightened at the sound.

"My Lord, can you hear me?" Bal-Simba didn't shout, but the timbre of his voice carried to the very bones of the hearers.

"Ahh, okay, yeah." Jerry seemed to relax into the bed then his eyes flickered and opened.

"Welcome back, My Lord," Bronwyn said warmly. She motioned and one of the apprentices handed her a bowl. "Drink this." She held it to Jerry's lips. Jerry swallowed, gulped, wrinkled his nose and sneezed. From where she stood, Moira's dragon sense of smell caught a whiff of the bowl's contents. She could not blame him at all.

"Gahh! 's awful."

"It will help you recover," Bronwyn told him, handing the bowl back to the apprentice.

"Where am I?" He turned his head. "Infirmary, right?"

"Just so," Bal-Simba told him.

"How long?"

"Were you gone? About three days."

"Wiz?" Jerry slurred. "Malkin?"

"Not here," Bal-Simba told him.

"Where are they? Are they all right?"

"They are safe and well. But they have gone on a mission."

"Where?"

"To the City of Night to face the thing that did this."

"No!" Jerry struggled to sit up, paled and sank back into the pillows. "Won't work," he gasped. "Can't do it that way."

"They do not intend to confront our enemy," Bal-Simba said. "They only go to scout, to bring us back a better picture of what it is we are fighting."

Jerry clutched at his arm. "You don't understand. The thing *absorbs*. If Wiz and Danny get too close it will suck them in, make them part of it. That's nearly what happened to me."

"Wiz drove the things off before they could finish," Moira told him.

Jerry looked at the dragon. "Hallucinating?" he mumbled.

"There was an accident," Moira told him. "Or perhaps intentional action."

"The Enemy has taken her body," Bal-Simba said. "That is why Wiz and the others have gone there."

"They can't do it!" He broke off in a fit of coughing. "Get them back," he said hoarsely.

Bronwyn moved to the head of the bed. "My Lord, unless you have pressing questions you had best let him rest. He is still very weak and somewhat disoriented."

Bal-Simba nodded and touched the dragon's shoulder. "Very well." He nodded to Jerry. "We will talk later."

"Get them back," the programmer entreated to their retreating backs. "Call them off."

Arianne was waiting for them in the corridor beyond the sickroom.

"More news from the Watchers?" Bal-Simba asked as soon as the door was closed.

"There is another complication, My Lord. We have not only lost contact with Wiz's party, we cannot reach them along the Wizard's Way. We can still penetrate the things attacking the castle, but apparently the Enemy found their entry and blocked it. The Watchers are still trying but so far they cannot reach them by any means."

Moira drew back her scaly neck and hissed like a berserk tea kettle. "A trap! The whole damned thing is a trap!"

"So it would appear," Bal Simba said grimly. "Our enemy seems to have a special fondness for traps."

"If we do not find them and get them back—or at least warn them . . . " The thought hung unfinished.

"Then we will just have to bring them back or warn them—somehow."

## EIGHT

# UNDER SIEGE

"My Lord?" Arianne asked.

"Hhhmpf?" Bal-Simba refocused his eyes and looked at his assistant.

"I asked if you were ready for luncheon."

"I am sorry. I was thinking. Piecing together what we know and what we do not."

Arianne recognized the tone and saw that lunch would be delayed for a bit.

"Our attacker's magic is of a type which is unknown to us, although it appears to be based on the new magic. Juvian and Agricolus have done much good work on that. So far his primary weapon appears to be this fog, which is attracted to magic, which seems to explain why it clings so close to the castle."

"Which we know it does thanks to the page Brian," Arianne added. "He went out no less than three times yesterday. Now we are using dismounted dragon riders to survey the fog's extent. He will be serving us for a while, by the way, part of his reward."

Bal-Simba nodded.

"But most of this we knew as of this morning," Arianne added. "From your manner I suspect you have discovered something more."

The wizard's brow furrowed. "Not discovered, exactly, but I did have a thought. Obviously our adversary has access to the Sparrow's new magic. Perhaps that would be a fruitful line of inquiry."

"Lord, the new magic is fairly widespread by now," Arianne pointed out. "The Sparrow and his friends have been teaching it to any who would learn and they in turn have been teaching it to others."

"True, but whoever is behind this has unusual abilities with it. Perhaps it would be well to make inquiries, delicately, as to the activities of the especially apt pupils."

"Yes," the blond woman said slowly. "If done quietly it costs us little enough and may perhaps offer a clue." Her expression changed.

"A thought of your own?" Bal-Simba asked.

"Perhaps," Arianne said slowly. "It was unwise of them to step into the Enemy's jaws unknowing."

"Let us hope it was merely unwise," the big wizard said to his assistant. "You may have noticed that prudence is a characteristic notably lacking in Wiz and his friends. Their magic is powerful, but their method of training does not teach them the value of patience and caution in great matters."

"I have noticed. So, apparently, has the Enemy. My Lord, has it occurred to you that this is a trap which would not work against most wizards? Only against Wiz and his friends?"

"I had not thought of that, but you are quite right."

"And that, in turn, implies a knowledge not only of the new magic but of the wizards of Wiz's world."

"I take your point."

"In fact," Arianne went on, "there is one such here within our walls who might bear examination on both accounts."

"Mikey? But he has the mind of a child."

Arianne made a graceful gesture.

"You are right, of course." He struck a crystal bell on his work table and Brian appeared in the doorway.

"Go find the chief healer and have her examine the foreign wizard we hold prisoner," he told the page. "Then have her report to me."

Brian bowed and dashed off down the corridor.

"Are there any from the Wizards' Keep who have

learned the new magic whom we cannot account for?" Bal-Simba asked.

"I will have to check but, off hand, I cannot think of any. One or two have died, of course, but . . . No, wait! There was one several years ago, the apprentice Pryddian who disappeared about the time Wiz was kidnapped by the remnants of the Dark League. His whereabouts were never discovered."

Bal-Simba snorted. "I remember that one all too well. As I recall his skill was in stirring up discord, not magic. Still," he went on, "there was a suspicion he had rifled the Sparrow's desk and taken some manuscripts with him." He sighed. "A slim lead, My Lady."

"We have few better, My Lord."

"I think . . . " Bal-Simba began slowly, but he was interrupted by a strong knock on the door. It was Bronwyn, the council's chief Healer, tight-lipped and white-faced. "My Lord, I think you had better come look at this." Bal-Simba hesitated. "Now."

With Bal-Simba and Arianne in tow, Bronwyn led them up the winding stone stairs to the door of Mikey's cell. The door was open and the two guards outside were clearly uneasy.

Once Mikey had been a skilled programmer and, as "Panda," one of the best system breakers in Silicon Valley. But the shock of his final battle against Wiz and his elven allies had left him with the mind of a four-year-old. Now he spent his days playing with blocks and toy soldiers in a prison-cell-cum-playroom in one of the Keep's towers. He was fed, cared for and guarded, but otherwise ignored.

Now he was slumped in the corner, surrounded by a scattering of blocks. His eyes were closed, his head sunk on his chest and his breathing deep and regular.

Bronwyn knelt and pulled open an eyelid. Mikey did not stir. She looked up at Bal-Simba. "An empty shell, Lord. There is nothing left here at all."

"When did this happen?"

"Sometime in the last two days. He sat in a corner all that time, but that was not unusual for him. The guards were becoming worried because he had not eaten." She rose and looked down at him. "Before, he had the mind of a child. Now he has—nothing."

Bal-Simba frowned "Did he still have his knowledge? Before this happened, I mean."

Bronwyn shrugged. "Since we never knew just what was wrong with him I cannot tell you. Certainly he did not have the mind to use it. But as to the knowledge itself . . . " She shrugged again.

"I think we can assume he still had at least some of it." Bal-Simba rubbed his chin.

"And now we can assume the Enemy has that knowledge," Arianne added.

Bal-Simba nodded and looked down at the not-quite-human thing at his feet. "Come, Lady, we have work to do."

"And him?" Arianne asked.

"I will make him comfortable," Bronwyn said grimly. "He will not last long like that."

Malkin stopped and touched Wiz's arm. "It's getting light up ahead again," she whispered.

Wiz strained to see beyond the magic light's glow. "More bugs?"

The thief shook her head. "The light's not as blue and the shadows are sharper."

*Now what?* Wiz thought. He looked over at Danny. The younger programmer checked his magic detector. "A lot of magic, but it's not immediately dangerous."

It wasn't the most reassuring report Wiz had ever heard but he motioned the group on and they crept down the tunnel.

Ahead of them the tunnel grew brighter and the air around them grew warmer. Suddenly they turned the corner and found themselves staring into the mouth of Hell.

The very walls of the tunnel glowed incandescent. Orange and red, yellow and white, churned and roiled on every side. Instinctively the party flinched back as if from a blast furnace and retreated around the corner.

"No heat," Wiz said wonderingly as soon as they were back around the corner. He stuck his hand around to make sure. "There's no heat."

"It's magically blocked," Danny said, checking his magic detector. "That tunnel must run right through the heart of the volcano, but magic keeps the heat away." He looked at the magic detector again. "Tunnels, I mean. There's a whole pile of them out there."

"Another maze."

"A hotter-than-hell maze," Danny agreed.

"Well, we've got an answer to that," Wiz said as he fished in his pouch. "I have here the granddaddy of all maze solvers." He held up a demon that looked remarkably like a white rat.

"Put that away," Malkin said firmly.

Wiz frowned. Malkin had her faults, including kleptomania, but squeamishness wasn't one of them.

"It's not a real rat," he explained, "it just looks that way because . . . "

"I know what it is," the tall thief said. "There is a trap here and that thing may trigger it."

"What kind of trap?"

"Magical. Beyond that . . . " She shrugged.

"How do you know?" Danny asked.

"Because I know. It is my business to know and this is not the place for magic."

Wiz looked at the rat demon, which twitched its whiskers. He put it back in his pouch. "Okay, let's take a break while Danny and I see what we can learn."

Half an hour later a grim-faced Wiz and Danny called the others to gather around them.

"This is the cutest thing yet," Wiz told them. "All these tunnels are kept open by magic, very carefully balanced magic. Too much additional magic will upset the spell and they'll collapse."

Even Glandurg looked uneasily at the glowing red magma beyond. "Better it were that we use no magic then."

"We won't, mostly. Danny and I have a spell running to strengthen the tunnels, so it's not quite the trap it was when we came in, but any large expenditure of magical energy is still likely to bring the place down."

"So we feel our way through magicless," Malkin said.

"Not exactly. With the tunnels reinforced Danny and I can use a real low-power spell to narrow our choices."

"You say that as if there is a problem."

Wiz frowned. "Not a problem exactly, but there is a consideration. The spell is sensitive and people throw it off. It will work best if Danny and I go ahead alone while the rest of you wait here."

Malkin's face didn't move a muscle. "Is that wise?" she asked neutrally.

"About as wise as a lot of the rest of this expedition," Wiz told her. "Anyway people, stay close and we'll be back as soon as we can. Above all, use no magic you don't absolutely have to use."

It took several minutes to get the details sorted out and somewhat longer to convince June she had to stay behind and not go with Danny. That done, the two wizard programmers started off down a likely tunnel.

It wasn't a pleasant experience. The heat from the walls beat in on them and soaked up through the soles of their boots until Wiz was reminded of bread in an oven. There was no noise through the insubstantial walls, but there was a low vibration as if hundreds of tons of melted rock around them was flowing and shifting under some unimaginable pressure. Sweat streaked their faces and soaked into their clothing. Even Wiz's socks soaked until he squished in his boots with every step he took. Here and there a trick of the light turned a patch of wall into a mirror that threw back a distorted funhouse reflection of the pair.

Nor was the maze easy to unravel. It was mostly on one level, but it twisted and turned and divided and rejoined in a way that was not only confusing, it was downright unpleasant. For all that, Wiz and Danny made good progress. Their spell allowed them to eliminate first large chunks of the maze and then successively smaller sections. Once or twice Wiz got an uneasy feeling they were being followed, but they saw no one and they heard nothing.

Of course, because the spell was so weak it was not infallible. Time and again, they found themselves headed in the wrong direction or caught up against a dead end.

"The exit should be right up ahead here," Wiz said at last as they moved down a twisty, glowing corridor. They turned another corner and found themselves face to face with a rock wall.

"Dead end," Danny observed needlessly.

Wiz shrugged and turned to start back down the way they had come. There was a noise down the tunnel. A noise like heavy footfalls. A lot of them. Wiz motioned Danny to silence and peeked around the corner to see what was ahead.

What was ahead was goblins. Big, hairy, nasty goblins armed to the fangs. The tunnel was packed three deep with them. The light from the molten rock reflected redly off the creatures' armor and made their little pig eyes seem even redder. They were still some ways off and they apparently hadn't seen the humans yet, but there was no place for them to go wrong.

"Oh boy," Danny said quietly. "Oh boy."

The breath caught in Wiz's throat. He had plenty of spells that would deal with a mere pack of goblins, but the more magic they used, the more chance the tunnels would collapse and engulf them in molten rock. But without magic both Wiz and Danny together probably weren't a match for just one of the oncoming goblins.

Wiz raised his staff and prepared to fight. "Well, we can't delay the inevitable."

"Let me try something first, okay?" Danny said. Wiz raised his eyebrows and nodded. Out of the corner of his eye Wiz saw Danny gesture with his staff as he said something unintelligible. Wiz took a tighter grip on his own staff and both stepped out to face the oncoming monsters.

Only the goblins weren't coming any more. They stopped dead in the center of the tunnel. Then they huddled together. Then they turned and ran screaming from the two humans.

Wiz lowered his staff and looked after the fleeing monsters.

"What the heck was that all about?"

Danny looked smug. "A little something I cooked up. Look at yourself in the wall there."

Wiz moved over to the stretch of reflecting wall Danny had indicated. Staring back at him was a *Thing*. It was big and amorphous and tentacled, and clawed and fanged and looking at him with hundreds of beady red eyes. It had pincers, and stingers and hair and scales and fins and teeth. Lots and lots of teeth. After several years in this World, Wiz knew Things. This was an E-flat, full-bore, world-class *Thing*.

"Holy . . . " Wiz jumped back.

"That's what they thought," Danny said smugly. "Oh relax, it's just a seeming, a minimum-magic disguise you might say."

"A nightmare you might say," his friend corrected shakily. "Where did you come up with that thing?"

Danny smirked. "My imagination."

Wiz looked at the younger programmer and frowned. "You know, there are times I really wonder about you. Now let's find the exit and get back to the others before something wanders by that doesn't frighten so easily."

## NINE

# KILLER VEES

It took another hour to get through the magma maze. Beyond were more tunnels, and beyond them a series of natural caves variously modified. They made their way without incident until they came to a crudely hacked-out tunnel connecting the second and third caves.

"Wait a minute guys," Danny whispered, "I think I've got something—or nothing."

The party clustered around as Danny checked his magic detector.

"Well, which is it?" Malkin asked.

Danny looked up. "Both. The whole area up ahead is magically dead," Danny reported. "I mean not a spark anywhere that I can see."

"Not even the normal background magic?" Wiz asked.

The young programmer shook his head. "Not a sign."

Wiz noticed Malkin make sure her rapier was loose in its sheath.

"Okay then. Let's take the hint and move slow and careful."

Again the tunnel widened out into a cavern and again the party moved ahead by the light of a single magical globe. Strain as they might they could hear nothing but their own footfalls and what sounded like rushing water faint and far ahead of them.

Halfway across the room they found the source of the sound. A chasm divided the cavern and from the bottom, faint and far away, came the sound of the water.

"How deep do you think that is?" Danny asked as he squinted down into the blackness.

"Too deep," Wiz said.

"Too wide besides," Malkin added as she looked across the gap. "I don't think our ropes will reach, even if we could find something on the other side to secure them to."

Wiz thought of crossing the dizzying blackness on a rope and got a distinctly queasy feeling in the pit of his stomach.

"Let's assume ropes are a non-option," he said.

"Well, I've got something for this," Danny said. "Watch." He lifted his staff and pointed.

The hair on Wiz's neck stood up and he started to protest, but he was too late.

Rocks and boulders on both sides of the gap glowed blue, then rocked in their places and rose gently into the air. Danny waved his staff like a conductor's baton. Waves of magic twisted and congealed into invisible forms as the rocks floated out into empty space and settled in place according to some unseen plan. More waves of magic as the rocks locked together and a great arched bridge began to take shape. More magic and smaller stones rushed to fill in the gaps. A final burst of magic and a bridge sat in place, glowing from the unnatural forces that held it together.

"There!" Danny said proudly.

"Come on then," Wiz said unhappily. "Let's get over this as fast as we can."

The bridge was solid enough beneath their feet as the party started over.

"Beats a rope, doesn't it?" Danny said gaily. "It's a variation of a spell I worked out for Ian's toy blocks. Just scale it up, and hey . . . "

"Takes a lot of magic," Wiz said.

"So? We've got power to spare here."

The magic globe lighting their passage flickered, then

flickered again. Wiz saw something like a moth flit around it. Then another and another and another.

Something stung Wiz on the back of his neck. He slapped at the spot and felt something small and furry under his fingers. He jerked his hand away and shook his fingers and a scrap of black fluttered out of them.

*"Get off the bridge!"* he yelled and charged ahead. Caution forgotten, the rest of the party charged after him, swatting at the things around them.

As soon as they were on the other side, Danny gestured and the rocks went thundering into the canyon. But by that time the entire party was under attack.

In swarms and hordes and legions the tiny black things came on, diving mindlessly to the attack and sticking where they landed to bite and chew. Each of them was no larger than a mouse, but they struck with blind ferocity.

Wiz laid about him with his staff, striking great swaths of the creatures down by magic. Malkin turned out to be a surprisingly good swordswoman. Her long arms gave her reach and her wrists were like iron. She used her reach to keep the things off and the edge of her rapier to take out several at once. June was a whirling dervish with her knife, slicing in a dozen directions at once. Danny also struck out with magic. Glandurg flailed about him with Blind Fury. He never hit what he was aiming at, but there were so many of the things that each stroke felled half a score. Along the way he also brought down two good-sized boulders and a stalactite, but he barely noticed.

The light in the cavern dimmed as the creatures mobbed the magic globe, like a pack of enraged moths. Wiz struck out desperately again and again. Caught in the open as they were the things could attack from any direction, including driving straight down. Even the ones who had been knocked from the air crawled toward them to continue the attack.

A fireball whizzed past Wiz's ear and singed the hair

on the left side of his head. He turned his head to glare at Danny and the thing that was diving on him missed his eyes and latched onto his ear instead. Danny shrugged and went back to throwing fireballs.

The little things were so thick in the tunnel there was really no place to aim at, but it didn't matter. As soon as each fireball emerged from Danny's staff it was surrounded by a horde of suicidal batlets who dived to their destruction in it. Wiz, seeing what was happening, began dividing his time between beating off attackers and throwing fireballs. The cavern filled with rank smoke and the reek of ozone and burned flesh. Gradually the attackers became fewer and fewer and finally there were none.

The party found themselves standing back to back in the cavern, surrounded by a haze of stinking smoke and a carpet of dead creatures. Wiz realized he had been bitten in a dozen places or more. He could feel the blood oozing down both cheeks and a wound in his forehead was trickling blood into his eyebrows. Most of the others appeared wounded in several places as well.

"What where those things?" Danny panted, as he wiped blood from his eyes. June was instantly at his side with a cloth, cleaning the wounds on his face and ignoring her own.

Wiz bent down to examine the litter of corpses around them. Each of the things had the form of a tiny bat, perhaps half as long as his little finger. The mouths sported a pair of outsized fangs and even in death the little eyes showed a glazed malevolence. He picked one up and showed it to the others.

"Little vampire bats," Danny said. "I wonder if these things carry rabies."

"Rabies we can handle," Wiz reminded him. "Healing magic, remember?"

"Speaking of which . . . " Malkin said, looking at the bloody wounds on the back of her hand.

As one person, the party sank to the ground where

they were and started rummaging through their packs for what Wiz persisted in thinking of as "first aid kits."

On an impulse Wiz tried a listing and scowled at the result.

"More weird code," Danny said and then winced as June dabbed a healing salve on a wound on his neck.

"So the Enemy sent these things against us," Malkin said.

"If I had to guess I'd say they weren't exactly sent," Wiz said. "This part here looks like another variation on the watcher spell and there doesn't seem to be a lot of code for remote control."

"Meaning?" Danny studied that section of the listing.

"Meaning I think these things operate independently. If I had to guess, and that's pretty much what it is at this point, I'd say this part here is a magic detector and they home in on magic. What's more, magic seems to rouse them to a rage. You'll notice Malkin wasn't the focus of an attack and they didn't go after Glandurg until he got Blind Fury into action."

"Kinda like leaving hives of killer bees around as guards," Danny said. "Cute."

"Ugly," Wiz corrected. "Especially since the same principle could be applied to other critters. Nastier ones."

Danny nodded. "Let's get out of here then. There may be more on the way and I'm not sure I'd want to face a horde of maddened dragons."

"And no more magic," Wiz admonished. "Not if it attracts these things."

"Our steel and our courage alone shall carry us henceforth," said Glandurg.

"Well," Wiz amended, eyeing Blind Fury, "we don't have to swear off magic completely."

## TEN

# ENTER THE LOBSTER

"Moira," the wind moaned. "Moira, Moira, Moira, Moira."

It keened around the towers. Frigid fingers clutched at the banners and tugged at the windows. It could not find purchase against the wizards' spells, but it kept on.

Moira went to the window and tried to look out, but a dark formless thing beat upon the pane, as if to strike her, and she turned away.

"Is it getting worse?" she asked Bal-Simba.

"It gets no better. That in itself means it will get worse. Like a starfish on an oyster. It pulls and pulls and eventually the oyster weakens."

The dragon hesitated. "Then perhaps I should go out there," Moira said.

"And give our enemy the advantage he seeks? An unwise move, My Lady."

"Then what shall we do?"

"Work. Wait. Perfect the spells to drive this thing from our door."

The dragon did not turn its head. "I wish Wiz was here."

Bal-Simba sighed. "So do I, My Lady. So do I."

Their first warning was the way sounds changed. Careless footsteps or dislodged pebbles rang sharper and more hollowly. Wiz was still trying to puzzle out the difference when they came around a bend in the tunnel and stepped out into a new world.

The cavern was immense. Stalactites and sheets of

flow stone rippled from ceiling to floor in pastel pinks and yellows. They made weirdly distorted shadows in the light from Wiz's glow globe. In spite of the steady illumination the shadows seemed to flicker and dance in eerie motion. The air was heavy with damp and utterly still. Occasionally a foot would dislodge a pebble and the sound would ring through the emptiness.

They picked their way along for perhaps two hundred paces and then, suddenly, there was no floor before them.

It took a minute for Wiz to make a coherent picture out of the sense impressions, like staring at an optical illusion. Finally the elements snapped into focus and he realized they were standing at the edge of a cliff thickly coated with onyx flowstone. By directing the magic light out over the darkness he could see that the face was a steep cascade of the same orange, pink and white material as the surface they were standing on. He could not see the other side and the light did not show him the bottom, but his magic detector pointed straight out across the emptiness.

"It looks like we're going to have to climb down," he said to the others."

"Fine," Malkin said, shedding her pack and unhooking a coil of rope from it. "I'll go first."

Wiz wasn't exactly overjoyed at the prospect of climbing down a slippery cliff in the dark, but he felt he had to assert himself as leader. "Why you?"

Malkin looked up at him. "Because you're a klutz. Now help me find a rock to tie off on."

That was true enough that Wiz didn't argue. But he was a little surprised she knew the word.

Malkin selected a convenient boulder, looped the rope around it and secured it with a particularly complicated looking knot. Keeping the rope taut in one hand she stepped back and admired her handiwork.

"All right everyone, I'll go first. Be sure to keep

tension on the rope and whatever you do don't let it go slack and then jerk it."

"Why not?" asked Danny.

"Because if you do the knot comes undone. That's how we get the rope down when we're at the bottom."

Danny looked at the knot again.

"It's perfectly safe," Malkin assured him. "The next person to go down stands by the rope and keeps the tension on. Just keep doing that and we'll be fine."

The thief rigged a harness from a shorter piece of rope and attached it to the main rope with a peculiar looking knot.

"I'll take a light with me and signal for the next one to follow," she said, and with that she stepped backwards into the blackness and disappeared from view.

Danny kept tension on the rope as she worked her way down. The others watched the rope twitch as Malkin worked her way down the cliff face. Finally it lay still and they heard her call up to them.

"Okay. It's about a hundred paces down. There's plenty of rope and its an easy descent. Come on down one by one."

Since he couldn't lead, Wiz figured the leader's next logical place was as rear guard. He let Danny and then June go down. Glandurg disdained the rope and scrambled down the cliff face like a fly. At last the rope was still again. Wiz picked up Malkin's pack, slung it over one shoulder and started to work his way down the cliff.

In the back of Wiz's mind a small voice kept telling him all this was wrong. You don't find limestone caves beneath volcanoes. Halfway down the rope Wiz decided this was arrant pedantry and told the small voice to shut up.

The rope firmed and steadied as someone took hold of it from the bottom. With that aid Wiz made good time the rest of the way down.

"Thanks," he said as his feet touched the ground. Behind him the rope holder snorted.

Wiz turned to look. His first impression was of Malkin in a silver fright wig. His second impression was of a lot of teeth, claws, blazing red eyes and really awful breath.

He yelled and ducked as the thing took a swipe at him. He fumbled for his staff, but the thing was too close, so he settled for tripping backwards and going flat on his back. The thing closed in for the kill and the world blinked.

*The protection spell,* Wiz thought. *The protection spell kicked in.* His second thought was that he wasn't wearing the magic ring, so he must have been stunned by his fall and before he had time for a third thought, a liquid voice broke in.

"Oh, I hope you are all right. Not damaged in any way? Here, let me help you up."

"Thanks," Wiz said, taking the proferred hand.

It wasn't a hand, exactly. It was a claw. A very large claw. At the other end of the claw was a lobster—about thirty feet of lobster.

"Uh, thanks," Wiz said again.

The lobster waved an antenna. "Think nothing of it. All in a day's work, I can assure you." Its voice was a warm rich baritone, not at all the way Wiz had expected a lobster to sound. Although come to that, Wiz realized, he didn't really have an idea how a lobster should sound. "Terribly sorry about that," the lobster went on. "Those creatures have no manners at all, not to mention absolutely no taste! Tasteless."

The lobster gave Wiz's hand a little squeeze before releasing it. "Oh, and you're molting too," the lobster said delightedly. "How wonderful. You're especially tender at this stage." The lobster sighed. "And the shells are such a bother."

It occurred to Wiz that he might not be out of trouble yet.

"Uh, where are my friends?"

"Oh, they're off chasing the rest of those things. They attacked them, you know." A sniff of disdain. "Tasteless. Utterly tasteless. No matter how much garlic and herbs you use, it's like eating old leather."

Wiz remembered the guardroom with the dismembered skeletons.

"Now you, on the other hand! Oh, think how wonderful you'll smell all boiled up with lemon pepper and a bouquet garni of herbs."

Wiz scrambled back up the slope away from the huge claws. "Look, can't we talk about this?"

"But it is the function of humans to be served up on a plate with garlic butter and surrounded by parsley," the lobster protested as it moved toward him. It paused. "Ah, you don't happen to have any parsley with you? Pity. I'm out."

The lobster extended his enormous pincers and advanced on Wiz. "Now, I assure you, your nervous system is so primitive you won't feel a bit of pain."

"I'll be the judge of that," Wiz said, continuing his backwards scramble. "Did anyone ever tell you it's impolite to eat your acquaintances?"

The lobster sighed gustily through its gills, giving Wiz a whiff of iodine-scented "breath." "You humans have the most curious notions. We have always believed that a little light conversation before dinner allows you to fully appreciate the meal. But not too much. Come on now, into the pot you go."

Wiz kept backing up. There wasn't anyplace to run to and the lobster seemed to move over the rocky ground more easily than he did.

"You're being quite unreasonable, you know." The lobster sounded almost hurt. "After all, humans eat us."

"But you give us heartburn."

"That," said the lobster smugly, "is the advantage of a superior constitution. We don't get heartburn."

A fireball whizzed over the lobster to splatter against the cavern wall above them.

"Oh, drat!" said the lobster and scuttled backwards at astonishing speed as Malkin, Danny and the others came up the tunnel.

"Boy, am I glad to see you guys!" Wiz said as the rest of the party gathered around him.

"We had a little butt-kicking to do," Danny explained.

"What was that?" Malkin demanded. "The Enemy?"

"No, that was a lobster. I think it was here before the Enemy took over. Local color you might say."

"I'd like to color him," Malkin retorted fiercely. "Boil him in a pot until he's bright red."

"Yeah, well the feeling is mutual," Wiz told her.

## ELEVEN

# Lateral To the Real World

*I wish these things would run straight for a while,* Wiz thought irritably. But the tunnels down here didn't and this was an especially twisty part. Wiz's inner ear was starting to send queasy messages to his stomach because of all the sharp turns.

Then the tunnel opened out into another room, an enormous, echoing black space that yawned before them in all directions. Wiz hastily ducked back around the corner and dimmed the magic light. Then he motioned for a huddle.

"What does the magic detector say?"

Danny squinted at the device. "That there's something magical around here that probably wouldn't be too glad to see us." He cocked his head and squinted some more. "But it's not real active and it doesn't seem to be directly in our path."

Wiz peeked around the corner again and listened intently. The silence was as overpowering as the darkness. He looked at Malkin, but the thief shook her head.

"Nothing," she said quietly.

"Okay folks, single file and move softly. We don't want whatever's out there to surprise us."

Wiz considered leaving the light off, but he decided the danger of falling into a hole outweighed the risk of alerting whatever was in the neighborhood. With a gesture he sent the globe of light floating above them. *I gotta figure out a way to make these things directional,* he thought as he followed Malkin out into the room.

The room was huge. After nearly a hundred paces the light no longer showed the walls or ceiling, only the uneven, stalagmite-studded floor, glistening with moisture. It occurred to Wiz that the detector might be pointing toward their ultimate destination rather than toward the exit. If that was true they could spend hours searching for the way out and if there was more than one they could be thoroughly lost before they knew it.

Out in the gloom was a heap of something. It wasn't rocks and it didn't seem to be alive, but aside from that Wiz couldn't make out just what it was. With a gesture he increased the brightness of the magic light and was rewarded with a glint from the heap.

At first Wiz thought the pile had caught fire. Then he realized it was his own light reflected back at them, glittering off the objects in the pile.

Another gesture and the light grew even brighter. Now there was no doubt at all what the heap was.

Gold winked yellow or glowed ruddy in the light. Gems flashed green and red and wine-purple fire. Pearls and opals threw back a soft luster. There were ingots and cups and brooches and rings; candlesticks and platters and coins and gems loose like marbles. Wiz even caught a glimpse of a full suit of golden armor, studded with precious stones and filigreed with enamel. All of it piled head-high in a loose, careless mass.

"Look at that," Wiz breathed.

The others could only stare. Malkin started edging toward it, only to be pushed aside roughly by Glandurg in his haste to reach the pile.

"Glandurg! Get back here. We're not here for gold."

"What kind of adventure is it if you don't get the treasure?" the dwarf grumbled. "Uncivilized, I say."

"Boy," said Danny, "I always knew dungeons were supposed to have treasure, but this . . . " He waved his arm in awe. June stayed behind her husband, obviously torn between wonder at the sight and distaste at his reaction.

Wiz noticed that there were no containers in the pile. No chests, no bags, nothing that could be used to transport or contain the hoard. It was as if it had been carefully brought here and emptied out and then the containers removed.

"Where do you suppose this came from?"

"Your dark wizards, or whatever." Malkin ran her fingers through the pile. "Whoever it was is long gone."

"You hope," Wiz retorted.

With a clatter and the ringing sound of falling gold hitting the stone floor, Glandurg burrowed into the pile like a homesick gopher. Suddenly his head emerged from the top, sending a shower of wealth cascading down the mound. He spat out a ruby the size of a hen's egg and grinned gleefully.

"Look, people," Wiz said, "this isn't what we're here for."

"But it doesn't hurt," retorted Malkin, who was already elbow-deep in a mass of gold coins.

Danny threw himself down in the treasure, scooped up handfuls and poured it over his head. He winced when a particularly heavy and tasteless gold goblet hit him on the head. "Hey, Scrooge McDuck was onto something with his money bin."

Wiz hesitated. He didn't like this at all and he sure didn't want to be encumbered by a lot of dead weight. But obviously the attraction of all that loot was an irresistible force for Glandurg and Malkin.

"We need a way to carry this stuff," Malkin said.

"If you think I'm going to whomp up a levitation spell just so we can take that along with us, you're crazy." Malkin and Glandurg looked at him.

"Okay," he sighed, "you can take what you can carry in a cloak."

It took Malkin and Glandurg a minute to decide whose cloak was bigger. Then they started shoveling gold, jewels and other treasure from the pile. When the heap on Malkin's cape was about three feet high in the center they stopped for breath.

"Now try to move it," Wiz said.

Dwarf and thief each seized an edge of the cloak and gave a mighty tug. The pile moved perhaps six inches.

"What you need is a cart," Danny suggested.

"Won't work. Floor's too rough."

"Okay," Wiz said, "if it will get us moving again, I've got a spell that reduces friction to almost nothing. That will make the cloak easier to haul. But we're burying the stuff the first chance we get."

He stepped forward, raised his staff and spoke a few words.

"There, it should pull easily now."

Malkin tugged on the edge of her cloak and nearly went over backwards when her hands slipped off the material. Glandurg grabbed and yanked and went careening into Malkin when his hands slipped. Both of them landed in a tangle on the rocky floor and glared at Wiz.

"Okay, let me modify the spell."

He drew a breath to list out the spell, but before he could exhale he heard a noise from beyond the circle of light. Something was moving out there in the dark.

"Ah, folks . . . " Danny began. He never finished the sentence. He didn't need to.

Wiz didn't know if it was the biggest dragon he'd ever seen or not. For one thing, the cavern was mostly dark. For another he couldn't see all of it. But primarily, he was too scared to take accurate measurements. If it wasn't the biggest dragon he'd ever seen it would do quite nicely for now.

The dragon spouted a gout of flame that illuminated the cavern to its corners and left a dark smear of an afterimage clouding his vision. He tried to raise his staff to cast a spell and realized he was magically frozen in place. Out of the corner of his eye he saw the others straining to move as well. The dragon fire had been misdirection while the creature pinned them where they stood with a spell.

Its enemies neutralized, the dragon lumbered forward for the kill.

Wiz muttered under his breath.

Talons extended, the dragon's left front paw landed on the cavern floor and promptly flew out from under him, dumping the beast on his nose. The great muzzle slipped on the floor and left the dragon lying spread-eagled and neck extended on the glistening limestone.

However dragons are not so easily defeated. The huge talons on all four feet dug into the limestone as if it were soft clay and the beast levered itself erect. It crouched to spring across the intervening distance at its prey, but its purchase failed just as it leapt and the dragon went sprawling and slithering across the cavern. Wiz and the others watched fascinated as the dragon slid helplessly by, hit the cave wall behind them and rebounded back into the cavern like a pool ball coming off the side rail.

Wiz had cast the reduce-friction spell not on the floor, but on the dragon. That not only made the dragon slippery all over, but it charged the beast to a high magic potential—and made every stalagmite, stalactite, flowstone and ordinary rock in the cavern repel him violently. The creature had put enormous power into his spring and lost almost none of it in the inelastic collisions. As a result a very unhappy dragon went caroming off everything he hit, and he managed to hit just about everything in the cave except Wiz and his friends.

Every time the beast struck a rock it let out a roar and a gout of flame, making the walls ring and lighting the cavern to its edges. The result was like being in a giant pinball machine during especially active play.

Finally the dragon slid backwards into a tunnel off the main cave. A quick, precisely aimed lightning bolt struck inside the tunnel and collapsed the mouth into a pile of rock. Behind the landslide they could hear the faint roaring of a very unhappy dragon.

"Dragon in the side pocket!" Danny whooped. "Awesome."

Wiz discovered he could move again. "Let's get our awes out of here before that dragon digs himself out. Move it people!"

"But the treasure!" Malkin protested.

"Mark it on the map and we'll pick it up on the way out. Now come on!"

Everyone complied, but Wiz noticed that Malkin and Glandurg clinked suspiciously as they hurried down the tunnel.

There was a dragon asleep beside the fire, with only an occasional tail twitch or foot thump to show he was dreaming dragonish dreams.

It was in fact an achingly normal scene for the programmers' workroom, if you could ignore the whispering shadows outside the windows.

Jerry Andrews stared at the four screens hanging above his desk and bit his lip. As decoration they were spectacular, all neon colors ranging through the whole spectrum with annotations and hypertext links in other glaring colors. As information they were just about useless.

"Shit," Jerry exclaimed, throwing himself backwards so hard his chair creaked.

The dragon lifted his head questioningly.

"My Lord?" Moira asked as her personality asserted itself.

"It's been a long time since I've felt this frustrated."

As a hacker's significant other, Moira recognized the signs. Jerry needed a sounding board. She also knew that a sympathetic ear was more important than cogent advice. A Siamese cat would do the job nicely if it meowed in the appropriate spots.

"A difficult problem?"

Jerry grinned but there was no joy in it. "I don't even know enough to know that." He spun around in the chair to face the dragon on the hearth.

"Normally on a job like this where you've got a pile of observables—stuff—and no paradigm, you just grab hold of anything that looks likely and see where it leads. You poke and prod at it and see what happens and eventually you can make sense out of what you're seeing. Here—" he waved a hand expressively. "Here no matter where I grab and how much I poke and prod I don't get anything that makes sense."

He spun back around and waved at the light show above his desk. "Ninety percent of this sort of project is getting inside the other guy's head. Eventually you've got to be able to see the code through his eyes, to understand a little of how he thinks. Only here, no matter how hard I try, I can't make any sense of what I'm seeing. Some of this stuff is truly elegant, some of it is a triumph of development over design, some of it is awfully crude and some of it is pigeon droppings. And there's no sense to any of it, no rhyme or reason, no overriding structure."

"Well, Wiz always said you start with what you know."

Jerry spun back to her. "I know enough to know I'm out of my depth on this. We need help, heavy-duty help from our world."

"Another programming team?"

Jerry shook his head. "Not that simple. We need someone who can get his mind around this thing."

"Another wizard programmer?"

"No, we need someone even more powerful. We need a programming legend, a code demigod"

"Do you have anyone in mind?"

Jerry thought for a minute. "That's a problem. You can't very well go up to someone like Ken Thompson and ask him to take a sabbatical from Bell Labs to go off to another world to solve a problem involving an evil magician."

"You mean he might not believe you?"

"I mean the paperwork would be a little excessive. People of this caliber don't grow on trees and a lot of them are key figures at their companies, teaching at the university level or in jail for getting cute with someone else's computer. In any event they're not available."

"Are there some who are not occupied?"

"Yeah, a few." He thought for a minute. "Well, Tom Digby isn't available right now, so the best is probably Taj."

"Taj?"

"E.T. Tajikawa, the Tajmanian Devil. The guy spends most of his time surfing the far, far end of the bell curve, out three sigmas west of Strange." Moira didn't know what that meant but it sounded powerful, So she concentrated on the part she thought she understood.

"E.T. Is that like the movie Wiz likes so much?" Moira asked.

"No, it's E.T. as in Elvis Twitty." Jerry shrugged. "His mom was Korean. She didn't speak English real good but she loved country music and she wanted to give her son an American name.

"Taj used to teach an extension class in debugging down in the Valley. I learned a hell of a lot from him, but for the first four weeks I thought I'd wandered into a 'Kung Fu' episode. He started us off with Tai Chi exercises and quotes from Bugs Bunny cartoons. We ended with five minutes of meditation while he rang this little bell. And crazy as it sounds, it all tied together."

Moira, who didn't know what Tai Chi was and to whom a lot of programming was a mystery anyway, was willing to take his word for it.

"His power isn't in his techniques. It's in the way he *sees*."

"That sounds like Patrius," Moira said.

"The wizard who brought Wiz here in the first place?

Yeah, from what I've heard of him he would have liked Taj."

"What would it take to get him?"

"Mostly you'd have to catch his interest. But that's hard to do. Last I heard he was hip-deep in a six-figure design project for a gaming company."

"Would it hurt to ask him?"

"No," Jerry said slowly. "No, it wouldn't hurt." He brightened. "Thanks, Moira, you're a genius."

Moira took the compliment without comment. "You had best ask Bal-Simba before you talk about bringing another through from your world."

"Right. I'm sure he won't have any problem with it."

In a matter of minutes Bal-Simba was summoned and he listened carefully, if somewhat sleepily, to Jerry's proposal.

"If you think it will aid us, by all means ask this person to come here," he said when Jerry finally wound down.

"Even if he can't physically come to us we can probably do a lot over the Internet. But it would be better if he can get free for a while." He looked at Bal-Simba. "Can we still do a Great Summoning to bring someone over from our world?"

"Almost certainly. The shadows do not seem able to block that path."

"Well, let's find out then." Jerry picked up the telephone sitting incongruously on his desk and began punching in the number. "I'll put it on the speaker. I hope it's late enough in the day that he's up."

"Hallo," came a female voice with a hint of Scandinavian accent. In the background he heard the steady click of computer keys.

"Is Taj there? This is Jerry Andrews, jerry@thekeep.org, I'm kind of a friend of his."

The keystrokes didn't even slow. "Oh yah, I remember you, I think. From alt.comp.lang.theory.wild_blue. This is Sigurd, you know, Sig@miskatonic.frodo.org."

Jerry remembered Tajikawa's girlfriend/soulmate/companion/secretary/keeper. "Hi, Sigurd. Is Taj there?"

"He's at Comdex. He's not gonna be back until, like, a week from Sunday."

"Oh. Well, is there any way to reach him?"

"I don't think so. He said he was gonna beg crash space off a friend. Didn't say who and I don't think he knew himself."

"Didn't he take a celluar phone?"

"Well, kinda. He's got a loaner from MMCC—you know, the Mini-Microcell-Communications Consortium—that's running a demonstration network at the show. They're setting up stations at all the major hotels. Only, one of their crates got lost in transit, then they had a problem with some weird connectors and had to have replacements airfreighted from Taiwan. Plus their directory software apparently has some kind of suicide pact with their hard drives and . . . "

"So their phones aren't working," Jerry cut in.

"I understand the hotel books are giving eight to three that they won't have them working before the show ends."

"Well, what about e-mail? Is he going to be on-line?"

"Well, he took his laptop but I don't think he's got the modem working. It's a new machine with a Type III PC Card modem, only the card services for Linux are, like, flatlined. He was going to hack a driver but he didn't have time before he left."

"That's too bad. Look, do you know who's he's going to be seeing? It's really important that I reach him."

"He wanted to check out some scientific visualization software, but other than that he didn't say. I'm sorry."

"If he does check in have him contact me. It really is a matter of life and death. Have him send to jerry@thekeep.org."

"Okay, let me open a window here." There was a brief

pause then more clicking of keys as she took the address. "If I hear from him I'll sure give him the message."

"Shit," said Jerry as he broke the connection.

"What now?" Bal-Simba asked. "Will another serve?"

"There aren't any others in Taj's class," Jerry said, "at least none that I know of who are available."

"Is there any other way to contact him?"

"We can put out the word on the Net, but I'm not sure how long that will take and we'll probably get a lot of bogus reports. Taj is pretty famous." He thought. "Comdex only lasts a week so he should be home next Monday at the latest."

Bal-Simba considered. "I am not sure we can wait that long. These things press us relentlessly and ever closer despite our efforts."

"Can we hide Moira somewhere?"

"I do not think there is any place in the World where these things could not find her," Bal Simba told him.

"Okay, then. There's only one thing to do."

Wizard and dragon looked at the programmer expectantly.

"We," said Jerry, "are going to Comdex."

# Part II: Queen of the Strip

## TWELVE
## Another Quest

For a minute no one said anything. For a long minute.

"That does not seem terribly practical," Bal-Simba said at last. "A dragon cannot survive where there is no magic."

"Normally no, but I think I have an answer to that. You know how our method of getting into the other world's telephone system works?"

Bal Simba looked at him. "No."

"Basically we use magical energy to influence semiconductors on an atomic level—well, really it's subatomic because what we're doing is analogous to actualizing virtual particles out of the quantum froth. You see . . ."

Moira cleared her throat significantly. It was especially impressive coming from a dragon.

Jerry took the hint. "Ah, right. Anyway, we have found we can leak a little magic across if the conditions are right. That's how we signal back to this World for a Great Summoning to bring someone through from our world. We can apply the same principle to draw magical energy from this World to support the dragon's metabolism."

Bal-Simba only nodded. "I will take your word for it. But tell me, are there any other difficulties?"

"Well, one. The magic flow messes up the signaling scheme for a Grand Summoning. There are only a few points on our world where we will be able to signal you that we're ready to return. Vortex points, they're called. There's a big one out in the desert about a hundred and fifty miles north of Las Vegas. That area's practically uninhabited so we won't have any trouble getting back through it." He stopped. "There was another one a few hundred miles away in Sedona, Arizona, but they built a McDonald's on top of it."

Bal-Simba rubbed his chin. "This spell of yours does not sound stable."

"It will hold for a few days. Once we get on the ground that should be all we need to find Taj. Meanwhile it will take the pressure off the Wizards' Keep."

Bal-Simba turned to the dragon. "My Lady, how do you feel about this?"

"I am not sure," Moira said. "This is the first I have heard of such a thing. It seems . . ." She fell silent for a minute and then the dragon's head came erect, chin out in a gesture that was achingly Moira. "It seems to me this is our best chance, is it not?" Jerry and Bal-Simba nodded. "Then this is what we should do."

Jerry felt a sudden pang of conscience. "Uh, I ought to point out this is still experimental. Things could go wrong."

The dragon snorted. "My Lord," Moira's voice said bitterly, "they could not go any more wrong than they have already."

*Another day, another maze,* Wiz thought, looking around. In the light of the magic globe he could see no less than six different tunnels leading off from the one they were in, including one in the roof. The whole area was like that, twisty, turning, branching and rebranching. He had been in the lead with the magic Moira locator for most of the morning as the group picked their way along, stopping every few feet while he consulted the device to see which way to go. It seemed as if they had barely made a quarter of a mile the whole day and Wiz was fuming with impatience.

"I mislike this place," Malkin said quietly over Wiz's shoulder. She had taken the number-two position to let Wiz guide the party.

"Not my favorite piece of geography either, but what's your point?"

The tall thief looked past him, eyes never still as they talked. "There are far too many openings here. Ideal for an ambush."

Wiz hadn't thought of that. "Danny hasn't seen anything on the magic detector." Malkin looked at him as if he was stupid. "Okay, pass the word to close up, and no straggling."

There was a sound behind them, a scuffle and then Danny yelled. They both whirled to see June locked in a deadly embrace with a tall figure in rags. Her knife was flashing as she struck home again and again but the thing kept its grip on her.

There was another sound and Wiz and Malkin whirled again to face a new danger from the front. A figure in black armor was closing, almost on top of them, sword raised.

Like a striking snake Malkin's rapier darted over Wiz's shoulder and thrust into the attacker's face. The armored figure never flinched and brought his own sword down in a vicious overhead blow aimed at Wiz's skull.

The cut was clumsily made and poorly aimed. The sword slid along Malkin's rapier and off past her side. Before the attacker could recover Wiz hit it square on with a lightning bolt and it burst into flames.

Even that didn't stop it. Slowly, deliberately, it brought its sword back and above its fiery body to strike again. Then it tottered and fell backwards as fire reduced its substance to ashes.

Beyond it there were other figures in the corridor. Wiz didn't hesitate. He sent bolt after bolt of lightning flashing down the tunnel to consume the others even as they shuffled forward.

And then it was quiet again. There was no sound but the labored breathing of the adventurers and June's knife, striking again and again into the dismembered body of her foe. Danny went to his wife's side and gently pulled her off the still quivering body.

"It's all right," he said, "it's dead."

"A long time dead," Malkin amended, studying the body. "This was not a living man. It's an animated corpse."

"Zombie?"

"Why not?" Wiz said grimly. "The Enemy probably had a lot of corpses to work with here."

"I would suggest," Malkin said with equal grimness, "that we get out of this place as quickly as we can. We do not want to be set upon from all sides at once by things like this."

Night had fallen over the Wizards' Keep, though its inhabitants needed magic or a sand glass to tell them that. Outside, the unremitting gray fog beat against the castle, pushing, squeezing, trying to insinuate its tentacles into the structure.

The great hall was lit by magical glow lamps. At each of the eight cardinal points stood one of the Mighty, staff in hand. Within the inscribed circle stood two men, a woman and a dragon.

"May Fortuna aid you all," Arianne said to Bal-Simba, Jerry and Moira as she finished giving them final instructions.

"We'll be all right," Jerry said. "I just hope you can do something on this end while we're gone."

"The other wizards say that given time they will be able to control this thing, at least here."

Silence fell over the group. Unconsciously they turned to watch the sand trickle out of the glass.

"There is still time, My Lady," Bal-Simba said quietly. Moira shook her head. The big wizard breathed a gusty sigh. "Well, then. I believe we are ready."

"Merry part," Arianne said to them.

"Merry meet again, Lady," Bal-Simba replied.

Arianne stepped out of the circle, being careful not to scuff it. As the sand ran from the glass the wizards threw back their robes to expose their arms and raised their staffs. As the final grains fell to the bottom they began to chant.

The world wavered, dissolved and suddenly they were in a narrow alley between blind wooden walls. It took a moment for Jerry to realize the walls were really shipping containers stacked six high.

Jerry and Bal-Simba were dizzy and a little disoriented. Moira seemed to be worse affected. The dragon leaned drunkenly against the crates, making little pawing motions with his front claws.

"My Lady, are you all right?" Bal-Simba asked.

The dragon shook his head feebly, as if trying to clear it. Then he heaved himself upright. For an instant Jerry was afraid he would fall, but the dragon steadied and seemed to draw inner strength.

"How do you feel?" Jerry asked.

"Let us get on with it," Moira said grimly.

Jerry was relieved both at the dragon's apparent recovery and at Moira's response. He hadn't been absolutely sure that Moira would be able to talk to them in this world.

"Where are we?" Bal-Simba asked, craning his neck to look at the three-story-stack of crates surrounding them.

"We're in a storage area next to an exhibit hall, but I don't recognize which one."

He looked around trying to orient himself. It wasn't

easy. The view at ground level was completely blocked by the stacks of crates. Beyond the crates on one side was a solid brick wall, perhaps four stories high. Above that were two hotel towers perhaps twenty stories high each. Scanning the horizon over the tops of the crates he could see mountains in the distance and here and there tall buildings, obviously more hotels. The sky above was pale turquoise blue with just a few wisps of high clouds.

"I don't recognize this at all," Jerry said. "This isn't the Convention Center. It must be one of the new hotels."

"What do we do first?"

Jerry looked at Bal-Simba in his leopard-skin kilt, bone necklace and blue cloak. "First we get some clothes. No, first we get some money."

It took them a while to find their way out of the wooden maze. Finally, with the help of some rather profane instructions from a startled forklift driver who nearly ran over them, they found a gate and stepped into a parking lot dominated by a fleet of semis, trailers and satellite dishes.

"Okay," Jerry said, looking around, "this is the Paladin. That tells me where we are, more or less."

Bal-Simba and Moira didn't say anything. They were too busy staring.

There was reason to stare. Off in one direction a castle raised pinnacled towers to the pale blue sky. In another a giant lion of blue glass crouched, and off to the side stood a glittering black pyramid. A tropical rain forest rose under a glittering dome, a gigantic brightly striped pavilion stood in another direction. Off in the distance there were more spires and domes. That all these wonders were accompanied by nearly identical blocky high-rise towers sheathed in golden glass did nothing to dim the effect on Bal-Simba and Moira.

"Amazing," Bal-Simba said at last. "Moira may have seen its like before, but it is new to me."

"This is unlike what I saw before of this world," Moira told him.

"This is Las Vegas," Jerry explained. "It's unlike just about anything." He looked around, getting his bearings and then patted the brown suede purse that hung from his belt. "Come on, let's go around to the front."

They trudged across acres of asphalt crammed with automobiles, threaded their way between the towering hotel block and a multi-story parking garage and finally emerged at the front of the hotel.

As soon as they came around the corner their surroundings changed completely. Jerry led them up a walkway beside a winding drive, past groves of palm trees and stands of giant bamboo springing from an impossibly green lawn. They passed statues in classical poses, a compound holding several white tigers, crossed over a bridge above a pool housing a number of dolphins, passed an artificial geyser at a discreet distance and finally came to the bank of glass doors leading into the hotel proper.

"Moira, you'd better wait outside," Jerry told the dragon. "I'm not sure what their rules are on animals and I don't think we can pass you off as a seeing eye dog."

"Well enough, My Lord," Moira said. "It sounds excessively noisy in any event."

"I begin to understand why the search will be difficult," Bal-Simba said as soon as they were through the door and out of Moira's earshot. "This place is larger than I had imagined."

"Oh, this is only one of the places we've got to look. There are maybe a couple of dozen more this big or bigger. One of the problems we've got is that the show is spreading out again. For a while they had all the exhibits concentrated in just two big exhibit halls and the Hilton next to the Convention Center," Jerry said. "But those overflowed and they've had to start using the hotel exhibition space again."

Bal-Simba started forward toward the line of clerks and away from the racket in the casino, but Jerry stopped him.

"No, this is just the registration area. What we want is probably the teller's cage. That's over this way."

Bal-Simba frowned slightly but followed Jerry out into the maze of the casino.

Everywhere there were lights, colors and noise. It took Jerry a minute to realize the casino didn't have many players.

"The casinos hate the show even if the hotels love it," he told Bal-Simba as they maneuvered through the aisles and past the occasional slot player. "Most of the attendees don't gamble—well, except for the startups and product rollouts on the show floor."

Bal-Simba nodded as if the comment made perfect sense.

The cashier's office was off at one side of the casino so it only took about ten minutes and three sets of directions from change girls and a guard before they found it.

The cage manager was well-groomed, well-mannered and impossible to surprise. The sight of a couple of characters in Halloween costumes with a bag of gold they wanted to change into money didn't so much as turn a hair. He laid out the terms for them as if this happened every day. Looking around the casino, Jerry reflected that maybe it did.

"Ten thousand dollars maximum," the manager told them. "Market less twenty-five percent." He shook his head. "I'll tell you right now you can do better in most of the pawn shops."

"We need some walking-around money."

The manager shrugged. He led them around the corner, past two armed guards and into a small room where a clerk was waiting for them with a tabletop full of machinery.

The clerk was not as well groomed and considerably less mannered. He took the coins and ten by ten put them in a large piece of equipment in one corner.

"Neutron spectroscope," the manager explained. "We get a lot of Asian customers with gold."

It took time to test the coins and more time to count out the cash. In the process Jerry had to sign a statement saying who he was, that the gold was legal and that he had paid all the applicable taxes. He noticed that the manager didn't ask them for identification.

"Now do we begin our search?" Bal-Simba asked as they threaded their way back through the casino.

"Now we go get our credentials," Jerry said. "That will take a good chunk of this money."

"Excuse me," said a woman's voice off to one side. Both men turned and took a blinding light full in the face.

"Thanks," said a shadowy form perfunctorily as she lowered her camera and pushed by them.

Bal-Simba blinked as he tried to get his sight back. "What was that?"

"That was a reminder that we need some different clothes." Jerry frowned. "But that's going to take more time and . . . " Then his rapidly returning sight fell on an arcade of shops off beyond the registration area. "Come on. It'll be expensive, but we need to save time more than we need to save money."

The shopping arcade angled off from the registration area leading to one of the hotel towers. Beyond the frozen yogurt shop, the jeweler's, the furrier's and the "art gallery" selling brightly colored paintings whose kitsch was only exceeded by their prices, was the men's store Jerry had known had to be there.

The place had an Italian name that Jerry thought was some kind of sausage, but he wasn't picky. The interior was all white and old gold and decorated in a way that for some reason reminded Jerry of a tapestry woven of polyester. The salesman was tall, lean and dressed in an extreme version of Italian style. He was also showing a five o'clock shadow.

"May I help you?" he said in tones that indicated he probably couldn't, but he was going to go through the motions anyway.

"Uh, my friend and I need some clothes."

The man looked them up and down. "I'll say."

"They lost our luggage and all we have left are our costumes. We need something for street wear."

"Hmm," the man said. "Hmm," he said again. "Hey, Meyer, can you come out here a minute?"

Meyer was a wizened old man with thick glasses set low on his nose. His trousers were dusty with chalk and he wore a tape measure draped around his neck like a shawl.

"They need some street clothes," the younger man told him.

Meyer looked them over with an obviously professional eye. "Come on back into the fitting room and let's see what we can do."

"He keeps me around for color," the old man confided as he led them into the back. "Pfafh! Like I'm a museum exhibit or something."

Like its inhabitant the back room wasn't nearly as fancy but looked a lot more businesslike. Meyer whipped the tape measure off his shoulders and began to lay it against Jerry's body. "My nephew. He should have learned his trade at his father's knee—God rest him—but instead he goes off and gets an MBA. An MBA! Better he should learn tailoring to run a haberdashery, no? But kids, you can't tell them anything. So, you want suits or what?"

"Something less formal," Jerry said.

"Hmm," the old man said without stopping his measurements. "Pity. I could do some real good things for both of you in suits." He sighed. "But these days, you don't get a chance to show off what you know. Well, at least it's not leisure suits any more."

Museum exhibit or no, Meyer knew his business. With hardly a pause he had both Jerry and Bal-Simba measured and the sample book laid out for them to pick the cloth.

"Here you go. Not a thread of polyester in the bunch. Just show me what you want and in two, three days we'll have you turned out sharp."

"We were hoping for something today. Something we can wear out of here."

"You want miracles too?"

"We can't go walking around like this."

"I don't see why not. You look like a bartender from the Excalibur. That's a hotel," he added at Jerry's puzzled expression. Then he nodded toward Bal-Simba. "Him, he's a problem."

"It can be just about anything. We're kinda desperate."

He looked at Jerry. "In that case, you I can fit off the rack, almost. Your friend—" He shrugged. "That's special."

"How long will it take?"

"So you're in a hurry too?"

"Look, if it's a matter of money . . . "

The old man waved him to silence. "It's a matter of possible. A challenge like this I haven't had in a long time, but even so . . . " Again the shrug. Then he brightened. "Wait a minute. I do have something a customer never picked up. I can even make you a price on it."

A few minutes later Jerry stepped out of the dressing room the picture of Las Vegas casual. His polo shirt and slacks fit him beautifully. The clothing felt odd after the loose shirts, tunics and breeches he had worn for so long at the Wizards' Keep. The shoes were stiff and pinched a little after the soft leather boots of the other world, but he could get used to it.

"Are you ready?" he called into the dressing room where Bal-Simba was changing.

"I believe so," Bal Simba said, somewhat hesitantly.

Bal-Simba emerged wearing a puffy-sleeved pink shirt open to the navel. A fancy vest fitted tightly over the shirt. Tight tan bell-bottoms stretched across his ample rear. He had left his bone necklace around his chest and a snap-brim hat with a leopard-skin band completed the outfit. Meyer fussed around him, pulling down the vest here and tugging the shirt into position there.

Jerry looked his friend up and down. "We don't have to guess the guy's profession, do we?"

The old man shrugged. "So who asks? Now come on up front and we'll get you taken care of."

Jerry gulped when he saw the bill, but he peeled off hundreds without comment. "The rest of the stuff, four o'clock tomorrow," Meyer admonished. "I swear not a minute sooner."

They found Moira outside by the dolphin pool, posing for pictures with a family of tourists while a couple of bemused security guards looked on.

"Don't you need a leash for that thing?" one of the guards asked when Jerry came up to rejoin her.

"Audio-Animatronics," Jerry explained.

"No kidding?" one of the guards said. "Like the showgirls?" Jerry wasn't sure whether he was joking or not so he just smiled.

There was a covered slideway from the lobby to the street, but Jerry led them down the ordinary sidewalk beneath it. He wasn't sure how his friends would take to a moving walkway and he wasn't at all sure Moira would be able to keep her tail out of the gears.

"How do we begin our search for this wizard?" Moira asked as the three made their way out to the street.

"First things first. We gotta get registered. We do that at the main Convention Center."

"Where is that?"

"There." Jerry pointed to one of the towers springing up out of the desert. "It's further than it looks."

"How will we get there?"

"Walk. I don't think they would let a dragon on a shuttle bus. Besides, we don't have credentials so they won't let us in either."

Bal-Simba nodded and the strangely assorted trio joined the knots of business-suited convention-goers drifting down the sidewalk toward the distant tower.

You would think that a twenty-foot dragon parading down the main street of a major American city would attract at least *some* attention. You would be wrong. Anyone who's been in Las Vegas more than forty-eight hours has found stranger things than that on the breakfast buffet. The only interest came from the occasional gawker in a car stuck in traffic, and truth to tell they seemed more taken with Bal-Simba.

"What is all this for?" Moira asked as they walked along. "Wiz compared it to the Winter Fair once, but I never understood."

"It's a trade show for the computer industry," Jerry said. "All these people are connected with computers somehow."

"And they are here to buy and sell them?"

Jerry shrugged. "Well, they used to be. Then the distribution channels got better established and most of that business moved elsewhere. Then for a while everybody came to see the new products that were being announced. But the show got so big and there were so many announcements that most of the really big ones aren't made here any more. Then it was the place to meet people. But now it's so big you have trouble doing that." He fell silent.

"Then why do people come here?" Moira asked.

"I guess," Jerry said slowly, "because it's here."

The air was cool and the desert sun merely warm

rather than blazing. Even so, Moira was showing signs of stress before they reached their destination.

"I am sorry, My Lord, but this body cannot go much further," Moira told them finally. "It is worn out and I, I am feeling unwell."

The way she said it made Jerry wonder about what happened when a dragon barfed. He decided not to be in front of her if it happened.

"That's okay. I told you it was further than it looked." He glanced down the street. "Look, the Convention Center is right down there. Why don't I go ahead and you two follow when she can? I'll have to wait in line for a while anyway."

Registration was in a big blue-and-white tent erected in the parking lot at the Convention Center. Jerry breasted his way through the thickening crowds around and inside the tent to get a place in line to register.

"How many?" the woman behind the counter asked.

"Two, no make that three sets."

"Fill out the forms over there and when you get done bring them back here."

Secure in the knowledge that no one would pay any attention to what was on the forms until he was away from this world, Jerry indulged in an orgy of mendacity. By the time he was done he was president of his own company, Bal-Simba was "Wizard In Chief" and Moira bore the title of "Exhibit A."

Since he had signed them all up for the seminars as well as the exhibit halls, the bill was in four figures. So much so that he was momentarily taken aback.

*What the heck,* Jerry thought, *it's only money.*

By the time he emerged, the better part of an hour later, Bal-Simba and Moira were waiting for him.

"Here." He handed Bal-Simba a paper bag of literature. "Most of this is junk but we can go through it later."

Next he gave Bal-Simba his badge. "Don't lose this. You have to have it showing all the time."

The big wizard raised his eyebrows.

"It's, uh, a talisman, to get you into the exhibit areas."

Bal-Simba nodded and clipped it to his vest.

"Where shall I attach mine?" Moira asked.

"Just clip it to your . . . Ah, right. That is a problem."

Then it occured to Jerry there might be a bigger problem. Even with a badge it would be hard to get a dragon into the exhibit areas.

"Wait a minute," Jerry said, "I've got an idea."

Ignoring the thronging crowds, Jerry went over to a banner decorating the side of the building. He quickly cut the ropes and gathered the banner as it fell.

"Here," he said to Bal-Simba, "help me drape this over her." With Bal-Simba holding one side of the sign, he threw the other over her back and crawled under her stomach. He barely missed being decapitated when Moira involuntarily raised a massively clawed hind foot.

"Be careful, will you?"

"Well, it tickles," Moira said.

With a little tugging and trimming he managed to get the cords tied under the dragon's belly. That left the sign draped like a horse blanket over her sides. As a finishing touch he pinned Moira's badge to the banner.

In the process Jerry noticed they had gathered a knot of onlookers.

"A dragon?" he heard one of them say.

"That's the code name for IBM's third-generation Personal Digital Assistant," announced woman in a serious gray business suit with Raiders shoulder pads and a pale silk jabot tied like a bow tie. "They're pre-pre-announcing at the show to build momentum."

Her companion, a middle-aged man in a three-piece suit and a pony tail, looked unimpressed. "I think they should have stuck with the Little Tramp."

"I thought Harris was the company that used the dragon," said another bystander.

"See?" Jerry said softly to Moira. "This way everyone will think you're advertising for a product."

"But the people who own the sign will know she is not with them, will they not?"

Jerry smiled up at the dragon. "Forget it. It's IBM. They're so big and so confused everyone will just think it's from another division." He turned to Moira. "If anyone asks tell them you were part of the Lotus acquisition. That'll really keep 'em guessing."

Dragon and wizard in tow, Jerry made for the main entrance. The closer they got the thicker the crowds became. Although most of the throng was white and in business suits it was a wonderfully diverse group. Perhaps a quarter were women, dressed in everything from business suits to bunny suits (literally—someone had a product code-named "Easter"). There were Indian Sikhs in business suits and turbans, American Sikhs in cotton pajamas and turbans, there were Chinese (both kinds), Japanese and Koreans from the Far East dressed in business suits. There were Chinese-Americans, Japanese-Americans and Korean-Americans, mostly in the American techie outfit of short-sleeved sport shirts and slacks. There were impeccably tailored Europeans and rumpled Americans. There were full beards and pony tails, although both were tending to gray and the pony tails started further back on the head than Jerry remembered—a reminder that the original technically oriented generation was being replaced by the corporate types, which made him a little sad. Here and there you could see the long white robes of an Arab or the rainbow robes of a West African.

They were standing in line waiting for shuttle buses, sitting on the grass eating off paper plates, leaning against the building resting their feet, handing out newspapers, rejecting newspapers, and talking, talking, talking. In addition to English of every conceivable variety, there were French and Spanish, Chinese and Korean, Japanese and Hindi, German and Russian, and a couple of things Jerry wasn't even sure were languages at all.

He drank it all in in passing and flowed with the current of humanity toward the glass doors that led into the exhibit hall.

Three steps through the door and Jerry was in information overload. The place was not merely packed, it was *stuffed*. There were thousands of people in every direction, crammed shoulder to shoulder and seemingly all in motion. You couldn't stand still unless you sought the lee side of an object to protect you from the flow.

"My Lord, I do not think I have ever seen so many people in one place at a time," Moira said in Jerry's ear.

"Neither have I," Jerry told her. "They're estimating two hundred and fifty thousand attendees this year."

"I see why you said this would be complicated," Bal-Simba rumbled.

Jerry flicked him a tight smile. "This isn't the complicated part."

Their first stop was the message center, in the hope that Taj had left someone a message saying where he was. Jerry didn't have a lot of hope for that and he was right. After battling their way through the crowd and waiting in line at a terminal, Taj's message box contained nothing but a couple of junk-mail announcements.

As they turned away and prepared to press onward, a man stepped in front of them waving his arms.

At first Jerry thought he was a high-tech mime. He had the jerky arm motions and sudden head movements.

"Amazing, isn't it?" said a voice in his ear. Jerry turned and saw a man standing beside him with an armload of literature. He was trapped and he knew it.

"It's the first completely integrated Cybernautics

system," the man said as he pressed a glossy brochure into Jerry's hand. "There's a P6 with a graphics accelerator in the backpack, transparent LCDs in the goggles and the gloves are 3-D pointing devices. There's also a high-bandwidth cellular modem so you're always hooked up. Right now he's net surfing, playing Doom II and watching the Browns play the Bears, all at once. The next step is to install the ultrasonic proximity locators and the differential GPS system so he'll never get lost."

In spite of himself Jerry was impressed. The demonstrator continued waving his arms and jerking his head, oblivious to the conversation and the crowd.

"What do you do? Besides hand out literature."

The man looked apologetic. "I'm his guide. Without the ultrasonic locators he keeps bumping into walls."

Suiting his actions to his words, he took the cybernaut's elbow and steered him away through the swirling throng.

"I think," Jerry said to Bal-Simba, "that's a concept that needs a little development." Then he was all business. "Now let me see the show guide. Sigurd said Taj was interested in scientific visualization software."

If anything the human mass was thicker and more congealed flowing through the doors of the main exhibit hall. Once inside things opened out slightly and the aisles were merely packed. Their first stop was a "booth," actually a carpeted area cut up by movable walls, about a third of the way in and halfway back. There were oversized television screens showing a dizzying array of images, and workstations on pedestals displaying other images, but not many people. The area on the carpet was relatively uncrowded and Moira breathed a sulfurous sigh of relief. One or two of the employees started to drift toward them but Jerry kept scanning, paying special attention to the feet.

Finally he spotted an attractive blond woman in a

tan business suit who had just finished talking to two other employees.

"Excuse me," Jerry said. "I wonder if you could help me."

"That's what we're here for. Has, ah . . . " She gave a quick glance at Jerry's badge. "Magic Dragon got a need for visualizaton software?"

"Sort of. I'm Jerry Andrews, CEO of the company, and this is, uh, Mr. Simba. He's our chief wizard."

"Elaine Haverford," the woman said extending her hand. Then to Bal-Simba she said "Jambo. I like the title. I may steal it."

"Jambo," Bal-Simba repeated, for all the world as if he knew what it meant. "And you are welcome to the title, My Lady, if it pleases you."

Elaine Haverford took the wizard's polite address for a compliment and dimpled.

"Actually, we were supposed to meet one of our consultants here," Jerry went on smoothly. "E.T. Tajikawa. But we seem to have missed connections."

"Taj? He was here yesterday, but I haven't seen him today. Hey, Henry!" she called over her shoulder, "have you seen the Tajmanian Devil around today?" Then she shook her head at the answer. "Not today. I think he said something about attending the Mauve reception at the Towne Centre, though."

Jerry handed her a card, fresh out of the vending machine in the registration booth. "If you see him could you have him leave us a message on the board saying where he's going to be? We really can't move on the visualization software without his advice."

"Sure will," Elaine Haverford said. "Meanwhile, if there's anything I can help you with," she handed over one of her own cards, "just ask."

"Excuse me, My Lord," Bal-Simba said as they pushed out into the aisle again. "Why did you ask that person and not one of the others?"

Jerry, an old hand at trade shows, recognized the question as a sign of severe information overload. When you're overwhelmed, you concentrate on the little things, even the irrelevancies.

"Her shoes."

"But she was not wearing any."

"Exactly." Jerry looked smug. "A woman's shoes are a giveaway at a trade show. See, high heels are murder on these concrete floors and you walk a lot, so the only women who wear high heels are the booth bunnies—hired models—and the low-level employees. If a woman wears flats she's with the company and probably has some status, an engineer maybe. Running shoes and she's probably high-level management. Now she—" he jerked his head back toward the booth. "She was barefoot with her business suit."

"Which means?" Moira asked, intrigued in spite of herself.

Jerry tapped Ms. Haverford's business card. Dr. Haverford, he saw. "Which means she owns the company."

Moira sighed and shook her head. In doing so she took her eyes off the crowd and nearly collided with an eight-foot-tall man in a gorilla suit. The dragon reared back and hissed in surprise and the man inside the gorilla suit nearly fell off his stilts.

"Forgive me, My Lord . . . " Moira began.

"Why don't you watch where you're going?" demanded the man in the gorilla suit, a former professional wrestler who had been hired for his size more than his temper.

"She said she was sorry," Jerry snapped, but the potential confrontation was cut short by a blaze of light.

The news crews at the show were desperate for visuals. Because of its importance everyone felt they had to cover it. But for all its importance, the computer show was one of the most relentlessly un-visual of all trade shows. After you had gotten your crowd shots, your geeks-playing-computer-games shots and your booth-bunnies-in-revealing-costumes shots there was almost nothing worth picturing. A giant ape and a dragon together were irresistible. A dozen flashguns and two sets of TV lights zeroed in on the accidental pair.

The dragon reared up and let out a steamwhistle hiss, which only brought a new round of flashes and even more TV lights. Except for his tail, Fluffy wasn't dangerous, but Jerry had visions of thousands of computer types trampled in a panicked stampede—the physical equivalent of what happened every time Microsoft introduced a new operating system. Fortunately, Moira was able to bring the body under control and they moved away as quickly as they could.

"What's this for?" asked a blond TV reporter, shoving a microphone under Moira's nose. The dragon blinked and flinched under the sudden glare of the TV lights.

"The new IBM announcement," Jerry said hurriedly as he stepped between Moira and the crew. "Excuse us, please, we're late."

"What new . . . ?"

"The kits are in the press room," he called over his shoulder.

Normally TV reporters aren't so easy to discourage, but the press of the crowd made it hard to follow them and Bal-Simba was bringing up the rear.

"That will be all, My Lady. Please." He emphasized his request with a polite smile.

Since Bal-Simba was about six-foot-eight and decked out like a 1970s pimp, he was hard to argue with. When he smiled and showed teeth neatly filed to points the TV crew lost all interest in the little group.

Meanwhile the gorilla's handlers, recognizing a heaven-sent opportunity, buttonholed the reporters, shoved press kits on them and began to explain

Gigantopithecus Software's latest announcement in multi-part high-decibel technobabble.

"What was that about?" Moira asked as they got free of the knot of people.

"Advertising. He's promoting something." Jerry paused and looked back and squinted to read the sign on the giant's back. "'Sasquatch.' I wonder what that is?"

"Forgive me if I do not share your curiosity," Moira snapped. "In fact I can think of nothing which is likely to have less bearing on our search."

"Yeah, but still . . . "

"It is utterly irrelevant. Now please, let us at least find a place where we can rest for a moment."

Jerry looked closely at her. Even though he wasn't used to judging the moods of dragons he could see she was tired.

"Sure, Moira. Come on over this way."

Off at the edge of the hall was a space between the booths for a fire door. The guard looked at them suspiciously as they made their way through the crowd into the temporary clearing, but since none of them sat on the floor or otherwise blocked the exit she didn't say anything.

"Hi there." Jerry turned and found himself right across the table from a couple of guys in the booth bordering the fire exit. He was trapped and he knew it, so he resigned himself to listening to a sales pitch.

He smiled as if he might be interested and studied the pair. One was hefty, slicked back and smarmy and the other was skinny, chinless and frenetic. Jerry couldn't read their badges so mentally he dubbed them "Leisure Suit Larry" and "The Squirrel."

"Are you interested in imaging?" Larry began. "If so we've got the hottest product at the show."

"It's truly revolutionary," The Squirrel picked up. "They're cracking down on adult GIF files on bulletin boards, right? Okay, with Peeping Tom's Inverse

Steganographic technology you don't need a GIF. Any data file of more than two megabytes is displayed as an X-rated picture."

Jerry nodded in spite of himself. "GIF," of course, was a standard encoding method for storing and transmitting pictures for personal computers. He was trying to piece the rest together when The Squirrel went charging on.

"You know about steganography, right? How you can encode a message in a picture file like a digitized TV picture so it looks like noise or just part of the picture?"

"I've heard of it."

"Well," said The Squirrel triumphantly, "this is the same thing only backwards. Instead of specifying the encoding scheme and using the picture as the variable—the cyphertext— to get the plaintext, we take the file as the given and apply various decoding schemes until we get the appropriate plaintext—the picture. With Peeping Tom's Inverse Stenographic technology, combined with our easy-to-use Windows front end, you select the kind of picture you want as an output from our menu and Peeping Tom goes until it finds it."

"Are you saying," Jerry said slowly, "that you can always find a dirty picture, ah, 'adult GIF' in any data file?"

"Guaranteed," Leisure Suit Larry boomed.

"Assuming the file's big enough," The Squirrel added. "Over two megabytes."

"And this is going to avoid censorship?"

"Hey," Larry said virtuously. "Can we help it if those files contain dirty pictures?"

"Yeah," The Squirrel chimed in, "we just decode them."

There was a flaw in that argument, but just then Jerry didn't have the time to go looking for it. However his curiosity was piqued.

"How big is the program?"

"It takes ten Meg of disk space," the big one said.

"Yeah, but how big's the executable, the main program file?"

"About five Meg," The Squirrel put in.

"What happens if you feed it the executable?" Jerry asked. "You know, let the program examine itself?"

"We didn't put any pictures in there," Larry said. "Nothing but code."

The Squirrel, however, looked puzzled. "Hmm. I never thought of that. Let me try it and see."

"We're running a show special," Larry said as his companion began pounding the keyboard. "Just $199 for the basic package. Runs under 3.1, NT and Windows 95 and . . ."

"*Jesus Christ!*" The Squirrel yelped. "Hey, take a look at this!"

Sales pitch forgotten, his partner rushed to join him at the screen. "Wow," Larry said reverently after a minute. "I mean I'd heard the expression, but I didn't think anyone could really *do* that."

Between their heads Jerry caught a glimpse of the screen and blanched. He didn't know if you could get busted for pornography in Las Vegas, but what was on that screen had to violate *some* law and he didn't want to be around when the cops figured out which one. "Come on, folks," he said to Bal-Simba and Moira, "I think it's time we moved on."

The rest of the day wasn't much more productive. People at one or two of the booths they visited had seen Taj the day before, but no one had seen him today. Jerry guessed he was visiting one of the other exhibit halls, but that didn't help much.

The fact was that they could spend the rest of the week at the show and never catch sight of E.T. Tajikawa. Jerry had known that before they came, but the physical reality of the place drove the point home like a pile driver. Not only was it too big, it was too spread out and too crazy. It was going to take either blind luck or a really clever piece of strategy if they were going to find him.

He explained all this to Bal-Simba and Moira on a snippet of lawn outside the exhibit hall. The late-afternoon sun was casting lengthening shadows over the lengthening lines of showgoers who were trying to get seats on a shuttle bus back to their hotels. The buses roared in and out of the rank constantly but still the lines grew.

"Basically, we're going to have one more shot to try to find him tonight," Jerry told the pair. "That's at this reception downtown." He didn't say what they'd do if they didn't find Taj there and the others didn't ask.

"How shall we get there?"

Jerry looked at the dragon and sighed. "I'm sorry but there's only one way. We'll have to walk again."

It was a hike of several miles and they took it slowly, resting every few blocks for Moira's sake. The sun sank, the shadows deepened and Las Vegas lit up for the night.

"This is truly a wonderland," Bal-Simba said at one of their rest stops, awed by the explosion of colored lights and rivers of traffic around them. "Your world is indeed a fantastic place."

"Well, this is fantastic even by the standards of our world," Jerry said. "Like I told you, Las Vegas is unique."

"Is it all like this? The town, I mean."

"Oh no. Most parts of Las Vegas are really quite normal. It's supposed to be a pretty nice place to live, actually."

"Will we go there? The normal parts, I mean."

Jerry looked at the twenty-foot-dragon and the giant black wizard dressed like a 1970s pimp. "Nooo, I don't think so."

It took them several hours to reach the Towne Centre hotel in the older "Glitter Gulch" downtown casino district. By now it was full dark and so late Jerry was afraid they might miss the reception completely. An even bigger worry was Moira, who was obviously getting more and more run down. Even with more frequent rests she was nearly punchy by the time they reached the alley behind the hotel.

"Why don't you wait out here?" Jerry suggested. Moira just nodded.

"Perhaps I had best stay too while you go inside," Bal-Simba said.

Jerry considered. Anyone who found Moira by herself probably wouldn't ask questions. Bal-Simba, on the other hand, would be expected to answer them. While Jerry had great confidence in the big wizard's brains and judgment, he was much less sure of his ability to concoct a story that wouldn't get him hauled off to jail by Las Vegas' finest. Especially in the get-up he was wearing.

"I think you'd better come with me," he said. "Moira, you stay here. No, over here next to the dumpsters. Stay out of that yellow painted area, otherwise they're likely to tow you away. If anyone comes by, just freeze like a statue. Pretend you're not alive. We'll try not to be too long." Moira nodded and sank down in the space beside the dumpsters.

Bal-Simba's size and appearance may have attracted attention, but it made it remarkably easy for them to get an elevator. In fact as soon as the door opened on the first car the four tourists in the front row took one look at them and bolted. The other passengers pressed back against the walls, leaving them plenty of space.

They paused just outside the elevators and Jerry briefed Bal-Simba on their mission.

"Okay, this is going to be a little tricky since we're not on the invite list. So we'll just have to fake our way in. Act like you belong, smile a lot and be noncommittal."

"Will they not know we do not belong?"

"They'll know we're not on the guest list, but they can't be sure we won't do them some good. We only need a few minutes to find out if Taj is here anyway. Follow my lead. And remember, smile a lot and say as little as you can."

Putting his advice into practice Jerry smiled at the people manning the table outside the door and picked up a press kit as if he was interested. Then they walked into a wall of noise.

If the show floor had been a madhouse, this was bedlam. Up on stage a lounge band was backing a female impersonator belting out torch songs. The place was packed, of course, and everyone seemed to be trying to talk over the band and each other. Along the walls four bars were going and a huge buffet table dominated the center of the room, complete with a melting ice sculpture of what was probably supposed to be an orchid. There were orchids everywhere. Clouds of them. Wreaths of them. Garlands of them. Orchids as boutonnieres, orchids as corsages. Orchids as centerpieces. And where there weren't orchids there were crepe streamers in orchid purple and white.

Jerry parked Bal-Simba by the bandstand and set out to work the room in search of Taj. Trying to look inconspicuous, he jammed into the crowd around one of the buffet tables and scarfed a handful of shrimp. The crab claws were already gone he saw, so the party had been going on for a while. Meanwhile he scanned the crowd, hoping to see Tajikawa, or at least a friendly face.

He couldn't see either and the more he looked the less likely it became. This wasn't the right kind of party. The ratio of suits to ponytails was way too high and there was hardly a laptop open anywhere.

He was still scanning, looking for technical types amid the noise and chaos, when a perfectly coifed woman in a blue suit slid in next to him.

The woman smiled brightly. "Snarf mafoozle gleeber justik," she said.

"I beg your pardon?"

She leaned closer and raised her voice to be heard over the din. "I said what did you think of the big announcement?"

It occurred to Jerry that he was laboring under a severe disadvantage here. Not only didn't he know what the "big announcement" was, he'd never even heard of Mauve Technology. And hadn't the faintest idea what—if anything—it made. He thought about opening the press kit and actually reading it but he discarded the notion instantly. For one thing the light was so poor he wouldn't be able to read anything and for another it would make him suspicious. He decided to play it safe.

"Really something. Pretty ambitious, isn't it?"

"We have to stay on the leading edge. I'm sorry I don't recognize your company name. Are you a distributor or a VAR?"

"Uh, we're kinda a technology partner. Actually I was hoping to meet someone here. E.T. Tajikawa."

"Oh, is he with our West Coast sales office?"

"Uh, not exactly. Your software people know him."

"You wait right here and I'll go see." With that she turned and dived into the crowd. Jerry made to follow her but before he could take a step, a large man in a suit stepped in front of him and stuck out his hand.

"Perry Jacobs," he boomed, "vice-president of sales." It was both a greeting and a challenge and Jerry was acutely aware of how little he fit with the business-suited crowd swarming around them.

Jerry smiled brightly. "Cantraf colgain esper jokake jon," he mumbled, as if it meant something.

"Glad you're enjoying it," the other boomed. "Here let me give you one of my cards."

Jerry extended one of his. "Meeper gleeble ranamuck shusur."

"Yeah, I've gone through a pack of them, too," Jacobs boomed.

✧ ✧ ✧

Meanwhile, Bal-Simba was enjoying himself, in a bemused sort of way. The singer, a Judy Garland impersonator, was taking advantage of his size and appearance by playing off him, flirting with him as he sang, flicking him with his silk scarf and vamping outrageously. When the number ended the singer blew Bal-Simba a kiss and scampered offstage. That was the cue for the band to take a break, and for the first time in several minutes Bal-Simba could hear himself think.

"I said, quite a show isn't it," said a voice at his elbow.

The wizard turned and saw a small man in a bad toupee standing beside him.

"It is indeed," Bal-Simba agreed, which seemed safe enough.

"They're going all out," his new acquaintance said. "They missed the top of the IPO cycle, their quarterlies are off and if this doesn't fly big they're probably going to have to gobble up a couple of startups with good stories to save their offering."

Bal-Simba nodded sagely.

The man extended his hand. "Peter Saperstein, of the Saperstein Group. You know, the *Saperstein Technology Letter.*" Bal-Simba nodded again.

"So, who are you here for?"

Bal-Simba took the first name he could think of. "IBM."

"That's not what it says on your badge," Saperstein shot back.

Bal-Simba realized he had blundered.

"You weren't supposed to say that, were you?"

If there was one thing the big wizard knew it was when to keep his mouth shut. So he just smiled slightly at his new acquaintance.

"Look," Saperstein went on, "I know you can't say anything, non-D and all that, but just let me lay a scenario on you."

"I cannot stop you."

"First off, it's gotta be big if you're here under a cover name." Saperstein thumped the big wizard on his chest where his badge was pinned. "Your badge doesn't say IBM. But it does say 'wizard,' so you're obviously in software development and you sure as hell don't work on the AS400 if you're walking around dressed like that. So you gotta be blue-sky and if you're here, that means edutainment and that," Saperstein concluded triumphantly, "means a partnership arrangement with Mauve."

"That is a great deal of speculation," Bal-Simba said mildly. Anyone who knew him would have recognized the reproof in his voice, but Saperstein didn't know him and wouldn't have wanted to spoil a hot story even if he had.

Saperstein craned to look through a random rift in the crowd. "Excuse me, I gotta go talk to someone."

Bal-Simba nodded, not realizing he had not only made his acquaintance's evening, but saved Mauve Technology as well.

". . . unique market position with the possibility for strong leverage of our technology through the channel," Jacobs was saying.

Jerry nodded and smiled. So far he'd managed to keep from revealing his ignorance, but it was getting harder. For one thing, since the band had quit playing he'd actually had to talk to Jacobs. For another, Jacobs was angling hard for some kind of commitment. Since Jerry still didn't have the faintest idea what the company did he couldn't agree to anything without giving himself away.

"Well," Jerry began, "you have to understand our position vis-à-vis the market."

"Excuse me." Jerry found himself shouldered aside by a small middle-aged man in an expensive suit and cheap toupee. "Peter Saperstein, of the Saperstein Group. You know, the *Saperstein Technology Letter*?

What's this about a joint game venture with IBM's European division?"

"Where the hell did you hear that?" Jacobs demanded.

Saperstein shrugged. "Around. So there is something to it?"

"No. I mean, I can't comment even if it was true."

"When are you going to make the announcement? Not at the show, is it? So that means sometime in the next quarter, right?"

"I can't say."

"A little further out then."

"Uh," Jerry said, "if you gentlemen will excuse me . . . " But neither was paying any attention.

He was heaving a sigh of relief when someone touched his arm. It was the woman in the blue suit.

"I checked with the software people. They say Mr. Tajikawa isn't here."

"Oh, well thanks anyway."

She smiled a thoroughly professional smile. "Don't mention it. If there's anything else I can do . . . " and with that she was lost in the crowd.

The band had struck up again and "Judy Garland" was back on the stage, flirting with Bal-Simba as he swung into his first number. Jerry collected his friend and they made for the door.

"Forgive me," Bal-Simba said when they were out in the corridor and could talk in normal tones again, "but is there something peculiar about that woman?"

"For starters, it's a man."

"Ah," Bal-Simba said mildly, "I see," and seemed to lose interest. Jerry thought about trying to explain and then realized that to Bal-Simba a female impersonator was probably the least peculiar thing he seen had all day.

Moira was waiting for them where they had left her. "Well?" she asked.

"No sign of him. We're going to have to look elsewhere." He frowned. "This isn't a real good strategy to find Taj anyway."

"What would you suggest then?"

Jerry had pulled out his exhibitor book and was thumbing through it in search of inspiration.

"Look, there are a couple of more companies on the hospitality suite list that Taj has a special relationship with. We can call them and see if they know where he is. It'll take some calling around to track them down, but it will be faster than trying to hit all these exhibits."

He closed the book and looked up. "Meantime, we can't stay here. Too public. Let's get a few blocks away from the casinos and find a place where Moira can hole up and rest for a few hours while we hit a pay phone. It's getting late enough for that."

"My Lady?" Bal-Simba asked.

The dragon nodded "Forgive me, My Lords, but this body is not as strong as it looks."

"We understand," Bal-Simba said gently.

"Yeah," Jerry added. "The last time I was here I would have collapsed if I'd done half as much walking as we have already."

"Then lead on," Bal-Simba said. Jerry picked a direction and led them off away from the maze of casinos and neon.

Just a few blocks from the downtown casino district the scene changed radically. From bright lights and constant bustle it became a run-down area of progressively cheaper motels and shabby buildings. The character of the people on the streets changed as well. In the next several blocks Bal-Simba's appearance got them a number of interesting business propositions—both buying and selling.

Bal-Simba and Moira didn't know enough to see it as unusual, but Jerry was getting progressively more nervous. At six feet three and well over two hundred pounds he was the least physically impressive member of the trio, but even so he did not like the looks of the neighborhood. "There's a mini-mart down the block," he said finally. "It should have a pay phone."

A small sign informed them that the pay phones were inside.

"Wait here. I'll see what we can find out." He paused and looked at Bal-Simba. "No, you come with me. Moira, you wait here." The dragon settled down in a parking space and Jerry and Bal-Simba went into the mini-mart.

In the event it took longer than Jerry had expected. The hotels were overworked and the switchboards were glacial. Even when he did find where the companies were staying, the phone would ring forever before someone answered it and it would take somewhat longer to find anyone who knew the Tajmanian Devil and could tell Jerry that he wasn't there. Jerry kept pumping in quarters, but it was slow.

Meanwhile, things were quiet outside and Fluffy was exhausted. So Moira lay down in the parking space and drifted off to sleep.

Fluffy was big enough to fill up the parking space, but down on all fours he wasn't visible over the cars on either side. Incautiously the dragon let his tail trail out behind him, making him longer than the parking space.

If Moira had thought about it she would have tucked the tail back around Fluffy's body. But she was dead beat from all the walking, ill from the effects of being a magical creature in a non-magical world, and generally not thinking very well. All she wanted to do was to curl herself into a little ball of misery and let the body relax.

Moira wasn't the only one who felt that way. The couple in the Mini-Winnie had driven straight through from Los Angeles and the driver wasn't as awake as he might have been. Besides, he was distracted by the simmering argument with his wife over finding a campground. As a result he didn't see the thing lying in the parking lot until it was too late.

The motor home ran over the dozing dragon's tail and all hell broke loose.

Fluffy jerked up with a roar of pain and rage. Moira was slow to regain control of the body so, for the first critical seconds, the dragon reacted out of instinct.

Unfortunately the dragon's instinct was to lash out at his tormentor. Fluffy's tail slammed into the side of the motor home again and again, caving in some of the thin aluminum paneling and rocking the vehicle so violently it teetered on the brink of overturning.

Moira quickly discovered she didn't have as much control over the dragon as she thought, especially when the dragon was frightened or angry. Although dragons are physically tough, the young ones are more vulnerable psychologically. In general they do not take well to new experiences and they are somewhat skittish in strange circumstances. Fluffy had been a pampered pet almost all his life.

Again and again the dragon lashed the motorhome with its tail while the occupants screamed and Moira tried desperately to regain control

Jerry and Bal-Simba came running out of the store into a scene of complete and utter chaos. There was already a small crowd gathered at a safe distance and almost as soon as they stepped out of the store the first police car arrived, quickly followed by two others. The lights and sirens did nothing to calm the hysterical dragon.

Shotguns at the ready the officers advanced to the rescue.

By this time Moira had gained partial control and Fluffy lay panting on the pavement.

Jerry held his breath. If they could just get the

situation calmed down, then maybe . . . An odd corner of his brain wondered what it would cost to bail out a dragon.

He never had the chance to find out.

The cops were understandably nervous. Even lying down, a dragon looks dangerous and there were a lot of civilians around to protect. When Moira suddenly heaved the dragon's body back on his feet the logical conclusion was that it was getting ready to attack, especially since the dragon's open mouth was treating the cops to a spectacular display of fangs.

One of the cops with a clear shot pumped a load of buckshot into Fluffy at close range.

This was a spectacularly bad idea. The shot was #6, enough to drop a deer or a man in their tracks, but only enough to sting the scaled hide of a dragon.

The results were equally spectacular. With another steamwhistle roar, Fluffy went berserk, charging directly at the police officers closing in. Two more rounds of buckshot did nothing to stop him. A lash of the scaled tail and the policemen went flying like tenpins. A few of the spectators applauded, it being that kind of neighborhood.

"Get animal control. We need a tranquilizer gun," one of the officers yelled into his microphone.

"Tranquilizer, hell!" one of the other cops shouted. "We need a goddamn tank."

One of the officers, with more courage than tactical sense pulled her police cruiser into the parking lot to block the dragon's escape. Fluffy stopped, hissed in breath, drew back his head and for the first time in his life, breathed flames.

It wasn't much of a blast by dragon standards, weak and low temperature, but the gout of yellow fire did quite a nice job of igniting the police car. The officer bailed out the driver's door as the opposite side of the car erupted in fire.

"Act inconspicuous," Jerry hissed. "Us they can arrest."

Bal-Simba leaned nonchalantly against the side of the building. The effect wasn't exactly inconspicuous, but it wasn't that out of place either.

The best thing Moira could think of was to get out of there. Since that accorded perfectly with the dragon's instincts, she had no trouble commanding the body to run. Moira put her head down and galloped straight at the crowd.

One spectator decided this was the Las Vegas version of the running of the bulls and stepped in front of her waving a jacket with a red lining like a bullfighter's cape. For his pains he got thrown nearly ten feet by a quick toss of the dragon's head. No one else seemed disposed to follow, not even the police.

Jerry nodded to Bal-Simba and the two of them drifted off around the other side of the building. Once they were out of sight they ran after the disappearing dragon.

They found Moira in an alley a block and a half away, leaning against a fence, her sides heaving.

"Are you all right?" Jerry asked.

With an effort Moira raised the dragon's drooping head. "I am sorry, My Lord. I could not control this body."

Jerry looked back at the glow from the burning police car. "Well, thank God no one was killed. Now come on."

They made their way down the alley and paused in the shadows at the next cross street until there were no cars coming. Then the two men and the dragon sprinted across the street and into the next alley. They did it twice more before they ran out of alley at the blank rear wall of an apartment building.

"I take it we are not yet out of danger," Bal-Simba said as they made their way back to the mouth of the alley.

"They'll be searching the whole city for us and we're not exactly going to be hard to spot. We can't keep walking around, not with the cops looking for Moira."

"Is there someplace we can hide?"

"Well, we could stash her among the life-size animated dinosaurs in the Las Vegas Museum of Natural History, but we'd have to get her there first." Jerry frowned. Then his frown cleared and he looked past Bal-Simba out of the mouth of the alley.

"Wait a minute. I think I see the answer to our problem."

The guy at the truck rental place was remarkably uninterested in his customers. All he wanted was a driver's license and a cash deposit. Fortunately Jerry's California license hadn't expired yet. *Gotta find some way to get that renewed*, he thought.

"Just make sure you bring it back clean," the clerk said dubiously, eyeing the dragon.

"Don't worry, she's housebroken," Jerry assured him. Moira only sniffed.

In just a few minutes the contract was signed, Moira was loaded into the back of a twenty-four-foot truck with the slogan "Land of Enchantment" and a picture of New Mexico scenery painted on the side.

"Well, that's one less problem anyway," Jerry said as he watched a police car cruise by in the opposite direction.

"Now what?" asked Bal-Simba, who was hunched down on the passenger's side.

Jerry glanced at the time display in front of a bank. "It's too late to do much tonight. We'll have to get some sleep and try again in the morning."

"At least this place has many inns," Bal-Simba said as he looked at the row of neon signs stretching away before them.

"Forget it. You can't get a hotel room in this town this week for love or money." He paused. "Well, maybe for love, but you've got to rent it by the hour and, come to think of it, that's for money too."

Bal-Simba looked at him. "I take it that is not practical."

"Most working girls don't like threesomes and if we try to bring a dragon into the scene—well, yeah it's not practical."

The watch commander for the police department was having a hard night as well. Except he knew where he was going to be spending most of it.

"Take over," he said to his sergeant as he picked up his hat. "I'm going to the scene."

"What do you want me to do about this thing in the meantime?" his sergeant asked.

"Nothing. We're not doing anything until I debrief those officers and find out just exactly what the hell we're dealing with here."

The watch commander knew his men and he trusted them—within broad limits. However, whatever this was pretty clearly went beyond those limits. Obviously *something* had happened at that mini-market, but equally obviously there was some sort of failure of communication. He was not about to put out an APB for a mythical creature until he'd had a good long talk with the officers and the witnesses.

In the event that proved more difficult than he had anticipated. No one in the crowd would admit to seeing anything, the clerk in the mini-mart could suddenly only communicate in an obscure dialect of Farsi and the tourists in the Mini-Winnie were still hysterical. The physical evidence was impressive enough, what with the burned-out police car and the scorched and dented motorhome, not to mention the scrapes and bruises on the officers who had been knocked around. The testimony of the officers was more equivocal. None of them really liked the idea of what they had seen, or thought they had seen, so they were very careful in their descriptions. The watch commander collected numerous statements about the poor light in the parking lot, the stress of the encounter, the lack of a good view and such. But of the nine officers present not one of them used the word "dragon."

It was nearly dawn when the watch commander decided that the official story was going to be that someone had a large alligator that was causing trouble. That's the way it went down on the blotter and incident report where the media would see it. Privately and unofficially he passed the word to the next watch commander and left it to him to pass the word privately and unofficially to his officers. It wasn't the first time that the official version and the truth had differed significantly in this town.

Jerry, Bal-Simba and Moira spent a miserable night parked in a patch of desert a few miles out of town. Moira slept in the back of the truck, Jerry curled up in some old moving pads underneath and Bal-Simba tried to sleep in the cab. Moira was too sick to sleep well and the others were too uncomfortable. The November desert at night is bone-chillingly cold and Jerry kept thinking about scorpions.

Wiz and the other humans awoke that morning stiff and sore from another night sleeping on the rocks. At least the humans awoke stiff and sore. Glandurg seemed as relaxed and fresh as ever.

Fresh was definitely something the rest of the party wasn't. Wiz wondered why dungeon-delving games never said anything about what the participants smelled like after a couple of days of hard work and no baths.

After a quick breakfast of vegetable porridge everyone crowded around Wiz while he checked the locator crystal.

"It says we go off this way," Wiz told the others.

"How close are we?" Malkin asked.

Wiz looked back down at the crystal and frowned. "Still a ways to go."

Danny looked down at the glowing object in Wiz's hand. "It doesn't seem any brighter than it was when we started. Shouldn't it get brighter as we get closer?"

"We still have some distance to cover. These caverns are big."

"Are you sure this thing knows where it's going?" Danny grumbled.

"It's set to home in on Moira," Wiz replied with more confidence than he felt. He was developing a nagging suspicion about where the magical compass was leading them. Either these caverns were much bigger than he remembered them or they were being taken on the scenic route. Considering all the stuff they'd run into so far that was a distinct possibility.

*Or maybe there's just a lot more stuff down here,* he thought as the party moved along a tunnel as wide as a four-lane highway. *I wonder how you estimate the monsters per square kilometer in a dungeon. Or should that be per cubic kilometer because the place has so many levels it's really three dimensional?*

The air was getting more humid as they went along. At first there was a nasty, cold clamminess that seemed to cling to them. Then it got warmer until all the humans were sticky with sweat. Finally, after two more turnings into smaller tunnels they were surrounded by a thick, warm mist.

"I hear water up ahead," Malkin said softly. Wiz nodded and took a better grasp on his staff.

Suddenly the tunnel opened out into a cavern. The far wall and the ceiling alike were lost in billows of mist. The sound of trickling, splashing water was loud before them.

They paused while Danny surveyed the area with his magic detector.

"No sign of anything," he said at last. "Whatever's up ahead of us is natural, not magic."

"Natural hot springs," Wiz said. With a gesture he

increased the intensity of the light from the magical globe and the party stepped into the cave.

They looked around and gasped.

Brightly colored flowstone had congealed like melted candle wax in opalescent patterns. The fog and mist made the place look like a Hollywood soundstage.

"It's beautiful," Danny said softly. June said nothing, but clung open-mouthed to Danny's arm, staring wide-eyed like a child on Christmas morning.

"Quite something," Malkin said. Wiz looked back and saw her standing arms akimbo and feet spread. She was also eyeing the scene as if she was trying to figure out how to take the place home with her. Wiz decided that where Malkin was concerned, larceny was the sincerest form of flattery.

"Stay close people," Wiz admonished. "Just because there's no magic in here doesn't mean there's nothing dangerous."

The room was not as big as it had seemed, being much longer than it was wide. The tunnel they had entered from angled in on the long side and in perhaps fifty paces they were across the room.

"Here's your hot spring," Malkin said, gesturing at a place where the water trickled out of the rock wall. From there it ran along the floor of the cavern and gathered in a series of pools before disappearing through a crack in the floor.

Danny mopped his sweaty brow on his wet sleeve. "Whew, this place is like a sauna."

"Yeah," Wiz said slowly. "Or a hot tub. Come on, let's see how hot it really is."

The water at the seep was scalding, but by three pools down it had cooled until it was just barely tolerable. Wiz stuck his finger in and nodded.

"Are you thinking what I think you're thinking?" Danny asked.

Wiz just gestured at the pool. "Looks big enough."

"Right," Danny said, dropping his pack and staff and stripping off his outer tunic. Wiz and the other humans followed suit.

Glandurg eyed the water with distaste. "Another of your mortal customs, eh? Fear not. I'll guard the door while you pollute yon stream." With that he turned his back and disappeared into the steamy fog.

They kept their shirts on for modesty's sake, but the thin fabric clung to their bodies as soon as it got wet and the result was more like a wet T-shirt contest than swimming suits. The pool wasn't even waist deep, but the four lowered themselves into the steaming water with much "oohing" and "aahing" and made themselves comfortable on the smooth flowstone of the bottom.

For several minutes no one said anything, letting the heat and warmth soak into their bodies.

"First time I've even been on a quest with a hot tub," Danny said at last.

Wiz sighed deeply and relaxed further into the steaming water. "Civilized though."

Malkin ducked under the water and came up with her long dark hair streaming behind her. She was the picture of ease but Wiz noticed she never strayed more than a foot from her rapier. She shook her head vigorously to clear her eyes, splashing everyone else with droplets flung off from her raven hair.

"Jerry told me that in your world you have such things built into your dwellings," the thief said. "Now I see why."

"We ought to put one of these in at the Wizards' Keep," Danny suggested.

Wiz didn't say anything. He leaned back, rested his head on the rim and let the hot water drain the tension from every muscle.

A fine sifting of dust was falling from the ceiling. Wiz brushed it out of his hair absently and sneezed as the pungent dust tickled his nose. He wet his finger and caught a speck of the dust on the end. His eyes wrinkled at the sharp taste and then widened as he recognized it. Lemon pepper!

A broom-sized bundle of herbs dropped from above and splashed into the pool next to him.

"Look out! It's the lobster again."

There was a mad scramble for weapons and wizards staffs as the pool emptied almost instantly.

"Oh, pshaw!" came a crustacean-accented voice from the misty darkness above.

Glandurg came pounding up through the fog, waving Blind Fury as if to decapitate the foe—or someone—with a single stroke. The others moved around to the opposite side of the pool, well out of range.

"What happened?" the dwarf demanded.

Wiz pointed to the bundle of herbs floating in the pot of would-be Cannibal Soup Mix. "The lobster. He must have come across the roof of the cave."

Glandurg looked up and snorted. "The craven creature was afraid to face my steel. Little did I expect the foe to crawl along the ceiling like some verminous spider. But never fear. I shall be ready if he returns."

Wiz glanced at the pool, already filling the steamy air with the spicy aroma of herbs, pepper and lemon. "Never mind. I think I've had all the swimming I want."

"What now?" Bal-Simba asked Jerry after they had stashed the truck with Moira in it in a hotel parking lot.

"Back to the convention, I guess. We'll start working the outlying halls. That's where they put the newcomers to the show and Taj is more likely to be hanging around some of the more innovative startups." He sighed. "This isn't working very well. I'm sorry."

"There is nothing to be sorry for," Bal-Simba said. "The obstacles are clearly very great."

"Thanks, but we can't keep going like this. Not with the cops looking for us."

"I do not believe Moira can continue here either. She grows ever sicker and weaker. It is well that she can sleep the day away, but even so . . . " He shrugged.

"Yeah. Okay, let's try today, and if we haven't found him by evening we'll just head north to the power spot and go home."

Even the smaller halls were jammed and, if anything, the crowds were more colorful than at the main exhibits. There was a higher ponytail-and-T-shirt to suit ratio, Jerry noted approvingly, and here and there someone was sitting on the steps or a bench with an open laptop actually hacking code.

Their first stop was the message center, more out of optimism than genuine hope. There was still nothing for Taj, but to his amazement Jerry found a message for him from Elaine Haverford.

Their second stop was the line at a pay phone. After twenty minutes, Jerry paid a scalper twenty dollars to use a cell phone that had been hacked to have a fire marshall's priority so its calls would get through.

Dr. Haverford answered on the second ring. "Oh yes, Mr. Andrews, I did see Taj last night. He was at the chili cookoff. Were you there?"

"Ah, we were having a hot time of our own," Jerry told her. "Did you talk to him?"

"Only for a minute. He placed second in the relativistic Tetris competition, you know, and he didn't have much time. But I did find he's staying with the people from, ah, Bizzareware at the Paladin."

*Shit!* Jerry thought, *right where we started.* "The Paladin? Okay, thanks, Dr. Haverford. We'll get in touch with him right away and set up a meeting with your folks later. Thanks again."

"We gotta do something nice for that company," Jerry said as he handed the phone back to the scalper.

"What now?" Bal-Simba asked. "I believe you told me that everyone is at the show all day and unreachable at their lodgings until evening."

"Most people are," Jerry corrected. "But it's barely ten. If I know Taj he's still asleep, especially after a relativistic Tetris tournament. So let's pick up the truck, head for the Paladin and set up a meet."

"Why not call him from here?"

"Because," Jerry said grimly. "If he doesn't agree to meet us, we're going to waylay him in the lobby and kidnap him. I don't want to take a chance on waking him up and letting him get away before we get there."

It took nearly fifteen rings for someone to answer the phone in the Bizarreware suite at the Paladin. All the while Jerry fidgeted and Bal-Simba merely waited.

"Hello," came a muzzy voice at the other end of the line.

"Is Taj there?"

"This is Taj. Whaddya want?"

"My name is Jerry Andrews, jerry@thekeep.org, and I've got to see you right away."

"Hey, it's not even noon yet."

"I know, but this is important."

Taj's voice hardened. "And you'll only take five minutes of my time, right?"

"Actually," Jerry said, "it'll probably take a couple of weeks of your time, but you'll hate yourself if you don't meet me."

The voice sighed. "Well, that's original anyway. Okay, I'll tell you what. Let me get a shower and some breakfast and I'll meet you in the lobby, by the bird cage, say, in an hour. Okay?"

"Fine. We'll be there."

## THIRTEEN
# Making a Deal With the Devil

"It has been longer than an hour, has it not?" Bal-Simba asked nearly two hours later.

"Yeah, but don't worry. If he said he was coming, he's coming. Probably. It's just that time doesn't mean the same thing to him it does to you or me."

Bal-Simba nodded. "Elven blood."

Jerry didn't have a chance to respond before someone called out "Mr. Andrews?" and Jerry turned to see the object of their quest.

Seeing him once again Jerry appreciated how he got the nickname "Tajmanian Devil."

E.T. Tajikawa was rather over six feet tall and loose-limbed without being gangly. But it was the face that got you. It was thin, with an unusually aquiline nose, high cheekbones, narrow lips and topped by a pronounced widow's peak of black hair. The only thing that kept him from looking positively satanic was the perpetual expression of bemused interest.

"Jerry, please. And this is Bal-Simba."

"Cool." Taj shook hands. "Now what's this big deal?"

"Come on out back. Part of the problem's in a truck."

"What are you guys gonna do, kidnap me?"

"Only if we must," Bal-Simba said mildly.

"No, no," Jerry put in hastily. "Nothing like that, but there's something out there you gotta see."

Taj eyed them suspiciously. "Prototype hardware?"

"Kinda. Ah, look, have you heard anything about a dragon at the show?"

"Is that you? I'll say! You guys are causing more of

a stir than anything on the show floor. Even Intel's pre-announcement leak of the Octium-and-a-half."

"Octium-and-a-half?" Jerry asked as he held the door open for Taj.

"It's a P8 with a couple of extra ALUs, a bigger lookahead cache and another pipeline. Even in simulation the original was a slug, barely 300 MIPS. Anyway," Taj went on without a break, "there are stories about that dragon all over the show. There's also a bidding war going on for the video game rights. If you guys don't have an agent . . . "

"Right now we've got bigger problems," Jerry said.

All through this Bal-Simba had been behind Tajikawa, studying his ears closely for signs of points.

"What's with him?"

"He thinks you're an elf."

Taj looked over his shoulder at the wizard. "I've got some friends who are Radical Faeries. Does that count?"

When they got to the truck, Jerry rolled up the back and Fluffy's head jerked erect.

"My God!" Tajikawa said.

"Get on in. We don't want too many people to see this." He and Bal-Simba followed the Tajmanian Devil into the truck and rolled down the back behind them.

By that time Taj was already examining the dragon. "Someone did a hell of a job on this skin," he said. Then he reached out and grabbed Fluffy's foreleg just above the joint and kneaded the flesh experimentally. The dragon drew back its head and hissed, giving Taj a faceful of sulfurous breath and a close look at a dragon's dental equipment.

Taj didn't so much jump back as levitate retrograde. "My God!" he yelped. "It's real!"

"I'm sorry, My Lord," Moira said contritely. "I am not always the master of this body's reflexes."

"But you're a real dragon!"

"Actually," Moira said sadly, "I am a witch, trapped in a dragon's body."

"That's part of the problem," Jerry said. "But only part of it."

"So? Don't you need a wizard or something to handle this, not a programmer."

Jerry jerked his head at Bal-Simba. "Actually he's a wizard. But where we're from a programmer is also a wizard. That's part of the problem as well."

Taj cocked his head and Jerry congratulated himself. The trick had always been to get Tajikawa to buy into the deal once they found him. So far that part was going nicely.

"I know you've been up to something," Taj said. "There are all kinds of rumors about you and Wiz Zumwalt flying around the net." He looked behind Jerry at the twenty-foot dragon. "But I guess the rumors didn't have the half of it."

"We've got a really weird problem."

Taj looked at the dragon again. "I'll bet."

"No, I mean *really* weird. And we need help."

"No kidding?" Taj sounded intrigued. "Tell me about it."

"It's so weird I can't even describe it to you. You've got to experience it."

"No kidding," Taj said again.

Jerry tried to keep a poker face but he was smiling inside. *Gotcha!*

*Blue eyes crying in the rain . . .*

Michael Francis Xavier Gilligan concentrated on the way the neon lights reflected off the ice in his highball. It hadn't been raining when they had parted, but Karin's blue eyes had been full of tears. So had Gilligan's.

A smattering of computer chatter drifted over from the group in suits at the next table. That was the other thing. The whole damn town was full of computer types.

Lines were terrible, traffic was more than normally awful, there were no rental cars to be had and hotel rooms were at a premium.

It was too damn early to be drinking, he knew, but what the hell else was there to do in this place? *What I get for volunteering to come in a week early*, he thought sourly.

Gilligan was in Las Vegas on business as well. Next week, after the computer show ended, was the Western Air Show. The aerospace company he joined after leaving the Air Force had needed someone to come in early and get things set and ready. It seemed like a good idea at the time. An extra week in sunny, exciting Las Vegas at company expense plus an opportunity to visit some of his old Air Force buddies stationed at Nellis.

It hadn't worked out that way. Not only was the town jammed, but it wasn't as exciting as he remembered from his last tour here. Half the people he had known at Nellis were gone, assigned to other bases scattered halfway around the world. But worse than that was the gulf that had opened between him and the other pilots. Oh, they still liked him well enough, but he didn't strap his ass into a high-performance jet every day and let it hang out. He wasn't a member of the fraternity any more and that left an awkward hole in the relationship. After a couple of painfully clumsy visits, Gilligan had begun avoiding the base and his old friends.

*Blue eyes cryin' in the rain . . .*

That left him nothing to do but drink, and brood. Las Vegas was a great town for doing both, he was discovering.

He hadn't been much of either a drinker or a brooder before, not even when his marriage broke up. But then he'd drawn a mission out over the Bering Sea, come out on the short end of a dogfight with a dragon and met Karin. He couldn't stay in that world, but he had promised to return as soon as his tour in the Air Force was finished. The programmer/magicians there had even given him a phone number he could use to call them when he was ready.

Well, he got ready. Then the number hadn't worked! When he tried to use it he got a visit from a couple of very serious FBI agents who questioned him about possible involvement in telephone fraud.

So here he was, left with nothing but memories. Nothing to do but remember, and drink. God, he hated himself when he got maudlin like this.

*Blue eyes cryin' in the rain . . .*

The security guard wasn't looking for dragons. In fact he was checking for people sleeping in their cars in the parking lot.

With hotel rooms completely unavailable it wasn't unknown for Comdex-goers to live out of their cars. Cars were fairly easy to spot on regular rounds, as were motorhomes. Vans were special objects of attention.

As the guard came closer he heard several voices coming from the back of the rental truck. So naturally he jumped to the obvious, and wrong, conclusion.

"Hotel security. Open up in there."

He yanked the back of the truck up and was promptly trampled by a panicked dragon.

"Ah, Mick."

Gilligan looked up from the remains of his drink to see Ivan Kuznetsov standing at his table. He didn't really feel like company, but he waved the Russian to a seat anyway.

Kuznetsov was a bit of a character. According to rumor he had defected from the Soviet Union a couple of years before it fell apart. Now he was using his connections in both the former Soviet republics and the West to put together aviation-related "deals" of much import but vague content. Their paths crossed repeatedly on the air show circuit and Mick had found him a more congenial drinking partner than most of the executives he met.

"You have an interest in dragons, yes?"

Gilligan nodded, vaguely recalling a drunken conversation one night in Brussels.

"Then you might want to look out front. Police are chasing a dragon around the building."

Jerry, Taj, Bal-Simba and the dragon had ducked through the first open door they could find. Unfortunately that led right into the main casino.

"Oh, shit," Jerry breathed. "Just act natural and head out the other side."

As casually as they could, the three men and the dragon strolled across the casino floor. The slot players paid no attention, of course, but the guards started grabbing for their radios and moving toward them.

The magic field that kept Fluffy alive had some rather interesting effects on the laws of probability. The dragon waddled through the casino leaving a string of jackpots in his wake. In fact every slot machine he passed suddenly started paying off.

The effect was as instantaneous and predictable as gravity. The machines were mobbed by slot players determined to cash in on the sudden bounty. Since in Las Vegas "monomaniacal slot player" is a redundancy, not one of the converging crowd was willing to let a little thing like a dozen cops stand between them and riches.

The leading guard nearly fell over a tiny blue-haired woman in pink shorts who was making for a dollar slot still pouring out coins. She didn't even look as she elbowed him expertly and sidestepped his falling body to beat out a Chinese man for the machine by perhaps one pace.

The guards behind fared even worse as the crowd congealed, blindly determined to reach those machines.

The police weren't so much thrown back by the determined gamblers as they simply bounced off the writhing mass of humanity. One officer shouted into his walkie-talkie, trying to make himself heard above the din of the suddenly bountiful slot machines.

Never ones to question the dictates of fortune, Jerry, Bal-Simba, Taj and Moira made for a side door. They had barely turned the corner when they found themselves face-to-face with a wall of casino security guards, all looking very determined.

"Stand aside," commanded the guard in the lead and the phalanx swung around them without a second glance, intent on reaching the chaos on the casino floor.

Jerry looked at Bal-Simba and Taj and shrugged. Then the four bolted out the door and dashed for their truck. In the distance the sirens were getting louder.

Moira and her companions had barely gotten out the door when à mob of police erupted around the corner. The group did a fast 180 and ran the other way, cut off from the truck in the parking lot.

"Hey! Over here," a voice called as they rounded the corner ahead of their pursuers.

Jerry saw a man holding a side door open and beckoning them.

*What the heck? Any port in a storm.* The group made a mad dash for the door and Fluffy's tail disappeared through it just as the first police were coming around the corner.

"Quick, this way," Gilligan said to the oddly assorted group. He led them down a corridor and stopped at one of the hotel's freight elevators. Taking a key from his pocket he used it to summon the elevator. As soon as the door opened he piled them all in.

"We're setting up exhibits on the third floor and I tipped a little extra for my own key," he explained to the others. "Once we get there we'll make for the passenger elevators. You can hide in my room for a while."

There were several workmen in the exhibition area, preparing for the next show. They stared incuriously at the four men and the dragon who emerged from the freight elevator and headed down the hall.

With most of the rooms taken by show attendees and almost all of them at the show, the hotel corridors and elevators were deserted. It took two cars to get the party up to the twentieth floor where Mick's room was, but they met no one on the way.

"Thanks," Jerry panted as soon as they were inside and the door was locked. "But why . . . ?"

"Let's say I have an interest in dragons," Gilligan told him. "And the people who associate with them."

"Hey, Mick, open up," came a Slavic-accented voice. The others started, but Gilligan motioned them to be calm and opened the door. There, in addition to Kuznetsov, was his friend and business associate, Vasily.

"How'd you know where to find us?"

"You are not very good at this game," Kuznetsov told him. "Too predictable."

"Great," Gilligan muttered.

"You had better think of something fast," the Russian added. "They are already starting to search the hotel."

Gilligan looked around. "I don't suppose that dragon can fly?"

"Too young," Jerry said.

Before Gilligan could think of anything else there was another knock on the door. "Hotel security," a voice called. "Open up, please."

Like most Las Vegas hotel rooms the bathroom and dressing area were next to the door, forming a short corridor and shielding the beds from direct view of the door. While everyone else crowded around the corner, Gilligan pulled his shirt from his pants, kicked off his shoes and went to the door, rumpling his hair as he went.

"Yes?" he said, trying to sound sleepy, as he opened

the door a crack. There was a man in a hotel blazer and two armed guards on the other side.

"I'm Mr. Masterson, the assistant manager," the man in the blazer said. "Have you seen anything, ah, unusual in the last few minutes?

"I've been asleep."

"Yes sir. Do you mind if we come in and check things out? Just as a precaution you understand."

"What's wrong?"

"Please open the door, sir," one of the guards said firmly.

"Who is it, honey?" came a sleepy female voice from inside the room. An amazing voice, oozing sex and promise.

"Ah, it's the hotel," Gilligan said, managing to keep his wits about him.

"Oh, what do they want?" Now there was a note of sultry disappointment. "Can't you get rid of them and come back to bed?"

Gilligan looked at the manager and shrugged. "This is really inconvenient, you know. My wife, she's just joined me, and . . . "

"Oh come on, honey," came the steam-heated voice. "Just tell them to go away."

The manager, who didn't believe this stuff about a dragon anyway, jerked his head. "Sorry to disturb you, sir. If you see anything please call the desk." The guard glowered, but moved back from the door.

"Sure, sure," Gilligan said as he shut the door. Then he leaned against it and let out a deep, heart-felt sigh.

"Okay people, they're gone."

"Thank you for rescuing us, My Lord," the dragon said in an everyday version of the voice that had gotten rid of the searchers.

"Uh, you're quite welcome," Gilligan said. *A talking dragon,* he thought numbly, *a talking dragon with a voice made for phone sex.* Of course.

The dragon's eyelids dipped demurely. "I did not think they would be so base as to disturb a couple intimately engaged."

"Ah, right," was all Gilligan could manage. "By the way, I'm Mick Gilligan." He looked closely at Jerry. "I think we met once before, just briefly. Ah, someplace else."

Jerry looked at him and his mouth dropped open. "The fighter pilot! Right, I remember you."

"And I am Ivan Kuznetsov."

From somewhere Gilligan remembered that "Kuznetsov" meant "Smith," so the Russian's name translated as "John Smith"—a fact which reinforced Gilligan's speculations about the man's background. Jerry didn't seem to notice. He shook the man's hand vigorously. "Pleased to meet you."

The other Russian was older and leaner, with the leathery skin of someone who had spent most of his life outdoors and the studied, unobtrusive manner of someone who preferred not to be noticed. For some reason he reminded Gilligan of the instructors at Air Force survival school.

"This is Vasily Gregorivich, my associate."

Jerry put out his hand. "Pleased to meet you Mr. Gregorivich."

"Vasily," the man corrected, taking it.

"Gregor is his father's name, so Gregorivich is his patronymic," Kuznetsov explained. Gilligan realized he had never heard Vasily's last name. He wondered what it was, but Vasily didn't seem inclined to volunteer the information and besides, he suspected it would probably turn out to be the Russian equivalent of "Jones."

"I am called Bal-Simba." The wizard extended a meaty paw.

The Tajmanian Devil waved. "Taj."

"And I," the dragon said, "am called Moira. I believe we also met before, but I was in my proper body then."

Gilligan looked hard at her.

"Normally she's a redhead with green eyes and freckles," Jerry explained."

"Oh! Right. The Sparrow's wife."

"Even so," Moira said sadly.

"Now," Gilligan said. "Suppose you tell me just what the bloody hell is going on around here?"

The explanation took several hours.

## FOURTEEN

# FUDWARE, FANTASY AND AREA 51

They broke for lunch in a cul-de-sac with a convenient jumble of rocks to serve as table and chairs. The fare was the usual cracker bread and dried meat with magically heated herb tea.

"Okay, people," Wiz said as they waited for the tea to brew, "strategy session. So far we've only been reacting to what we've encountered. I think we need to start taking the initiative."

"Meaning what?" Malkin asked.

"For starters let's look back over what we've run into down here and try to see the pattern to it all."

"Well," Danny said slowly, "leaving aside the lobster, we haven't run into the same thing twice."

"I think the lobster's a special case," Wiz said. "So the similarity is that they've all been different."

"There is something else," Malkin said quietly. "They haven't ganged up on us. Usually the first time you have a run-in with a guard his fellows come running. So far it seems we have faced only those things we have encountered by chance."

"And that's not good news?" Danny asked. "That we haven't been mobbed?"

"I mislike it."

"They fear our steel," Glandurg said confidently.

Somehow Wiz didn't think that was the answer.

"There's another possibility," Danny said. "Maybe these things all have separate patrol areas they won't leave. That's the way a D&D game is set up. Most of your monsters are tied to their rooms, or a stretch of corridor, and there're only a few roamers."

Malkin rubbed her chin. "It would keep all the guards from being drawn off by a distraction, but it still seems a strange way to protect something."

"Whoever's running this show does a lot of strange things, so think about it and see what you can come up with," Wiz said. "Anyway, there's another implication to that strategy."

The thief looked at him questioningly.

"In a D&D game the monsters get tougher as you get closer to the treasure."

". . . so anyway," Jerry finished. "All we've got to do now is get to this place in the desert where we can make the jump back to our world." Jerry spread out a Nevada road map. "It's a couple of hours north of here." He put his finger down. "Right here on this dry lake bed."

"Oh boy!" Gilligan said almost reverently.

"Boshemoi!" Kuznetsov added.

Jerry looked up from the map. "Now what's wrong?"

"That's part of Nellis Air Force Base," Gilligan said. "Restricted area."

"Worse than restricted," Kuznetsov said. "That is Area 51, Groom Lake. Top-secret testing area for F-119, SR-25 and other aircraft your government swears do not exist. That is most tightly guarded piece of land in whole country. Almost as tight as places in Soviet Union—when there was a Soviet Union."

The Russian looked over at Gilligan. "He cannot tell you this because of agreement he signed when he left Air Force. Me, I signed no such agreement."

"Well, we don't have to come in through the front gate. It looks pretty deserted out there and we'll be gone within a couple of minutes of reaching the power vortex."

Gilligan kept a poker face. Kuznetsov just grinned. "As soon as you set foot on land they will be after you.

Whole place is loaded with sensors. They get lots of experience chasing tourists who come to watch secret aircraft flights."

"Not to mention Soviet spies," Gilligan added.

Kuznetsov's grin grew wider. "No need for Soviet spies to sneak in that way. Anyway, it is too far to go before they grab you." He quit smiling. "The guards are also authorized to use deadly force."

"But we've got to get in there! It's the only way we're going to get back."

Kuznetsov considered. "Okay. Only one thing to do. We fly in."

"That's nuts!" Mick Gilligan protested.

"Maybe nuts, but here," he stabbed his finger down on the map, "is close enough we can maybe get in and land before we are stopped." He considered. "That is if they do not shoot planes down without warning for trespassing."

"That was your trick," Mick said sourly. Kuznetsov was beginning to wear and the whole conversation was making him profoundly uncomfortable.

"So we have to get three people and a dragon into this super-secret base in an airplane."

"Four," Gilligan said. "I'm going with you. All the way back." He looked at them. "That's my price for helping you."

"You know you may never be able to return," Bal-Simba told him.

"I thought of that."

The wizard looked at him closely and then nodded. "Very well. You are welcome."

"We," Kuznetsov said with a gesture at Vasily and himself, "will go with you."

Gilligan scowled. "Why?"

"Technical expertise. You need someone who knows the area—" he glanced at Gilligan significantly "—and will tell what he knows." Then he shrugged. "Besides, thumbing your nose at authority is a Russian thing. You would not understand."

Mick shook his head. "This particular nose-thumbing is gonna get you thrown out of the country—or worse."

Kuznetsov grinned broadly. "That is why it is Russian thing. It is no fun thumbing nose at authority unless you can get in big trouble for gesture."

"Then," Mick predicted, "you're gonna have more fun than you've ever had in your life. You may even die laughing."

The Russians only grinned.

"Okay, so we've got to get six people and a twenty-foot dragon in there and land on a dry lake bed. That's going to take a pretty special plane."

Vasily, who had been leaning up against the wall spoke for the first time. "I think I know where."

"So far the buzz is positive." Mark Toland gestured toward the Hilton suite's window and the Convention Center beyond with a wave of his champagne glass. "Everyone's impressed and no one's quite sure what we've got." He smiled broadly. "FUDware at it's finest."

Toland had coined the term FUDware in a speech to an industry conference several years ago and he used it whenever he could. In this case he was justified. Gigantopithecus Software's pre-pre-beta technology direction disclosure of its new API had sown Fear, Uncertainty and Doubt—FUD to connoisseurs—among potential customers, technology partners, retailers and VARS. FUDware was the equivalent of a rolling artillery barrage on the computer battlefield. Its purpose wasn't so much to cause casualties as to pin everyone down while the attackers moved in for the kill. The software being shown in another suite here at the Las Vegas Hilton was packed with nifty features. Better, it was far enough along that it might be the prelude to a real product. Then again, it might not, and that was better yet.

As a result Sasquatch was performing its intended job of paralyzing the market, exciting the trade press, and making buyers hold off committing to a competitor and stretching everyone's acquisition cycle.

Keith Malinowski slumped down on the couch and grunted. He was wearing his "Save The Sasquatch" sweatshirt over his hand-tailored sport shirt. His champagne was going flat.

"The beauty is we caught Microsoft and IBM/Lotus in mid-FUD cycle," Angela Page, his marketing VP put in. "It will be at least eight weeks before they can counter with FUDware of their own."

"But when are we going to release it?" asked Joe Kroeber from the suite's bar. He was head of software development, and pouring the drinks for everyone was part of his job at these things.

"Second quarter of next year," Page told him. "It's in the briefing sheet we use to leak to reporters."

"No, I mean when are we *really* going to have it ready?"

Page and Toland looked at Kroeber like he'd farted. Malinowski ignored them.

*I should have stayed behind and gone sailing*, he thought. Three years ago he would have been bouncing up and down like a miniature poodle at an industry coup like this. Now it was flat as his champagne. Even the knowledge that he'd put the screws to Microsoft, his former employer, just didn't thrill him. The millions more this would add to his net worth were even less important.

These days Malinowski thought of himself as a cryptozoologist more than a software entrepreneur. Ever since he was a teenager he had been convinced the planet was teeming with undiscovered animals, from Sasquatch in the Pacific Northwest and as far south as

Arizona to dinosaurs in central Africa to serpents in the seas.

The zoologists of his acquaintance thought he was a nut, but that didn't bother him in the slightest. Like a lot of people in the computer industry, Keith Malinowski had spent his whole life being the smartest person in the room, and like most of his fellows the experience left him with a rather high opinion of his opinions.

With his newfound wealth Malinowski also had the ability to back his beliefs with more than on-line arguments. In the last two years he had sponsored expeditions to places all around the world, provided computer and technical support for the people who claimed to have seen something or thought they might have gotten something on film or tape.

The ringing phone at his elbow jarred him out of his ruminations and nearly made him spill his flat champagne. Before he could focus, Toland grabbed it like the well-trained subordinate he was. He listened for a second, then put his hand over the mouthpiece and turned to his boss.

"It's Al Benedict. He wants to talk to you."

"Who?"

"Al Benedict, the guy who's handling on-floor PR. He insists on talking to you."

Malinowski frowned. *Jesus, what now?* He knew from experience that a call from the show floor usually meant he was going to have to pay out a lot more money. But that didn't bother him as much as having to fight another fire at the behest of someone he didn't even know. There was a time when he knew all his employees by face and name. Now he couldn't even tell which building they worked in. *What the hell,* he decided, *it's better than sitting here watching champagne go flat.* He nodded and reached for the phone.

"Keith?" The voice on the other end was high-pitched with excitement and nearly drowned out by the combination of background noise and a lousy cellular connection. "It's me, Al." Vaguely Malinowski remembered a frenetic little fox terrier of a man with a rusty beard and an exaggerated interest in his boss' hobby. "Listen, we, uh, ran into something on the show floor."

"Yeah?" Keith said flatly.

"No, not like that. Or not really anyway. This was two guys with a dragon. A real dragon!"

Suddenly Keith was like a beagle sniffing on a hot trail. He was up, he was excited, he was alive! FUDware and the eternal Darwinian software struggle paled to insigificance. This was *important.*

"You're sure this wasn't some kind of robot?" he demanded.

"It was definitely real. It's not real tame either. It nearly knocked our guy off his stilts."

"Old Cheng was right! They do still exist. This is fantastic!"

"I think it's genetic engineering of some sort," Keith's informant added, but Keith was gone in transports of ecstasy. Suddenly life had meaning again!

"We've had reports from remote areas of China."

"Yeah, well . . . "

"There's even a rumor that a top-secret Air Force project in Alaska got a picture of a dragon in the air a few years ago. But to find one, and here of all places. It's just unbelievable."

By this time Page and Toland had figured out the subject of the conversation and they exchanged looks. "Unbelievable" was the word they would have chosen all right, but obviously their boss did believe it. They had been sounding out major investors about replacing Malinowski for a couple of months because of his diminishing interest in the business and growing weirdness. If they handled this right it could be the capper for their campaign. Meanwhile, he was still the boss and they had to act like this was important.

"Anyway," the voice on the phone went on, "I checked and found out more. The authorities have known about it for a couple of days and they're keeping it quiet. Meanwhile, the police are hunting for it."

"The police?"

"Yeah. They want to kill it because it's dangerous."

Malinowski unfolded off the couch as if it had exploded under him.

"We can't let them do that! Angel, get our lawyers on the phone. Joe, use the phone in the other room to call Bill Reeves at Interior. We've got to protect this thing."

"You really think you can get the government to move on this?" Toland asked.

Keith paused, phone in hand, to look at him. "They'd better, after all I did for that twit in the White House." Malinowski had been one of the high-technology business leaders the incumbent had paraded during the election to support his "new technology vision for America." Like a lot of them, Malinowski had been sorely disappointed with the results. After the election they discovered their guy thought high technology meant anything with a lot of blinking lights and he couldn't use his computer consistently because he kept putting floppy disks in upside down. His computer problems got significantly worse after his teenaged daughter went back to school.

"Maybe that dope will be good for something after all," Malinowski said as he reached for the phone.

The rest of the day passed uneventfully, if not smoothly. By dint of a little fast talking, steadfast denial of any knowledge of anyone in the truck and a firm promise to get it off the hotel grounds immediately, Jerry was able to recover the vehicle. By waiting until the hotel corridors were packed with Comdex attendees, shielding Moira in the back of an elevator behind himself, Taj,

Bal-Simba, the Russians and Gilligan, and employing a few other expedients, they were able to get Moira out of the hotel and into the truck a few hours later. Then he and Bal-Simba made arrangements to meet Vasily's friend with the airplane that evening and drove off with Moira safely in the back, hidden behind a stack of boxes salvaged from the dumpsters.

Jerry was getting a headache.

They were sitting in a lounge off the casino at the hotel. Perhaps a hundred tables were packed into a space big enough for fifty. Each table would have been small for two normal people and, while Mick was a little on the short side, Jerry definitely was not and Bal-Simba was huge. As a result things were decidedly crowded. The Russians were sitting at the table just over Jerry's shoulder, and when he leaned back he bumped heads with Kuznetsov. Moira was waiting in the rented truck.

It was early evening and the other tables were mostly occupied. Occasionally a burst of laughter or a snatch of conversation would rise over the level of the general racket, but mostly it was just noise with a country-western beat. The band may not have been good, but they fulfilled one of the primary requirements for any lounge act by being loud, almost loud enough to drown out the unrelenting cacophony from the slot machines on the other side of the railing.

"My head hurts," he muttered.

"Best place for a private meeting," Kuznetsov told him. "Noise drives listeners crazy and even digital signal processors have trouble picking out one conversation."

"How do you know that?"

The Russian just smiled. "Heads up everyone. Here comes our contact."

Jerry turned in his seat and saw a man pushing his way through the crowd. Save for bushy white eyebrows and an enormous white mustache there wasn't a hair on his head. He looked like a walrus, if you can imagine a sunburned walrus wearing aviator sunglasses and an orange flight suit decorated with a wildly improbable collection of patches. Jerry saw insignia from everything from the 23rd Fighter Squadron to something called Miz Lil's Cottontail Ranch and Sporting Club. He looked over at Gilligan.

"I don't know and I don't want to know," Gilligan muttered.

The man nodded to the Russians and pulled a chair over to the table where the others sat. "Charlie Conroy," he boomed, extending a paw that was sunburned as pink as the rest of him. "My friends call me Cowboy."

As Jerry shook the proferred hand he saw the wrist was decorated with a watch the size of a can of snuff, with dials and buttons and hands galore.

Almost as soon as Charlie sat down a waitress wearing not much, and that black and slinky, slithered up to take his order.

"Honey," he boomed, "bring me over one of those Tanqueray and tonics. Make it a double." The waitress reflexively avoided a pat on the rump and swivel-hipped off through the tables.

He turned to the Russians. "Vaseline you old commie, how's it hanging?"

"Okay, sky pirate. Burned any babies lately?"

"Naw, I got out of that end of the business. How 'bout you, Ivan? Still doing them dirty deeds?"

"I get by," Kuznetsov said with a slight smile. Jerry got the impression he wasn't nearly as charmed by Conroy's antics as his partner. Gilligan was obviously un-charmed, but he was keeping his mouth shut.

"Hell of a crowd, ain't it?" Cowboy boomed to Jerry and Bal-Simba. "Between the tourists and the computer geeks, whole damn town is packed. I ain't seen anything like it since the fall of Saigon."

The waitress returned with Charlie's drink and Jerry

paid for it. Charlie emptied the gin and tonic in one gulp and held up the glass. "Fill'er again will you, darlin'?" Obviously he had never heard of the "twenty-four hours from bottle to throttle" rule either.

"Now," he said, setting the glass on the tiny table, "I understand you boys want to make a little excursion."

"Yeah," Jerry said, glancing around the table. "Four of us and, ah, some cargo. About five hundred pounds of it. We need to make one trip to a place about a hundred and fifty miles from here."

"No problem," Charlie said. "But there are some conditions." He leaned forward and put his meaty forearms on the tiny table. Gilligan grabbed his drink just as it was shoved off the edge.

Their guest was oblivious. "Now understand, I don't smuggle dope. Leastways not for strangers. And I won't stand for murder on my airplane. Beyond that—" he shrugged. "I don't see nothing and I don't hear nothing."

That, Jerry reflected, was probably going to be the most important characteristic of all.

"Where are we gonna make pickup and will it be a day or night flight?"

"You can pick us up at the airport," Jerry said. "Day is probably better than night. It's the destination that's a little tricky."

"Where you going?"

"Uh, Groom Lake, Area Fifty-One."

"Just outside inner fence toward the end of runway," Kuznetsov added, leaning over from his table.

Charlie looked at the Russian narrowly. "This cargo don't explode does it? 'Cause as a patriotic American and a veteran of four wars I don't hold with blowing up US air bases."

"It doesn't explode," Jerry assured him. Then he thought of the Las Vegas police car. "Well, not unless you get her angry."

"Her?"

"The cargo's kind of livestock."

"I may charge you boys extra for mucking out the airplane. Can this thing be trusted to use a sick sack?"

"Well, she's a flying creature anyway," Jerry said, "so I don't think she's subject to airsickness."

"What the hell is this critter?" Charlie roared, just as the music ended and there was a lull in the casino racket. "A five-hundred-pound canary?"

Suddenly half the people in the bar were looking at them.

Jerry turned beet red under the attention. "Uh, something like that," he whispered.

Charlie grinned and leaned back in his chair. "Boys," he boomed, "I think I'm gonna enjoy this little trip."

Looking at their pilot, Jerry wasn't so sure he would be able to say the same.

## FIFTEEN

# Biplane Bye-Bye

The morning was bright, cold and crystal clear. The mountains on the other side of the airport looked like they were only a mile away.

When the truck pulled up to the gate on the general aviation side of the field, Jerry and Taj were in the front seat as the least conspicuous of the group. Moira, the Russians, Taj and Bal-Simba were in the back.

The guard came out of the shack huddled in his flight jacket, his breath leaving little puffs in the frosty air. He kept his hands in his pockets until he needed one to hand the clipboard under his arm up to the cab.

There was a sign by the gate informing them that all vehicles were subject to search when entering and leaving. For an instant Jerry was afraid the guard was going to ask to look in the back of the truck, but he only nodded as he retrieved his clipboard.

They'd be more likely to check them on the way out, Jerry decided. But that didn't matter.

Jerry pulled the truck into a parking space in back of a row of tan metal hangars. Although there were a number of cars in the parking lot, the place looked deserted. Then he remembered that pilots liked to take off at dawn. Those cars probably belonged to people who were already airborne.

Quickly Jerry and Taj rolled up the truck's tailgate. "Okay. We're here."

"About time," Kuznetsov said as he hopped down. "The dragon is getting carsick."

Moira followed him out, gulping deep lungfuls of air

and looking decidedly green around the gills, even for a dragon. "I am sorry, My Lord. I am not used to riding in closed conveyances and this body is unwell."

"No harm done," Gilligan assured her.

"But five minutes more . . . "

"Never mind that," Jerry cut the Russian off. "Let's go find our ride."

Just at that moment Charlie came around the corner of the hangar wiping his hands on a rag. In the light of day his orange jumpsuit looked even gaudier than it had in tho cocktail lounge. He saw Moira, did a double take and got his composure back.

"You folks ready to go?" he asked, staying well clear of the dragon.

"All set," Jerry assured him.

Charlie eyed Moira. "Don't you need a leash for that thing?"

"I am quite under control, thank you." Moira said with a sniff.

"Holy shit! She talks! Uh, no offense ma'am."

The dragon nodded. "None taken."

"Well, come on then. I got her gassed, oiled and preflighted. She's right around here."

Charlie led them around the hangar and pointed proudly. Although the ramp was occupied by the usual gaggle of Pipers, Cessnas and Mooneys it was obvious to all of them what he was pointing at.

It was a biplane. A very big biplane with an enclosed cabin, a radial engine and a dull-green paint job. Next to the civilian registration numbers on the body was a large red star. "AN-2 Colt," Charlie announced proudly.

"That's a Russian plane!" Gilligan almost shouted.

"This one's Polish, actually," Charlie told him. "Design's Russian though."

Mick groaned. "We're going to fly into a restricted area in a Russian plane." He looked over at Kuznetsov. "Why didn't you get us a Mig 29 escort while you're at it?"

"No Mig 29s in town until air show next week," the Russian deadpanned. "Besides, we cannot get dragon into a Mig 29."

Mick just shook his head and turned away.

"Be reasonable, Mick," Kuznetsov said. "There are not many planes that can carry all this and still land in dirt."

"Reasonable?" Gilligan yelped. "*You're* asking *me* to be reasonable?"

"Ivan's right," Charlie said cheerfully. "These babies were made for hauling cargo in and out of rough fields. She'll land on a dime and give you back a nickel's change."

"Besides, I don't think we've got much choice," Jerry said. "There's no time to find another plane and we're probably going to have company faster than that."

Gilligan looked at the others and his shoulders slumped. "That thing's got a radar cross-section like a barn door."

Charlie grinned appreciatively but Gilligan just snorted. "What about you?" he asked Charlie. "Are you gonna come all the way?"

"They don't have airplanes in this place?" Charlie asked.

"No," Jerry told him. "Just dragons."

"Dragons, hell!" He nodded to Moira. "Uh, no offense ma'am but it don't sound like my kind of place. I'll just drop you folks off." He took a map from the leg pocket of his flight suit and unfolded it on the ground, nailing a corner of it with his knee.

"Okay," he said as the others gathered around, "our best shot is to head north to about here." He stabbed a finger down on the map. "Then we drop to minimum altitude, pop over that ridge and run straight for the target."

"How fast can they intercept us?" Jerry asked.

"Fast," Kuznetzov put in. "Once they see us, first fighters arrive in three point five minutes."

Gilligan looked at the Russian oddly, but he was oblivious.

"Now the way I figure it," Charlie went on, "we can get to this place with, oh, two-three minutes to spare." He looked at Gilligan and his friends. "But son, this dingus of yours had better work because there's no way in hell we are gonna get back out."

"How are you going to explain this?"

"Simple. I'll tell them I was drunk and I did it on a bar bet." He smiled broadly. "No way in hell they won't believe me. You people were just sightseers who were along for the ride. You didn't know what I was gonna do until I did it."

"You know you're going to lose your license over this."

The old man's grin faded. "Son, I'm gonna have to give it up when I take my physical next month anyway. When this is over I'll move to Costa Rica or someplace where they don't have all these pissant rules for pilots."

There was also an excellent chance he would go to jail, but Gilligan didn't mention that.

"Don't worry, it will work out." He glanced over Gilligan's shoulder toward the rear of the plane. "As long as that talking lizard isn't around. I'm a good bullshitter, but I'm not that good."

"That's okay," Jerry told him. "She won't be there when the cops arrive and neither will we."

"Well, let's do it people," Charlie said. "I hear sirens and I don't think they're fire engines." He looked at Gilligan. "You take the right-hand seat with me. The rest of you get in the back.

"That ground isn't that smooth," Gilligan said as Charlie refolded the map. "We're gonna land pretty rough."

"Nahh, don't worry," Charlie said. "They built these things in a tractor factory."

"Actually tank factory," Kuznetzov told him. "Tractor factory was cover story."

The sirens were getting closer. Jerry looked back toward where the truck was parked.

"Now what?" Kuznetsov demanded.

"I was just thinking. We really should turn the truck back in. Or at least call them to tell them where they can pick it up."

"Jerry."

"Yeah?"

"Shut up and get in the damn plane."

As Jerry scrambled aboard and Vasily slammed the door behind him, Charlie reached down and hit the starter. The big Kuznetsov radial chuffed two or three times as compressed air from the starter tank turned it over. Then one cylinder caught and fired, then two more and then the aircraft was filled with the roar of the engine.

Slowly, the plane turned out of its tie-down spot and started down the taxiway. Charlie used the rudder pedals to wiggle the nose from side to side so he could make sure the way was clear. From instinct Mick swiveled his head to check for possible interference. The older man was talking into his headset, obviously communicating with the tower, but Mick couldn't make out the words over the engine.

They reached the turn-in and Charlie ran up the engine while standing on the brakes, scanning the gauges as he did so. Satisfied, he backed off on the throttle and turned the plane onto the runway.

"Okay folks, here we go," Charlie bellowed over his shoulder and shoved the throttle forward again. The engine noise rose to a crescendo and the big biplane began to gather speed. Out his side window Mick could see a couple of police cars coming out onto the field with their red and blue lights flashing.

*If those damn police cars don't interfere,* he thought.

It occurred to Mick, who hadn't had so much as a parking ticket since he sold his sports car, that he was now involved in about half a dozen felonies. He found it was an odd sensation. He also realized he didn't much care, not if it got him back to Karin and a place where magic and dragons ruled the skies.

The police never had a chance. In what Mick thought was a suicidally short distance, at what he was sure was an insanely low airspeed, Charlie hauled back on the wheel and the plane swooped into the air, hanging on the big prop. Lift and thrust battled drag and gravity and for a stomach-churning instant Mick was sure gravity would win. Then the plane seemed to find itself, steadied, and began to climb like a contented cow on a hilly pasture. Now the only way to stop them was to shoot them down, Mick thought.

Then he remembered that could very easily happen.

## SIXTEEN

# LORD OF THE FLIES AND THE LORD OF THE FLIERS

*It was the flies,* Peter Hanborn told himself. *I'm being punished for the flies.*

He was a thin, serious man with intent brown eyes behind heavy spectacles. He was not yet thirty but his increasing baldness made him look ten years older. Just now he felt about a hundred years older.

Well, damn it, an endangered species is an endangered species. And the Southern Nevada Garbage Fly was certainly endangered. He still didn't regret his attempt to get the fly listed under the Endangered Species Act, despite the hundreds of editorials, two Congressional inquires and thousands of angry letters which had deluged his department as a result. To this day he didn't accept the taxonomists' opinion that his proposed endangered species was really just a sub-population of ordinary house flies with a slightly different distribution of characteristics as a result of generations of breeding in a landfill in the middle of the desert.

But that didn't mean he was looking forward to this. He glanced over at McWilliams, the government's counsel for the petition. The older man seemed as cool and unruffled as if this were an ordinary case instead of this, this travesty. *At least I had solid population data when I made my proposal,* Hanborn thought. This thing wasn't even supported by a headline in the *National Enquirer*.

Not that there wouldn't be headlines in the *Enquirer*, not to mention the *Weekly World News* and every fringe publication from here to London. Twisting around to look at the half-dozen spectators on the hard wooden benches he wondered which of them was the stringer for the tabloids.

The state was opposing the motion, naturally. They considered it such an open-and-shut case they sent their newest attorney, a kid named Sculley, to handle it. It didn't help that Sculley looked and acted like Jimmy Olsen from the old Superman comics.

Hanborn was so sunk in his own misery he missed the bailiff entering the courtroom and had to scramble awkwardly at his announcement.

"All rise. Court is now in session. The honorable Judge Margaret Schumann presiding."

Judge Schumann was a tall, slender woman with iron-gray hair and a demeanor to match. "Be seated."

*It had to be Maximum Mazie*, Hanborn thought miserably as he sagged back in his seat. Now there was a very real possibility he would not only be a laughingstock, he would go to jail as well. He slumped even further until he was almost sitting on his shoulder-blades.

Judge Schumann was oblivious. "Counsel ready?" she asked, flipping through her copy of the petition. Both lawyers rose and nodded. "Let's begin then. Now the government," she gestured at McWilliams, "wants an injunction to protect a new and possibly endangered species. The state opposes, is that correct?"

"It is, your honor," Sculley said. "We feel . . . "

"We'll get to what you feel in a minute, Mr. Sculley." She kept her attention on McWilliams. "Doesn't the Endangered Species Act have provisions for emergency listing of a species?"

"It does your honor," McWilliams said, "but we are asking for protection for this animal until the emergency provisions can be invoked. We have reason to believe that the few surviving members of the species, perhaps the entire remnant population, is in immediate and dire danger."

"Your honor," Sculley cut in. "The state contends that if this animal does in fact exist there is absolutely no evidence to show that it is entitled to protection under the Endangered Species Act. Further, the thing, if it exists, is dangerous and the state must be able to protect its citizens."

Judge Margaret (Maximum Mazie) Schumann hadn't made it to the federal bench without a finely tuned set of antennae. These endangered species cases were tricky. They usually meant someone was trying to build something someone else didn't like. In Las Vegas, where development was nearly as big an industry as gambling, that usually meant a lot of money was at stake. It was even worse when you were asked to issue an injunction for an animal that wasn't even officially listed as endangered. Besides which she recognized the clown sitting beside the government's lawyer as the nut who tried to get the flies at the local landfill declared an endangered species.

"Someone trying to build a golf course?"

"No, Your Honor. The species is being hunted to possible extinction by the Las Vegas police."

"What is this thing? King Kong?"

A couple of spectators chuckled.

"It's, uh, a reptile," the plaintiff's council said. He looked at his Fish and Wildlife expert for support.

"A large reptile," Hanborn added miserably.

For the first time the judge looked interested. "What kind of reptile?"

"Uh, if Your Honor will just read Exhibit A attached to the petition you'll find a description."

Judge Schumann flipped through the document. *Reptile, large, species unknown. Wings . . .*

Maximum Mazie Schumann jerked her head up and slammed her gavel down. "Court's in recess." She glared down at the counsels' tables. "I want to see the parties in my chambers. Now."

Mazie Schumann had started out as a dancer in the Las Vegas shows. While she was strutting it by night she went to college by day and then to the University of Nevada law school. When she graduated she traded feathers and beads for a gray wool suit and a job with the Clark County District Attorney's Office. Thanks to her abilities, drive and political skill she eventually wound up on the Federal District bench. If she was not a towering legal scholar, she was smart, politically savvy, and a hard-boiled no-nonsense judge who retained a streak of the theatrical. The media loved her, lawyers respected her, criminals feared her and nobody, but nobody, trifled with her.

Just now Maximum Mazie felt she was being trifled with.

"Now," she demanded as soon as her clerk closed the door to her office. "What the hell is this? A publicity stunt for a casino?"

"No, Your Honor," McWilliams said smoothly, "it's not a publicity stunt. It's . . . "

"Crap," Judge Schumann finished. "That's what this is. Mr. McWilliams, do you know how long it takes to bring a civil case to trial in this district?"

McWilliams knew almost to the day, but he also knew when to shut up and take his licking. "No, Your Honor."

"Nearly two years. Two blessed years to get a serious case to trial and you come marching in here wasting this court's time with crap. I know a load of crap when I see it. And this," she said, tapping the petition with a blood-red fingernail, "is prime-cut, table-grade crap."

"Precisely, Your Honor," Sculley said. "That has been the state's contention . . . "

"Don't gloat, counselor. You're as much a part of this as they are." Sculley went from gloating to wilting in one smooth transition.

Judge Schumann cocked an eye at McWilliams. "Anything from the petitioner?" McWilliams was more experienced than Sculley and he knew when to keep his mouth shut. Hanborn shrank into his chair and devoutly wished he was somewhere, anywhere, else.

"All right. I'm going to grant this petition. That makes it a matter of public record. And I wouldn't be at all surprised if the newspapers don't get hold of this." She glared at Hanborn and McWilliams. "As a judge I can't comment on the matter to the media. That means you two will have to explain this pile of horseapples to the taxpayers."

Sculley shifted in his chair. "Ah, Your Honor . . . "

"Mr. Sculley, you are trying my patience. That is the second time today and no one has ever done it a third time. Now get back out there, all of you, and let's get this farce over with."

They were still in the traffic pattern when Charlie got a radio call that obviously displeased him. He reached over to the microphone jack and wiggled it firmly. "Say again tower, you're breaking up. Over." Thanks to Charlie's fiddling the transmission was nicely garbled.

The old pilot chewed his mustache for an instant as he listened to the transmission, then he reached down and switched off the radio. "Pissants," Charlie yelled to Mick.

Charlie did not waste a lot of time gathering altitude. While they were in the tower's control zone he made a pretense of staying above the FAA minimums. As soon as they were beyond visual range of the tower and over the open desert he pushed the wheel forward.

As an ex-fighter jock, Mick Gilligan was a member of the high-and-fast school of flying. Charlie, on the other hand, belonged to the "low and slow" school. Gilligan had no objection to flying low—within reason. But he considered having to pull up to get over barbed wire fences decidedly unreasonable. A couple of times

Gilligan saw puffs of dust where the Colt's wheels had touched the ground. After that he tried not to look.

Back in the cabin the other passengers had their own problems. Flying sideways is unsettling, the noise and vibration were terrible, and the humans were sharing the space with a dragon who'd never been in an airplane before.

Fluffy didn't get airsick, but he wasn't a very good traveling companion. Although he was too young to fly the dragon had the reflexes of a flying creature, which meant he kept trying to use his body to control his "flight." Moira tried valiantly to keep the body under control, but with very mixed success. Every time the plane lurched, Fluffy instinctively tried to spread his wings. After being smacked in the face a couple of times, the occupants of the seats learned to duck when the plane lurched.

"They're not responding," the air traffic control supervisor told his visitors.

Like most air traffic controllers, the supervisor had a strong sense of what was proper. In his book having a bunch of police and other gawkers invade his control center was highly improper. However, as an ex-Air Force controller he was disinclined to argue. The best he could do was keep them out of his people's hair, be civil to them and hope they would get out of his control center soon.

"Isn't that illegal? Ignoring air traffic control?" asked one of his visitors, a blocky middle-aged man in an expensive suit. The supervisor had already sized him up as the one who was running this show. The police captain and other officers, as well as the gaggle of civil servants from federal and state agencies, didn't seem to count for much.

"Maybe their radios are out," the supervisor said, more to annoy his unwanted guests than out of any belief. Charlie had only been in town for a couple of weeks on this visit, but already the controllers knew him and his plane.

"Where are they going?"

The supervisor glanced over a controller's shoulder. "North and a little east."

"Didn't they file a flight plan?'

"Yeah, but they've already deviated from it. Besides, according to the plan they're coming back here."

"Well, stop them," the suit snapped. The supervisor just looked at him until he realized how stupid that was and reddened.

*It's easier dealing with the DEA,* the supervisor thought.

"I mean, can you alert the airports within range and have them report when it lands?" the suit asked in a lame attempt to cover himself.

"If they land at an airport. From the looks of that plane it can set down on any strip of flat desert from here to Idaho."

The suit clearly didn't like that. The police captain, on the other hand, seemed less concerned. Clearly he was just glad to get the problem out of his jurisdiction.

"Well," said the civilian, obviously trying to control his temper, "can you follow them on radar?"

"For a while. But they're descending rapidly. If they get right down on the deck we'll lose them in the clutter."

"How fast can you get a plane after them?" one of the lesser suits asked.

The supervisor shrugged. "Ask the police, or maybe the DEA. Or you may have to rent something."

The suit turned to look at the police captain.

"We've got an air unit that can follow them for a while," the cop said.

"Don't worry about following them too far," the supervisor told the visitors. "They're headed into restricted airspace. If they don't change course pretty soon the Air Force will take care of them."

"What will they do?" the suit asked.

"If they don't break off? Then they're going to overfly Area Fifty-One. The Air Force is *real* touchy about uninvited visitors there."

The suit looked apprehensive. "But what will they do about it?"

"Intercept them. Try to get them to land." The supervisor shrugged. "In the worst case they'll blow them out of the sky."

"We are getting close," Kuznetsov yelled in Mick Gilligan's ear.

Mick didn't recognize the terrain, but he didn't need the Russian to tell him where they were. They'd crossed the highway some time back, pulling up so they didn't collide with any cars or trucks and scaring the heck out of a couple of tourists. By now they had to be inside the restricted airspace that surrounded the base and soon they'd be over the line on the base itself.

The Russian leaned over Mick's shoulder and pointed at a nondescript building on top of a nearby mountain.

"Radar station," Kuznetzov shouted over the noise of the engine. "Normally would have been eliminated by speznatzii, but no speznatzii, so . . . " He shrugged.

Gilligan turned in his seat to look at him closely. "What in the hell are you?" he yelled.

"I told you," Kuznetsov shouted back, "I am a businessman."

"Yeah, but what did you used to be?"

"Used to be businessmen were parasites and enemies of people. So I was good Communist like everybody else."

"Heads up!" Charlie called. "Here comes company."

It only took Mick an instant to pick up the two dots headed toward them. They quickly grew and resolved into the gray shark shapes of a pair of F-16s.

*This is a nightmare,* Mick thought. *I'm going to wake up soon and find out this whole thing is just a nightmare.* But the F-16s kept coming.

*I should have gotten out back in 1978 when I was still a captain,* Major General Paul Manley thought as he stared at the radar plot. Outwardly everyone in the command center was cool and professional, but you could feel the tension rising. Right now the tensest place in the room was the pit of General Manley's stomach. Unusually for the Air Force, General Manley was not an experienced combat pilot. Even his tour in Vietnam had been spent pulling pilots out of the jungle with Air Rescue rather than dropping bombs. For the first time in his career as an Air Force officer he was probably going to have to kill someone.

"Break off, you damn fools," he muttered at the dot on the scope. But the point of green light kept coming straight for the smear of the mountain range and the base beyond.

One of the problems with running the most highly secret military base in the United States was the tourists. Groom Lake was so secret it was regularly written up in national magazines. So naturally it drew military buffs, peace protesters, flying saucer fanatics and assorted religious cranks, crazies and general-issue looney-toons like a magnet draws iron filings.

That in fact was one of Groom Lake's functions. While there was some very secret work done here, the focus of developing the next-generation aircraft had shifted elsewhere. General Manley knew that the next generation was really being developed in an industrial park in Los Angeles by a weird mix of civilian engineers, "retired" military officers and science fiction fans, most of whom thought they were working for a private foundation running on a shoestring.

There was also the "agricultural experiment station"

up in northern Idaho where the *really* secret work was done. That was so highly classified the general could hardly bear to think about it. While the work went on there, all the flak came to Groom Lake, and it was part of General Manley's job to catch it.

The most dangerous of the groups were the military buffs who prided themselves on collecting every scrap of information about programs they were supposed to know nothing about. By combining everything from chance sightings to seismic records of sonic booms they had pieced together remarkably detailed pictures of several of the craft that actually existed at Area 51, as well as equally detailed pictures of several that had never existed, including one that had started out as a practical joke in the Nellis AFB officer's club.

Those people the general could almost sympathize with. The most irritating ones, and the most persistent, were the space nuts who kept insisting that the government had a flying saucer hidden in one of the hangars. Their latest tactic had been to file a lawsuit claiming the saucer's force fields were making people sick for miles around. Lawyers for the saucerians had been combing the sparsely populated desert around the base seeking people with illnesses, real or imaginary, that they could blame on the presence of the alien spaceship. The next step would be a class action suit against the government with all kinds of discovery motions.

Was this more saucer folk, General Manley wondered, or was it another camera crew from a tabloid TV show? Using a Russian airplane would appeal to those bozos.

Whoever it was was in for a big disappointment even if they lived to get here. The truth was there was nothing to see. The plane was so slow the base had plenty of time to get anything sensitive under cover—a well-practiced maneuver because of Russian spy satellites. Besides, nothing interesting happened outdoors in the daytime.

Off in the background a phone rang. The general gritted his teeth and wished he hadn't quit smoking.

If he thought that plane represented a threat to his command he would have ordered it shot out of the air without hesitation. But unless there was a nuclear weapon on board there wasn't a damn thing it could be carrying that would seriously hurt this base. He knew it, everyone in the command center knew it and the pilots hanging off the intruder's wings knew it. But everyone also knew the standing orders. The fact was he'd need a damn good reason *not* to shoot that plane down.

"General," the lieutenant holding the phone said hesitantly. She was young, fresh-faced and buxom even through her flight suit. She reminded the general of his daughter, who was also a lieutenant training at fighter school at Luke Air Force Base.

"Sir, it's the XO."

General Manley glared. "Sir, he says it's urgent," the lieutenant offered.

The general sighed and extended a hand for the phone. "Sir," the XO said, "I've got a lawyer on the phone. And I've got the Pentagon on the other line telling us to cooperate with him 'to the maximum extent feasible.'"

*Oh Jesus,* the general thought, *what now?*

Wiz was still wondering about it when the scenery changed again. This section of tunnel was neatly floored and walled with blocks of worked stone. Columns stood along the walls supporting groined vaulting overhead. After all the different kinds of tunnels they had seen, Wiz wasn't particularly surprised, but he was reminded of pictures of the crypts under a Gothic cathedral.

Just to be sure he motioned to Danny. The younger programmer swept his magic detector back and forth across their path and then shook his head. No magic before them.

Wiz took three steps before Malkin grabbed his arm.

"Freeze," she commanded.

"What's wrong?"

"Your trusting nature, for a start," the tall thief said.

"But there's no magic here."

Malkin looked amused. "Do you think that's the only danger we face? Look at this place. Why do you think it's built like this?"

"To hold the roof up?"

"Perhaps. But why here and nowhere else we have seen? Give me more light, if you can." With that she picked her way ahead, studying the floor before her intently and occasionally poking and prodding with her rapier.

She got perhaps a dozen steps beyond Wiz before she stopped dead and looked around. Finally she reached into her pack and pulled out a rock the size of her fist. She tossed it underhand at a perfectly unremarkable section of stone floor a couple of steps ahead of her.

As soon as the rock struck there was a creak and a section of the floor swung downward, leaving a gaping blackness beneath. Far below Wiz thought he heard the sound of rushing water, but he heard no splash from the stone. Then there was another creak and the stones swung back into place, leaving the floor looking as perfect as before. Malkin looked smug.

"How did you know that was there?"

"The stonework was too regular," she told him, leaving Wiz to try to determine why that section of the paving was any more regular than any other.

"Now listen," she said. "I'm going to go ahead to find the traps. I'll mark the safe path and then you come through one at a time. No more. We want as little weight on this floor as we can."

As Wiz and the others watched, Malkin picked her way over the stone floor. Twice more she marked hidden traps with a bit of charcoal stuck on the point of her rapier, and once she skipped neatly out of the way as a blade swung down from the ceiling on a long rod.

"All right," she called back as the blade slowed. "The place is so big we'll have to do this in stages. The first one of you follow my path to here. The next one come to that white stone just in front of the second trap." Wiz picked his way forward and Danny followed. By the time he had reached the now-still blade, Malkin was up ahead, dodging in and out of the forest of columns.

They watched intently as she spotted another trap, then she stepped behind a pillar and they couldn't see her anymore.

"Hey!" they heard her yell. "What . . ."

With that Wiz and Danny were off and running. They stayed on the safe path Malkin had marked for them but they were almost side by side when they reached her.

They gasped when Malkin stepped out in the light. Her entire right side was splattered with blood. Gore was matted in her hair and dripped down one side of her face. But she strode toward them strongly, rapier in hand, apparently unaware of the extent of her injuries.

"We," she announced, "have got to do something about that lobster."

*Shock,* thought Wiz numbly. *She's in shock.* He and Danny rushed to meet her and half-carried her back to the others. Malkin was apparently too dazed to appreciate their help. She struggled and protested all the way back.

"Will you to let go of me!" she demanded as they laid her down on a cloak. Danny managed to get her rapier and Wiz tried to hold her down so June could work on her. Malkin was having none of it. She pushed and shoved and tried to knee Wiz in the groin.

"Have you run mad?" she demanded.

"Take it easy, you've lost a lot of blood."

"What blood? The thing never touched me. I'm fine I tell you."

Wiz looked more closely. In spite of the amount of clotted red all up and down her side there was no sign of fresh blood. He dropped his arms to his sides and stood up.

"You're all right?"

"Of course I'm all right. I came around the corner and the damn bug squirted me with something."

"But it's red, and it's . . ." Wiz extended a finger to touch Malkin's gory torso. He drew it back, rubbed the red substance between his thumb and forefinger and sniffed it. "Cocktail sauce," he concluded.

Wordlessly, June produced a hand mirror and held it up before Malkin.

"Oh Fortuna!" the thief exclaimed at what she saw in the mirror. "And you thought I . . ." She broke up laughing and Wiz, Danny and June all joined in.

"I'm going to kill that lobster!" Malkin growled. "Try to serve me up with cocktail sauce, will he?"

"I never did like lobster," Wiz said. "Always gave me gas."

June handed Malkin a cloth and she began wiping the sauce off her face. "I think I'm developing a taste for lobster." She looked down at the red-smeared cloth. "If I can watch him boil," she added savagely.

Danny was still laughing. "Hey, what's the matter? I heard you like being smeared with stuff."

"That was honey," Malkin said with some dignity. "And it was completely different. Besides, it was Jerry's idea."

"*You what?*" General Paul Manley roared into the receiver.

The lawyer on the other end was unperturbed by Manley's rank or his command bellow.

"That aircraft is carrying a member of an endangered species," he repeated. "We have a federal court order protecting it. Under the terms of that order you cannot harm it."

"What?"

"Specifically," the lawyer went on, "you can't shoot it down."

"That's the biggest goddamn load of bullshit I've ever heard in my life!" General Manley roared. He went on in that vein for several minutes. Then he slammed down the phone.

"Order the CAP not to fire," he said to the controllers. "We've got orders from Washington not to down that plane." The controller turned back to her radio to relay the message and General Manley grinned. Then he caught the lieutenant looking at him and scowled again.

"Get the ready squad loaded and in the air," he growled. "If that turkey lands I want him surrounded and arrested."

The Colt roared over the mountains so close Gilligan could have reached out and touched the rocks. Ahead lay a flat tan plain dotted with occasional greasewood bushes. Almost lost in the distance and the dark backdrop of mountains was a cluster of low buildings including several hangars and a control tower. As soon as they were over the ridge line Charlie pushed the wheel forward and sent the plane into a sickening swoop, sticking so close to the mountainside that, for an instant, Mick thought he was going to set down on the slope. Gilligan decided to look up instead but the view wasn't any less menacing. The F-16s came flashing over the mountain at a much more reasonable altitude, then banked sharply to come around toward them.

General Manley studied the approaching speck through his binoculars. That was a bit of an affectation since he could have gotten a much better view from the optical sensor displays on the console. Heedless of the F-16s buzzing about, the lumbering biplane droned on like a bumblebee on a summer's day.

"Alcatraz," General Manley growled.

"Sir?" the lieutenant asked.

"When I get that pilot I'm gonna send him to Alcatraz for the rest of his miserable life."

"Sir, they closed Alcatraz prison years ago."

"We'll reopen it," the general growled, clamping the field glasses to his eyes. "When I get done with him, that bastard's never going to see daylight."

"Okay folks, almost there." Charlie chopped the throttle and the big biplane settled toward the desert floor at an unnerving rate. Gilligan resisted an urge to close his eyes.

The lake bed was flat and the Colt was made for rough-field landings. Charlie took full advantage of the plane's ruggedness and brought them in steeply and hard. Gilligan's teeth rattled and Jerry lost his grip and landed in a heap against Moira.

Charlie was unfazed. "I'm going to taxi right up against the thing," he yelled over the engine noise. "As soon as we get there everyone get the hell out." With that he stood on the rudder pedal and gunned the engine to send them bouncing over the desert at a speed that threatened to ground-loop them at any instant. Off in the distance Gilligan could see columns of dust rising where vehicles left the pavement and raced toward them. He looked sideways at Charlie, but the old man seemed oblivious to the approaching danger.

"There!" Jerry yelled in Charlie's ear, pointing past his head to an utterly unremarkable spot in the desert. Charlie nodded, kicked the pedals to bring them around and gunned the engine for one last burst of speed.

Then he stood on the brakes, chopped the throttles and the Kuznetsov radial died in ear-shattering silence.

"Everyone out folks," Charlie called back into the cabin. "Come on. We're gonna have company in just a couple of minutes."

Gilligan was out of the seat and back into the cabin in a flash. Jerry fumbled with the door until Vasily reached past him and opened it with a practiced twist. Then the dragon, wizard, programmer, pilot and Russians all piled out onto the dusty lake bed.

The desert was chilly, but the glare from the bare soil was disconcertingly bright and the dust kicked up by the prop stung their eyes and skin.

"Is this the place?" Gilligan asked. "If so, do it quick."

Coming over the lake bed were three Blackhawk helicopters painted in green camouflage. Squinting, Gilligan thought he could make out door gunners. Two more columns of dust marked where vehicles were speeding toward them across the desert.

"Stay where you are!" the loudspeaker on the first helicopter blared. "Put your hands up and stay where you are."

"Everyone ready," Bal-Simba boomed.

"My Lord, the circle . . ." Moira began.

"No time," Bal-Simba said, raising his staff. "Stay close," he roared. The group huddled together at the sound of his voice.

As the F-16s circled and the helicopters flared for a landing, the wizard raised his hands and began to chant.

The security forces, mistaking Bal-Simba's gesture for surrender, barreled in. They couldn't hear his voice rising and falling and when the air around the group began to twist and shimmer it looked like heat rising from the desert floor.

As they dropped lower the helicopters kicked up clouds of fine, powdery dust. Even before the wheels touched, the combat-equipped Air Police were jumping from the ships to secure their prisoners.

By the time the dust cleared there was nothing in the desert but a dozen bewildered Air Policemen with M-16s at the ready.

## SEVENTEEN

# HOMECOMING

The world twisted, darkened and lightened again, leaving the party dizzy and blinking. Instead of the brilliant desert sunshine there was the softer light streaming through the windows of the Great Hall.

At the eight points of the compass wizards gaped at them. Behind them, a crowd of castle folk gaped too.

There was plenty to gape at. Unfortunately, the summoning spell wasn't precise without a physical circle to delimit it. Fortunately, the great hall of the Wizards' Keep was very large. Fortunate because when Bal-Simba looked over his shoulder he saw he had brought Charlie, biplane and all, with them.

As the castle folk gaped at the arrivals, most of the newcomers gaped back.

"Boshemoi!" Kuznetzov gasped.

"Holodeck City," Taj said, looking around. "Awesome."

"Son of a bitch," Charlie said softly. "Son of a goddamn bitch."

Mick Gilligan didn't say anything. He had done this before, after all. Instead he craned his neck, searching for a familiar head of blond hair.

Arianne advanced across the now-useless circle to greet them.

"Merry met, My Lord," she said to Bal-Simba. "Was your quest successful?"

"I believe so, My Lady." He turned and gestured. "This is E.T., the one we sought."

"Stunned," said the Tajmanian Devil.

Arianne dropped a graceful curtsy.

"Charmed, too," he added.

"Forgive me, My Lord, but we were not expecting so many." Arianne was doing her best to ignore the airplane and Bal-Simba's rather improbable outfit.

"Things became a trifle complicated," the big wizard said dryly.

"Karin?" Mick called into the crowd gathered behind the wizards.

"Mick! Oh, here Mick."

A blond woman in dragon rider's leather detached herself from the crowd and threw herself into his arms.

"You came back! Oh, you came back."

"Hey, I told you I would, didn't I?" Mick Gilligan said softly. "Just took a little longer."

"Have the shadows come back?" Bal-Simba asked his assistant.

"Somewhat. But we have better spells to hold them off, thanks to the time you bought us."

"Any word from the others?"

His assistant shook her head.

"Well then." Bal-Simba sighed. "We had best get our new guests settled and then decide how to proceed."

"I will have their quarters prepared immediately," Arianne said, gesturing the seneschal forward. Then she paused.

"My Lord, just one other thing."

"Yes?"

"How are we going to get this," she asked, gesturing at the airplane, "out of the hall?"

Bal-Simba pursed his lips. "That may pose a problem," he said at last.

It was a wonderful, glorious morning when Mick Gilligan awoke after a wonderful, glorious night. The sun was well up and the whole world was so perfect Gilligan thought his heart would burst.

He propped himself up on one elbow to admire Karin

beside him. She responded by snuggling closer, a wisp of straw-blond hair falling across her lightly freckled cheek. He leaned over and gave her a wake-up kiss. A long, lingering wake-up kiss.

"Hmm," said Karin, stirring beneath him and kissing him back. Then her eyes popped open and she broke the clinch.

"Good morning, beautiful."

"What time is it?" she responded. "Oh, I'm sorry Mick." She gave him a quick kiss. "I've got to go look after Stigi. I should have been down to the aerie long ago." She threw the covers back and swung her long legs over the side of the bed, giving Mick a wonderful view of her trim, athletic back.

"Oh," said Mick, deflated in more ways than one. "I'll wait here for you then."

She turned to look at him and the view from that side was even better. "Oh, come along. This won't take more than a few minutes." She searched briefly on the floor before finding the chemise she had dropped there several hours before.

"Yeah," Mick said, "but Stigi doesn't like me. I think he's jealous." He didn't add that the feeling was mutual.

Karin pulled on her flying breeches and cinched the buckle. "Pooh. Stigi didn't dislike you. Besides, I'm sure he's forgotten all about you. Dragons aren't very smart, you know."

"You don't have to be smart to dislike someone and that dragon doesn't like me."

"Come on, get dressed. I'll show you how wrong you are."

As he hunted up his clothing strewn about the floor Mick remembered how his ex-wife used to make jokes about being jealous of his F-15. Mick was beginning to suspect that those jokes had been more pointed than he knew.

✧ ✧ ✧

Wiz was dreaming of Moira. She was with him again and they were back in their chambers at the Wizards' Keep, all tangled together in the big bed with the feather comforter. Moira was in his arms and she was kissing him all over.

As she covered his body with warm, wet kisses Wiz smiled and groaned in his sleep. He knew it was a dream, but he didn't want to wake up from it, ever. It was so real, so vivid. He could not only see Moira and feel her moist tongue as it stroked his flesh, even the smells were real.

Especially the smells. In fact Moira smelled like she'd had spaghetti with a particularly aggressive marinara sauce. She reeked of garlic.

Something tickled his nose and he opened his eyes to sneeze. The first thing he realized was that Moira wasn't there. The second thing he realized was that the lobster was. In fact, the lobster was basting him with garlic butter.

Wiz let out a yell and rolled away from the lobster.

The noise woke Glandurg, who threw off his cloak and grabbed Blind Fury in a single motion. Unfortunately the cloak landed on Wiz so he was temporarily immobilized.

The dwarf sprang to his feet, brandished his weapon and charged.

"Die, vile crustacean!" he yelled, just as he stepped in the puddle of garlic butter and went flying. He landed flat on his back and the lobster vanished into the darkness.

"Run, you damned bug!" the dwarf yelled after the fleeing shadow. "You'll taste my steel yet!"

"My, don't we smell delicious?" Malkin said as she came hurrying up. Wiz glared. "There's a pool back that way," she continued. "You better wash that stuff off before something comes wandering by and decides you're good enough to eat."

"Hmpf!" said Wiz, and worked his way carefully to his feet.

The aerie was an enormous gloomy cavern that stank of dragon and reminded Mick irresistibly of the hangar deck of a medieval aircraft carrier. Men and women in the plain tunics of keepers and the leathers of riders bustled about caring for their charges. Occasionally the silence would be punctuated by the scrape of a manure shovel on rock, or the bass rumble of a dragon, but for the most part the place was quiet. Even the soft leather boots of the riders made no sound on the rocky floor.

"Why do you keep it so dark?" Mick asked, thinking of the brightly lit hangars of his own experience.

"The dragons prefer it," Karin told him. "And keep your voice down. They don't like loud noises either."

They skirted three harnessed dragons on the great central floor of the aerie, keeping well clear of the powerful tails. Their riders stood by the dragons' heads petting and talking to the beasts. Mick noted the ready patrol was spotted so the dragons were well separated. Probably to keep the dragons from fighting, he decided.

Karin took something that looked like an iron rake from a rack and hefted a leather sack from the row of similar sacks beneath it.

"Currying iron," she explained. "Stigi likes to have his back scratched."

"Do you do this every day?"

"Unless I am ill or we are in the field. Contact helps build the bond between dragon and rider. Now, walk to the outside, away from the stalls. Dragons prefer those who are familiar to them."

"How long will this take?"

"Oh, not long, love. A day-tenth or so. Then I shall be free for the rest of the day." She gave him a sultry look past lowered eyelashes. "I've made arrangements with my squadron leader."

She led him along the far edge of the chamber, past the shallow caves that served as stalls for the dragons.

"We're almost here," Karin told him. "I'm sure Stigi has forgotten all about you. You'll see."

They stopped in front of a stall no different from any other. Dragon tack hung next to the entrance, clean, oiled and ready for instant use. From within came the sound of gentle snoring—*loud* gentle snoring. Through the gloom Mick could see the dragon curled up like an enormous house cat.

"Oh, Stigi," Karin called gently.

At the sound of his rider's voice, the dragon stirred lazily and opened one eye. Then he saw Mick. His head jerked erect so fast it slammed into the roof of the stall and he let out a roar that made the cavern ring. Alarmed, other dragons took up the challenge until the place echoed and re-echoed with the steam whistle bellows of upset dragons.

"He remembers you," Karin shouted over the chaos.

# Part III: Queen of the Night

## EIGHTEEN
## Life As We Wish We Didn't Know It

"So anyway . . ." Charlie leaned back against the bar and gestured expansively. "There I was at fifteen thousand feet. Nothing between me and the ground but an air mattress."

The walls might be hung with squadron banners, old riding leathers, weapons and bits of dragon harness. The floor might be stone, the ceiling hewn beams and the leather-clad men and women dragon riders, but it was still a pilot's meeting place and Charlie fit right in, international orange flight suit and all.

Two or three of the dragon riders were gathered around him at the bar, listening intently. Several more were scattered around at the tables paying half attention. Off in the corner Mick and Karin were enjoying each other's company.

"Did he really do all these things?" Karin whispered.

"They're flying stories," Mick whispered in her ear, pausing to nibble a bit on the lobe. "You know the difference between a fairy tale and a flying story? A fairy tale starts 'Once upon a time . . .' and a flying story starts 'No shit, this really happened . . .'"

Karin turned to grin at him. The move deprived Mick of an earlobe but the tradeoff wasn't that bad. "We have a similar saying. He does it well, though."

The room exploded in laughter as Charlie reached the punch line.

"Oh, he's entertaining," Mick said quietly.

"But you don't like him?"

"Let's say our styles are different. We have another saying. 'There are old pilots and there are bold pilots but there are no old, bold pilots.' Charlie's one of the, ah, boldest pilots I've ever met."

"He is not young either," Karin pointed out.

"He's lucky then. But luck runs out, especially if you push it."

The programmers' workroom was as warm and cheery as the tavern, but there were only two inhabitants. Moira had long since excused herself and now only Taj and Jerry remained. Jerry was hoarse from talking and beginning to fade around the edges, but Taj was as eager and alert as a beagle on the trail of a rabbit. There were no less than eight "screens" hanging above Jerry's desk, most tiled with several windows, as Jerry led Tajikawa through the basics of the magic compiler and how to write software for magic. Taj already had a pile of scrolls beside him to read later and he was pushing Jerry hard on subtle points of the system.

"Well, then there's this for example." Taj pointed to a section of the compiler code written in glowing letters in thin air. "It's in here but you don't seem to use it."

"Oh, that's an indeterminate instruction," Jerry told him. "You've heard of the DWIM instruction, Do What I Mean? That's kinda an 'IDAIDWP.'"

Taj cocked an eyebrow. "Ida id wip?"

"I'll Do As I Damn Well Please. You can't be sure what it will do from one time to the next."

"Cute, but why'd you write it that way?"

"We didn't. Remember, the bottom layer of the compiler, the elements we built the rest of it from, are tiny spells that exist here naturally. But we only use a subset of what's available. Some we don't use because they're redundant, as far as we can tell. But some of them, like this one, don't produce reliable results. We think it's something analogous to a quantum uncertainty effect operating on a gross level."

He pointed to the fiery letters again. "This one was particularly tricky. Most of the time it works consistently, which is why it made it into a beta of the compiler. But about one time in a hundred it does something else. Which is why we didn't use it."

"Have you got a list of those things?" Taj asked.

"The indeteriminant instructions? Some of them. Mostly we didn't bother. Why?"

"I want to play with them a little."

"Be careful. Some of those things are damn dangerous and we don't know all the dangerous ones. Why mess with them?"

"Because," the Tajmanian Devil said, "you learn the most about a system by observing it when it becomes unstable."

"Yeah, well just remember that around here when the system becomes unstable you can get caught in a system crash. It nearly happened to us once and it wasn't fun." He leaned back and rubbed his eyes. "Look, I'm about done in. How about we continue this tomorrow?

"You go on. I want to go on with this stuff a little."

Jerry hesitated. "What did you have in mind?"

"I was thinking I'd just take the docs and dive right in."

Jerry frowned. "That's not a real good idea. Danny

tried that when he first got here and ended up stuck in a DO loop."

"So? That happens."

Jerry shook his head. "You don't understand. When I say he got stuck in a DO loop, I mean *he* got stuck in a DO loop, repeating the same action over and over. Someone else had to get him out of it."

Taj looked serious. "I take your point. But I still want to keep going."

The big programmer considered. "Probably the best thing to do is start you out with some simple little nothing spells so you can get the feel of things. He glanced around and spotted some pieces of wood on Wiz's desk. "Wait a minute, here's something." He picked up a stack of slats with writing on them and handed them to Taj. "Study these and the docs tonight and we'll take a crack at them tomorrow."

The Tajmanian Devil looked at the strips of wood and cocked a quizzical eyebrow.

"This is a spell one of the wizards wrote. Only there's something wrong with it and it doesn't work. It's pretty harmless stuff, it just brightens and dims the lights, but it will give you some practice with the tool kit and the language."

"Sounds good. Where shall I work?"

"You can use Wiz's desk. Tomorrow I'll get you in on his system. When you've got that problem spotted, I've got a couple of other things around here. But don't try to do anything tonight on your own. Remember, this stuff's dangerous."

It was June who heard it first. They were picking their way down a straight section of tunnel when Danny's wife hissed and suddenly her knife was in her hand.

"What?" Wiz asked over his shoulder.

"Shut up!" Danny commanded. Everyone froze. "I hear something down that way."

"What?"

"I don't know. Shut up and let me listen, will you?"

Instinctively the group had arrayed itself facing the side tunnel. There was a faint scrape as Malkin's rapier cleared its scabbard. Glandurg strode to the front, hand on the hilt of Blind Fury.

"**\light exe!**" Wiz commanded and a globe of blue light sprang from his fingertips. He gestured and the witch light began to float down the side tunnel toward the source of the sound.

At first there was nothing to see. The tunnel was empty as far as the globe's light reached. But no, there was something . . .

For an instant Wiz thought the tunnel was carpeted in brown-and-gray fur. Then he realized the carpet was writhing as if alive. As the mass moved out into the light he saw that it was an army of rats, packed shoulder to shoulder and climbing over each other in their eagerness to get at the humans.

"Rats!" Danny yelled and he and Wiz raised their staffs simultaneously.

"**lightning rapidfire exe!**"

Lightning bolts flashed and scythed through the charging mass, slaying hundreds, but the rats closed ranks and came on. Their eyes glowed feral red in the magic light.

Wiz gestured to the floor and the earth shook, bringing dust and clods of dirt down on the party. A chasm opened before the oncoming army. The rats took no notice and kept coming. Row after row of them disappeared into the crack in the earth, but others leapt across, some of them pushing off from the backs of their fellows as they tumbled into the pit.

With a flash of steel that nearly took Wiz's nose off, Glandurg drew Blind Fury and waded into the survivors. The blade's curse kept him from hitting the rats he aimed at, but it didn't matter. No matter where he struck there were rats aplenty.

Malkin stepped forward and lashed out with her rapier, skewering rat after rat. When she had three or four writhing on her blade she flicked it back toward the mass of rats, sending her victims twisting through the air and back into the horde.

Still the rats came on. Now a dozen or more of them were scrabbling up Glandurg as if he were a ladder, seeking chinks in his armor. Danny and June were laying about, he with his staff and she with her knife. But for every rat they struck down three more charged in.

Glandurg and Malkin were in front so Wiz couldn't get a clear shot. He danced back and forth, trying to find an opening for a lightning bolt. Then suddenly he had a better idea. He raised his staff and began to chant.

The oncoming wave of rats convulsed, stopped and then turned tail and ran squealing. As quickly as the tunnel had filled with rats it was empty, save for the corpses and a few survivors locked in combat with the humans.

Three or four rats were still clinging to Glandurg, including one with its teeth buried in his cheek. Without wincing the dwarf reached up and jerked the rat free. Then he held the squealing creature up before his face and glared at it. With a single quick motion Glandurg bit the rat who had bitten him back, taking off the animal's head with a single chomp. He spat the head out and tossed the corpse away.

"Impudent pest," he muttered.

"Outasight," Danny breathed. "Say, do you listen to Ozzie Osburne?"

The dwarf only scowled. For once Wiz was glad Glandurg was on their side.

Malkin was breathing heavily and bleeding from several bites on her arms and legs. "What did you do?"

"Jamming spell," Wiz panted. "I figured those things were being driven by magic, so I interfered with any magic in the area. Once the spell was broken the rats panicked."

"Nice trick," the tall thief said as she resheathed her rapier. She looked at the bites on her sword arm. "Pity you didn't think of it sooner."

"I'll try to do better the next time," Wiz said without a trace of irony. "Meanwhile people, let's get out of here. All that magic is likely to attract more trouble."

Several hundred yards and dozens of twists and turns later, the party found a cul-de-sac where they felt safe enough to rest and treat their wounds. June had some of Moira's salve in her pack and she applied it to everyone's rat bites. Even Glandurg consented to have his wounds smeared with the pungent brown ointment. The sharp, minty smell and the plain little pot from Moira's stillroom brought a lump to Wiz's throat. He noticed that even as she treated their wounds June didn't turn her back on the tunnel entrance.

"Any idea where we are?" Wiz asked Danny.

"Lost," the younger man said as he fished into his tunic for the magic compass. He looked down at the glowing disk. "I don't know where we are, but what we're after is off that way."

"Any sign of anything else?"

Danny squinted at the detector. "Not that I can pick up. This whole area's lousy with magic, but none of it seems immediately hostile." He dropped the talisman back on his chest. "This thing's getting less effective because of all the magical interference. Pretty soon it's not going to work at all."

That was unwelcome but not unexpected so Wiz didn't reply. "Okay, spread out. Danny you take the lead this time. And look out for those side tunnels."

"Remember," Charlie told Malus for about the hundredth time, "that baby's fragile."

"Fear not, My Lord," the apple-cheeked wizard assured him. "We will be as gentle with it as a queen cat with her kits."

"I mean, I've put that baby into places it was hard to get out of, but this is ridiculous."

"It has posed a bit of a problem," Malus admitted, "but I believe we have solved it to everyone's satisfaction."

They rounded the corner of the hall in time to see an apprentice wizard moving several of blocks of stone. He was walking backward holding a wand and the blocks were bobbing along behind him like ducklings behind their mother.

Charlie stopped dead at the sight. "What's holding those rocks up? Skyhooks?"

"That is not what we call the spell," said Malus.

Charlie's eyes followed the line of floating stones across the courtyard. "You could put a bunch of helicopter pilots out of work with that."

The doors of the great hall were large enough to accommodate a cavalry dragon, but the creature would have to stoop and bend to get through. Charlie's biplane couldn't stoop and bend, so a team of workmen and a couple of wizards had spent the better part of two days taking off the doors and removing stones to expand the opening.

"We're ready, Lord," one of the workmen said as he came over to join them.

"All right," Charlie said. "Let me get into the cockpit and you put your guys on the lower wing. I'll take the brakes off and you can push it out."

"Then what, Lord?" asked the foreman.

Charlie looked around the stone-walled court and sighed. "Then I guess she'll just sit there on gate guard. No other use for her here," he added sadly.

That evening Wiz called another council of war.

"Okay people, you know we're running low on food?"

Nods all the way around. The dried vegetables, fruit

and grains that constituted this world's "iron rations" were easy to carry, but there was still a limit to how much they had brought with them.

"Well, on the theory that we'd have to head back, at least to replenish our supplies, I ran some tests this afternoon."

"Tests?" Danny asked.

Wiz grinned but there was no humor in it. "I'm developing a nasty, suspicious nature down here. I wanted to make sure we could walk the Wizard's Way with no trouble."

"I take it there was trouble?" Malkin asked dryly.

"In spades. I can't open the way. It's closed. Blocked by some kind of magical jamming."

Everyone was quiet for a moment.

"So we can't go back?" Danny asked at last.

"Looks not."

"This smells like a trap," Danny said. "Like we've been lured in."

"Lured?" asked Glandurg. "We have had to fight every step of the way. Only the power of Blind Fury has brought us this far."

That wasn't the way Wiz remembered it, but he didn't object.

"This reminds me of Shiara's tale of the cursed tomb that took her sight and magic," Malkin said quietly. "That was a trap too, but the trap was cloaked by a series of other traps designed to eliminate those who were not clever and possessed of strong magic."

There was silence while they all considered the possibilities. June moved closer to Danny and he slipped his arm around her shoulders.

"So what do we do about it?" Danny asked finally.

"Well," Wiz said slowly, "we can't go back." He looked around the group, hoping someone would dispute the point, but no one did. "So we've got to go forward against this thing."

"Seems to me we've got just one chance," Danny said at last.

"What?"

The young programmer flicked a tight little smile. "We're gonna have to be a whole lot tougher than the thing that set this trap in the first place."

"Yes!" roared Glandurg and brandished Blind Fury aloft. The gesture drove the sword into the tunnel roof, knocking a liberal shower of fine, choking dirt down on them all.

Spitting, sneezing and brushing dirt out of their eyes, the other members of the group glared at the dwarf. He grinned sheepishly and carefully returned the sword to its scabbard.

"This stuff's trickier than I thought," E.T. Tajikawa said when Jerry broke to refill his tea mug. For the last two days he had been working his way systematically through the compiler and development system, coming back to Malus' light dimming spell from time to time.

"It has its peculiarities," the big programmer agreed as he ambled over to look at Taj's work. "What's the problem?"

Taj grinned sheepishly. "Probably really simple because I can't find it. The listing looks fine."

For an instant Jerry wondered if Taj was really as good as his reputation. "Well," he asked carefully, "how does it fail?"

"That's the nasty part. It's apparently an intermittent because I can't get it to fail at all."

Jerry leaned over Taj's shoulder and peered closely at the program, running down the instructions. "That's funny. I don't see anything there that would cause an intermittent."

"You mean you don't know what's wrong with it?"

"Well, no," Jerry admitted. "Wiz was working on it when . . . well anyway. Let's see."

A quick command and Jerry executed the program. The lights in the workroom brightened promptly.

"That's real weird."

"You mean it isn't me?"

"No. That's what it's supposed to do. Except Malus said it didn't work."

"I think," Taj said slowly, "maybe we'd better have a talk with this Malus character."

Jerry hesitated. Of all the problems they faced, a sticky light switch spell was far and away the least important. But Taj was quivering like a bird dog and the truth was that Jerry wasn't getting anywhere with what he was doing. *What the heck?* he thought, *we might learn something.*

They found Malus in the Wizards' Day Room, digesting lunch and talking to a few of his fellow wizards. Winter sun filtered weakly though the large diamond-paned windows and a small fire in the carved stone fireplace took the chill off the air. Magic provided most of the heat and light but the fire and windows added warmth and coziness.

"Malus, could you try this spell again?"

"Certainly, My Lord," the wizard said, getting up from his chair. "Have you found the problem?"

"I'm not sure. I want to see you do it."

"Very well."

Malus picked up the wooden strips, arranged them on a small table and then spoke the command.

Instead of brightening, the magic glow lamps in the Day Room flickered, dimmed, brightened and then dropped to a febrile glimmer.

Jerry and Taj looked at each other in the sudden gloom.

"Let me try," Jerry said.

This time the spell worked perfectly.

"That doesn't make . . ."

"Wait a minute!" Taj cut him off. "Do you each have physically separate copies of the compiler or are they all just instantations of the same compiler?"

Jerry looked at him. "I don't know. I never thought about it"

"Might be interesting to find out," Taj said.

"My Lord," Jerry said to the little wizard, "will you list out the compiler for me?"

It was Malus' turn to frown. "Very well. "**Emac.**"

Instantly a little demon with a green eyeshade popped into existence. Jerry noticed it was rounder than the ones he was used to. In fact it looked a lot like Malus himself.

"**?**" the demon said.

"**list compiler exe**," Malus pronounced, and the demon removed a quill pen from behind a large bat-like ear and began to scribble lines of fiery letters in the air.

The compiler was big and took a while. By now several other wizards had gathered around to watch.

"Shall I list out the libraries and include files as well, My Lord?" Malus asked when the Emac at last completed its task.

"No, this is fine for now," Jerry told him. "**Emac**." he commanded, and proceeded to order the demon to list out the compiler again. Taj watched closely, but aside from the fact that Malus' Emac wrote in letters of golden fire and Jerry's preferred electric blue he couldn't see any difference.

"Now," he said, as the second demon finished.

"**Emac**."

The blue fire superimposed itself on the yellow. Suddenly several sections of the code stood out in brilliant green.

"Your version of the spell compiler. It's different." Jerry checked the changed sections against Malus' spell. "Your spell didn't work because something messed with your copy of the compiler. The program was fine but the tool was broken."

"But, My Lord, I can assure you I have done nothing to change it!"

"I believe you," Jerry said. *And,* he didn't add aloud, *that's what scares me.*

A quick check of the other wizards present in the day room showed that two of them had compilers which had suffered minor changes, but none so great as Malus'.

"I wonder how many other broken copies of the compiler are loose around the castle? Or broken anything else?" Jerry said as the last wizard in the group checked out clean. "I think we'd better start a sweep of the software."

"You go ahead," Taj told him. "I've got some stuff I want to check up on."

Jerry was so engrossed in the problem he only nodded, forgetting his objections to Taj going out on his own.

"Well," Jerry said tiredly a few hours later, "we were lucky. So far we've only turned up a half-dozen infected programs." He leaned back in his chair and rubbed his eyes. "Maybe more than lucky. We didn't exactly build the spells to be virus-proof but we were real conservative in our design. There's an error-correcting code built into every spell and if the check sums and such don't match it won't execute. Plus the critical stuff uses triple redundancy."

"I noticed," Taj said. "Is there any pattern to what's been attacked?"

"Not that I can find. There's a lot of stuff here that's been nibbled around the edges but aside from Malus' copy of the compiler nothing else serious is really broken. Damn! I wish Wiz and Danny were here."

"Need some more insights, eh?"

"That's part of it. But now I'm going to have to go

through and design anti-virus software to protect every spell we've got. It would be easier if there were three of us doing it."

Taj looked at the changed code again. "Who's writing these puppies?"

Jerry shrugged. "If I had to guess I'd say it's our enemy in the City of Night."

"Seems kind of piddly for a deliberate attack. Are you sure none of your students worked these up?"

Jerry shook his head. "You don't understand how seriously these people take magic. This isn't like a bunch of bored high school kids or out-of-work Bulgarians. Everyone here respects magic too much to do something like this for the hell of it."

Taj looked skeptical. "This thing came from somewhere."

"Yeah," Jerry said. "And that's what worries me. One more thing that worries me."

*Moira rose dripping from the bath. The water streamed off, making little rivulets between her shoulderblades and breasts, splitting at her swelling belly and dripping off her sparse orange thatch of pubic hair. She stepped out onto the tiled floor and a skeletal hand offered her a towel.*

*She accepted it without noticing either her attendant's appearance or smell. In life the zombie maid had been a harem attendant for a mighty wizard of the Dark League. She had died on the surface when her master's palace collapsed and had lain there until the new master of the City of Night had claimed her. Even in this cold land, decay had set in while she lay dead on the surface and now that she was often in the steamy atmosphere of the bath her rotting flesh seethed with maggots.*

*Neither sight nor smell mattered to Moira's body or the intelligence that animated it. Bathing was necessary for human health, so Moira bathed, following barely remembered rituals gleaned from the dead brains of its other servants.*

*In the same way the body was fed, exercised and rested, cared for as a brood mare is cared for. Not for the sake of the body, but for the sake of what it would bear. Or more correctly, what would be torn from it at the proper time, since natural childbirth played no more role in the Enemy's plans than did a normal child.*

*Oblivious, unseeing and uncaring, Moira finished rubbing herself down and accepted the shift and long, fur-lined black robe from her shambling attendant. Then she sat as the decaying creature tenderly but clumsily pulled on her boots.*

*Warmth is important to human health as well.*

"Okay," E. T. Tajikawa said, "there's part of your problem."

Jerry, Bal-Simba and Moira all crowded around the table. Jerry squinted at the glowing letters over the Tajmanian Devil's desk. Some of them were the conventional magic notation used for writing spells in the code compilers. Others were odd symbols he had never seen before. The result made no sense at all.

Squatting underneath was the demon the code fragment manifested.

It had a nasty sneer on its face—or at least on its top, Jerry amended. The thing sat on six spindly legs like a demented version of a Lunar Lander. The main body was cylindrical and semi-transparent. Inside were vague outlines of something coiled into a long spiral. The top, where the face was, was a regular geometric solid, a dodecahedron, he realized after making a quick count of the edges on each surface.

"What the heck is it?"

"It's a virus," Taj told him. "You've got an infection in your system."

"Holy shit," Jerry breathed. "But how?"

Taj just shrugged.

Jerry tore his eyes away from the demon and examined the spell more closely.

"Does that make any sense to you?" Taj asked.

Jerry just shook his head. "For one thing it's not entirely in standard magic notation. More than that, well, it just doesn't make a lot of sense. What does it do?"

"It attaches itself to a spell and starts shifting instructions around or combining them."

Jerry bit his lower lip. There was something terribly wrong with this but he couldn't quite put his finger on what yet.

"Could it be a weapon?"

"If it is it's a piss-poor one. The thing's not very destructive and it's hardly hidden at all. It doesn't polymorph and if you know the sequence you can **grep** it out of any spell it's in."

Everyone was silent for a moment.

"There's something not right about this," Jerry said finally.

"That appears to be an understatement," Bal-Simba said mildly.

"No, I mean there's something *really* wrong here. Something we're missing."

Moira cocked her serpent-like head. "Another of your premonitions?"

"More like a feeling, but yeah. That sort of thing."

Moira furrowed her scaly brow. She had been more intimately associated with the programmers than Bal-Simba or any of the other wizards and she knew Jerry's knack for spotting problems even if he couldn't quite grasp the whole.

"You've never had a virus here before?" Taj asked.

Jerry shook his head. "Now that it's happened I can see how it could, but no."

"Hmm," Bal-Simba said, staring at the glowing letters. "Do you think it is related?"

"Directly? No. But I suspect it's a manifestation of

the same kind of underlying phenomenon. Sort of the fundamental particle of your problem."

"And it works by sticking stuff together," Jerry said in an effort to forestall the inevitable. "Let me guess, you call this a glue-on, right?"

Taj brightened. "Hey, that's a good name for it."

"Me and my big mouth," Jerry muttered. "Anyway, it still doesn't explain who our enemy is."

"What about," Taj said slowly, "the possibility that the glue-on arose naturally? It's not very complicated. Only about a dozen basic instructions."

"I suppose that's possible," Jerry said equally slowly. "Like I say, we've never seen that. But we really haven't been here long."

"Where do you suppose all these complicated magical phenomena come from?"

"Around here that's like asking why the sky is blue. They just are."

"The sky's blue for a reason," Taj pointed out.

"It's something we never really wondered about."

Taj smiled, looking more satanic than ever. "Those are the ones that get you in the worst trouble."

While Jerry chewed on that Taj went back to wandering about the room restlessly, looking at things without quite seeing them. He came to rest in front of Danny's magical fish tank and suddenly froze like a bird dog coming on point. The rainbow denizens of the tank were oblivious to him, but everyone else in the room was suddenly watching him intently.

"Those fish aren't natural, are they?"

"No, that's something Danny was working on for his son," Jerry told him.

"Do they change?" he asked in a peculiar voice.

Jerry frowned, remembering his earlier misgivings. "Yeah. He made them so they'd change over time. They kinda mutate."

"But they don't follow a pre-programmed pattern?"

"I don't think so."

Taj turned back to the fish tank and stared fascinated.

"Bingo!" he breathed softly. "Oh, boy howdy!"

"You've found something?"

"Alfie."

"Huh?"

"Alfie—A-Life, you know artificial life."

"What do you guys know about artificial life?"

Jerry shrugged. "It only got hot after we came here. We've been following the newsgroups on the net."

"It's a very rapidly developing field."

"As good as its hype?"

Taj snorted. "Get real. But they're still getting some interesting results, especially with evolutionary systems." He paused. "What's more, I'll bet your enemy isn't 'someone', it's 'something'—the mother of all artificial life programs."

*Zombie army ants.* The phrase flashed in Jerry's mind.

"Meaning the thing's not alive?"

Taj shrugged. "Define 'life' and I'll tell you. What it definitely means is that you've got stuff breeding out there."

"Wait a minute, A-life has to have a purpose. There's a design."

Taj gave another of his satanic smiles. "Teleological reasoning. The A-life we're familiar with is designed originally because humans created it. But there's nothing that says there has to be a designer. If you've got the right conditions and the right precursors it could arise spontaneously." He looked over at the fish tank. "Offhand I'd say you have the right conditions here.

"From what you've told me, there's natural magic everywhere, but the spells didn't combine very well. So now you guys come along and develop your spell compiler that sticks little spells together and eventually these things pick up the trick."

"But we didn't write anything like that," Jerry protested.

"Not necessary that you do. This kind of genetic crossover has been known for a long time in bacteria and a couple of workers have produced it in artificial life programs." He frowned. "So then the question is, how much available resources do they have? You sort of indicated that magic is an infinite resource here, right?"

"Well, not exactly. Some areas are more magical than others. There are dead zones all through the Wild Wood, for instance. And at times you can produce something like a magical drain effect and some resources become scarce. Wiz did that in his attack on the City of Night." It was his turn to frown. "But that kind of thing is rare. There's an awful lot of available magic out there."

Taj nodded. "Makes sense. If you're really resource constrained it's hard to get any kind of complex development. You get the equivalent of lichens and algae. If there's no constraint you lose a potent driver for evolution. But if there's a lot of resources before you hit the constraints . . ." he shrugged.

"Jeez," Jerry muttered.

"Okay, now suppose that these things are out there, these little spells, competing for resources. It becomes survival of the fittest. The things that can grab the most resources and hold on to them best survive longest."

"And we started that?"

Taj pursed his lips. "Actually that probably pre-dates you. I suspect that's where this world's naturally occurring demons and such come from. What you added were code fragments that made it easier for pieces to combine."

"So we are responsible."

"Law of nature, man. You can't do just one thing. Anyway, eventually this proto-evolutionary process turns out our friend the glue-on." He nodded toward the desktop where the virus sat. Jerry thought it didn't look like anyone's friend, but before he could say that, Taj was off again. "Now you throw in something like this recombinant virus and the things that survive are the ones that get reproduced."

He shrugged. "Kind of like an artificial life version of Core Wars, only we're in the core." He laughed. "Evolution in action. I'll bet by now there's a whole ecology out there."

"Wonderful," groaned Jerry.

"That too," Taj agreed, obviously having missed his tone. "The big question is how high a lambda have you got?"

"Lambda?"

"Information mutability. If information is hard to change you stifle any kind of evolution. If it's too easy to change self-organization doesn't have a chance. There's a fairly narrow band where A-life is possible."

Jerry thought about that. He didn't like it, but it made sense. "We know some areas are less magical than others. The whole place around the City of Night is an especially magically active zone. Plus there's a lot of leftover magic down there from the days of the Dark League."

"And we have kept scant watch there," Bal-Simba rumbled. "My fault, I am afraid."

"So," Taj said, "these things had the equivalent of a petri dish where they could grow and evolve. And now you've got something that's looking to spread out."

"Why is it so hostile?"

"Because that's the way it evolved. Maybe it gives the thing an edge in surviving, maybe it's an accidental characteristic, like something it picked up along the way."

"Point is, that it's out there and that's the most likely explanation for what's going on here." Taj shook his head. "Boy, what the guys at the Santa Fe Institute wouldn't give to see this."

"What we wouldn't give to see the last of it," Jerry retorted. "The real question is how do we stop it?"

"Now that," said the Tajmanian Devil, "is going to take a little thought."

"More strangeness, Lord."

Bal-Simba had had about all the strangeness he could stand in the last few weeks, but he forbore to say so to the chief Watcher. "What and where?" he asked.

Erus, the head of the watchers, was a lean gray-haired man with a broken beak of a nose and fierce blue eyes. Years of stooping over a scrying crystal had left him with a permanent slouch.

"Where is to the south, out over the Freshened Sea. As to what . . . " He shrugged. "They travel in groups, and they seek darkness or clouds, but each day they range further north."

Bal-Simba grunted. "Enough of both at this time of the year, what with long nights and winter storms over the Freshened Sea. You say you have never encountered them before. What are they most like?"

Erus hesitated. Like most of those in his line of work he disliked making guesses, but for him as for all of them guessing was part of the job. "Lord, they appear to be ridden dragons, at least for the most part."

"For the most part?"

"There are other things as well, but not so many. Mostly they seem to be dragons, but of an odd sort."

"Odd in what way?"

"Like the rest of this thing's magic—cold." He looked up at Bal-Simba. "Lord, I have never seen anything like it. Nor have any of the other Watchers."

"What do you think they are doing?"

"I cannot say with certainty, but it appears they are scouting, perhaps testing our defenses. At their present rate they will reach our lands ere long."

Bal-Simba considered. "Then best we seek these things out to see what they are. Order our patrols south again, but cautiously. And try to steer them to a small group they can meet in overwhelming strength."

"Jerry tells me you have developed a weapon against our enemy," Bal-Simba said without preamble as he walked into the programmers' work room.

"Yep," Taj said proudly. "It's a lysing virus. Or maybe a self-reproducing restriction enzyme would be a better way to describe it."

Jerry squinted at the code hanging above the desk Taj was using. "Describing it in English would be better yet."

"Okay," Taj said. "Basically the problem is that this virus of the enemy's glues spells together, with some transcription errors. Then those new spells compete against each other in what amounts to a Core Wars tournament where only the fittest survive. Eventually the winners get big and nasty."

He gestured to the code. "What this virus does is exactly the opposite. It breaks spells into pieces at certain specific points, sort of makes them come unglued."

"What's going to prevent this thing from running wild and reducing every piece of code to rubble?"

Tajikawa smiled, looking more satanic than ever. "It won't affect a piece of code smaller than a certain size."

"Wait a minute. How do you keep the anti-virus from mutating?"

Again the satanic smile. "You can't. It has to mutate if it's going to do its job because the sticky virus is going to mutate. But we can make sure it won't attack anything smaller than the limit. Here, take a look."

Jerry scanned the indicated portion of the code.

Taj reached past him and pointed to several sections of the listing. "You will note that there is *not* a test in there for code size. Nor is it localized to one part of the program. It's more subtle than that."

Jerry nodded. "Clever."

"As far as we know there are no programs that big. None of yours anyway. It won't prevent things from forming, but it will limit their size and that will probably limit their power."

"Probably?"

Taj shrugged. "Theoretically these things could become efficient enough to be pretty potent within that limit, but with the smaller code sizes the global minima tend to be in pretty steep wells on the state surface. Plus there are a lot of local minima to act as traps. A genetic algorithm might reach a minimum but it would be pretty much a random event. Like the monkeys at the typewriters trying to produce Shakespeare." He frowned. "Of course there is a question of how many monkeys and typewriters we've got here." He got a faraway look as he considered the problem.

"Will this thing leave us worse off?" asked Bal-Simba, who had understood perhaps a quarter of what Tajikawa had just said.

"No."

"Then we will do it." He paused. "How long will it take for this thing to work?"

"It starts as soon as we tell it to execute," Taj said. "It will start here and then spread like the original virus did."

"Wait a minute," Jerry said, "how long will it take to affect what's in the City of Night?"

"That's a ways from here right?"

"And it's protected by some kind of magic barrier."

"Oh, the barrier shouldn't be a problem. Eventually it will diffuse through or be carried through by an infected spell."

"How long," Jerry asked slowly, "is eventually?"

"Fermi numbers, around ten years."

Bal-Simba looked at him. "What kind of numbers?"

"Fermi numbers. You know, within an order of magnitude."

"In other words," Jerry added, "it could happen in anywhere from one year to a century." He shook his head. "But even a year is way too long."

"Well, if you're closer it would strike faster. If you're right next to this thing when you invoke the program it would get it right away."

Jerry sighed. "Okay then. We're going to have to get in there to make this work."

"That will not be easy," Bal-Simba told him.

"Wiz and the others did it."

"I am afraid that way is blocked now," Bal-Simba told him. "We cannot walk the Wizard's Way and the city is ever-more-strongly guarded by the Enemy's non-living servants."

"There's another problem," Taj pointed out. "This thing's likely to react to your presence, right?"

"I would call that an understatement," rumbled Bal-Simba.

"Well, understand, it's going to take the lysing virus a while to work on anything that's fairly complicated. If this thing has developed something like an immune system to keep it from being taken over by the competition, it may take a few hours, or even days." He caught the others' expressions. "Too long, huh?"

"For the main enemy, way too long. The first thing it will try to do is eat our lunch—and us with it. We can't wait hours, we need to knock it down immediately."

"How inorganic," Taj sighed. "All right, let's go back and take it from first principles again."

They took special care to find a secure resting place that evening. Malkin seemed abstracted all through the dinner meal, but she didn't say anything until they were finished.

"I have been thinking about what you said, about the monsters getting more dangerous as we come closer to our goal," she said to Wiz as they cleaned the last of the dinner dishes.

"And?"

"Have the monsters been getting more dangerous?"

Wiz thought about it. "No, not really."

"And have we encountered greater numbers of them?"

An ugly little prickle of his neck hair told Wiz he wasn't going to like where this was going. "No," he admitted.

"Then," Malkin asked, "are we sure we are getting closer to our goal?"

"Well, the seeker says we're going in the right direction."

Malkin just looked at him.

"I'm really beginning to wonder about that seeker," Danny said. "I know this place is big but we should be at least a little closer to Moira than when we started."

"Maybe it's been getting brighter so slowly we didn't notice," Wiz suggested.

Malkin reached out and tapped his shoulder. "The glow only extends out to this smudge on your right breast. That's where it was yesterday and the day before."

"Are you sure?"

"Trust me. In my profession you notice these things. You always hold the crystal in the same place, straight out from your breastbone to the length of the cord around your neck."

Wiz thought about that. Then he looked down at the crystal. Then he thought about it some more. Not very pleasant thoughts.

"Let's see something."

"**Emac**."

Instantly a two-foot-high demon with a big bald head, flapping ears, glasses and a green eyeshade appeared before him.

"?," said the little demon.

**"backslash list find_moira exe."**

The creature took a quill pen from behind one enormous ear and began to scribble fiery letters in the air. Wiz and his fellow adventurers were soon bathed in warm yellow light from the golden letters hanging before them.

"Wait a minute!" Danny said almost as soon as the Emac finished writing. "That doesn't look right." He pointed with his staff at a section of the code.

"It's not," Wiz said sourly. "Neither is that," he added as his staff jabbed out, "that or that."

"The spell's been sabotaged!"

"Who?" demanded Glandurg. "Who has played such a foul trick upon us?"

"If I had to guess, I'd say the Enemy," Wiz said. "Okay folks, gather around, it's conference time."

The party sat down on a convenient patch of rocks and all of them looked at Wiz expectantly. "Well," he said to break the silence, "what are our options?"

No one wanted to mention the obvious one: Give up, try to make their way to the surface and wait for rescue.

"Dwarves can find their way underground," Danny suggested. "Perhaps Glandurg can guide us?"

"I would have to know where we were going," the dwarf said shortly. "Impractical."

"Besides," Malkin said, "he tends to get lost."

"Slander," hissed the dwarf.

"Okay, settle down, people. The important thing is it won't work." Glandurg and Malkin glared at each other but obeyed.

"What about re-casting the seeker spell?" Malkin asked after a minute.

"Hard to do. We could write a new spell easily enough, but we need something like a lock of Moira's hair to focus the spell." He sighed. "If Moira's personality were still with her body we could work something up to seek that, but otherwise we've got to have something intimately connected with her."

"Her cloak," June said from her place beside Danny. "Like mine."

"Similarity isn't good enough I'm afraid."

"From the same cloth. Made at the same time."

With a pang Wiz remembered the long summer afternoons when Moira and June had sat together under a rose bower at Wizards' Keep, sewing the matching cloaks for the coming winter and watching Ian and Caitlin romp among the rose bushes. Sometimes they had worked together, with a cloak stretched across their knees as they sat side by side or across from each other.

"Wait a minute! You both worked on Moira's cloak, didn't you?"

June nodded.

"Did you ever prick your finger while you worked and get blood on the cloak?"

A hesitation and then another nod.

"Jackpot! Okay, we can do this then."

Everyone looked at him. "DNA," he explained. "If June got blood on the cloak her DNA is still on there."

"Washed it," June said defensively.

"I'm sure you didn't get it all out. We can home on your DNA."

Danny grinned. "Yeah, and because it's uniquely hers it will stand out almost as strongly as a true name." Then his face fell. "Wait a minute. How are you going to make it sensitive enough to find June's blood on Moira's cloak with June standing right here?"

"I've got a way to make a spell directional, like an antenna. As long as June's not in the beam, her presence won't interfere."

"Let's get to it, then."

In the event it took several hours to produce and check the spell. Part of that was because Wiz and Danny took good care to armor the code against tampering and to sprinkle alarms throughout the program to warn of attempted subversion. Part of it was the usual quota of unexpected problems and glitches. Part of it was simply that it's harder to work sitting on rocks in a cave than it is in your own workroom. So while Glandurg fidgeted, Malkin watched and June did whatever June did, the pair turned out a new spell.

The only real difficulty came in drawing a sample of June's blood for comparison. June was so eager to help she slashed a four-inch gash in her arm and Wiz and Danny had to break off preparing the spell to give her first aid.

Finally they held up the finished product and commanded it to find Moira. Almost instantly the pointer lit up and swung around, pointing almost back the way they had come.

"Wonderful," Danny said glumly. "We have been going in the wrong direction."

Wiz ached to get going in the new direction but common sense prevailed. "In the morning. Let's get a good night's rest and then we'll head out. And this time we'll be heading for Moira."

Honesty compelled him to admit that what they'd actually be heading for was Moira's cloak. There was no guarantee Moira would still be with it. He tried very hard to push that thought out of his mind.

They moved out the next morning in good order and somber spirits. Once again Malkin led the way and Wiz followed, staff at the ready. His senses were alert but his mind was elsewhere. Malkin was right. The defenses of this place didn't make any sense in the real world. They made sense in terms of a fantasy role-playing game, but there weren't any fantasy role-playing games here. The only people in this World now who knew about such things were Danny, Jerry and himself. There had been Craig and Mikey, two computer crackers who had come to this World and hooked up with the forces of prima chaos. But Craig was dead and Mikey was a mindless husk held under tight guard at the Wizards' Keep. So where had the idea come from?

*Damn,* he thought for about the thousandth time, *I wish we knew what we are fighting.*

"Well," E.T. Tajikawa said, "there's your weapon."

On the table sat a golden globe about the size of a softball.

"Behold the Holy Hand Grenade of Antioch," Taj said with a sweeping gesture. "It's what you might call an anti-takeover device—a poison pill."

"You intend to poison the Enemy?" Bal-Simba asked.

"Actually we're going to hand him a retrovirus and he's going to do a number on himself."

Both Bal-Simba and Jerry waited for him to continue.

"It started with those indeterminate instructions, the ones you call I'll Do As I Damn Well Please, IDAIDWP."

His audience looked apprehensive. "Go on," the big wizard said slowly."

"Okay, first I divided them into two categories: Regular IDAIDWP and FU-IDAIDWP."

"Foo ida id wip?" Jerry asked.

"Eff you ida id wip," Taj corrected. "What you might call IDAIDWP with an attitude. Anyway, I rolled the FU-IDAIDWPs into the nastiest package I could dream up, added some interface code to make it easy for the Enemy to absorb and wrapped it in the prettiest package I could find." He gestured. "Viola."

"That's voila."

Taj gave him his satanic grin. "Not the way I play it."

Taj looked at Jerry. "Okay, you say this thing's instinct is to absorb whatever's tossed at it?"

"Well, humans that attack it, anyway."

"Close enough. Essentially what this thing does is to insert a sequence with a bunch of indeterminate instructions into the thing's code. You feed it to The Blob out there and the critter self-destructs."

"Nasty," Jerry said. "I like it." He paused. "What's the downside?"

Taj pursed his lips. "Well, there is one thing that might be a problem. It's got to be absorbed all at once so we've got to get pretty close to make it work."

"How close?"

"For immediate effect? About hand grenade range."

For a minute no one said anything. "So we've got to jump down this thing's throat, right?"

Taj shrugged. "If you want it to work right away and if you want to be sure you get the main bad guy."

No one said anything. "There's another problem," Taj added helpfully. "This thing's been bred to learn quick. If you don't make it the first time it will be a whole lot harder the next time." He paused and looked hard at them. "Basically I'd say we've got one shot at this."

Another pause. "I believe," said Bal-Simba, "this is what Charlie would call a sporty proposition."

# NINETEEN
# Operational Plan

With the weapon came the stirrings of a plan. Soon the Wizards' Keep was abuzz with preparations. Since the Watchers were still unable to establish communication with Wiz and his party, the first order of business was to combine an attack on the Enemy with a rescue operation. In his or her own way everyone readied themselves for what was to come.

"So this is what the enemy stronghold looks like?" Kuznetsov asked Jerry as they walked down the stone-walled tunnel.

"Something like this. Only smaller and not as neat."

The Russian sized up the space with the professional interest of an engineer who had been given the job of building the place—or a sapper who had the job of blowing it up.

Kuznetsov had wanted to see what the "battlefield" would look like. The closest thing Jerry could come up with was the cellars and storerooms under the Wizards' Keep. It wasn't that close to the tunnels beneath the City of Night, but Kuznetsov assured him it would help.

"Now there're a lot more levels and twists and turns," Jerry added as Kuznetsov knelt down to examine the way the stones fit. He produced a knife and scratched at the space between the rocks, held the scrapings to his nose and sniffed them.

"But just this mortar? No concrete?"

Jerry thought for an instant. "I've never seen concrete in this World."

Kuznetsov grunted, stood up, and then said something quickly to Vasily. The other Russian nodded and set off down the tunnel.

"And these lamps." Kuznetsov indicated the magic glow light that floated above their head. "This is standard illumination?"

"Yeah. What's Vasily doing?"

"We are seeing how close enemy can get before we see him. This is very important in urban combat."

"This isn't exactly a city."

Kuznetsov grinned. "I believe your saying is 'Close enough for government work.' " He looked down the tunnel and motioned to his partner. Peering out past the edges of the light, Jerry couldn't see him, but apparently Kuznetsov could.

"Now he comes back hiding behind cover and in shadows," Kuznetsov said without taking his eyes off the tunnel. "The way an enemy would approach."

By straining his eyes Jerry thought he could detect an occasional flicker of movement down the corridor. Finally, when Vasily was almost on them he caught a glimpse of him sidling along a wall and whipping into an open storeroom.

"He's really good."

"He was a specialist," Kuznetsov said, and smiled as if he had made a joke.

There was an explosion of Russian from the storeroom and Vasily came charging out with no attempt to hide. He pointed back to the room and spat out something long and complicated in Russian.

Kuznetsov whistled. "Da shto ve gavorete?"

"Po pravda!" Vasily confirmed.

"What was that about?" Jerry asked.

The Russian looked at Jerry strangely. "Let us say we just discovered that our paths have crossed before indirectly. You might even say that you are the ones who got us started in our present line of work." He waved away Jerry's frown. "Never mind. It was another time and another country."

The Russians were silent as they climbed the stairs from the cellar. They declined Jerry's offer of a warming drink.

"Comrade Major, do you realize what this means?" Vasily hissed in Russian as soon as Jerry turned the corner.

"It means we have solved another mystery my friend. Now we know how the computer disappeared from the airplane."

Kuznetsov sighed and grinned. "It takes you back, does it not, to the days when the world was young, our hearts were pure and there was no problem in human relations which could not be solved by the application of sufficient quantities of high explosive?"

He sighed once more. "Life was so much simpler then."

"Complexity?" Bal-Simba echoed in bewilderment.

"Complexity," Taj repeated with a satanic grin. "The weakness of all centralized systems is that they cannot handle complexity beyond a certain level."

"And you are certain of this?"

He spread his hands. "It's inherent in the state equations. If we wanna give this boy indigestion we start by giving him a nervous breakdown."

"What in the world are you doing?" Jerry asked as he walked into the workroom.

"Origami," Taj said cheerfully. "Great way to relax."

Jerry looked over the collection of cranes and other creatures scattered over the benchtop.

"Parchment's kind of scarce. We can't waste it on stuff like that."

"Oh, it's not a waste," Taj said cheerfully. Then he held up his latest creation. "See, here's a dragon."

Jerry looked past the long-necked shape at the litter of parchment scraps on the table. "It's still not a very good use for parchment."

Taj smiled evilly. "Wanna bet?"

The rhythmic scrape-scrape-scrape told Gilligan that Vasily was sharpening something. When he got close he saw it wasn't a knife or a sword. It was a small shovel with a two-foot handle. An entrenching tool in fact.

"Where'd you find that?"

"Castle smith made it for me," the Russian told him. He laid the stone aside and sighted down the shovel blade, turning it slightly so the light struck the edge. "Almost ready now."

"Going to dig your way out of trouble?"

In a single cat-like motion Vasily twisted and hurled the entrenching tool overhand. It flew end-over-end and buried itself in a post twenty feet away with a *twang*. The shovel stuck there with its handle vibrating from the force of the impact.

"Good for digging, too," The Russian said. Then he walked over and wrenched the blade out of the timber.

Gilligan nodded. "Where's Kuznetsov?"

Vasily inspected the edge of the blade critically. "With the big wizard," he said without looking up.

Gilligan himself had spent a good part of the time trying to figure out how he could get into the battle. As a pilot with nearly two thousand hours in Air Force fighters he felt supremely confident. Unfortunately riding a dragon takes a different skill set than flying an F-15.

Besides which, the dragons didn't like him. Every time he entered the aerie he was greeted by growls and roars from the monsters. Gilligan suspected that Stigi had been talking. Karin said that was impossible, but Gilligan knew better.

✧ ✧ ✧

Of course planning was the major form of preparation.

"It is in our favor that nothing has tried strongly to breach the physical barriers," Bal-Simba told the group assembled in his work room. "The Enemy has not had the opportunity to learn how to defend against it."

"It seems to have put up defenses enough," Dragon Leader remarked as he studied the magical map showing the known patrol routes from the City of Night.

"We think that's more reflex than planning," Jerry said. "If you'll notice these tracks pretty much match the Dark League's patrolling when they controlled the city. But circumstances have changed and that leaves holes here," he said as he stabbed a finger onto the map, "here and especially to the south."

"What's more, they're not flying smart," Gilligan said, "at least not from what the Watchers have seen."

"We have not been allowed to test these fliers yet." There was a note of reproach in Dragon Leader's voice.

"That will come soon enough," Bal-Simba told him. "Meanwhile we do not want to, ah, 'tip our fingers.' "

"That's tip our hand," Jerry corrected. "Yeah, we want them dumb when we hit them."

Bal-Simba caught his air group commander's expression. "Never fear, you will have the opportunity to test them very soon, but under controlled conditions."

"Meanwhile," Jerry said, "the basic plan for the main attack will be to lure him out over the Freshened Sea with a dummy strike and then hit from another direction."

"Bakka Valley," Gilligan said.

Kuznetsov nodded. "*Konyechno*. We spoof them to show themselves and then the second wave eliminates them."

Dragon Leader nodded. "We can expect most of their air power to be drawn north, but that still leaves their ground defenses, plus whatever they hold back for point defense."

"Well, there's a trick we used on the second Schweinfurt raid," Charlie said.

Gilligan did a quick calculation and gave Charlie a hard look.

The older man caught it. "Okay," he amended. "*Someone* used it when the Eighth hit Schweinfurt the second time."

Dragon Leader ignored the byplay. "There is still the problem of the inner defenses."

"We may just have to fight our way through those," Bal-Simba said. "Expensive, I know."

"Maybe we can come up with something as we go along," Jerry added.

Dragon Leader looked thoughtfully at the map.

# TWENTY
# SKY ZOMBIES

*Well,* Dragon Leader thought, *at least the rain has stopped.* Not that much of an improvement. The air was clammy with moisture and the cold and damp seeped into everything. There were no warming spells which might give them away to the enemy they sought so carefully.

Dragon Leader pulled his inner flying cloak closer about him, breathing in the odor of lanolin as he drew air through the thick wool to try to keep out the cold. Behind him nearly a full squadron of the North's dragon cavalry spread out in stepped formation. It was no comfort to him to know the riders were all as miserable as he was.

Somewhere ahead of them lay—what? The forces of the Enemy. Probably other dragon cavalry, so the Watchers said, but his job was to find out for certain. His other job was to be cautious in doing it. Well enough, this wasn't the time for open battle if it could be avoided, and he and his troop would go carefully.

He scanned the sky ahead, eyes always moving, looking off the center of his vision to catch any movement. Not that he could see far. The wan winter sun was nearly at its zenith, but below them was a solid gray mass of fog-like cloud, tinged with rainbow where the sun caught it right.

Dragon Leader shifted uneasily in his saddle. He didn't like this at all. Fighting in clouds was bad business and according to the Watchers their quarry preferred clouds and darkness to light. That was odd, but not unknown.

Dragons, being sight hunters, preferred to fly by day. Just one more peculiarity to weigh upon him.

"Dragon Leader," came a voice in his ear. "Dragon Leader, we have your target at widdershins low. Range about three leagues." Dragon Leader did not break communications silence to acknowledge the message. Instead he rose in his stirrups and signaled his squadron into attack formation. The less magic used now the harder it would be for the enemy to detect them.

Behind him the squadron tightened up and sorted itself out into pairs and simultaneously into a box formation. Almost, Dragon Leader nodded approval. Weeks of hard drill had paid off. The movement was as smooth and precise as any veteran squadron during the long war against the Dark League. The dragons were carefully spaced to provide the maximum amount of maneuvering room consistent with interlocking fields of fire. Dragon Leader reached behind him in the saddle and drew his great bow from its scabbard. Then he selected an iron death arrow from the quiver by his right knee and fitted it loosely to the string. With a practiced motion of the right hand he pulled the straps securing him to the saddle tight, but not too tight. Then he turned his full attention to scouting ahead.

The white crystal set into his saddle horn began to darken on the left side. Magic in that direction, then. He signaled the squadron onto a new heading. The magic detector was passive and emitted almost no magic of its own, but it was not very sensitive. He knew that the Watchers in the Wizards' Keep were following them closely, but at this distance they could not follow the battle in fine detail. Once the enemy was sighted they would be able to see through the eyes of the dragon riders but for now they could not help them locate the enemy.

Following the directions of the detector Dragon Leader led his squadron lower until his dragon's wingtips almost touched the rainbow-tinged clouds. Still no sign of the enemy, but something was making the dragons very nervous. Dragon Leader's own mount nearly shied beneath him and out of the corner of his eye he saw others toss their heads in unease.

One of the flight leaders waved, relaying a signal from further out in the patrol. Dragons in sight! Dragon Leader strained his eyes and saw dark, amorphous forms rising out of the clouds toward them. With a touch of his knees he wheeled his mount around to set up an attack as soon as the enemy came out of the clouds.

Definitely ridden dragons. But there was something strange about them. Dragon Leader pushed the uneasiness out of his mind and drew his war bow. Ahead of him the leader of the third, left-most, flight lined up for the first attack.

The enemy dragons glided up out of the clouds with their wings outstretched. First one rider's head broke the mist, then another and another. Apparently oblivious to the threat above and behind them they continued to climb into perfect position for the ambushers.

Dragon Leader watched as the leader of the third flight led the attack in a fast, shallow dive, aiming to fire on the rearmost of the exposed dragons and then swoop away without dropping into the concealing clouds. The rest of his flight would follow him in, each taking the next dragon left in line. If the enemy was really unaware, the lead dragon might not realize the formation was under attack until all his fellows were down.

The flight leader's attack was textbook perfect and his release beautifully timed as he fired the iron death arrow into the enemy dragon's flank. Even from the distance Dragon Leader saw the arrow strike home.

The enemy dragon reared its head against slack reins and looked back over its shoulder at the attacker. Then a burst of dragon fire caught the flight leader and his dragon as they climbed away from the formation, sending them plummeting from the sky in a blazing mass. Unconcerned by the deadly arrow sticking in its side, the dragon turned to face the oncoming foe.

Another death arrow struck the dragon, and another and another as the remaining members of the flight hastily shifted their aim. One of them tore a hole in the dragon's wing and one pinned the rider to his saddle. The rider was no more bothered than his mount. He merely swiveled in his saddle to send off his own arrow over the dragon's flanks. The draw was stiff, the release jerky and the arrow wavered past its intended target without effect. But by this time another Northern dragon and rider were down and the melee became general.

Jerry and Taj were hard at it in the programmers' workroom when Bal-Simba sought them out. The giant black wizard looked as grim as Jerry had ever seen him.

"There is a new factor we must consider in our planning," he said without preamble. "The enemy has a weapon we were not expecting."

Jerry's first impulse was to say something like "what else is new?", but the look on Bal-Simba's face stopped him. "What?"

"Animated corpses. Our enemy wakes the dead."

"Zombies?"

"Dragons and riders alike." The distaste was plain on Bal-Simba's face. "Such—things—are not unknown. But not even the Dark League meddled with them overmuch."

Jerry bit his lip. "We haven't either, except in movies."

"No one in the North has experience with them," Bal-Simba went on. "There are tales, however. They all agree they are difficult to create and harder still to control. Nor do they make satisfactory servants. They are merely puppets dancing on strings."

"Maybe this guy's found another way to make them work," Taj suggested.

"So it would seem. A strong patrol of dragon cavalry engaged a flight of the Enemy's this afternoon and we lost six riders and as many dragons." The corner of his mouth quirked up in what might have been an attempt at a smile. "Our riders were using death arrows."

"And you can't kill a zombie," Taj said. "So how do you stop them?"

"The body must be destroyed so as to render it useless to the animating intelligence. We were finally able to do so, but at a cost far too high. Such things are very hard to stop."

Jerry and Taj looked at each other.

"If you will excuse me, My Lords, I must call upon the families of the riders we have lost. Should you require further information Arianne will be able to assist you." With that he turned and left the workroom.

## TWENTY-ONE

# Stand to Your Glasses

The wing gathered in the tavern that night, but no one was drinking.

Off in the corner three squadron leaders sat with their heads together, talking in low tones. Occasionally one of them would make the hand motions which are the universal language of fliers. Some of the others gathered in twos and threes to talk quietly as well. Most of the riders just sat. Occasionally there would be an outburst of wrath and the sound of a mug shattering as it was thrown against a wall. Dragon Leader stood alone by the bar, sunk in a brown study.

You could have heard a pin drop when Charlie walked through the door.

Seemingly oblivious to the mood of the place he bellied up to his accustomed spot at the bar.

"Heard you boys had a little scrap today," the old pilot said."How many did you lose?"

"Six," the man at the bar said shortly.

Charlie gave a low whistle. "Tough. Really tough. But I've seen worse, believe me. One time in Korea we were still flying P-51s, we got jumped by a bunch of Migs and lost half our squadron."

Still no one said anything.

"Aw, hell. Come on boys, the drinks are on me. Barkeep, set 'em up!"

No one moved. No one said a word.

"My Lord."

Charlie turned and found Dragon Leader standing too close behind him. "This is not the time or place for you," he said quietly. "It would be best if you go somewhere else."

Charlie opened his mouth, perhaps to apologize, and Dragon Leader moved even closer. "Now," he said.

Charlie closed his mouth and left.

Karin was late getting home that evening and for some reason that troubled Mick. She had been working with Stigi as she did every day. Since the first time Mick had stayed away from the aerie.

He had heard about the battle and the losses, of course, and he expected she'd spend some time with her squadron mates in the complex, wordless process of pilots' grieving for those fallen. But it was very late indeed when she finally returned to their quarters.

"Hi, beautiful," he said and took her in his arms, only to feel her tense.

"Mick, we need to talk."

*Uh-oh,* thought Gilligan, who had been married long enough to know what that meant.

He sat down at the table. "Would you like some tea?"

Karin shook her head and settled into the chair across the table from him. "I've asked to rejoin my squadron."

"What?"

"That means I must move back to the barracks," she rushed on, "so I can be ready to fly at an instant's notice."

"That's pretty heavy," Mick said at last.

Karin leaned forward to put her hand on his arm. "It won't be that bad. There'll still be time to see each other and I'll only be at ready six or seven days out of ten."

"You know that's not what's worrying me." *Well, not the main thing,* he thought.

She hesitated. "Mick, we lost too many riders to the zombies. We need every dragon and every experienced rider now."

Mick didn't say anything.

"This is not like the machines you flew. It is no more dangerous than riding horseback."

*And how many people have been killed falling off horses?* But he didn't say it.

"There's a big operation coming up," he said finally.

"And you thought I would stay out of it?" The color drained from her cheeks and she pressed her lips together in a tight line. "What do you think I am? Did you honestly believe I would desert my mates at a time like this?"

Gilligan gave her his best winsome, little-boy smile. "Well, I could hope."

As soon as he said it he knew it was wrong. Karin went even whiter and stood up so fast she almost knocked the chair over.

"I must return to my squadron," she said woodenly. "I will be back later for my things."

Gilligan opened his mouth to apologize, to say the words that would make her stay. But there were no words, so he just nodded and looked at his hands.

Sometimes it's worth freezing your buns off just to be alone. Jerry stood on the battlements and stared off into the night. The stars were back again, shining like bright, hard bits of metal in a crystal clear sky. The air smelled of cold and nothing else. Even the sounds were gone.

Jerry slipped one hand out of the relative warmth of his heavy cloak and pulled the fur-trimmed hood closer around his nose. The fur smelled faintly of cedar even in the nose-numbing cold. He made no move to go back in.

*So stand to your glasses steady . . .*
*This world is a world full of lies.*

It was Charlie, obviously very much the worse for wear. From the way he was staggering Jerry was afraid he was going to fall off the walkway into the courtyard two stories below.

He was bareheaded and wearing only his flight suit and flying jacket; not even gloves. The old pilot must be freezing in this weather but he seemed too full of drink and his own concerns to notice.

"How ya doin'?" he slurred as he came up to Jerry.

"Okay," Jerry said neutrally, hoping he'd take the hint.

He didn't. "I got my ears pinned back good an' proper tonight," Charlie told him with an air of alcoholic confession. "I butted into something that wasn't my affair, squadron business, and I got what I damn well deserved."

Jerry nodded and didn't say anything.

"A squadron's like a family, son. There's times outsiders are welcome and there's times they ain't. Forget that and you're gonna get slapped down."

Some comment seemed seemed called for. "You must have run into that in Vietnam," Jerry said.

Charlie leaned on the parapet and stared out into the freezing night.

"I wasn't in Vietnam," the old man said softly. "Hell son, I didn't learn to fly until I was thirty-two." He turned back to look at Jerry.

"You know what I was? I was an accountant. A goddamn accountant! But I got lucky and I was in the right place at the right time and when we went public I walked away with nearly twelve million bucks.

"A good chunk of that went to my second wife, but I was still left with more money than any normal human being can spend in a lifetime of trying. The day we closed the deal, I came out of the lawyer's office, tore off my coat and tie, threw 'em in a trash can and I vowed I'd spend the rest of my life doing exactly what I wanted.

"Oh yeah, I got what I wanted." He smiled off into the darkness but there was no humor in it. "Maybe what I deserved."

Charlie hawked and spat out into the crystal night.

"Thirty years of doing just what I wanted and you know what that adds up to? Not a bucket of warm piss.

"I'm sixty-three years old, I got a drinking problem, diabetes and a cardiac arrhythmia that's probably gonna kill me if the other stuff don't get me first."

"Sounds like you had fun, anyway," Jerry said neutrally.

Charlie turned to face him. "You know what I found? Too much fun ain't fun any more. You need some kind of purpose to make it all mean something."

He waggled a finger under Jerry's nose. "Now you, you've been dragged from pillar to post. But you know what? All of that was for a cause. It means something.

"Like this here. You're gonna go charging off to rescue your lady love and maybe save the world.

"Maybe you'll win, maybe you'll lose. But when it comes to the end you're gonna be able to look back on your life and say it meant something.

"Son," the old man said, "from where I stand you've got nothing to complain about."

## TWENTY-TWO

# FINDING A PLACE

Mick Gilligan peered down onto the floor of the aerie, trying to pick a familiar blond head out of the dozen or so mounted dragon riders assembled below for the dawn patrol. But the aerie was softly lit and the observation balcony where he stood was high. He thought Karin was the third in line, but he couldn't be sure.

At an unheard command the first dragon lumbered forward, spreading its great bat wings as it picked up speed. In five strides it blocked the daylight and then it was out of the cave, its wings beating strongly. By that time the second dragon had started its run and the third was straining forward. One by one the beasts and their riders poured out of the door and vanished into the bright blue beyond. Mick waited until the last of them had gone and turned away as the grooms and other ground crew swarmed out onto the floor to prepare for further operations.

"Forgive me, My Lord," came a gentle female voice behind him. "You seem troubled." Gilligan turned and started when he found himself face-to-face with a dragon.

"Yeah, I guess I am," Gilligan said, ignoring his questioner's physical form.

"You are worried about Karin, are you not?"

"She asked to be put back on flying status. We had a big fight."

"She is a dragon rider, after all," Moira said gently. "As a flier, surely you can understand how she feels."

"Yeah, but it's different from this side of the fence.

I'm getting some of my own back." His mouth quirked bitterly. "You know something? I don't like it."

*Shit! Telling my problems to a dragon.* Well, it was no crazier than the rest of this place.

"We seldom do," Moira agreed. For a while both of them stared at the bustle of activity in the aerie below without talking.

"What brings you here?" Gilligan asked.

"Watching the dragons. I enjoy it—or rather this body enjoys it." She sighed. "Sometimes I am not sure of the difference any more."

Charlie was at Bal-Simba's door early the next morning. That was surprising because the old man had established himself as a late riser. Looking at his generally disheveled condition and smelling the alcohol on his breath, Bal-Simba surmised he hadn't been to bed yet.

"I need to talk to you," Charlie said without preamble.

"I am at your disposal, My Lord." Bal Simba gestured to a chair but Charlie kept standing.

"You've got a big show coming up," Charlie said. "I want a piece of it. Flying."

Bal-Simba cocked his head. "On a dragon? I believe your machine will not work here."

"You mean it won't fly under its own power," Charlie corrected. "But if you guys can float a big rock you can float a plane."

"Perhaps, but—without meaning offense— what can your craft do that dragons cannot do better?"

A broad smile spread over Charlie's face. "Confuse the hell out of 'em."

"Eh?"

"You need a distraction, right? Okay, Mick and the nerds tell me that comes down to an ECM problem. Electronic Counter-Measures," he added quickly at Bal-Simba's puzzled look. "You need something that will spoof them into thinking you're coming at them from one direction when you're really gonna hit them blindside." He leaned forward and put his hands on Bal-Simba's work table, heedless of etiquette. "So we load the Colt up with all the magic it can carry and your wizards wave their wands to make it fly. I go blasting toward the Enemy, radiating magic like it was going out of style. They'll know something is coming, but they won't know what. It will be radiating enough magic to cover every dragon in the North."

In spite of himself, Bal-Simba nodded.

Charlie grinned. "The best part of it is that even once they acquire me visually they still won't know what the hell they've got. They can't just break off like they would with a drone."

The big wizard grinned mirthlessly. "You mean they would continue to pursue you and try to destroy you. We cannot spare the dragons to protect you. Not a safe position, I fear."

The old man grinned back equally mirthlessly. "It's sporty son. Downright sporty."

Bal-Simba looked more closely at the pilot, and thought hard. The man was apparently sincere and undoubtedly sober enough to understand what he was suggesting. Having such a strange thing at the center of the magic would indeed confuse the Enemy.

"I will see what I can do," he told Charlie.

Dragon Leader ignored the constant boom of the sea as it crashed on the nearly vertical rock. He was not much given to conversation and there was no need as long as he kept an eye on his wingman. His wingman had climbed to the top of the pinnacle to watch for intruders. Dragon Leader surveyed the jagged fissures, overhangs and holes in the rock.

Their dragons were resting in the great crack that nearly cleaved the place in two. They were invisible, save from the proper angle at close range.

They had not sought a confrontation with the Enemy's dragons this time. Instead they had sneaked south by a roundabout route to this place and several others similarly situated.

The Executioner was as bleak and unattractive as its name. A snag of red-black volcanic rock thrusting above the restless gray sea like a monstrous fang. All around it lay Murder Shoals, the names a tribute to the terror these places inspired in those who sailed the Freshened Sea.

Even here, as far "inland" as it was possible to get on this place, spray stung his eyes. The chill, wet air sucked the heat from his body. It was not a comfortable place, but he had known that before he came. Comfort was not one of the parameters he was interested in.

Dragon Leader nodded to himself. The place would do.

Mick was having a drink in the pilot's bar. It was the one place in the Wizards' Keep where he felt really comfortable—as long as Karin and the members of her squadron weren't around.

*Drinking by myself again,* he thought. *I gotta cut this out.* It wasn't as bad as Vegas. He wasn't drinking as much and it was brown ale rather than whiskey—which apparently didn't exist here—but he'd still rather be doing other things.

Part of it was that he felt like a rat and he didn't know how to apologize, or even if the apology would be accepted if he could find a way to make it. He'd have to get Karin alone and try sometime soon, but she was avoiding him and staying down in the pilots' quarters.

He took another swig of ale as someone came over to join him. Looking up he saw it was one of the squadron leaders from the air wing.

"Join you?"

Gilligan waved him to a seat.

"The wing was out practicing today," said the man, whose name, Gilligan remembered, was Martinus or something like that.

Gilligan nodded. "I was watching from the war room."

"What did you think?"

"Still needs a little work."

"They say you've done operations like this before," Martinus said.

"Something like."

"This complicated?"

"Pretty much."

"How do you keep it straight?"

Gilligan considered. Although the dragon riders were skilled fliers and sometimes fought in wing or multi-wing strength they apparently seldom coordinated more than a squadron attack at once. More, the idea of closely coordinating forces which were out of sight of each other was completely alien to them.

"Practice is part of it, of course," Gilligan said, "but scheduling is more of it. One of the things we've found is that scheduling is a force multiplier. It lets us put maximum effort on the target at the right times."

The other looked interested and said nothing.

"So the first thing we do is draft an ATO, that's an air tasking order, that coordinates the entire operation. That comes down from the very top with basic assignments, timetable and such. Then each lower echelon fleshes it out so it all works together."

"Could you draft this—ATO—for this operation?" Martinus asked.

*Traditional role for grounded pilots,* he thought to himself, *pushing paper.*

"Sure, but it'll take time. Normally we've got software to help us."

Off in the corner a tall blond woman in a wizard's robe was listening intently. Mick vaguely recognized her as someone he'd seen hanging around with Bal-Simba.

"Basically it's a matter of deciding what you want to do when and working backwards."

"It sounds complicated."

"Used to take a whole room full of staff officers to do it. Now we have specialized software, but before that we used to do it on spreadsheets."

The other nodded. "It would take something the size of a sheet to write all of this down."

"No, it's a piece of software, a program. But you don't have those here do you?" He thought for a minute. "You know, I'll bet Jerry and his friends could turn one out in no time."

"The Mighty are all busy at their own tasks," the other grunted.

"Forgive me, My Lords." Mick turned and saw the blond woman had joined them. "I could not help overhearing and I think perhaps we can convince the wizards to give you what you want." She turned toward Mick. "You are the Great Gilligan, are you not?"

It took Mick a second to recognize how his rank had transmuted. "That's major. Actually I'm retired. Call me Mick."

The woman waved it off as if it were of no moment. "Very well, Mick. I am Arianne, Bal-Simba's assistant. I wonder if perhaps you could help me."

# TWENTY-THREE
# Enter the Dwarves

Arianne growled in frustration and tossed her pen aside.

"Trouble?" Bal-Simba asked mildly, looking up from his own work.

"This plan of Gilligan's makes my head hurt."

"And mine as well," the big wizard agreed. "'Tis said that simple plans work best. But here we must have complexity if we are to attain our goal." He gestured at the glowing letters. "So . . ."

"This is far more complex than anything we have ever attempted and it must all work perfectly."

Bal-Simba nodded. "Complex indeed. But then we face a situation of unprecedented complexity. Indeed, I cannot see how matters could become more complicated."

He was about to go on, but Brian came dashing into the room. Then he remembered his lessons, pulled himself up short, squared his shoulders and pulled his tunic straight.

"Excuse me, My Lord, but the seneschal says there are a hundred dwarves here to see you."

Arianne cocked an eyebrow at the big wizard, who shook his head and rose from his seat. "Foretelling the future was never my strong point," he said, and sighed.

Either Brian had understated the case or Wulfram miscounted. There were actually 128 dwarves waiting in the great hall of the Wizards' Keep. All adult males, since women and children never left the dwarven holds. All of them armored in knee-length byrnies of chain or heavy leather, all of them wearing steel caps and all of them with their traditional dwarfish battle axes strapped to their backs. Since their round shields of iron-rimmed oak were slung over the axes and since the axes were tied fast to their baldrics by peace bonds, it was obvious this was not a war party. Just what it was, Bal-Simba and the other wizards weren't sure. Dwarves seldom left their delvings and never in human memory had so many been seen at the Wizards' Keep.

As Bal-Simba entered the hall behind Wulfram the dwarves arrayed themselves in parallel lines with an older dwarf at their head. From his position and stance, Bal-Simba took him to be their leader, a notion confirmed by the circlet of red gold fitted around his steel cap.

"I am Tosig Longbeard, King of the dwarves," the head dwarf proclaimed as soon as the wizard gestured for him to speak. "Here to reclaim my rightful property."

Bal-Simba looked blank. "Property, Your Majesty?"

"The sword Blind Fury, the greatest treasure of my tribe."

"Ah," the giant wizard said softly. This was beginning to make sense.

"My idiot kinsman stole it from our treasury. We have traced him here. Now give me the sword—and while you're about it you can turn over my kinsman for punishment as well."

"I am afraid neither is here," Bal-Simba said. "They were here but they have departed."

From the way the news left Tosig Longbeard unmoved, Bal-Simba suspected he already knew that neither the sword nor the dwarf were at the Wizards' Keep.

"Where?" he demanded, gimlet-eyed. "Where did they go?"

"The dungeons beneath the City of Night. Your kinsman—Glandurg?—wished to accompany our folk on a hazardous mission there."

"A quest, eh? For what treasure?"

"No treasure, just great danger and a mighty foe."

Bal-Simba didn't need a mind reading spell to see Tosig didn't believe that. Not even his moronic nephew would go charging into someone else's dungeon unless there was treasure involved. The fact that the humans denied it only meant they didn't intend to share if they could avoid it. To the dwarf king that was perfectly reasonable, but it only made him more determined to get part of the loot.

"We will follow him, then."

"That may be a trifle difficult," Bal-Simba said mildly. "The lord of the dungeons has closed the path to any who try to enter. Not even dwarfish magic may force the way, I fear." For a moment wizard and dwarf regarded each other.

"Well?" Tosig Longbeard said finally.

"I beg Your Majesty's pardon?"

"Well, what's the rest of it? You wouldn't tell me that for no reason and you obviously don't expect me to pay for that information. So you want something. What?"

Bal-Simba didn't even try to disabuse him of the notion they were bargaining. The dwarf wouldn't have believed him, and besides . . .

"No bargain, but I do have a suggestion. Soon we shall attempt a strategem to force our way into the dungeons. If you would care to accompany us, we would be glad for your help. Meanwhile, please stay with us in the Wizards' Keep as our guests."

There was silence again while the king considered. "Very well," he said at last. "If you do not delay too long we will combine our forces to breach this fortress and recover our property."

"I will have the seneschal prepare accommodations."

"We will camp amongst the trees across the river," Tosig Longbeard said. "This whole place stinks of dragons." With that he turned and marched between the ranks of his followers and out of the hall.

"A hundred dwarves," Bal-Simba murmured once the last mailed warrior had followed his king out of the hall. "And the Sparrow thought he had trouble with only one."

"A hundred and a score and eight," Arianne corrected. "Do you think they will be much help?"

Bal-Simba sighed. "I told you I fared poorly at predicting the future, Lady. I only know they will do less damage to our cause if they go with us rather than preceding us on their own and stirring up the Enemy." He eyed the door where the dwarves had passed out. "Probably," he added.

## TWENTY-FOUR

# Operation Winter Storm

Although not bound to their tunnels, the dwarves were uncomfortable away from them. Clearly Tosig's men would rather be back at their shafts and forges than preparing to battle an unknown enemy half a world away. Still, dwarves are stoic by nature and none has ever faulted them for lack of courage.

There was snow in the wood, piled up under the trees, and a skin of ice lay on all the ponds and streams. The dwarves didn't seem to notice as they bustled about, felling trees and digging into the frozen soil to make crude dugouts. Before the sun completed its short journey to the horizon, a section of the wood had taken on the appearance of a semi-permanent and none-too-uncomfortable camp.

Tosig Longbeard was standing in front of a camp fire, overseeing the last of the work and warming himself when Durgrim, captain of the dwarven guard and his military second-in-command, approached him.

"We are almost done with the sleeping holes," Durgrim told his king. "Another day-tenth and the last of them will be done and the evening meal will be ready."

Tosig Longbeard grunted assent. Durgrim paused, judging the king's temper.

"Your Majesty," he said slowly, "I have been thinking about this, and the place on the Southern Continent where we are bound."

"Speak your mind," invited the dwarf king in a tone that suggested his lieutenant had better be careful about what he said.

"Even before mortals started using it, the place had an evil reputation," the other dwarf told him. "I am sure human occupation has not improved it."

"Unsurprising if it were so. You have an alternative to propose?"

Durgrim paused again, obviously gathering his courage. "Your majesty, can we not simply bargain with this enemy, buy the sword back?"

Tosig Longbeard glared at him. "Do you think I'm simple? I've tried that already. Whatever this creature is, it will not treat with us at all. Besides," he continued, the anger leaving his voice, "even if he would deal the price would undoubtedly be too high."

The dwarf king scowled back into the fire. "No, there is no help for it. With or without the mortals we must penetrate this place to recover the sword."

Being dwarves and with dwarves' careful sense of property rights—not to mention their greed for treasure—it never occurred to either of them to simply leave the sword in the Enemy's hands.

Charlie brought the Colt around in a wide, easy turn. He lined up on the white expanse between the rows of leafless trees and settled to the snowy earth lightly as thistledown. The big biplane rolled perhaps a hundred feet across the field before it stopped.

Malus stood at the edge of the field, blowing on his hands to warm them. As the plane rolled to a stop he crunched across the snow to meet Charlie.

"Still feels a little funny on the controls," Charlie told the tubby little wizard as soon as he stepped down from the door. "I don't think you've got the center of lift quite right over the wings yet."

"I can adjust the spell again," Malus said.

"No, it'll fly fine the way it is. If it ain't too broke, then don't go fixing it, that's my motto."

"Is there aught else then?"

"Yeah, one thing. The propeller. It doesn't rotate."

Malus spread his hands. "It is not necessary that it should spin. Magic now moves your craft through the air."

Charlie looked at him. "Just do me a favor. Make it spin."

Gilligan was in the "war room," going over the details of the air operation and the scheduling software with Jerry when Bal-Simba entered.

"Merry meet, My Lord. How goes the plan?"

"Well enough, I guess," Gilligan said with a sigh.

"What is worrying you?"

"You mean in general? Nearly everything." He grinned. "That's part of my job."

"Specifically, then."

"Well—" He hesitated. "Has it occured to you that this might be another trap? That the whole purpose of this thing might be to lure as many of us as it can into those caves so it can snap us up?"

Bal-Simba's smile had no warmth. "Constantly. It is our greatest fear. Yet we have little choice. We must strike soon and with all our strength or this thing will overwhelm us. We have taken what precautions we can, but this still remains the best course of action." He looked at Mick. "Is there aught else?"

Mick sighed. "Charlie. He isn't a programmer, he isn't a magician and I don't think he's ever really flown in a combat environment before. He's going to have a lot to do up there. Do you think he'll be able to handle it all?"

Jerry looked at Mick and smiled. "Taj and I have rigged up a custom user interface to help him."

It was getting colder. Except for occasional spots like the hot springs or the lava tunnels, the caves had never been really warm but now they were getting more and more frigid. Wiz could see his breath in puffs before his face and he hugged his cloak tighter about him to try to keep out the frigid chill.

He tried not to think how hungry he was. Since their discovery that they were cut off, the group had been on "half rations" that had grown steadily skimpier. Glandurg was not eating at all and Wiz suspected that half of Danny's ration was going to June.

They were even short on monsters. It had been nearly two days since the last attack. Wiz wondered if that meant they were headed in the wrong direction, but the new Moira seeker was pointing resolutely the same way.

Wiz went around the corner and came face to face with a cloaked, hooded figure. He drew back and Malkin's rapier sprang free before they realized they were seeing a reflection. Motioning Malkin to stay on guard, Wiz advanced, staff ready, toward the mirror. As he drew closer he saw it was no mirror. Instead there was a rough reflective coating on the rocky wall of the tunnel.

Wiz touched the glistening surface. "Ice," he called back to the others. "Ice under a volcano."

"Perhaps our enemy likes it cold," Danny suggested as the group came close.

Malkin arched an eyebrow. "Makes it easier to keep the zombies fresh, no doubt."

Wiz drew his hand under his cloak to warm it. "Or maybe it just makes things more uncomfortable for us." He looked around. "Well, let's get going. They say exercise helps keep you warm."

There was more ice as they went along. Here it glistened as a thin film on the rocky walls, there it made a treacherous coating over the floor of the tunnel. Occasionally there would be a solid vein of ice, filling a crack in the stone like some strange glistening mineral. Now the air was so cold the adventurers could see their breath before them.

Glandurg seemed unfazed, but the others kept their cloaks wrapped tight around them. Still the cold seemed to steal through to sap their very strength and leave them weak and shivering.

Nor did the tunnel cooperate. It seemed as though every few steps they had to crawl over a pile of frozen debris or climb a slope so steep they must go on all fours or squeeze between unrelenting walls of rock. Places with level footing were few and far between. Even without the ice and cold it would have been difficult. With them it was exhausting. They saw and heard nothing for the rest of the day, save the occasional drip, drip, drip of not-quite-frozen water. Still, their senses were alert and straining and that added to their fatigue.

Malkin was on watch, staring out into the dark, thief's senses alert. She neither turned nor moved as Danny came up behind her, but he knew she sensed he was there.

"Anything?"

She didn't turn, only shook her head slightly.

With a slight scrape he slid in beside her.

"How do you stay warm like that?"

Malkin flicked a bit of a smile. "I don't."

"I can't sleep," Danny said softly.

Malkin nodded, but said nothing.

"Malkin," he said at last, "do you think we're going to be able to rescue Moira?"

"That's what we're here for. That and to settle some scores with this thing."

Danny gathered his courage. "Yeah, but do you think we're going to be able to do it?"

"Are you so sure she wants to be rescued?" Malkin asked slowly.

"Of course Moira wants to be rescued."

"Moira herself might, but this thing has only Moira's body. The will is the Enemy's. I am not sure it will turn her loose that easily. The Enemy went through a great deal of trouble to get her. He obviously had some purpose."

"Yeah. Bait."

Malkin nodded, eyes never leaving the corridor. "Perhaps that too. But I think Moira, or Moira's body, plays a greater role in the Enemy's plans than mere bait."

"What are you getting at?"

"That we may not be able to rescue her. But I do not think we can afford to leave her here."

"Jesus," Danny breathed. "That's awful! Have you talked to Wiz about this?"

"He has problems enough and this is one he isn't going to think clearly upon." She turned to face him. "But we must think upon it, and decide what we're to do, should it come to that."

She turned her head to face down the dark passage and neither said anything for several minutes.

"That's a hell of a choice," Danny said at last.

"Hard choices must still be made."

"And you think we . . ."

"I doubt Wiz will be ready to make such a decision when we find her. Do not try to decide now. But think about it. And think about how to do what we must do if it comes to that."

"It won't come to that," the young programmer said firmly. "Wiz will find another way, or I will, or someone."

Malkin's expression did not change. "I hope you are right."

*It could not be said to be anyplace, really, for it had no sense of self as we know it. There was a nexus, but its senses were spread over more than a continent. There was no feeling for where it left off and others began, because in a very real sense there was no "other"—there was only that which had not yet been absorbed and turned to its purposes.*

*It had discovered the strategy long ago, in the brutal battles that had led to its supremacy. Better to absorb and adapt than to destroy, to incorporate and use rather than smash. It was a superior strategy and even if it had the gift of introspection it would not have troubled about the consequences. This frozen corpse contained magical knowledge it could incorporate. With that came a burning hatred seared soul-deep, a hatred that set it on its present course, but that was of no moment. Later the gleanings of a soulless husk far away reinforced that animosity as well as adding knowledge. That too was of no moment. They were simply things to be absorbed and put to use. That was enough.*

Wiz awoke still groggy, with an ache in his head and someone's foot in his face. From the way the rest of the pile shifted and grumbled he got the feeling they weren't in any better shape.

"Hmf," Danny grumped as he disentangled himself from the pile. "Another day, another monster."

"Not many of those," Malkin said.

Danny quirked a smile. "Hell, I even miss the lobster."

"I'm not so sure I'd go that far," Wiz said.

"I would," Malkin put in. "We could eat for a week off that bug."

Wiz really wasn't quite ready to go that far, but he could understand the sentiment.

Carefully he measured the grain and a little of the vegetables into the cooking pot and added ice. Then he gestured and a flame sprang up among the rocks. He set the pot with the ice on it to melt. He crouched over it, hands extended to soak up the warmth.

"That will tell the Enemy where we are," Malkin said, eyeing the magic flame and not quite protesting.

"The Enemy probably knows where we are already," Wiz growled. "We'll be in a lot better shape to face him if we're warm, rested and fed."

After breakfast the group continued on. Wiz was right. If conditions were no better this day, at least they felt better for the hot meal.

Wiz had Danny take the lead with Glandurg behind him. Actually that meant Danny and June were in the lead and Glandurg following them. Malkin brought up the rear and Wiz stayed in the center of the formation for a change.

Just before the break for the noon meal Wiz pulled Malkin aside. "I want to talk to you."

The tall thief saw his expression and nodded. "You heard last night?"

He gave a tight little smile. "I don't sleep real well when I'm cold."

Malkin cocked her head, waiting.

"I've been thinking about it ever since." Wiz drew a deep breath. "I just wanted to tell you, I think you're right. I think we can still get Moira out, but if we can't . . . " He stopped, gulped another breath and went on. "If we can't I want you to know I understand if you do . . . what has to be done."

"You want us to take action, then?"

"I know that thing about shooting your own dog, but I can't." He tried to smile again and the effect was ghastly under the bluish magic light. "Just don't do it unless you're absolutely sure, okay?"

Malkin nodded slowly, not trusting herself to speak.

"Now let's catch up with the others."

"He heard us," Malkin whispered to Danny later when she contrived to get him and June off to one side.

"And?"

"He does not like it but he sees the force of the argument. He only asks that we do it should it become necessary."

"I've been thinking about this too," the young programmer said. "I think maybe there's an alternative."

"If there is, well and good," Malkin told him. "But we do not dare leave Moira, or Moira's body, here."

"They say you're coming with us."

Mick looked up from his planning software to see Jerry and Taj standing before him. "There's nothing more useless than a staff officer when the battle's joined. So yeah, I'm going with you."

"We figured you'd need a weapon," Jerry said, handing him the box.

Mick opened it and inside was a military-issue Beretta semi-automatic pistol with a couple of clips of ammunition and a shoulder holster like the one he had worn in the attack on Caer Mort.

Mick slipped into the shoulder harness and hefted the pistol. "Thanks, guys. But didn't you say things like this won't work in this world?"

"Things like that work just fine," Taj said. "It's guns that don't work here."

"What he means is, it isn't what it looks like," Jerry explained. "It's actually a magic weapon that shoots lightning bolts. It just looks like a pistol."

"We could make it look like a Star Trek phaser if you'd prefer," Taj offered. "Or something really wicked."

"I think I'll stick with this, thanks." Gilligan slipped the weapon into his shoulder holster.

"Anyway," Taj said. "If you've got a few minutes we thought you might want to come down and watch the takeoff."

Mick looked at the spreadsheet hanging over the map. There were still things to do, but he realized that most of it was make-work. The ball was about to start rolling and things were moving increasingly out of the war room and into the real world.

"Yeah," he said, rising from his desk, "yeah, I'd like that."

The three made their way down into the depths of

the castle and into the echoing dimness of the dragon aerie. For Mick it was the first time he had been on the aerie floor since Karin brought him here the first day. He felt a pang at the realization.

Sitting in the middle of the aerie was Charlie's AN-2 Colt, newly equipped with a top turret, tail gunner's position and with what looked like science-fiction machine guns sticking out on the sides. The dragons eyed the newcomer and shifted and bridled uncomfortably. Clearly they didn't like this addition to their midst.

"That thing looks like a bomber," Gilligan said. "A B AN-2?"

"Actually it's a more like an EW AN-2," Taj said. "Except it's magic not electronic warfare, so I guess it's an MW AN-2."

"Why do I get the feeling this is never going to make *Jane's All The World's Aircraft*?"

"Different world?" Taj suggested.

"Here he comes," Jerry said. "And it looks like he's got his, uh, user interface with him."

Charlie stepped between the looming monsters and marched out to the group of waiting wizards and programmers. Trailing behind him were five bat-eared demons.

"My crew," he said to the group.

The first in line was a fresh-faced demon in aviator sunglasses, an officer's cap with a thousand-mission crush and a brown cowhide flight jacket with a Flying Tigers Blood Chit on the back and an Eighth Air Force patch on the sleeve. "Gerry O'Demon. My co-pilot."

Jerry groaned and threw an anguished look at Taj, who merely spread his hands and shrugged.

The next demon was short and slovenly with an unshaven chin and beady little eyes that never seemed to look at anyone straight on.

"That's Joe, my tailgunner."

Next in line was an older demon wearing a baseball

cap, coveralls liberally smeared with grease and chewing on a cigar stub that was disreputable even by demon standards.

"Kelly. He's my crew chief and waist gunner."

Next was a young demon in a fleece-lined leather jacket, baseball cap and a particularly goofy grin. "This is Sparks. He's radioman and handles the other waist gun."

Finally there was a slender, rangy demon wearing a leather flight jacket and a battered Stetson.

"Tex here's the turret gunner."

With introductions made, Charlie waved his "crew" toward the airplane. "Okay, boys, saddle up and let's ride."

"User interface, huh?" Mick said to Taj as they watched Charlie and the demons swarm over the plane doing last-minute checks.

"At least it ain't Windows 95," Jerry said.

"The best interface is the one that best fits the user," Taj added. "Can you think of a better interface for this job?"

At last Charlie and the demons were aboard and in position. Charlie slid open the cockpit window and signaled thumbs-up to the Flight Master, who controlled operations from the aerie.

As he had been taught, the Flight Master waved to Charlie to indicate all was ready. Charlie responded with a one-finger salute. The Flight Master turned to the door, dropped to one knee and brought his stiff arm down pointing at the entrance. On that signal Malus raised his staff and the big biplane shot the length of the aerie and out into the open air like an F-14 coming off the deck of a carrier. The cavern erupted into a deafening chorus of roars as the dragons protested an unfamiliar flying thing in their airspace.

As the grooms and riders fought to keep the dragons under control the plane disappeared below the rim of the entrance for a heart-stopping instant and then appeared again, climbing smoothly for altitude.

"Come, My Lords and Ladies," said Bal Simba. "We have our own work to do."

With a final glance at the rapidly vanishing speck in the center of the patch of blue, Gilligan turned and followed the group out of the aerie.

"Where's your girlfriend?" Taj asked as they climbed the stone steps back to the main keep.

"She left a little while ago," Mick said shortly.

*Deep beneath the ground the pale queen sat upon her ink-black throne. Light there was none, nor sound. Neither was needful.*

*Part of her was in this dark hall and other parts were in a thousand different places, sensing, observing and here and there acting. All of that was part of the dark queen just as she was part of all of it.*

*She could feel the pulse of the earth and the pull of the tides. She could sense the currents and eddies of magic which flowed through this place. She could sense her belly ripening even as desires ripened. All were good. All would come to fruition in the fullness of time.*

*The pale queen knew neither impatience nor haste. Only the pattern, changing, unfolding, becoming. That was all there was and all there needed to be.*

# TWENTY-FIVE
# THE FLIGHT OF THE OLD CROW

The sea was gray, the sky was pale, clear blue and all was quiet. Too quiet.

*I shoulda had the wizard do something about engine noise*, Charlie thought as the plane hissed through the air. The AN-2 was as rugged as a steel I-beam, but her Russian designers hadn't spared any attention for nonessentials like soundproofing. Flying a Colt and being able to hear himself think was a new experience for Charlie. He wasn't sure he liked it.

He flicked the intercom switch.

*Praise the Lord and pass the ammunition,*
*And wee'lll alllll stayyy freeee.*

None of the demons could sing worth a damn and that wasn't stopping any of them. In fact they'd been singing constantly since they launched out of the aerie several hours before. They'd started with "Remember Pearl Harbor" and worked their way through a medley of World War II patriotic songs, including a rousing number called "Bomben auf England" that Charlie was sure never graced the messes of the Eighth Air Force. When they reached the end of their repertoire they started over again. It wasn't such a large repertoire and Charlie had decided long ago he preferred the unnatural silence of the cockpit to the racket in the intercom.

Gilligan leaned over the map and put his fists on the table. "Okay, their forces are deploying. We've got six, eight, it looks like about ten squadrons of dragons moving into range of Charlie."

"What is Dushmann doing?" asked Kuznetsov.

Gilligan looked puzzled.

"The enemy," the Russian explained. "'Dushmann' means the Enemy."

"In the air over the city, not much. There are only scattered indications from the City of Night. It looks as if they only have a few sentries up." He looked over at Bal-Simba. "I'd bet he's got forces still on the ground and ready to launch. But the ones that are homing in on Charlie are probably out of the battle. They can't get back in time."

Moira thrust her scaly head between Gilligan and Kuznetsov. "Has Charlie been warned?"

"He knows they're there," the American said dryly.

Everyone watched silently as the waves of red dots swept toward the lone green diamond.

"Six o'clock high," Tailgunner Joe sang out over the intercom. "Bogies. Multiple. They're going for a beam pass."

"I got 'em," Sparks shouted. "Here they come."

Charlie twisted in the seat to catch sight of the attackers. The undead dragons weren't as smooth as the ones he had seen at the castle. Their formation was ragged, they tended to slew in the turn and their flight was stiff. But all that only made them more menacing. He counted at least six as they swept around in a flat turn to come in on the Colt broadside. On they came, rising and falling slightly in the air currents, growing larger and more sinister as they bored in for the kill. Charlie saw the skeletal riders rise in their saddles to draw their great iron bows.

Just when it seemed they were too close to matter, Sparks opened up with the waist gun. The undead riders and their zombie mounts were immune to death arrows and hard to stop with dragon fire. They would have laughed at .50 caliber machine gun bullets. Energy bolts were another matter.

Lances of lightning stabbed toward the attackers. The afterimage burned purple in Charlie's vision of a dragon arcing its neck back almost on top of its rider in a lambent nimbus of brilliance. Then Tex joined in from the top turret and the brightness became too much to bear. Charlie blinked and shook his head, trying to see. The instrument panel was lost in the dark spots swirling across his vision. He drew a gasping breath and nearly choked on the ozone. The flat *crack-crack-crack* of the lightning bolts told him Sparks was still firing.

Suddenly it was quiet again. "Eight in, eight down," Sparks yelled into the intercom. Charlie looked out the side window and saw two splashes in the ocean below. One of them had a burnt relic that might once have been a wing disappearing at its center.

Back in the cockpit Gerry O'Demon, his copilot, was holding the controls straight and level as if nothing had happened.

"Good work, son," Charlie said into the mike.

"Don't get cocky," came Joe's growl from the tail position. "We got two more groups on our six."

Gerry leaned forward and squinted out the windshield. "Twelve o'clock high!" the demon called. "Multiples. Three squadrons at least. I think more behind those."

Charlie's eyes weren't as good as the demon's but when he looked hard he saw them too. He craned his neck left and right seeking more bogies. He didn't see any but there was an ugly looking thunderhead boiling up a couple of miles off to the left.

Normally Charlie would have avoided a storm cell like a temperance lecture. But the three squadrons of zombies were coming straight at them. He heard the *crack-crack-crack* as the squadrons behind them came within range of Tailgunner Joe's weapon.

"Really sporty, huh?" chirped his co-pilot.

"Tu madre," Charlie muttered. Then he kicked the rudder hard, shoved the throttle to the firewall and ran for the clouds for all he was worth.

Far above, the watching demons scanned everything that came within their purview. They were without emotion or even intelligence. They simply collected sense impressions and transmitted the information through intermediary demons back to the Wizards' Keep, where it was processed and displayed on the magic map in the war room.

Moira thrust her scaly head over Gilligan's shoulders. "It appears that Charlie has destroyed some of his attackers."

"He's got firepower in that plane," Jerry said.

"Every one he takes out is one less we have to worry about," Kuznetsov added.

Gilligan peered deeper into the tank. There were a lot of red dots closing in on the lone green diamond. "From the looks of it I'd say we're going to have plenty to worry about anyway."

"Are we ready for the next phase?" asked Bal-Simba.

Gilligan looked at Kuznetsov and both men shook their heads. "We want them committed as fully as possible before we spring our next little surprise on them."

"A while more," Kuznetsov said.

Gilligan watched the battle develop and tried not to think about Karin and what she was doing.

## TWENTY-SIX
# The Executioner

*No sea birds,* Karin thought, scanning the gray sky above the gray-green sea. She spared a glance down at the crag. *No nests and no signs of them.* Not even the deposits of whitewash left by birds using the rocks for fishing lookouts. The place probably smelled better for the lack, but it did not make it any less forbidding.

The Executioner's attraction was its geography and topography, not natural beauty. There were several reefs and bars within a two-hour dragon flight of the ruined City of Night, none of them big enough or high enough above water to be called islands. But the Executioner had one thing the others lacked: Hiding places. The volcanic rock was laced with crevices, blowholes, fissures and pumice caves that could keep a dragon or two and their riders safe from eyes in the sky.

Karin and her partner had been here for almost two days now, keeping concealed and waiting for the signal. Karin hugged the jagged rock and stared out over the sullen ocean, scanning from horizon to horizon and back again for any speck that might be an approaching dragon. But the sky was as empty as the sea. Finally satisfied, she twisted on the narrow ledge and waved to her companion below.

Senta was a small, dark woman who was unusual in being both a skilled magician and a dragon rider. Karin was with her as her wingman and to use her scouting skills to keep them undetected and out of trouble until they had done what they came for.

*I wonder where Mick* . . . But she pushed the thought from her mind and concentrated on the business at hand.

Down below, back under a lava overhang, Stigi and Senta's dragons were restive. They didn't like being on the ground when there were enemies about, and the undead dragons made them nervous besides. Well, that was fine with Karin. She was nervous too. As soon as they completed their job here she would be only too glad to be back in the air and winging her way home.

Back in the Wizards' Keep, the command group around the tank watched in satisfaction. The diversion had worked perfectly. The Enemy had thrown almost all his forces north, out over the Freshened Sea. Now those forces were fully committed and it would take time for the Enemy to recall them. Too much time.

Of course that also meant that one lone biplane was the focus for every undead dragon and rider the Enemy had in his first wave, and he had a lot of them.

Gilligan looked at the clocks on the walls. "Okay, initiate phase two."

He stared into the tank to watch the aerial ballet he had choreographed unfold. He tried not to think of Karin.

Karin spared another glance for Senta, standing now on the black rock and lashed by ocean spray. Now the signal had come and at last, *at last* they could do something besides wait.

Senta reached into her pouch and pulled out one of Taj's Origami dragons. She placed it in the palm of her hand, holding it against the wind with a curled little finger. She spoke a spell, blew on the bit of folded parchment and tossed it into the air with a cry of "oh-oh-oh-oh-oh-oh." As soon as it left her hand it began to grow and change. Now there was a dragon and rider swooping up past Karin to circle over their heads. Even this close the illusion was well-nigh perfect to Karin's senses, right down to the rush of air on her face as the "dragon" climbed past her. She only hoped it appeared as perfect to the Enemy.

Below her Senta selected another parchment dragon and repeated the process, this time crying "oh-oh-oh-oh-oh-eye." The next was "oh-oh-oh-oh-eye-oh" and the one after that "oh-oh-oh-oh-eye-eye," just as the foreign wizard, the one they called Taj, had instructed her.

Origami after origami was tossed aloft to shapeshift into the seeming of a dragon and rider and join the circling throng above the rock. Finally the last of the sixty-four "dragons" was launched and named. With a wave of her wand and another one-word spell, she sent the group on its way. As one the dragons sorted themselves out into squadron Vs and climbed toward the south, a non-existent armada flying straight at the Enemy's stronghold.

If Karin was impressed by the reality of the seemings, Senta was even more impressed by the magical skill behind them. Such ruses had long been common in battle, but they suffered a fatal flaw. A magician could not control more than one seeming at a time. True, such an illusion could appear to be an army or a horde of dragons, but magically it was all one unit, with but a single true name. A skilled magician could quickly detect the fact and even the greatest of wizards could only control a few such magical entities.

This group was different. Somehow by naming them as they had been named they had become part of an entity called "array," each separate, each with its own true name, yet all of them bound to perform collectively by a single spell. To Senta, this was high magic indeed.

She was still admiring her handiwork when Karin came sliding down the rock to join her.

"Perfect," the blond woman said. "Now let's get out of here before the Enemy decides to investigate this place."

Senta looked after her creations winging south. "I wonder why they call them drones when they don't make any noise at all?"

"Mick said . . . " Then she stopped, looking north. "Never mind that," Karin said flatly. "We've got a problem."

The other turned and saw a ragged line of black dots on the line where gray clouds met gray sea.

"Back under the rocks, quickly." Both women sprinted for the shelter of the crevice, hoping against hope that the zombies' senses were as uncoordinated as their movements.

Had the seeming been detected so quickly? It had to be an accident, Karin told herself firmly as she pressed against the spray-wet rock. Only by chance had these undead been near at hand when Senta activated the seeming.

But chance or plan, it put them in a precarious situation. They were caught on the ground, outnumbered and perilously close to the Enemy's base. If they were spotted . . .

From her recess in the rock she watched as the ragged V passed perhaps two dragon lengths above the tallest point on the reef, swinging around the crag in jerky precision. For a minute Karin thought the zombies had not seen them.

Then one by one the zombie dragons peeled off and swooped back toward the island.

"Shit," Karin breathed and pressed further back against the rear of the overhang.

Gilligan watched the second wave of dummy dragons soar aloft from the Executioner and aim straight for the City of Night. Almost immediately he saw a few ragged dots rise from the city to meet the suddenly-appearing foe.

"Okay," he said. "They're as fully committed as they're

going to get." He picked up the microphone connected to the communications crystal.

"Now," Gilligan said. "Tora Tora Tora." In the back of his mind he wondered if it had been such a good idea to let Charlie pick the code names. Then he focused on the display to the exclusion of everything else.

Charlie was in the middle of a heck of a fight. There had been perhaps ten squadrons of zombie dragons launched against him and the survivors pressed their attack ruthlessly.

Charlie put on a display of flying that would have been the hit of any air show—and gotten his license lifted immediately by the FAA. He hauled the big biplane around so tightly the whole frame shuddered, giving his gunners belly shots on three and four dragons at once. He dived for the sea and skimmed so low that the following dragons crashed into the waves. He zoomed for altitude and then hit his flaps far above the safe maximum speed so that his pursuers overshot him and fell to his turret gunner. He used every trick in the book and a few that never made it into the book.

The zombie attackers gave as good as they got and then some. Salvos of arrows struck the plane, without effect. The mechanical damage the iron arrows could do was minor and the plane itself was not complex enough to be killed by their death spells. Dragon fire was something else. In spite of the efforts of his gunners and Charlie's frantic jinking, the swarm of dragons drew closer and closer, swirling in about him and diving on the aircraft to deliver gouts of fire. The cockpit was magically protected against dragon fire and there was no fuel on board, but the fire of even undead dragons is hotter than a flamethrower.

Finally it was all too much. Trailing flame in half-a-dozen places, the AN-2 went down in a flat spin. As the plane hit the water the magic link broke and the green diamond on the display winked out.

"I don't suppose . . . " Moira said into the strained silence.

"We will do what we can," Bal-Simba said, "but I fear it is not much." He turned to issue orders to one of the Watchers.

The others continued to stare numbly into the inky water.

"I am sorry," Kuznetsov said at last.

"Don't be," Jerry said quietly. "It was what he wanted." He looked into the still black water in the bowl. "Maybe more than he ever wanted anything in his life."

"At least it will not be in vain," Moira said. "He has taken us the first step. Now we will continue what he has begun."

"Your part approaches, Lady," Bal-Simba told her. "The others have assembled in the great hall."

Gilligan nodded to the Chief Watcher. "You have the watch."

Erus inclined his head and stepped to the tank to watch and issue whatever further instructions might be necessary.

As he followed the others out the door Gilligan's feelings were decidedly mixed. His training told him he was abandoning his post at a critical time, but his reason told him there was nothing more he could do. Unlike a controller in his own world he didn't have the capability to shape the battle from here on out. The forces were launched and everything depended on the execution. Now he could go kick ass with impunity.

Gilligan wasn't the introspective sort so it never occurred to him to wonder how much of his decision was reason and how much was the driving need to actually do something.

Perhaps fortunately, he was gone by the time the tank showed the zombies closing in on Karin and Senta.

✧ ✧ ✧

Over the sea north of the City of Night a new battle was shaping up. The Enemy launched the last of its forces to meet the incoming squadrons.

The zombie squadrons bore north in ragged formation. These were the scrapings of the Enemy's aerie and many of the dragons and riders were so badly damaged they could barely fly, much less maintain formation. Still, under command of their guiding intelligence they all climbed and circled as best they could.

The League dragons came on in a smooth squadron weave. The defenders had height on them and the sun at their backs. Wings locked, they dove on the intruders.

A blast of dragon fire and a spark went tumbling from the sky. Another blast and another scrap of burning parchment went fluttering seaward.

In quick succession they knocked a dozen more "dragons" from the sky, all scraps of parchment.

That was proof enough even for zombies. As one they turned away from the drones and ran for the City of Night.

It was already too late.

The dragon cavalry of the League had trickled south under a cloaking spell, giving wide berth to the City of Night. Now they swept in around the volcano and over the City of Night on its slopes. Wing on wing of dragons soared above the Enemy's city and strafed anything that moved on the ground with bursts of dragon fire. The Enemy's aeries were empty and no dragons rose to oppose them. The zombies that trickled south from the decoy missions arrived in dribs and drabs and were easily burned from the air by dragon fire.

The great hall was not merely full, it was jammed. The eight wizards who would send the storming party on its way were pushed back against the wall by the crush. Besides a twenty-foot dragon, most of the castle guard was mustered, armed and ready, and another dozen or so wizards were scattered among them. Mick Gilligan was toward the center with his new pistol. Taking up half the space was a knot of 127 dwarves gathered close around their king and as far from the dragon as they could manage.

Kuznetsov and Vasily came pushing through the crush to stand next to Gilligan. From somewhere the Russians had come up with powder blue berets, striped jerseys and fatigues in a pattern of camouflage that Mick found just a little disconcerting.

"Brings back old memories, eh?" Kuznetsov said as they positioned themselves.

Around them the wizards raised their staffs and began to chant.

The Colt had sunk quickly, leaving only a small oil slick behind. Charlie had managed to launch the life raft before the plane disappeared, but with the zombie air force overhead Charlie had hidden under it rather than riding in it. The undead riders had made pass after pass on the bright yellow raft, tearing it to waterlogged shreds with their arrows. Then, as one, they had wheeled and headed south, leaving Charlie alone in the water.

As the last of the enemy dragons disappeared into the clouds, Charlie inflated his life jacket and surveyed his situation. He was hundreds of miles from land and already the chill of the water was starting to creep through his exposure suit. He had no food, no radio and nothing with which to call for help.

"Son," he said to the empty ocean. "It don't get any more sporty than this."

Then he saw dorsal fins slicing toward him.

## TWENTY-SEVEN
# SNEAK ATTACK

The whole purpose of the operation was simply to distract the Enemy for just this instant. Distraction enough so it wouldn't notice that Moira was arriving with company. Or what that company was carrying.

Although the Enemy was naturally multi-tasking, each new assault had spread it thinner and thinner. From the very beginning Watchers had been scrutinizing parts of it, judging its reactions, looking for signs of slowdown and confusion. When they came, when Bal-Simba judged the time was right, a dozen wizards struck against the Enemy's defenses to push the attackers through.

They were in an enormous echoing room in total darkness. Glow lights floated up from a dozen wizards simultaneously and the group realized they were standing in a gigantic limestone cavern. Even with a dozen lights the illumination barely reached to the edges of the room and threw eerie shadows into the parts it didn't quite penetrate.

According to plan the group divided up. Following separate magic detectors, Moira, Bal-Simba and half the guardsmen went one way, Jerry, Taj, the Russians and the rest of the guards went another. The dwarves formed into a column and marched off in their own direction.

"How do you think they will do?" Jerry asked the guardsman nearest him as they looked after the dwarves.

The man rubbed his chin where his chain mail coif met his jawline. "Either turn and run at the first opportunity or break off and start looting."

"Well then?"

The guardsman shrugged. "So we send them off independent. Can't hurt, should draw some of the Enemy off us." He paused, considering. "They may even do some damage."

"I still don't like this," Taj said to Jerry as the other parties moved off.

"Neither do we, but we don't have much time to search. This way we have a better chance of finding either Moira's body or Wiz and his group before the Enemy can seriously oppose us."

"Besides," Kuznetsov said, "this will confuse Dushmann. If we move quickly," he added significantly.

Jerry took the hint, checked his homing crystal and ordered his group to move out down a side passage.

"Sharp lookout now," Tosig Longbeard commanded. "And mind those side rooms. They might have something in them."

As the humans scattered in response to their magic detectors, the dwarves worked through the dungeons more methodically, checking each room and nook for valuables. Thus they moved more slowly and were closer to the arrival point when the Enemy's first counter-attack struck.

"Something's coming," Durgrim told his King.

"Sound the recall," Tosig ordered and looked around him.

It wasn't an ideal situation. Rather than being in a snug tunnel, the dwarves were in another large room where the enemy could come at them from all sides.

"Light," the dwarf king commanded, and the blackness of the cavern gave way to the twilight gloom dwarves prefer to daylight.

As the last of the dwarves scurried back to the safety of their fellows, Tosig's breath caught in his throat. From all sides ragged lines of shambling, twitching undead warriors were converging on the little band of dwarves.

Against human foes it might have worked. But dwarves are tougher than mortals and bonny fighters beside.

"Steady the shield wall," Tosig bellowed. "Here they come."

As if by instinct, the dwarves crowded into a tight circle two-deep in the middle of the cavern. Those in front dropped to one knee with their round shields before them. The rear rank shrugged their shields off their arms and stood behind the protection of their comrades' shield wall with both hands on their axe shafts.

Heedless of their opponent's new formation, the undead charged. There was no sound save the scuffling of feet on the cavern floor and the breathing of the dwarves. Soundlessly the zombies lurched forward and soundlessly they struck.

Then the cavern erupted in the clamor of steel on steel and dwarven battle cries as the undead warriors hit the 128-dwarf Cuisinart.

The zombies might be already dead and hence unkillable, but there are certain practical problems in attacking when one's arms have been lopped off at the shoulder or one's head is rolling across the floor. Further, zombies' muscle control is notoriously poor and this handicaps them in hand-to-hand combat.

The first rank of dwarves was safe, crouched beneath their shields. The second could swing their axes with full force, protected yet unencumbered. About the only weapons that could reach over the shield wall to strike the axe bearers were spears and halberds. But as soon as a polearm extended over the shield wall, the shield dwarves would reach up with their axes and hook it, immobilizing weapon and wielder and leaving both open to a counter-stroke by the axe dwarves.

Not that it stopped the zombies. Whole or hacked

up they continued to come on in deathly silence, pulling themselves forward to the attack with whatever limbs they had left. Again and again they pressed forward and again and again they were cut into ever-smaller pieces.

Finally, when the last zombie had been chopped into pieces too small to be dangerous, the attack stopped.

Tosig Longbeard peered into the darkness, seeking other foes. He was breathing heavily and the gold crown upon his helm was battered and scarred. Already those warriors with healing skills were tending to their comrades' wounds.

"Casualties?" He did not turn to look at his men.

"Six wounded," Durgrim told him. "Four will be able to walk once the healers finish with them. Two we must carry."

"Well enough then. Anything else about?"

"Nothing I can sense."

The dwarf king hawked and spat upon the still-quivering flesh of their late foes. "Pfagh! Animated corpses. These humans become ever more troublesome."

His second-in-command gestured at the pile of bodies strewn about them. "Human these were. Yet I am unconvinced a human animated them. The magic was wrong."

Tosig rubbed his chin. "This is a matter to be thought upon. Meanwhile," his voice rose so all his troop could hear, "stand up and prepare to march! But carefully now. We know not what else we may find in this place."

The magic detector tuned to Wiz led Jerry, Taj and his group down a side passage, through a series of natural caverns and finally to an iron-bound oak door that led off the side of a tunnel.

Jerry pressed his ear to the door and listened.

The wizard behind him, a young man named Elias, checked the magic detector around his neck. "There is nothing in there."

"Yeah?" Jerry hissed. "Well, that 'nothing' is breathing

awfully heavy." Elias frowned and tapped his detector on his palm.

Keeping his back to the wall, Jerry reached out and pushed on the door. It creaked, but it swung open smoothly, showing only darkness beyond. Now they could all hear the hoarse, heavy breathing.

"What do you think it is?" Taj whispered.

"I dunno," Jerry whispered back, "but it's cloaked, shielded and probably nasty."

Taj regarded the door. "So, do we go in or not?"

"It would be better if we sent something in ahead of us." He brightened. "And I've got just the thing."

A quick call for an Emac, a muttered spell and suddenly there was a fuzzy pink mechanical rabbit standing before them. The rabbit was wearing dark glasses and carrying a bass drum. But he also had a boonie rag tied around his head and an awesomely wicked looking weapon slung across his back. The rabbit did a quick half turn to orient himself and marched into the dark room, beating the drum.

Four beats later, the drum was drowned out by the roars, growls, snarls and liquid sucking sounds coming from the room. Then the corridor echoed and rang with gunfire and explosions until the watchers clapped their hands over their ears to save their hearing.

Then there was silence. After a few seconds the pink mechanical rabbit appeared out of the smoke. He blew the smoke from the barrel of his weapon, slung it back on his back, adjusted his drum and marched off down the corridor, beating his drum.

A quick peek around the corner showed there was nothing left alive in the room, although there were enough miscellaneous body parts to stock a good-sized zoo—or a terrific nightmare.

"Jeez," said Taj, as he stepped over something that might have been a tentacle and avoided a taloned foot that was still twitching, "what do you suppose this thing was?"

Jerry looked around. "As a friend of mine likes to say, never ask questions you don't want to know the answer to. Now come on. Let's see if we can find the others."

*Well, you wanted to die a fucking hero*, Charlie thought. Somehow his definition of a hero's death had never included being eaten alive by sharks. He could just give up, exhale and sink beneath the water, but natural orneriness in him kept him from taking the easy way out.

Damn! Why couldn't he have gone down with his plane? *At least I won't end up a zombie.*

The fins drew nearer and Charlie braced himself for what must come. Closer and closer they scythed until he could see the wet sheen on the black flesh of the fins and the smooth ripple of water before them. Barely two yards from him the nearest fin disappeared beneath the waves and Charlie gasped in anticipation.

Something broke water in front of him. After a second he opened his eyes to find himself facing a very unsharklike snout with the mouth pulled back in a toothy grin.

"Hello," the dolphin squeaked. Behind the first one, two other dolphins had their heads out of the water.

Charlie goggled. *It's a damn good thing I'm already wet*, was his mad first thought. Then he laughed in pure relief.

"Go home?" squeaked the dolphin. "Go home now?"

Charlie doubled over laughing and got a nose full of water. He choked and sputtered and the dolphins moved in to support him under the arms.

"Goddamn. You guys are Air-Sea Rescue, right?"

"Go home," the dolphin repeated.

"Okay, son, just lead the way."

Supported and pushed along by the dolphins, Charlie headed north, toward the lands of man.

"Hey, do any of you boys know . . ." He started to sing. *"Praise the Lord and pass the ammunition . . ."*

None of the dolphins did of course, but they were apt pupils and not in the least put off by Charlie's cracked baritone. By the end of the first mile they had joined in with their mosquito-buzz voices.

*". . . praise the Lord and pass the ammunition,*
*And we'll allll stayyy freeee."*

The Executioner's rock ledges were narrow and slippery and the zombies were clumsy. The second dragon misjudged the landing and was swept into the boiling sea before it could correct. Karin saw a dead man's head and a dead dragon's wingtip break the surface before being sucked under the foam. The other undead did not seem to notice.

They couldn't stay here. The rock was so small it would be the work of moments for the zombies to sniff out their cave. Once that happened they could be cooked by dragon fire in their lair. But there was no way to get airborne without being incinerated either.

"Do you have any magic for this?" Karin whispered. Senta shook her head.

Karin nodded and pulled her sword from its scabbard on Stigi's saddle. Senta did likewise.

Karin reached up and took Stigi's bridle. As quietly as she could, she turned the dragon around until he was facing out of the crevasse toward the zombies. Senta brought her dragon around. By jockeying and shifting the riders were able to get the dragons squeezed in side by side almost lying on each other but facing out the same way.

"Stigi," Karin whispered as the first zombies came into view, "fire."

Stigi needed no encouragement. A gout of flame swept down the ravine, incinerating the first of the undead dragon riders. As Stigi reached the end of his breath, Senta's dragon released his flame, causing Karin to avert her head and Stigi to bridle under the heat.

Twice more the dragons breathed fire turn and turn about and twice more zombies charred, burned and fell backwards into the foaming sea.

But it was a temporary victory and both of them knew it. As soon as the zombies got dragons aloft they would be incinerated in turn by dragon fire from the skies. Indeed, as Karin watched, one of the zombie dragons launched off the rock and flew low out over the ocean, wings beating to gain altitude.

A tentacle lashed out of the water and swept dragon and rider into the sea.

Another tentacle swept the cliff knocking another dragon and two more zombies into the water. Then another tentacle and another and another lashed onto the shore, seizing dragon and rider alike and sweeping them beneath the foam.

"Kraken!" Karin hissed. "Keep still!"

As the living dragons and their riders pressed back into the crevasse a forest of tentacles lashed from the sea and swept over the island, tapping, probing, searching for prey. The zombies did not scream as they were picked off the rock and dragged beneath the water. Their dragons did not roar. But one by one they were all taken as food for the monster of the reef.

Still the tentacles swept on, feeling for more. Several of them explored the crack where Karin and Senta hid and one of them came so far in that it actually touched Karin.

It took all her will to keep from flinching when the tip of a slimy tentacle brushed across her boot. She squeezed her eyes shut and bit her lip until she tasted blood to keep from whimpering aloud at the creature's foul touch. In the part of her mind that could still function all she could think of was Mick.

The tentacle passed on and withdrew down the crevasse. There were a few more tentative stirrings and then everything was still, save for the waves and the sea.

At last Karin dared to breathe again and she and Senta looked at each other across their dragons' backs.

"Fortuna," Senta breathed. "Let us be gone from here before something else happens."

Karin could only nod.

In spite of the glow lamp the tunnel ahead was dark, as if something was dimming the light. Taj started forward, but Jerry held him back. "Wait a minute. I don't like the looks of this."

"Bunny time?"

Jerry nodded and spoke the spell. First the Emac appeared and then the pink fuzzy mechanical rabbit, drum at the ready and gun slung across its back, obscuring its battery. The decoy spun mechanically and then marched down the corridor beating its drum. It had barely crossed the threshold when it disappeared in a blinding blue-green flash. Before the watchers recovered two more energy bolts smashed into the rocks over their head triggering an avalanche.

Jerry gestured frantically and the rocks seemed to bounce off an invisible shield to pile up and block the tunnel before them. Even after the rocks stopped falling the dust stayed impenetrably thick in the air, converting the humans to shadowy outlines.

The big programmer coughed and spat out a mouthful of dirt.

"Didn't work," he said unnecessarily.

"These things learn fast," Taj said. "That's probably built into their programs because it's a survival characteristic. I don't think we'd better use the same spell twice."

Jerry was still coughing and spitting, so he just nodded. "I think we'd better find another way through here," he said when he got his breath back.

✧ ✧ ✧

"Something in the tunnel up ahead," Shamus whispered. "Magic?"

Malus paused for an instant and then shook his head. A quick gesture from their commander sent the guardsmen shuffling into a new formation, shields to the front and spears and halberds behind. Malus stepped into the second rank, squeezed between two tall pikemen, and flipped back the sleeves of his robe to leave his arms bare for action.

One instant the tunnel before them was dark and empty and the next it was filled with nightmare creatures backlit by a weird blue glow. Instinctively the humans started and pulled tighter together at the sight of the insect-like horrors bearing down upon them.

A swipe of a halberd and an ant-thing was standing headless, arms and legs waving blindly. A man in the front rank screamed and fell as a stream of acid washed over him, leaving smoking holes in his clothing and skin.

Malus and the other wizards began throwing lightning bolts, death spells and everything else they could think of. The ant-things died in droves before the magic, and more died beneath the guardsmen's steel.

Step by step the humans were forced back by the oncoming waves of insectoid monsters. They left a trail of insect corpses behind them, but the pressure of the close-packed creatures was simply too great to withstand.

Thundering down the side tunnel came a column of dwarves, mailed, helmed and battle axes at the ready.

The dwarves hit the insect warriors about halfway down their column with an impact that shoved the bugs back against the wall. Streams of acid spattered off the dwarves. But dwarves are tough enough to handle molten metal and the steel of dwarfish armor is at least the quality of high-tech stainless. Save for an occasional lucky shot, the dwarves ignored the liquid.

They could not ignore the scything jaws and crushing

pincers of their insectoid foes, but they did not succumb to them easily either. Steel and leather protected the dwarves and a dwarf which could be reached with a pincer meant an insect which could be reached by an axe. Work-hardened muscles drove axes through the insects' chitinous exoskeletons and into the soft flesh beyond. The dwarves hewed legs, lopped pincers and chopped off heads with grim abandon, all the while forcing further into the main tunnel.

The charge split the enemy column in two and now instead of attacking, the front section was trying to defend on two fronts as the humans took renewed strength from the reinforcements. The tunnel grew slippery with blood and ichor as the distance between the humans and dwarves lessened. Finally there were only a couple of insect warriors left and the humans and dwarves were putting as much effort into avoiding each other's weapons as they were into killing bugs. Meanwhile, the back part of the insect warriors' column was being forced further and further down the tunnel. They were not retreating, but the dwarves were chopping through layer after layer of them.

Finally, at some unseen signal the remaining insects turned as one and ran down the tunnel, leaving the shorter-legged dwarves panting behind them.

"Thank you, Your Majesty," Malus panted.

Tosig Longbeard inclined his head in response. "We are allies." One of the dwarves pushed his way through the ranks and whispered in the king's ear. "Now if you will excuse us, there is—ah—a matter which we must investigate." With that he turned and signaled to his followers. As they fell back and the king strode to the front Malus caught a scrap of the messenger's words.

". . . piled clear to the ceiling . . . just everywhere."

"Well," said Malus. "If those creatures return they shall have to fight past the dwarves. Those will not give up treasure merely because of a horde of giant ants."

"Fine with me," said Shamus. "If they keep those bugs away from us they're welcome to all the treasure they can carry."

"Light up ahead," Malkin whispered to Wiz.

*What now? Giant ants or lava?* He tightened his grip on his staff and motioned the others to make ready.

The light was blue, but brighter blue than the fungus in the ant tunnels. It bobbed about as it came on, casting moving shadows on the floor and walls. Wiz scanned the shadows anxiously, looking for something hiding there.

Malkin was crouched to one side, rapier drawn and ready. When he looked back at the light he could make out figures in it. In fact . . .

Malkin screamed and dropped her rapier. Before Wiz could react she dashed forward bare-handed.

"Jerry!" she yelled.

Wiz looked again and sure enough, it was Jerry with a knot of people.

Malkin ran to Jerry and practically leapt into his arms. He hugged her and lifted her clear of the floor in a single sweeping motion. Meanwhile the others pounded up and there was a brief orgy of back-slapping, hugging and yelling.

"How the hell did you guys get here?" Wiz asked looking over the assortment of guards, wizards and others who were with his friend.

"We came looking for you," Jerry said, through Malkin's dark hair. Then he set her down and kissed her soundly. "Bal-Simba's here with Moira and a bunch of other people and, oh, Wiz, this is Taj, E.T. Tajikawa."

"The Tajmanian Devil? I'm honored to meet you, but how did you get here?"

"Let's just say they made me an offer I couldn't refuse," Tajikawa said. "No, not that kind of an offer," he said when he saw Wiz's expression. "They just dangled a real interesting problem under my nose."

"You know Major Mick Gilligan?"

"Good Lord? You're in on this, too?"

"It's a long story," Gilligan said, "and it's just 'Mick,' no more major."

"Let me guess."

"We found a solution, too," Jerry said. Then he explained to Wiz and the others about A-life and the probable nature of their enemy.

"It makes sense," Wiz said when the Taj and Jerry duet finally ran down. "It would explain a lot of what we've found since we arrived."

"I am glad it makes sense to you," Malkin said, still clinging to Jerry's arm, "because it's gibberish to me. All I know is we've got to find this thing and finish it."

"That's what it comes down to," Taj agreed. "Otherwise it will get bigger, meaner and nastier all the time."

"Yeah," Danny said, "and closer too. Look!"

Wiz turned and saw zombies bearing down on them.

"Quick," Wiz yelled, "down this tunnel." Programmers, guardsmen and wizards all dashed for the indicated opening. Jerry was the last in, backing down the tunnel for a distance before turning and running to join the others.

The zombies tottered out of the cavern and started down the tunnel, their sightless eyes fixed on their prey. Wiz stepped to one side, staff raised, ready to strike out at their undead attackers. Jerry put a hand on his arm to restrain him.

"Wait a minute," he said. "I may have something better." Wiz looked apprehensively at the oncoming horde but lowered his staff.

The first zombie tottered more than usual and stopped. He jerked convulsively as if trying to lift his trailing leg, but the foot stayed planted on the floor. By this time two other zombies had stopped, then three more. Before they were twenty paces down the tunnel all the zombies were stopped, doing a weird jerky twitch-dance like a demented version of a rock video.

"That should hold them for a while," Jerry said with satisfaction.

"What in hell kind of spell was that?"

"Crazy Glue," Jerry told him.

"Yeah, but how does it work?"

"Crazy Glue."

"No, not what you call it, but how does it work?"

Jerry held up a green-and-white bottle. "Crazy Glue. Jumbo size. I picked some up when we were in Vegas. I put drops of it all over the floor. Relax. They're not going anywhere."

"Until they cut their feet off and crawl after us," Wiz said.

Jerry looked back over his shoulder. "Don't give them any ideas."

"You know," Wiz said as they turned the corner out into another cavern, "those are the first zombies I've seen in a while. I wonder what happened to all the rest of them?"

"Oh, they were delicious," came a bubbling voice out of the darkness. The group turned and the giant lobster emerged from the shadows. "Such flavor, such character." He clicked his claws together in a way that reminded Wiz of a gourmet smacking his lips. "Humans improve tremendously with aging, you know." There was a pause. "Not much conversation however, and they simply *would* not stop wiggling."

Wiz turned slightly green. Something in the back of his mind kept reminding him that lobsters were carrion eaters.

The lobster clicked his claw more forcefully, with a sound that rang like a rifle shot in the cavern. "Oh, parsley! I don't suppose your friends brought any with them?"

"Not part of our MREs," Gilligan said, keeping his hand close to his pistol butt. "Sorry."

"Oh, well, one can hope, can't one? In any event, if you'll excuse me, I believe there are some more of them down this way." With that the lobster brushed by them and hustled off the way they had come, feelers atwitch with anticipation. Wiz, Mick and the others watched him go. Then Mick and the rest turned to look at Wiz.

"Uh, that's the lobster."

"Another ally?" Gilligan asked.

"Kind of. Just don't let him have you over for dinner."

## TWENTY-EIGHT

# THE END OF THE BEGINNING

They met Bal-Simba and Malus' group in another large chamber perhaps a half-mile on. There was another backslapping reunion and then a quick council of war to plan the final assault.

"Our detectors show the center of the thing—and Moira—are down that tunnel and in a large room beyond," Bal-Simba told the group.

"So do we sneak up on this thing?" Taj asked.

Wiz shook his head. "We're not going to surprise it. It knows we're coming." He looked around. "My suggestion is that we divide into two groups. One bunch of us will charge the thing and hit it hard. Hopefully that will keep it occupied. Meanwhile, the second group, with Bal-Simba and most of the wizards comes up behind, throwing as much magic at it as you can." He looked at the golden globe in the Tajmanian Devil's hand. "Taj, you go in tucked in behind the first line, ready to lob that thing at it as soon as we get close. With luck it will be so busy with the first and second lines it won't even see you coming."

"I claim quest companion's right to stand in the front rank," proclaimed Glandurg, stepping forward.

Wiz sighed and nodded. "Okay. Take the extreme right of the line then. Jerry, you and Danny stay to either side of me." Malkin stepped forward. "Malkin, you stay with Jerry." June moved up next to Danny and Wiz didn't waste breath trying to tell her where to stand.

"Now the first wave of the second rank will be mixed wizards and guardsmen. Shamus, I'll leave it to you and Bal-Simba to order that, but I want Bal-Simba and some of the Mighty behind them. Moira, you stay in the rear with the guardsmen and Bal-Simba."

He took a deep breath. "Okay, then. We go in fast and try to hit this thing hard and all at once. Our primary objective is to get Taj close enough to this thing to throw the grenade at it." Then he paused and looked at his companions. "Our secondary objective," Wiz said grimly, "is to protect the dragon from my wife."

No one mentioned the third objective.

Wiz looked at the people arrayed around him. One by one those in the first line signaled they were ready. He looked over his shoulder and saw the second line was ready to go too.

"Wait a minute," Jerry said. "I've got something to go in first." He spoke a phrase, gestured and suddenly there were hundreds of fluffy pink Rambo bunnies on the floor, with machine guns slung and drums at the ready. The mechanical rabbits turned and started down the tunnel in loose order, some going straight on and some dodging from cover to cover.

Wiz's eyebrows shot up, but he watched the "recon element" go marching, dodging and banging up the tunnel without comment.

"It knows how to deal with those," Taj pointed out.

"Yeah, but they'll give it something else to think about."

Almost immediately the tunnel was filled with smoke, gunfire, roars, screams and colored lights. Bits of bunny, pieces of monster, boonie rags, cartridge cases, chunks of rock and other, less identifiable objects came flying out of the tunnel.

"That's our cue, folks," Wiz yelled. "Hit 'em!" With a yell the group charged down the tunnel and into bedlam.

The surviving rabbits were still blasting their way forward but not all the defenders had been suckered into attacking them. Three steps into the tunnel a giant spider dropped from the ceiling, aiming for Wiz's face. He blasted it with a lightning bolt that sent showers of dirt and rock down on the party and kept going without breaking stride. Another step and a wall of flame came roaring down the tunnel, only to turn aside and break back under the impact of Wiz and Jerry's spells. Meanwhile, Malkin speared something on her rapier that writhed horribly and screamed like a dying child. Wiz had only a sickening glimpse of it before Malkin tossed it back into the maelstrom before them with a flick of her blade.

Two more steps and an undead dragon reared up before them. It took the combined fire of all the wizards and several mighty strokes from Blind Fury to cripple the monster and a liquid-oxygen spell from Jerry combined with a deluge of water from Wiz to freeze the thing solid. As they scrambled over the still-straining monster, the walls of the tunnel began to constrict on them like a throat. Jerry used a spell to force the tunnel to dilate, but he could only handle a few feet at a time. They pushed on step by step with Jerry dilating and Wiz freezing the tunnel in place repeatedly.

That left Danny to handle the attacking monsters, and his methods, while generally effective, tended to be chosen for creativity. Wiz was especially impressed with the spell that created four equidistant points of strong gravitational potential around the circumference of the tunnel. It not only ripped a herd of charging tyranosaurs into little, bloody pieces, but it plastered the remains tightly against the wall so the attackers didn't have to wade through them. His method of handling the giant acid slug left Wiz less impressed, primarily because the leftover slime was eating through his boots.

The Tajmanian Devil was busy, too, although Wiz couldn't be sure what he was up to. He thought Taj was responsible for stopping the horde of armored skeletons that fell apart into piles of bones as they came down the tunnel.

Wiz couldn't see what was going on in the back, either. However, the yells, screams, banging and other noises told him the other waves had their hands full as well.

The air began to grow clammy and the temperature in the tunnel dropped perceptibly. Then mist began rising from the tunnel floor. Jerry and Wiz dispersed it as best they could with their staffs, but it came back ever thicker until it was a wall in front of them. Then it grew thicker yet, until it swirled around them, confining each of them in their own little bubble.

Almost touching, but isolated by fog and freezing wind, the party forged ahead into the chamber. There were bits of ice in the fog that stung against skin and eyes, distracting them and making them lower their heads. Wiz gripped his staff tighter and held his cloak before him to try to shield himself from the magical storm. Dimly he could see Danny and Taj as darker forms forcing their way ahead on either side of him, but the rest of the party was utterly lost from view and hearing. Belatedly he realized they should stop and regroup, but there was no way to communicate with the others. So he lowered his head again and concentrated on putting one foot ahead of the other on the treacherous icy floor.

The going was easier for some than others. In a few paces their neatly formed line had grown ragged and then dissolved completely.

"Wiz!" Taj yelled, and tossed the sphere to him. Wiz caught it in both hands, juggling globe and staff as the wind whipped and lashed at him.

Suddenly the wind tore the fog away and there was Moira, sitting on a throne carved of black glass. Rising behind her was a black, gelatinous mass that shimmered and rippled as if from the wind.

His wife stood and held out her arms.

"Come, darling," she breathed. "Come to me."

Wiz's breath caught in his throat. She was as beautiful as ever. Her flaming hair a mane about her and her green eyes as wide and inviting as he remembered. Beneath the shimmering green gown he could see her belly swelling with new life. She extended her arms to him in open, aching invitation.

"Kiss me. Oh, kiss me, Wiz."

In spite of himself Wiz took a step forward, the grenade loose in his fingers.

Suddenly Moira froze. She twisted and shrank in on herself. There where Moira had been was a large green frog.

Wiz gasped and stepped back. Out of the corner of his eye, he saw Danny blow on his fingertips, like a gunfighter blowing gunsmoke from the barrel of his six gun.

"Ribbet," said Moira.

With a convulsive jerk, Wiz hurled the golden globe over Moira's head in the direction of the shining mass.

The sphere hit the dais beside the throne, but a hungry black pseudopod lashed out and scooped it up and into the glistening thing behind.

There were flashes within the ice, blue and green and red and orange, like the largest, most gorgeous fire opal that ever was. The cavern shook and a high, grating noise seemed to come from everywhere at once. The surface bulged and pulsed and heaved like gelatin going over speed bumps.

The mass seemed to slump in on itself and the flashes dimmed and died. Then it was an ordinary block of ice with shadowy forms embedded in it.

The wind died, the fog dissipated as rapidly as it had come and the party found themselves standing in a large room crudely hewed from the rock.

Moira was pirouetting in static little circles, her arms flung out.

"Free!" she crowed, a wonderful silvery sound, "I'm free."

She stumbled back against Wiz and he caught her close. "I'm also a little unbalanced," she said, looking down at her swollen abdomen. Wiz lifted her chin and kissed her passionately, holding on as if for dear life.

Fluffy let out a plaintive *wheep* as if to say he wasn't sure what had happened but he wasn't at all happy about it.

Wiz broke his hold on Moira and looked over her shoulder at Danny.

"If that change hurt the baby . . . "

"Relax," Danny said. "I didn't morph her. It was just an illusion." He gestured at Glandurg and the dwarf instantly shrank into a particularly warty and unappealing brown toad. Before anyone could react, he gestured again and there was Glandurg.

"Stupid mortal tricks," the dwarf muttered.

Moira laid her hand on her husband's sleeve. "No, I am fine. Honestly love. Never better."

"*You!*" came a roar from the cavern entrance. Wiz and the others turned as King Tosig stomped into the chamber with a half-dozen dwarves trailing behind. Their armor was bent, their shields were battered and their battle axes were nicked and scarred. Tosig's blade was as damaged as those of his followers and he held it aloft in a way that boded no good. Instinctively Wiz took a tighter grip on his staff and the guardsmen moved between the wizards and the oncoming dwarves.

Tosig ignored the mortals. "Come here, you," he roared, pointing at Glandurg. "I want to talk to you."

"Uncle!" exclaimed Glandurg, a little apprehensively. "I mean Your Majesty. I am here. . ."

"I don't care what you've been up to, you young hooligan!" King Tosig bellowed. "Come here and give me that sword!"

"Of course, Uncle." Glandurg whipped Blind Fury from its scabbard and brandished it aloft, nearly eviscerating King Tosig Longbeard in the process.

"Give me that, you silly nit!" the dwarf king snarled and grabbed the sword from his relative's hand.

"I was going to present it to you proper," Glandurg sounded hurt. "With a bow and all."

Tosig only snorted.

"Well, there it is."

E.T. Tajikawa stepped up and examined the glistening mass. "It probably wasn't alive anyway," Taj said.

Wiz looked at the wall of ice and the shadow forms embedded in it. So this was the Enemy. He knew he should feel something. Rage, triumph, something. But looking at the glassy mass he couldn't work up any emotion at all.

Then he turned back to Moira and all the emotions in the world overwhelmed him.

Meanwhile, the dwarves had been busy looting since the end of the battle. Parties of six or seven disappeared down every tunnel and poked into each room, returning laden with boxes, bags and chests. From the rapidly growing piles it appeared that they were almost as good at looting as they were at fighting. Malkin wandered over to inspect one of the piles, heedless of the dwarves' glares. Jerry could have sworn she kept her hands clasped behind her back the whole time, but she returned to him with a suspiciously lumpy tunic.

Bal-Simba turned to Tosig.

"Will you come back with us to the Wizards' Keep? We owe you a debt and wish to thank you properly."

"Alas, we must return immediately to our own land," the dwarf king said. "We will arrange our own transportation from here."

Down the corridor dwarves were carrying boxes and bales out of one of the rooms and stacking them in the middle of the floor. Bal-Simba pointedly ignored the looting.

"Mementos of our trip," Tosig said and Bal-Simba nodded.

"Do not delay your departure over-long. It is our intent to see that this place gives us no more trouble."

"Gone we shall be right enough," Tosig said and turned away. "Hey, you," he yelled to his scavengers, "hurry up with all that. We haven't got all day."

Wiz and Moira were still locked in an embrace, oblivious to everything around them until Fluffy pushed his head between them by main force and *wheeped* for petting and reassurance. Absent-mindedly Wiz compiled.

"Poor dragon," Moira said without taking her eyes off Wiz's face. "This must be so hard for him to understand."

"I'm not sure I understand it," Wiz told her. "Except that you're back just the way you were and all's well that ends well."

"Well," said Moira, green eyes twinkling, "to tell the truth, I do feel an urge to go chase a cat."

She laughed at his expression. "No, I am fine." Then she looked down. "Bloated, swollen, clumsy, but fine."

"You're beautiful," Wiz said with all the conviction in the world. "You've never been more beautiful than you are right now."

Fluffy *wheeped* because Wiz had stopped petting him. This time he was ignored.

"This isn't the end of it, you know," Moira said softly.

She was right. There would be others like this thing to deal with. This wasn't the last such entity that would come to be in out-of-the-way corners of the World. For the rest of his time here he and the others would face that problem and the problem wouldn't stop when he died.

Then Wiz Zumwalt looked down at his obviously pregnant wife and hugged her even tighter to him. "No," he said softly, "it's only beginning."